Moonlight Walk on the Turtlestones

OTHER BOOKS BY EILEEN RAYE

FOR ADULTS

Moonlight Walk on the Turtlestones

FOR CHILDREN

A Ghastly, Ghostly Night
Backyard Secrets Lost and Found

FOR YOUNG ADULTS

Alaine of Hawthorn
Lost in a Vampire Movie

MOONLIGHT WALK ON THE TURTLESTONES

EILEEN RAYE

PAGE TURNER BOOKS INC.

HENDERSON, NV
United States of America

Moonlight Walk on the Turtlestones, 2nd Edition.
Story concept, text, and cover concept © 2016-2024 by Eileen Raye.
Editing and print preparation © 2016-2024 Staback Author Services.
Back cover summary by Lady Leanne E. Staback, Ph.D.
Cover art © 2026-2024 by Eileen Raye and Lady Leanne E. Staback, Ph.D. (See Bibliography for downloaded artwork used on cover).

Books may be ordered through popular, online retailers, Page Turner Books, Inc.'s® online store, or by contacting the publisher at:

PAGE TURNER BOOKS, INC.®
170 S. GREEN VALLEY PKWY., STE. 300
HENDERSON, NV 89012-3145

Visit our website at www.ptbooksinc.com or
contact us via email at contact@ptbooksinc.com.

Page Turner Books, Inc.'s ® name and logo are copyright of Page Turner Books, Inc®.

ISBN: 978-1-958487-28-0 (Hardcover Edition)
ISBN: 978-1-958487-10-5 (Paperback Edition)
ISBN: 978-1-958487-11-2 (eBook)

Printed in the United States of America.
First Hardcover Printing: July 2024
Library of Congress Control Number: 2024934455

DEDICATION

This book is dedicated to my husband –
who has supported me in all things…

PROLOGUE

The heat of the July day had cooled. Breaths of the night air danced across the tall, field grasses and rippled the surface of the water. The moon was full and bright. High in the sky, it moved in its arc, casting white light on the landscape. The trees and fields were drenched in shades of silver and gray. The oval turtle pond was a pool of ink. The pathway, made up of the large, turtle-shaped stones, glistened in the moonlight.

It was well past midnight as she concealed herself in the shadow of the ancient, great, oak tree. Nearby, the natural spring spewed its water from the crevasse in the hillside's wall of granite. She was alert to the night and its sounds as she waited, silently watching. It was the season for witches. She knew well that their high, holy days approached. She did not fear them. She had faith in her strength against their dark spells.

She had known that there were trespassers on her land for some time. It was the magic of the grotto and the cycles of the moon that drew them here. At first, she had just noticed little things. She found paths of trodden grass. There was the scent of fresh fires recently extinguished. Then there came the more blatant signs of their presence. She had seen strings of lights bobbing through the back orchard late at night. Fence wires were cut. Sounds of voices were magnified into the night from the grotto's natural amphitheater. Lastly, there was the hen house gate left ajar with two birds missing. This was the closest the invaders had come to the house. They had no fear of her. They knew she was alone here. They almost dared her to confront them.

She had chosen her clothing carefully to help hide her in the darkness. She wore a black, long-sleeved top and her ankle-length, navy-blue skirt. She had put her long, white hair into a bun and covered it with a long, black scarf tied at the nape of her neck. Her shoes were soft-soled, allowing her to move quietly through the field. Tonight, she was determined to know who they were.

Now she stood very still, scanning the land for any movement. She watched as a coyote led her litter of three pups to the pond for a cool drink. As the moon hovered closest to the earth, its brightness would expose any prey, and the pups would eat tonight.

At last, she heard the muffled sounds of their approach. The quiet march of feet and small flickers of light moved through the orchard. They were moving toward her...heading to the grotto. Under the string of towering eucalyptus trees, leaves moved with a breeze, looking down on cloaked figures in shades of white and dark colors. The intruders entered through the opening in the circle of old willow trees. The willow's long bent branches with veils of vertical leaves shielded the twelve to fifteen figures as they filed into the grotto.

In silence, she stealthily clung close to the rock wall, and moved along its curved surface to find a notch providing a view into the circle. Her view was from the side, with the group of hooded figures looking forward. She could not identify any of the dark forms.

Rhythmic, soft chants from low, male voices had begun. A fire was lit, and the circle was cast by a figure facing the group, cloaked in white. He stood before the others, speaking in inaudible tones. The large, pagan amulet on his chest glowed in the firelight. He spoke his parts and his flock chanted back in return. The fire grew with flames reaching upward from its circular bed. The man in white raised his hands and lowered the hood of his cloak, bathing his face in firelight.

Melinda gasped, quickly moving her hand to her mouth. The recognition of the white-cloaked man produced an almost physical pain. Tears came to her eyes with a sharp sense of betrayal. She moved back to the darkness by the oak tree, not wanting to see any more from the grotto. She stood silently in the darkness for what seemed like hours, waiting for the coven to leave. She knew its leader, and a trust was broken. She wondered how many others of the men she knew. There was no doubt they knew who she was, and where she was. Now, whom could she trust?

EILEEN RAYE

1

THE FIRST CAT

Denia was in the kitchen of her Aunt Melinda's rural house in Solvang, California when she thought she heard a cat meowing nearby. She walked to the backdoor and looked out the curtained window. No animals came into view as she scanned the flagstone patio and the wide driveway that led to the back lot. An instant later, she heard the cry again. She walked back to the door and opened it.

Sitting on the doorstep was a skinny patchwork of black, orange, and white. It sauntered through the doorway and over to the front of the kitchen sink cabinet, where it sat staring at Denia expectantly. She had no idea what the cat wanted. Maybe it was hungry. Denia walked to the sink and opened the door to the cupboard under the sink. There she found dozens of neatly stacked cans of cat food. Next to them was a bag of dry cat food with a happy looking cat on the package.

Not knowing her aunt had a cat, this might explain all the little bowls she had found in the dishwasher. The cat certainly knew what it wanted; so Denia got out two bowls, one for dry food and one for water. Pulling up the tab, she opened the small can, scooping about half of the contents onto a saucer. Then the cat walked over to the refrigerator, and again sat down, waiting. It was the first time Denia noticed the oval mat on the floor, tucked out of the way next to the refrigerator. When the food was placed down, the cat quickly went to the saucer and began to eat. Denia had gotten to the ranch the day before and was still learning the lay of the land, or in this case, where things were in the house.

She wondered if the cat had been outside somewhere since her aunt's death. The patchwork feline would soon realize that its mistress would not be returning.

Denia went back to making her toast.

"Let's see, sixty calories per slice," she said out loud, while reading the bread wrapper.

She did have the habit of talking to herself whenever there was no chance of being overheard. Spreading butter on the warm bread, she pondered the choice between a jar of what looked like honey, or the one labeled in her aunt's writing as boysenberry jam. She decided on the jam. She also made a cup of tea, adding a dab of honey to the cup.

She knew that she would have to be careful. Her aunt had been a tall, thin lady, and there was no diet food in *this* house. Denia's battle with her metabolism was ongoing, with the dreaded morning weigh-ins. That reminded her, she would have to find a store in town to get a scale. She had not found one of those in her aunt's house.

Still in her nightgown and floppy slippers, holding her plate of toast and cup of tea, Denia wandered into the living room toward the sofa facing the old brick fireplace. She sank into the comfortable, well-used cushions covered with several homemade Afghans, and various pillows with needlepoint scenes on their covers. The coffee table was a dark wood, old and warn, strewn with candleholders and half-burnt wax towers of various colors. Magazines, knitting instruction books, and an old cookbook with papers and notes sticking out from the pages added to the clutter. She eyed a little, brass tool that looked like it was used to snuff out candles.

Hmmm, she thought.

Magazine covers stared back at her. *Life in the Circle? Woman of the Sage? Healing Arts at Home?* She had never heard of any of these, but they sounded exactly like the kind of things her aunt would have. Aunt Melinda was not from the usual cut of cloth, as her mother had always said. In fact, over the past seventeen years of her life there had been only polite contact between her mother's sister and the rest of the family.

The cat padded its way through the living room and across Denia's feet in front of the sofa. Without hesitation, it continued on to the large window that overlooked the expansive front yard. Up it jumped to the wide windowsill of the bay window where there was a small, braided rug folded in half. There, after two turns around the rug the cat snuggled down, resting on its front paws. Denia had not noticed the rug before, but this was obviously a favorite spot for a nap. The feline appeared to be willing to tolerate her presence, since its tummy was full. The cat watched her lazily, and they both knew that Denia was the visitor here.

"Okay, you'll get used to me," Denia directed at the cat. "I don't know what Auntie called you. Maybe Jorje can tell me who you are."

The cat ignored her. At the same time, Denia noticed that there were *two* small rugs under the windowsill. Was there another cat somewhere outside? Has it been alone out there for almost two weeks since her aunt's death? Maybe Jorje, the farmhand on the ranch, could help her. She would have to get dressed and search around outside.

First, she would finish her tea. Picking up her aunt's flowered mug, Denia sipped its contents. After a while, a lone tear made its way down her cheek. She finished the tea and tasted the honey on her tongue. It was still too soon. She was still in mourning. Her life was a mess! The wedding, the desolation, her aunt's sudden death…a murder; suddenly leaving her job and apartment and moving here.

All these events had happened over the past two months. Gazing out the window, Denia realized that she was slipping into the self-absorbed funk that had surrounded her for weeks.

Mentally, she shook herself. Time for the mantra: *I am*

changing my life. I am going to look forward, not back. Glancing about the room, she knew there was plenty to do around *this* place. Yes, she was going to find things to enjoy and be happy about every day. Already today, she became the caregiver to a rather scrawny looking cat. It was a good beginning.

Prompted by new enthusiasm, Denia knew she needed to get dressed and get started. She climbed the stairs of the old two-bedroom house and walked to what had always been *her* bedroom. It was the smaller of the two bedrooms in the house; but, as in the time when the house was built, bigger than the bedrooms in the newer homes built today.

In her aunt's generation, families were larger, and children shared a bedroom. More than one bed and one child would be comfortable here. This room with sky blue walls had not changed since she used to visit her aunt when she was a little girl. There was a full-sized bed with its blue, crocheted bedspread and a nightstand with an old-fashioned hurricane lamp. There was a white, five-drawer dresser with glass knobs. A small desk with a white, wooden chair, sat by the closet. An oval mirror was hung on the wall above the dresser. Other walls held framed pictures of girls from earlier times. Lacey, see-through curtains hung at the three windows. Denia could survey the front yard and road from two windows. From the other one, there was a view of the wide driveway that ran along the side of the house, leading to the back lot.

She knew she would need to move into the larger bedroom that had belonged to her aunt, eventually. But first, she would need to go through all her aunt's things and figure out what to do with clothes and personal belongings.

Fresh paint, maybe a new bed and mattress would be needed for that bedroom. For now, she almost liked living in her "little girl" room, with its soft, flowered rug on the floor and good memories floating in the air.

Rummaging through suitcases and boxes lining the wall, Denia searched for some clothes. She looked outside through the window assessing the weather. The August morning fog gave the yard an eerie look. Denia knew from past experience that the morning could be misty, but it usually burned off quickly for a sunny, hot afternoon. She grabbed her jeans, a short-sleeved, white top and a long-sleeved, lightweight, green shirt to wear on top.

While dressing, she made a mental note that she would have to put some of these clothes away in the dresser and closet. The previous evening, she had opened the door to the room's closet only to find it stuffed with clothes and boxes lining the floor. The many hooks flowed with scarves and carryall bags of many sizes. There was not an inch of space to put any of her things. In another corner of the room a pile of laundry was beginning to collect in a basket. It wasn't needed yet, but she hadn't seen a washing machine in the house. She would have to look in the garage.

Thinking back a couple weeks, Denia was rather amazed at how abruptly her life had changed. This morning when she first woke up, she had been a little disoriented as to where she was; but she knew this change was for the better. It had to be, even though it had come out of turmoil.

It had been Monday evening a week ago, when her mother had called her, obviously upset. At first, Denia had panicked thinking something may have happened to her father.

"My sister is dead," her mother had managed to get out. "They found her today, outside of the house. I just got a call from the Solvang Sheriff's Department. I have to go up there right away," her mother was saying, "tomorrow. I need you to go with me. I've already made reservations at a hotel in Solvang. You don't mind sharing a room, do you?"

Denia was trying to process the information quickly with images of the aunt she had not seen for years flashing to mind. Her thoughts quickly went to the regional quarterly financial report that was due on her boss's desk the next day.

"Mom, are you sure that you need me? What about Dad?"

"Your Dad is up to his neck at work and can't take off."

That made sense, since her father was a Vice President at the San Diego Energy Department and was frequently working when he was supposed to be off work. It *was* August in California. Demand for power was high, and there always seemed to be some crisis going on behind the scenes as the city's demand for air conditioning droned on.

"Besides, that stingy boss of yours can give you a few days off for a death in the family," her mother paused. "I really don't know what we're going to find up there," her voice sounding a little desperate now. "The person I talked to on the phone didn't seem to want to give me the details but told me to come to their office. Why wouldn't they tell me anything?" she asked, as if Denia would know.

"Okay, Mom," Denia relented, realizing that her mother probably did not want to be going through all this alone. "I'll call the office and tell them I will be gone for the rest of the week."

She had her laptop at home and could e-mail what was already done on the financial report to Ben. He was her co-worker at the same job level as herself, who was always finding excuses for getting out of the grunt work.

"Thank you, honey," her mother said, in a relieved tone of voice. "Bring at least one dress."

Her mother knew that she rarely wore dresses.

"I'm not sure if Melinda has made any funeral arrangements."

Then she added, "It's about a six-hour drive, so I want to leave early. Is seven good?"

Denia could hear all the wheels spinning in her mother's thoughts. She knew this could be a really miserable week.

"Yeah. Mom, do you want me to drive?" she offered, thinking of the long drive in her mother's cramped Prius.

"Would you?" her mother replied. "At least your car has some room in case we need to bring anything back."

Unlike her politically correct mother, Denia had a large, blue, five-year-old Explorer. She had not needed a big car, but she loved it. It was the first car she had bought on her own after college. It made her feel safe. She had no family to support, so paying for gas for the SUV was something she did not mind.

"Have a glass of wine, Mom, and try to get some sleep. I'll pick you up at seven."

She hung up and headed for the closet to find her suitcase.

The next day, the drive north had been quiet. Surprisingly, her mother had little to say during the drive. Was she reflecting on her childhood with her older sister? There had been an eight-year age difference between them. Was she feeling guilty for the lack of anything but the minimal connection to her only sibling for the last seventeen years?

When Denia was young, her mother and her aunt had a friendly relationship, but lived in different parts of the large state of California. They would visit each other from time to time. Denia remembered her aunt at Christmastime, sitting by the tree in their living room. Denia's parents had allowed her to visit her aunt's ranch for weeks at a time during the summers. It worked out for everyone since her aunt liked to have her visit, and her parents liked to travel for vacations; but the visits had ended rather suddenly when Denia was eleven years old, and she never knew why.

Through the years, Aunt Melinda had never failed to remember her February birthday. There was always a present that arrived by mail, many times something homemade, just for her. Denia had asked her parents about her aunt and the problem, but always received a brief response. Her mother seemed to get defensive whenever she mentioned her aunt, so she learned to avoid the topic. Occasionally, when her mother was speaking of her childhood, she would mention her sister, and then abruptly change the subject. Once, at fourteen, when having one of the usual mother-daughter disconnects, Denia had asked to stay with her aunt for the summer. She had been told that was not possible, with no other explanation. Even her father had not supported her request. She had always wondered what her Aunt Melinda had done that was so terrible to cause such a rift in their small family.

Now, Denia was angry with herself for not getting in the car and going to Solvang while her aunt was still alive. She was a twenty-eight-year-old adult. Her parents could not have stopped her. Unfortunately, she had been immersed in her own life, and it had been easier to let things go on as they had while years slipped by. Now, here she was, staying in her aunt's house with the mystery surrounding her aunt's death hanging over her head.

Remembering the drive to Solvang last week, they had done pretty well timewise coming up the infamous 405 Freeway, hitting bogs of traffic going through Orange County and crawling through the Los Angeles basin. Once they hit the 101 Freeway heading north, the heavy urban traffic thinned out and Denia was finally able to go a respectable speed. They stopped for brunch in Camarillo, both women needing a pit stop. When there was conversation, her mother spent most of the time talking about her job and plans for the September semester at State College.

Helene Rawlings was fifty-nine and proud of her job as Dean of Students. Denia knew her mother was nervous, speaking quickly, and avoiding any obvious conversation topics related to her sister.

Once on the road again, the drive up the Ventura and Santa Barbara coast had been breathtaking with cloudless, blue skies, and views of the Pacific horizon glimmering in the midday sun. This was the California central coast. When the highway turned inland, away from the coast, an even more rural landscape presented itself. Ranchland and farmland lined both sides of the highway. Dark green, pinion, pine trees hovered low in the open fields over the gold and brown natural grasses. Black cattle dotted hillsides here and there. Signs on the side of the road gave the mileage to Solvang, Santa Maria, and San Luis Obispo.

Her mother fidgeted with the air conditioning vent in front of her, and a building anxiety filled the air within the roomy car. Denia slowed down as the off-ramp for Solvang had come into view on the right, and the familiar windmill on the left side of the road. She remembered this place and the excitement she used to feel when nearing the town where her aunt lived. Turning right at the end of the off-ramp, she headed east on Route 246.

The highway headed directly to Solvang, and traffic slowed going through the small town. They had easily found the Grand View Hotel located by the local golf course. It was not far from the main tourist center of town. Once settled in their room, the receptionist at the hotel desk told them how to find the Solvang Sheriff's Station. They had passed it on their way to the hotel.

Once in the car, Denia drove back toward the center of Solvang. The rectangular modern building with its flat roof looked out of place in a town known for its unique

Scandinavian architectural attributes. Signage on the front of the Sheriff's Station told Denia she was in the right place as she pulled the Explorer into one of the available parking spaces.

Denia knew her mother was apprehensive as she stammered her name and reason for being there to the uniformed officer who sat behind the front counter. After a few moments, the policewoman led them to a very small office holding a desk, piled high with stacks of folders, and told them to have a seat in two well-worn office chairs placed in front of the desk.

A short time later, a tall, thin man in a khaki-colored uniform entered the room, passing by them to reach the chair behind the desk. He identified himself as Sergeant Nelson, stating that he had been the officer who called Denia's mother the day before.

After introductions, he offered his condolences regarding the death in the family. He pulled out a pad of paper and grabbed a manila folder on top of one of the piles on the desk. He cleared his throat, pushed his straight, blonde hair across his forehead, and picked up a pencil in his left hand. Denia looked at the small block of wood with black lettering sitting on the front of the desk that read: Sgt. Lee Nelson. Denia wondered if he was Danish, knowing that Solvang had been settled by a Danish group of settlers back in the early 1900s. She couldn't help but notice his clear, dark blue eyes and handsome face as he shifted his body slightly, prior to addressing her mother.

"Mrs. Rawlings, I asked you to come here today before you went out to your sister's house for a reason," he began. "We still have our perimeter tape surrounding the part of the yard where your sister's body was found. Your sister was very well known here in town, so her death has been the focus of gossip and speculation, spreading like wildfire around here since yesterday. I was out at the ranch this morning with one of our deputies to make sure we had gathered any possible evidence."

"Evidence?" Helene Rawlings asked, trying to clarify what the officer was saying.

"Melinda Greystone's death is currently under investigation due to the circumstances surrounding her death. Her body is at the Coroner's Office in Santa Maria. The coroner will probably have to complete an autopsy to determine the cause of death."

Helene Rawlings let out a small gasp.

"We are also trying to determine the time of death," he stated.

The two women remained silent.

"When someone dies suddenly at home, it meets the criteria for a referral to the coroner," he explained, softening his tone. "Yesterday morning, dispatch received a call from Jorje Hernandez, your sister's farmhand. He was crying and yelling for an ambulance. When they got out there, the paramedics called us. They had determined that your sister was dead."

The officer paused for a few moments and then continued.

"I've known Melinda for years. I went out there with my deputy, not knowing what we would find. Your sister was found outside her house, on the ground in the back lot, beside the old barn. There was no apparent reason for her death, no visible blood, and no obvious injury. We took pictures of the scene, and I called the coroner."

"Then why are you investigating?" Helene asked, not understanding the need.

"We are trying to rule out a possible homicide," he answered. "It looked to me like your sister's body may have been drug along the ground for some ways, and deliberately half hidden by the barn."

"Who would hurt a sixty-seven-year-old lady that has lived here for over thirty years?"

"Well, ma'am, that *is* the obvious question. I tried to interview Jorje yesterday, but he was so upset we thought we would have to take him to the hospital. We ended up taking him to the Urgent Care in town for the doctor to see him, and then Deputy Cleeves took him home. He's quite elderly - early seventies - and he has worked for your sister for over ten years. I went out to his house in Lompoc this morning to get a better picture of what happened when he found Melinda. He said he went over to your sister's house as usual, early yesterday morning. He started his daily chores with watering. He was headed to the barn to get some tools when he discovered your sister on the ground. He said that he immediately ran to the office building next to the barn to use the phone. He blames himself for not coming to the house first thing, and for not being in time to help. He said that he had been out in the orchard and had not heard anything in the yard prior to finding her."

The lawman paused, looked at Helene and said, "So now, we are waiting for the Coroner's Report."

He paused again, changing the subject. "Have you spoken with your sister recently?"

Denia noticed her mother's head come up.

"No, not since last month, the first part of July," she responded.

Denia looked at her mother in surprise.

"You told her?" she said in a demanding tone to her mother, momentarily forgetting she was sitting in a police station.

The good sergeant sat up in his chair with his full attention on Denia for the first time.

"Yes," her mother answered, turning to look at Denia. "She called me when she got the tea set you sent back after the wedding."

Then more to herself, "That was the last time I spoke to her."

Denia felt the heat and knew her face had flushed. Sergeant Nelson did not miss that there was some intrigue between mother and daughter.

"I was supposed to get married in June," Denia explained, looking directly at the man. "The wedding was called off at the last minute. I sent back all the gifts. Aunt Melinda had sent me a tea set."

The sergeant focused his questions back to Denia's mother.

"When you talked to your sister, did she mention anything to you that you think could be helpful? Were there any problems she might have mentioned?"

"We only spoke for a short time, mainly about Denia," her mother looked at her, with the beginning of tears forming in her eyes.

Then, after thinking for a moment, "She did say something that surprised me. She said she was thinking of selling the ranch. She said it was getting too much for her. I never thought she would think of selling the ranch. She and her late husband originally bought it back in the late seventies. She was very sentimental about the place and said years ago that she would die there."

Mrs. Rawlings stopped talking. No one would add the last obvious thought…she *did* die there.

"Are you staying in town?" asked the man with the blue eyes, looking at Denia for the answer as Helene appeared distressed, rummaging in her purse for a tissue.

"Yes, at the Grand View Hotel," Denia answered.

The sergeant stood up, indicating that the meeting was over.

"Well, I will let you know when I hear from the coroner. Melinda's attorney is Eugene Sorenson. Here's his phone number," he said, handing Denia a yellow, sticky-pad note. "You need to call him. He has your aunt's Will, and I think he knows about the funeral arrangements your aunt made. As a second thought, can I have your cell phone numbers, just in case I need to reach you?"

Denia provided the numbers to the tall sergeant standing next to her. She looked at her mother, who was emotionally upset and tearful. Denia quietly thanked the officer, gently taking her mother's upper arm, leading her out of the office.

Helene had been almost silent on the ride back to the hotel, introverted with her thoughts. Denia took the lead in getting in touch with the attorney, making an appointment for the following morning at nine-thirty. Neither of them had been hungry. The thought of going out to eat would have required too much effort after the wearing day. It was a quiet evening.

Back to her first full day on the ranch, Denia needed to finish dressing. She searched the floor of the bedroom for her shoes.

"Where did I take them off last night?"

No one answered.

She thought that she must have left them downstairs, so she headed toward the stairs. No, she found the well-worn tennis shoes when she glanced into the bathroom, right where she had taken them off. Retrieving them, she sat down on the edge of the tub to put them on.

Going downstairs, she noticed the cat was still on the windowsill, the living room was sheathed in morning light, and she was still hungry. Maybe a low-fat yogurt cup would hit the spot, she thought, as she headed for the refrigerator. She stood in the kitchen looking out the window over the sink. Her thoughts drifted as she ate small spoonfuls to prolong the enjoyment of the vanilla treat.

On Wednesday morning, two days after hearing about Aunt Melinda's death, and their first morning in Solvang, Denia and her mother had gotten coffee and some wonderful, freshly baked scones at a nearby bakery for breakfast. They easily found the attorney's office located in the nearby town of Santa Maria, not far from the highway. It was on the second floor of a modern looking office building. The wood-paneled reception area had the typical chairs found in doctors' and lawyers' offices – chairs that looked good but were not very comfortable.

Eugene Sorenson was the son of the founder of Sorenson Law Firm, and on that day, he arrived late to the office. As he entered, carrying a brown leather briefcase overflowing with files, Denia and her mother stood up. The receptionist introduced them, after which they followed him down a short hallway to a nicely appointed office.

Sitting in much more comfortable chairs across the mahogany desk from Mr. Sorenson, Denia and her mother waited as he located all the various documents. The lawyer was probably in his late thirties, and his clean-cut, good looks could not be denied. He was well-dressed in a blue suit, cream-colored shirt, and a tie with shades of blue gray. He was of medium height with wide shoulders and nice hands. His hair was dark brown, cut short and combed to the side. He wore no jewelry. Dark brows and lashes framed his chocolate brown eyes. His face was clean-shaven with well-set features, giving him the look of the modern male that could be found on the fashion pages of magazines.

Helene Rawlings fidgeted in her chair, trying to decide what to do with her purse. Denia peered out the window, seeing maple treetops, where late summer leaves were already starting to change from green to muted yellow.

She had met two men in two days, both attractive. The

fact that she even noticed might mean she was emotionally starting to move on after Jeff, she thought to herself.

After retrieving files and shuffling papers, the lawyer seemed to have all the items in order and was ready to address Denia and her mother. His tone was professional as he first addressed the funeral arrangements which had been made by Melinda Greystone. She had arranged for a cremation and had named Olson Mortuary in Solvang. She had also made arrangements for a small memorial service to be held at the mortuary. She requested that her ashes be released to her sister; and Eugene, as Denia decided to call him, handed her mother an envelope addressed to her.

Helene Rawlings opened the envelope and showed Denia the short, handwritten note that requested her sister to scatter her ashes at Melinda's beloved turtle pond on her ranch. Denia's mother started to cry. Eugene handed Helene a tissue and waited a few moments before continuing.

Speaking primarily to Mrs. Rawlings, "Your sister had a Will on file with us for many years. In fact, my father was the attorney who handled all the paperwork when Mr. Greystone died twenty-five years ago. Since then, we have handled all of Melinda's affairs," he waited to let that information settle.

"She came to our office in July, and to my surprise, requested that her Will be updated. She also wanted to establish a Trust. So, the Will that I have today is her last Will and Testament, which was recently changed to her specifications. Mrs. Greystone had her own copy, and I will provide the executor with a copy."

Using the traditional legalese, the attorney proceeded to read the document, stopping periodically to explain the meaning of some of the terminology. Denia was paying attention when the Will named her mother as executor. Her aunt had also named her mother as beneficiary to her life insurance of twenty-five thousand dollars and an account with stocks and bonds held with Cosmopolitan Financial. Eugene stopped to explain that the account had been specifically excluded from the Trust, which contained the rest of Melinda's estate. The stock account was worth over two million dollars. Helene opened her mouth in surprise as to the size of the account. Whatever had transpired between the sisters, there was still a strong connection to her sister as far as Melinda was concerned.

The Will also left the amount of ten thousand dollars to Melinda's dedicated farmhand, Jorje Hernandez. A sealed envelope with this money was included with the Will. It was to be given to Mr. Hernandez by the executor. The lawyer explained that this was unusual, but the gentleman was known to be afraid of banks and did not have a bank account. Melinda had always paid him in cash and goods from the farm.

This was just the beginning of the changes that took place in the office that day. The handsome lawyer went on to explain the Trust, what it was, and what was included under the Trust.

"All of the property, the house, the contents of the house, and the contents of Melinda's bank accounts were included under the Trust. As a surprise to both Denia and her mother, Melinda ran a successful, Internet, mail-order business called *Candles by Candlewick, Inc.*, which was also included in the Trust.

Looking at Denia the lawyer asked, "Are you Gardenia Rawlings?"

More than a little surprised at the use of her legal name, Denia nodded her head. No one had called her Gardenia from as far back as she could remember. She always tried not to disclose the regrettable choice of names, sounding like something left over from the nineteenth century.

"Denia is the name I use," she replied to the attorney, who was scrutinizing her from across the desk.

"Well, Miss Rawlings, your aunt must have thought very highly of you, because as of today with your aunt's death, you are the sole beneficiary of the Trust."

Denia stared at him, "What does that mean?"

"For all intents and purposes, you have inherited the bulk of your aunt's estate;" he said, in a matter-of-fact manner.

Denia was stunned and her mother was taken aback in her seat.

"You now own a ranch in the Santa Ynez Valley. It's a highly coveted area."

In complete surprise, Denia had not known what to say. Just the night before, her mother had assumed that the property was going to come to *her* and was remarking on what she was going to do with it. Not to mention 'getting rid of years' worth of junk in that house'.

Eugene went on, "Your aunt mentioned that she had an offer on the property last spring for over ten million dollars, but she had decided not to sell."

Then, looking at both women, who were trying to take in one revelation after another, he said, "Did something happen in the family this summer that could have made Melinda make all of these changes?"

Denia remembered her embarrassment at the moment. She decided that she was not going to tell this newly acquainted attorney about being dumped at the altar.

"Ten million dollars?" her mother had interrupted.

"Well, the property is over twenty acres," he explained, "and there is a natural spring and a pond on the property. The house could probably use a bit of updating, but the offer on the property was from a local winery in Santa Ynez, so they probably wouldn't be all that interested in the house."

A while later, after discussing all the next legal steps, the need for copies of the Death Certificate among other things, the attorney handed Denia another envelope with "Keys" written on the outside label.

"Here are an extra set of keys to the house, and here is my business card. We can work on getting all of this put into your name, and work with the banks to get access to the accounts."

Then, as an afterthought, "Did you plan on staying in the area?"

"I live and work in San Diego and this was *really* not expected, so I'm going to have to think about how to manage this," Denia explained. "I took off a few days, but I have to be back at work on Monday."

"Yes, I'm sure this was a surprise. Let me know if I can help you with anything. I've lived around here all my life."

Looking back at the documents before him, he added, "Oh, one more thing…I have an envelope addressed to you."

The last unopened envelope had '*Denia*' in a neat script on the front. Tears came to Denia's eyes as she recognized her aunt's writing. She had taken the envelope and put it in her purse. She did not want to read it there, or even when her mother was looking over her shoulder. She wanted to wait until she was alone.

Denia knew that her life had suddenly taken a turn – as sometimes happened - unexpected doors had opened.

2

THE BAT

Putting her dishes into the old porcelain sink and wiping down the gray tile kitchen counter, Denia was thinking about the possibility of another cat. She tried to review the events of her aunt's death. She was not sure how long a cat could live outside without food. There *was* water around. Feral cats managed to live outside on their own, she reasoned.

Denia mused out loud to the empty room, "Let's see, Auntie was found lying in the yard on Monday, we came up on Tuesday, and went to the attorney on Wednesday. Thursday, we met with Jorje, out here at the ranch. The coroner released Auntie's body to the mortuary on Friday and the sheriff came to the hotel. Dad drove up on Saturday and the memorial service was that evening. I drove back to San Diego on Sunday following Mom and Dad. That was seven days right there."

She remembered how the long drive south had allowed time for thinking about the new prospects for her life. By the time Denia reached her apartment, she had made up her mind to leave San Diego and return to Greystone Ranch. It was a chance for a new life. She was not sure if it was fate, predestination or kismet, but Denia felt strongly that it was the right thing for her.

Quitting her job had been easier than she thought it would be. Mr. Leven, her manager, had requested that she stay for two weeks, but Denia had explained about the ranch, the animals, and her need to get back right away. Her best friend, Heather, answered the call to help her pack and put most of her things in storage. The rest was packed into suitcases and boxes and loaded into the back of the Explorer. Heather was still living at home with her parents; so, she had jumped for the chance to take over the lease on the furnished apartment. Fortunately, the landlord had agreed rather than have the unit sit empty until it could be re-rented.

"It took three days to quit work and pack, and I drove back here yesterday," again she was speaking into the vacuum. "Today would be twelve days that a missing cat had been outside on its own."

The one currently curled up in the front room had been alright outside until this morning. She would talk to Jorje and try to find the second cat, if there was one.

Denia thought she also needed to call her mother this evening. She sent her a text when she arrived yesterday to let her know she had gotten there safely, but she should probably check in with a phone call. Her parents had been surprised last week, at her quick decision to leave San Diego. Her mother was trying to wrap her head around Denia being so far from home, and her life there. Her father had dubious feelings about Denia taking over a ranch and a business. Concerned as they were, they had to let her go.

Denia understood their reticence. The past week in Solvang, and the memorial service for Aunt Melinda had been especially hard on her mother. Friday had been a tragic day for them. That afternoon, Denia and her mother had just gotten back from lunch, when her mother got the call from Sergeant Nelson. He was on his way over to the hotel to discuss the Coroner's Report with them.

Helene Rawlings sat in a chair by a small desk and Denia sat on one of the beds in the hotel room. The Sergeant seemed very tall standing just inside the door, with his hat in his hand. The officer looked solemn as he removed his sunglasses and pushed the blonde hair on his forehead to one side. Maybe he too had been dreading this meeting.

The sergeant started by telling them about what the coroner believed was the time of Melinda's death.

Looking at Mrs. Rawlings he began, "We believe that Melinda died between five and seven Monday morning. She had been found fully dressed, so there was reason to believe she got up that morning, got dressed, and for some reason went out back."

Neither Denia nor her mother said anything, so he continued.

"Our Department will be ramping up our investigation of this case. According to the coroner, the cause of death was found to be asphyxiation, secondary to strangulation."

Both women expressed surprise, and Helene's hand automatically went up to cover her throat. Denia moved from the bed to stand behind her mother's chair.

"You think someone strangled her?" Denia asked, in a weak voice.

"Not only was she strangled, but the coroner also found a right occipital skull fracture. The thinking is that she was hit from behind - which may have knocked her to the ground - and then strangled. Melinda was tall for a woman, and in good physical shape. So, I'm guessing that the assailant was probably male. We found very little evidence at the crime scene. There were no discernable footprints since the dirt in the area in front of the barn was so well trafficked. I think she may have been killed near the barn, then dragged to a more concealed spot between the barn and the office building where she was found. There were marks on the ground that suggested this. We were able to get photographs and made a plaster mold of the drag marks. We did not find any possible weapons at the scene, and because there was no blood, we weren't aware of any head injury when we first went out there."

"What should we do?" Denia asked.

The officer looked at her with sympathy in his blue eyes.

"There is nothing you can do for now. As I said, we will be doing a full investigation. We'll get a deposition from

Jorje who, at the moment, is the only one we know of who was on the ranch the morning of the murder."

"You don't think *he* did it, do you?" asked Helene, remembering the kind, little man from their meeting the day before. He had offered to care for the animals, as usual, until decisions were made about the ranch.

"No. My deputy and I were with him for some time on Monday, and the man was in shock; but we still need to do a deposition. We will interview all of Melinda's friends and anyone that may have come in contact with her over the last few weeks. We will pull her bank and phone records. We'll have to come out and get her computer to see if there is anything of value on the files. It's going to take some time. We have a murder and no obvious motive or suspect."

Helene broke down crying.

"I can't believe this. Murder? I need to call your father," she said to Denia.

"I better get back to the office," the sheriff said. "I'm very sorry to have to bring you this bad news. The coroner has released the body to the mortuary, so you will need to call them."

He grabbed for the doorknob, started to open the door, and then turned back to face Denia.

"We will be keeping the details of the coroner's report confidential, and I'm asking you not to speak of it. This is a small town and most of the locals know each other. We want to gather as much information as possible prior to the facts of the case getting out. We want to find out who is responsible for Melinda's death before the case gets cold."

The details of the coroner's report had been shocking. A shiver of dread hit Denia, with the determination of murder being rather overwhelming. She had not heard anything from the Sheriff's office since that meeting, but Sergeant Nelson and his deputy had been standing on the sidelines at the memorial service and small reception at the restaurant afterwards. It was eerie to think that maybe the murderer had been there.

Now, still standing in front of the kitchen counter, she came out of her thinking mode as the sound coming from the driveway made Denia look out the front window. A car, followed by a dust cloud, had turned into the driveway from the road. The front yard was large, with the house set back from the road at least a hundred feet. The four-foot, stone wall that went along the front of the property allowed access by car on both sides of the front yard, via the two wide graveled paths. One led back to the garage on the right; and the other followed along the side of the house, leading to the spacious back lot behind the house. Both paths were intersected by a semicircular asphalt drive that bowed near the front door, defining the u-shaped front yard.

Looking through the windows, following the dust, Denia watched the purple PT Cruiser as it passed the turn for the drive to the front door, and continued straight on the wide driveway leading along the side of the house. The car came to a stop next to the small patio near the back door.

A head with a hat appeared on the driver's side of the car; but rather than coming to the back door, it took off toward the herb garden next to the patio. The hat passed the window in front of the kitchen sink and passed the window near the dining room table. Shortly, Denia saw the hat bobbing along the front of the house, passing the window by the front door and the large bay window in the living room, only to disappear around the side of the house. She had seen enough to know that this was the figure of a woman. In less than a minute, a knock was heard at the kitchen's back door.

Denia swung the door open to see the thin, wide-eyed owner of the olive green, cotton hat. Steel-gray hair frizzed out on both sides of the narrow face, which was accented by a long, narrow nose that ended almost in a point. Her cheeks were naturally pink. The mouth was upturned at the corners in a close-lipped smile. Over one arm hung several cloth grocery bags, and she held the familiar box of Morton Salt in her hands.

"Hi, Denia," said a rather high voice. "We met briefly at Melinda's memorial service. I'm Batty Henderson. Actually, it's Bathsheba, but nobody calls me that since my mother passed." She paused. "Today is egg day, and I knew that you wouldn't know that, so I thought I'd better come out."

The lady did look familiar to Denia; but she had looked so different, if Denia was remembering correctly. At the memorial service, she was one of many that had come and given her condolences to Melinda's family. Denia remembered Batty at the restaurant, where she and a group of other town ladies had put together a lovely coffee and pastry buffet for mourners. At that time, the fifty-something's hair had been neatly restrained with combs and clips, smoothed to the back of her head. She had worn a dark blue dress and low-heeled pumps. Her necklace had large chain links on which hung a silver representation of a half-moon. Denia remembered the necklace and the faceted crystal drops that hung from the moon's lower edge.

"Ah, yes," Denia said as she backed away from the doorway, allowing the visitor to enter. "We wanted to thank you and the other ladies for the beautiful reception that you put together after the memorial service."

"It was our pleasure, dear. We loved her," referring to Melinda. "I don't know how we'll get on without her."

Turning from Denia, she walked over to the utility closet at the back of the kitchen, went in and came out again, minus the saltbox.

"Mel always kept that blue trash can in the utility room for the recyclable trash."

She walked to stand by Denia, looking at her with large, round, gray eyes peeking out from under a wrinkled brow.

"Mel and I were like two peas. My heart is broken, but I do think that she would want me to help you get settled. She always hoped you would come up here."

"What is egg day?" Denia asked, feeling that the conversation was getting out of hand.

"Friday and Tuesday are egg days," she explained, one hand on her hip and the other elbow leaning against the kitchen counter. "Jorje collects and washes the eggs in the morning and puts them in the refrigerator in the office. Mel used to take fresh eggs to town twice a week. Solvang is known for the Danish pastries and other goodies, so there is always a lot of baking going on. That is especially true on Friday with everyone getting ready for the onslaught of weekend tourists."

"Well, I just got here yesterday, and I haven't gotten out back, yet. In fact, I was getting ready to go out just now. I haven't been into the office building."

A couple of short "mews" preceded the cat coming into the kitchen, having left its spot in the living room. The cat went directly to Batty's feet and rubbed against her lower legs. Batty bent down and scooped up the cat, cradling it to her chest.

"Hi, Mona, how are you doing, baby?" she said, talking to the cat. "You are going to have to keep Denia company, you know."

"Mona?" Denia asked. "She came to the door this morning. I think she's been outside all this time. The house was locked up when I got here."

"Actually, her name is Pomona, after the Roman goddess of fruit and nuts; but pretty soon after Mel adopted her, even *she* was calling her Mona."

The cat responded to Batty scratching her head with a couple of soft 'mews'.

"Have you met Isis yet?"

"If that's another cat, no," Denia answered, "but I *did* notice that there were two rugs by the window. I was going out back to talk to Jorje. I thought he might be able to let me know if there *was* one."

"Yes, Isis is another of Mel's cats. Let's go out back and find Jorje – maybe he's seen her. I'll show you the office."

Batty put the cat down and started out the door, only to turn around abruptly, heading to the pantry at the back of the kitchen. Confused, Denia followed her. The pantry was a small room lined with wooden shelves from floor to ceiling.

Denia groaned as she gave a closer look at the shelves packed to the brim with canned goods, empty and filled jars, and small appliances, and flower vases among other things. Here was another space that would need to be de-cluttered, she thought to herself.

Batty had stopped just inside the door where there was a rack labeled '*KEYS*' in large black letters, with several hooks protruding below holding different sets of keys.

"The ones with the Chevy key ring are for the garage and Mel's Range Rover. Here is the extra garage door opener - the other one is in the Rover. Oh, and here are the keys to the office. They have the crystal bead key ring. Jorje and Olivia also have a key to the office."

In a flash she was gone, past Denia and out the door, showing only the back of the blue, denim skirt. At least Denia would be able to put the Explorer into the garage tonight, she thought. That is, if the garage wasn't too full of stuff, which was a probability based upon the condition of the house.

Originally, the house had been built back in the nineteen-fifties, so there was no garage when Melinda and her husband bought the property. One of the first things that James Greystone had done was build a three-car garage with a small workshop on one side. Denia wondered if her aunt still had the old '64 Chevy Impala that Denia had seen in the garage years ago. Her aunt had kept her husband's favorite car after his death.

Denia headed through the kitchen door, onto the flagstone patio. Pots of red geraniums made a border on the edge of the patio beside the small, kitchen herb garden. The morning mist was gone, replaced by a bright August sun making its way toward a midday sky. She looked across the wide, open, back lot trying to locate the lady in the green hat.

Tall pepper trees lined the property line along the driveway from the road, almost even with the house. From there, a six-foot fence covered with boysenberry vines went all the way down the property line, behind the chicken coop, and continued to the five-foot, chain-link fence that crossed the back of the expansive open space. A large, chain-link gate allowed an opening to enter the back of the property, that her aunt called 'the orchard'.

Denia started toward the back of the large, dirt lot, extending the length of a football field behind the well-worn, two-story house. The chicken coop, about thirty feet past the house, was really the chicken *house*. This was no small coop. It was home to almost twenty chickens and was about eight feet high and twelve feet wide. It was made of wood, with a pitched roof, and painted with a redwood stain. Chicken wire covered three sides, including the large entry gate that was also covered with the wire known for its small weave. The nesting boxes lined the back, mounted on a solid wooden wall. Chickens milled about their familiar space, sharing conversations among themselves. The large, plastic flaps used for covering the open sides during the winter and inclement weather, were tied into long cylindrical rolls toward the top of the coop.

As Denia hurried across the dirt yard, a breeze blew strands of her straight, auburn hair across her cheek, escaping from the elastic band holding the shoulder-length mass at the base of her neck. It was warm outside, and she wanted to remove the long- sleeved shirt.

Batty was on her way down the long yard, arms flying at her sides, grocery bags flapping. She was heading toward a large, square pen built in the corner where the boysenberry fence met the chain-link. In the middle of the pen was a small, doghouse-type, wooden structure with a black-shingled roof. Batty stopped at the pen where Jorje stood leaning on the fence rail on the side of the pen. Standing on top of the little house was a goat - a small, white goat. Nobody had said anything about a goat, Denia thought with exasperation.

"Billy, get off of there!" yelled Batty at the animal, waving one arm.

The goat remained on the roof of the wooden shelter.

As Denia walked toward the batty lady and Jorje, she noticed that Batty and Jorje seemed to know each other well and were laughing at the little kid. Jorge opened the gate to the pen and the goat was off the perch and out the opening in a split second. It jumped up on Jorje's legs in greeting and followed him like a puppy dog as he went through the gate to the orchard.

"Keep an eye on her," yelled Batty to Jorje. "We don't need to have the vet out here again from her eating those apples on the ground."

Jorje waved to her in acknowledgement. Denia reached Batty and stopped next to her.

"A goat???" Denia asked in astonishment.

"Yeah, well it's a long story."

Denia waited in silence ready to hear it.

"Two guys showed up in a pick-up one day with this little goat and were trying to sell it to Jorje. Some of the Mexicans around here raise goats to sell for food," Batty explained.

Denia made a face.

"It's pretty common. Anyway, Mel was out here in the yard and was horrified at the idea of the cute, little thing being sold for food, so she bought it. None of us had any idea of how to keep a goat, but Jorje went to the feed store and got the right food and built a pen for it."

"What was my aunt going to do with a goat?"

"Oh, she had this harebrained idea of breeding her when she got bigger so that she could get goat milk. She was going to make soap using the goat's milk."

"Soap?" Denia repeated.

"I know," she said, commiserating, "but that was Mel for you. That was two months ago, and the little thing is growing like crazy. She gets into everything when she's out of the pen and eats everything. Mel had to have the livestock vet out here already. She ate so many apples off the ground when she was out back with Jorje, that she made herself sick - not to mention raiding Mel's new sweet potato patch *and* eating the lavender plants. She gets purple all over her face from eating the boysenberries off the vines along the fence; but she's sweet, she loves company, and she'll follow you around. I think she thinks she's a dog."

"So, she sleeps in the pen at night?"

"No, she sleeps in the barn in one of those old horse stalls. Jorje brings her out to the pen and feeds her in the morning," Batty explained. "She likes being out of the pen and makes a lot of noise until she's let out. Mel was letting her come into the office building, but I put my foot down on that. She's not housebroken and would do her business on the floor. Mel had to agree with me on *that* one."

Denia looked over at the large office building that had not existed the last time she visited her aunt. It was a tall, long building that had been built onto the back wall of the garage. The door of the office faced the dirt yard behind the house. There was a space the size of an alley between the office building and the enormous, old barn. The building was painted a light tan color, the same as the garage and house, and merged well with the landscape. A large, carved, wooden sign hung over the entrance. *CANDLEWICK* stood out in italicized, bright yellow letters against a black background. On the right side of the sign was an engraving of a lit candle in an old-style candleholder.

"Come on, let's show you the office," Batty said, grabbing Denia by the arm.

As they walked in a direct path toward the office door, Batty let go of Denia's arm and strayed toward the space between the office building and the barn. The space remained taped off with the police perimeter tape. Ducking under the tape, she stepped gingerly into the space and knelt down. She stretched out her hand, palm down, to touch the pebbled dirt. She sat there, very still. Denia was touched by the show of tenderness Batty displayed for her dear friend and allowed her the time in silence.

"Fly away, love, fly away…," Batty whispered into the cloistered air.

A moment later she stood and came back to where Denia stood waiting. The gray eyes with wrinkled corners were rimmed in tears. For want of a tissue, Batty grabbed the shirttail of her cotton blouse and used it to wipe her eyes. Smudges of mascara were left on the material.

"Well, let's go in," she said, in a pretense of cheerfulness.

When Batty unlocked and opened the oak door to the office, Denia was taken aback as she stepped over the threshold. The clean, modern feel of stainless steel assailed the senses while looking down the length of the rectangular space. Long, shiny utility tables, side-by-side and end-to-end, provided a lengthy, uninterrupted workspace that dominated the center of the room.

On the left near the door, was a room containing a cherry- colored, front-loading washer and dryer staring back at her with large, round eyes. A folding table and pull-down hanging racks took up one wall of the space.

"Here's the powder room," said Batty, opening a white door next to the laundry room.

A white pedestal sink, and toilet lined a beige wall. Wallpaper on the back wall presented variegated colors of white, black, and tan in a scene of birch tree trunks. A large, square, decorative mirror hung over the sink.

Outside the little room's wall, hovered a two-door, stainless steel refrigerator. Stacks of unfilled egg cartons leaned in a pile against the appliance. Along the wall, three short windows showing the side of the old barn, let in filtered light illuminating one of the biggest, deepest, steel sinks Denia had ever seen. Shiny faucets and spray nozzles rose up from the surrounding blue granite countertop. A dishwasher and white cabinets filled the long area below the counter. A microwave, toaster, and coffeemaker provided an improvised kitchen at the end of the counter; and a small, round table with three chairs, finished the back corner of the room.

The main feature of the back wall was a large, six-burner stove with bright, red, front knobs proclaiming its upscale brand. A large exhaust hood hung over the burners. Generous counter space hugged the stove on both sides. Below the counters, deep open shelves held tall metal pots. A bank of wide drawers stood at one end. Denia pulled open the top drawer which was filled with various sizes of long spoons, ladles, and cooking thermometers. At one side of the drawer was a partitioned space lined with black velvet used to hold scissors and two knives. Denia looked at the sharp blades with curiosity. Gleaming stones were inset toward the end of the black handles. She could not resist the urge to pick up one of the knives from its velvet bed.

Watching Denia, "Those are the athames we use to cut the herbs for the candles," Batty explained in response to Denia's unasked question. "Mel loved these."

Denia replaced the dagger into its nest. She had never heard of knives called athames.

The wall opposite the windows held three tall, metal cabinets, each clearly labeled: DYES, FRAGRANCE & OILS, and WICK SPOOLS.

What looked like old, wooden, clothes drying stands held sets of multi-colored tapers hanging by their wicks over the round bars of the racks. Next, stood wooden shelves about five feet in height, standing like library book stacks, perpendicular to the wall. There were narrow aisles between the stacks for ease of access. Again, each stack of shelves was clearly labeled: SCENTED, UNSCENTED, LAVENDER, and ROSEMARY.

The shelves held many different sizes and colors of wax towers awaiting their wrappers.

Beside the stacks of shelves was a horseshoe-shaped space dedicated to packaging. The workspace contained rolls of bubble wrap, stacks of folded boxes, rolls of tape, and more.

Denia was taking it all in. She realized that this was an active business space, producing a product. Batty came up the aisle and stood beside Denia.

"When Melinda first started Candlewick, it was a whim. She learned to make candles, wanting to use some of the lavender and rosemary she was growing here on the ranch. She moved her old stove into the workshop by the garage and bought a new one for the kitchen. She started building an inventory, and our friend John suggested that she go online to sell the candles. He set up a website for her and incorporated an ordering system with lots of doodads.

Orders for candles had started out slow at first, so Mel was able to keep up with them; but then, the orders really started to come in and the little workshop was just not big enough. She had stuff overflowing into the garage, and there was no good place to store the candles and supplies. So, she hired an architect, and they designed the office. After a bout of getting the permits and bids from contractors, it took about four months to finish the building. That was three years ago. This space has been wonderful. We've spent many hours out here," Batty finished on a nostalgic note.

They wandered along the room to the large, windowed cubicle that housed all of the accouterments of a modern office. A large, clean desk holding a laptop and flat screen monitor took up the space by the front window overlooking the back lot with the chicken coop across the way. The desk held a phone, two plastic trays, a file holder, and a round pencil holder. Sitting on the nearby windowsill were two small picture frames, one containing a picture of Melinda and her husband, and the other holding a picture of a group of women with Melinda sitting in the middle. The top of the desk was so neat and organized that it belied its owner.

Another small desk with a desktop computer and phone was just inside the doorway along the cubicle wall. A low cabinet next to the desk held two printers. The corner held a copy machine. Two short file cabinets lined the back wall.

Above the file cabinets was a large, framed canvas that demanded the eye of the viewer. Of course, everyone would recognize the subject of the landscape: Stonehenge, older than history itself. The scene on the Salisbury Plain showed the monument at the last glimmer of sunset. A clear, star-filled sky covered the upper limits of the picture, while shades of rose, red, and orange backlit the standing ring of stones.

"She promised me that we would go there when I retired," said Batty, gazing at the landscape. "She had gone there once with Jim back in the sixties. She called it 'awe inspiring'."

Denia did another look around the office.

"This place is so neat and organized. The house is such a cluttered mess. I never would have believed this."

"The house was her nest. She was sentimental and kept all that was dear to her there. She loved this office and was so proud of her business, but thought of this as a workplace," explained Batty.

"Is that a closet back there?" asked Denia, indicating the door in the back corner of the room.

"Oh, I have to show you *this*," said Batty with enthusiasm, taking off toward the door, talking with the assumption that Denia was right behind her.

"Your aunt planted a lavender field over between the garage and that steep hill that goes along the side of the property. It's so pretty when the lavender is blooming in front of the hill covered with golden grass. It looks like a picture of the lavender fields in France. Mel loved it," she paused to take a breath.

"Anyway, she harvests the lavender, dries it and stores it in wooden beer barrels. We use it in the candles and make sachets with it. Also, there is the rosemary, which she cuts the sprigs of when it's in bloom with the little blue flowers. We keep all the dried herbs and flowers back here in the storeroom."

She opened the door to the back room and the strong smell of plants permeated the air.

Denia was a few paces behind the batty lady, so when she entered the small room filled with wooden shelves on one side and a line of barrels on the other, she did not notice at first, that Batty was on her knees at the far end of the room.

"Oh, Isis! Isis, baby," she lamented, leaning over an outstretched form of black fur.

Denia knelt beside Batty, noticing that the prone animal was lying in front of an empty water dish. Batty tried to pick up the cat, which emitted a small sound when moved. Batty opened the cat's eye, and saw it dilate with the sudden light.

"She's still alive. Get me something to put her in. We have to get her to the vet."

Denia ran into the outer room and grabbed a bin from the lower shelf on the closest steel table. She emptied the candle molds onto the table and snatched a towel from the stove counter, putting it in the bottom of the bin while running into the storeroom. Batty lifted the limp animal into the bin and headed to the door of the office as fast as she could go, with Denia trailing in her wake.

3

THE SECOND CAT

Denia and Batty sat on the hard wooden benches on the CAT side of the veterinary office reception area. Other than a young woman with a nosey beagle on the DOG side, the reception area was empty. This day was definitely not going as Denia planned.

The ride to the vet's office had been spine rattling. Batty drove like she walked…fast! The ride had been a blur, with the low-riding PT Cruiser hitting every available bump in the road. Once off the rural road leading into town from the ranch, Batty had zigged and zagged through several of the twisted little streets of Solvang. Red, gray, and black-shingled A-framed roofs and decorative turrets of the quaint buildings went by the car window, as Denia tried to hold the container with the cat steady on her lap. Suddenly, the car came to a sharp stop, pulling into a driveway that led to a back parking lot behind a white office building.

When Denia went through the front door of the office, carrying the plastic bin holding the unresponsive cat, she went straight to the reception desk. The blonde girl in the green scrub uniform, with Molly on her nametag, saw the need for immediate attention for the animal. She grabbed the container and ran through the doorway leading to the back of the office. After a few minutes she returned to the front desk, telling Denia and Batty to take a seat.

"Dr. Anderson is assessing the cat," she explained. "Have you been here before?" Molly asked.

"No," Denia replied.

She handed Denia a clipboard with a form.

"The top form is to give us permission to treat the cat. We need that right away. The second form is your personal information and explains our payment policy."

"Actually, I just moved here, and I don't have a job here, but I'll do the best I can to fill this out."

Batty piped in, "She is Melinda Greystone's niece, so if you look under Melinda's name you will have the address and phone number. I am sure there is information on the cat because Melinda used to come here. The cat's name is Isis. Dr. Anderson will probably recognize her."

"That will help," said the receptionist, as she started searching her files for the cat's medical notes.

"Don't worry," said Batty speaking to Denia, "you will like Hans - I mean, Dr. Anderson. We were all happy when he decided to go in with Dr. Craig and stay local for his veterinary practice. Olivia, his mother, is a close friend of Mel and me. She comes out to the office at the ranch two days a week to check for new orders and get them sent out. We try to maintain a five-day turnaround time from when the candle order comes in to when we get it in the mail. Olivia is actually on the payroll for Candlewick," said Batty.

"It sounds like you both were very involved with the business," Denia inquired.

"Yes. I do most of the bookkeeping for the business, Olivia did a lot of the day-to-day, but Mel did the most work when it came to making the candles. I still work two days a week at the Harrison Accounting Firm here in town. I've been with them for over twenty years, and I haven't retired, yet - just cut down on the days I work. Olivia hasn't known what to do since Mel's death. It may be too soon, but you will have to let us know what you want to do about the business. For now, there's probably enough inventory to meet any orders that come in."

"I just got here. I need a little time to try to get my head around all of this," Denia said, her voice showing some stress.

"I understand," said Batty. "So, about Hans…he was away at college in Oregon and then he went to veterinary school in Kansas. He's only been back home since last spring. He didn't like Kansas. He likes to go surfing, and there's no ocean in Kansas."

Time passed. They watched as the lady with the beagle left, and the office was empty. Batty and Denia were quiet, waiting for word on the cat. Molly disturbed Denia's train of thought when she beckoned them to follow her into the back office. She led them down a long hallway and into a small consultation room with a raised, steel, examination table in the center.

No sooner had they gotten into the room, then a young man entered, saying 'hello' to Batty, and introducing himself as Dr. Anderson to Denia. He was a little taller than Denia, slight of frame, and had the tanned face of someone that went to the beach frequently. His straight, brown hair was long and tied in a band at the back of his head. He wore a blue lab coat over a striped shirt and blue jeans.

"Are you Melinda's niece?" The vet's blue-green eyes peered at Denia with obvious curiosity.

"Yes," Denia replied.

"I grew up knowing her. I was so sorry to hear of her death. She always encouraged me when I told her that I wanted to be a veterinarian. I'm very sorry for your loss."

"Thanks," responded Denia.

"Didn't you live in San Diego and were supposed to get married this summer, but the wedding ended up being called off?"

Denia could feel a flush rising to her face and was too surprised at the question to immediately answer.

"Sorry," he said, realizing that he had said too much. "My mother and Melinda were close friends, and I did hear about it."

"Hans," Batty interrupted, exasperated at the man's lack

of sensitivity, "what about Isis?"

"Isis, Isis," he said while getting back to the issue at hand. "*If* she makes it through this, she will have used up at least one of her nine lives."

He opened and reviewed the chart he was holding in his hand.

"I've given her a bolus of intravenous fluids and taken some blood for tests. She is severely dehydrated and is probably in kidney failure. I would say that her condition is guarded. We're continuing the IVs and we're now in a waiting game to see how she responds to treatment. She will have to stay overnight. I'll stay here with her. I can call you this evening to let you know how she's doing."

"What if she doesn't come out of it?" Denia asked.

"She's already responding to tactile stimuli, so I have some hope for her. We need to give her some time to react to the fluids. I'll do some labs again in the morning, and we can discuss her status then."

Denia realized there was nothing they could do at this point, and she might as well go home and wait for a call. Batty and Hans carried on a short conversation regarding his mother. They stopped at the front desk on their way out of the office, and Denia made a down payment on the services. Walking out to the car, Denia could not help but wonder how much all of this was going to cost. Since Isis was her aunt's beloved pet, she would just have to hope for the best.

Getting into the car, Denia pushed some of the items on the floor aside to make room for her feet. Batty grabbed a few of the bags and tossed them into the back seat. Denia had barely gotten her seatbelt fastened when the car jerked backwards out of the parking space, subsequently jerking forward down the driveway and onto the street. Once on the main street, traffic demanded a slower speed, which gave Denia a chance to take a closer look at some of the local businesses. Stopped at a red light, Denia broke the silence in the car.

"Why is it that everyone I meet in this town seems to know about my personal business? He is a stranger to me but knows that I was stood up at my wedding. It's embarrassing."

"I assume that you are speaking of Hans," answered Batty. "Don't fret, he's harmless, and a nice guy by the way. Mel knew a lot of people in this town, and Hans' mother was a part of her inner circle of friends. Mel had no husband or family here. I'm sure that it was hard for her, at times, to listen to all the rest of us birds running on about our children and grandchildren. So, when she spoke with your mother, she would share the happenings with the rest of us."

"By '*happenings*', you mean the details of my private life. What do you mean 'when she talked to my mother'? They barely spoke to each other," Denia asked.

"No, you are wrong there, Denia. They were sisters, and even though there was an age gap and some disagreements, they were the only family each other had. They spoke on the phone quite frequently. Your aunt was always interested in your mother and father, and what was happening in your life."

Denia sat in silence. Batty had revealed some food for

thought. Sometimes you think you know your parents, and then something happens to broaden your picture of them as a person. Obviously, her mother had kept some things to herself when it came to her relationship with her sister. Denia knew that her mother's distress over her sister's death was genuine over the past couple weeks.

The inside of the car was quiet. They were now on the road out of town and a more rural landscape came into view. Low hills with grapevines lined the side of the roadway.

Another thought came to Denia's mind prompting her to ask, "What was the salt thing?"

She was remembering Batty and the salt box from that morning.

"Oh, that was just a little protection charm," said Batty, looking at the road ahead. "It's been used for centuries, and hopefully for the good."

"A protection charm?"

"Yes, dear. You will just have to humor an old lady. Just a little added protection for you and the house," said Batty, with a dismissive tone.

As the car approached the front of the ranch, Denia had to admire the little house basking in the early afternoon light. The two-story building was set back from the road and faced the roadway. Its tan exterior was accented by white trim and a steep, charcoal shingled roof. A dining room window, front door, and living room bay window made up the lower level. Window shutters and the front door gleamed with black enamel paint. Three dormer windows accented the upper story. Rose bushes bloomed under the front windows. An ornamental, Japanese maple tree stood by the driveway. Small, well-trimmed boxwoods lined both sides of the flagstone path leading from the asphalt drive to the door. Denia was still trying to get used to the idea that this was now *her* house. No, it was now her new *home*.

As they pulled into the driveway, Batty insisted on collecting the fresh eggs and taking them into town. Prior to getting out of the car, Batty added Denia's cell number to her phone and wrote her number on a scrap of paper handing it to Denia.

"I'll call you in the morning to find out how Isis is doing," Batty said, getting out of the car with her bags in tow.

Denia stepped out onto the flagstone patio.

"I'll lock up the office," Batty called back over her shoulder.

Denia let herself into the kitchen, realizing she was hungry. She wandered into the pantry, scanning the shelves.

"Guess it's canned soup tonight," she said out loud, as she heard Batty's car leaving the drive.

Soon after the purple car pulled onto the frontage road, Denia heard the crunch of the driveway gravel. Looking out the front window, she saw a black and white police car pulling onto the asphalt drive in front of the house.

"Now, what?" Denia said and was already heading toward the front door when she heard the forceful knock.

Swinging the door open, Denia came face-to-face with

a deputy sheriff, whom she had previously seen with Sergeant Nelson at the memorial service.

"Ah, Miss Rawlings," he stated, rather than asked. "I'm Deputy Cleeves. We met at the restaurant, after the service for your aunt."

"Oh, yes," said Denia. "It was so nice of the town's ladies to put the reception together on such short notice."

"Sergeant Nelson asked me to come out here when he heard that you were staying at the ranch," explained the deputy.

"How did he know? I just got here yesterday."

"News travels fast around here," he retorted. "Besides, Sergeant Nelson had spoken to your mother today. She called to find out if there was any additional information related to our investigation of your aunt's death. She must have told him that you were here."

Denia sensed shades of an overprotective parent making sure that the police knew she was here. Denia regarded the uniformed officer standing on the small front porch. His face was tan, and his hair, brows, and neatly trimmed moustache were black. She could not help but notice the light blue irises of his eyes, surrounded by ink-black lashes. He was a good-looking man, under forty in age, Denia guessed. He was several inches taller than her, with a muscular build, with the muscular neck and arms of a football player. He wore a large aviator watch with a black band on his left wrist and was holding a clipboard.

"Did you need me for something?" Denia asked, noticing that the man was looking past her into the living space.

"Yes," he said. "Sergeant Nelson wanted you to know that we will be patrolling the roadway out front throughout the day and night, just to keep an eye on the place."

Denia again thought her mother might have had some influence.

"Also, I need to pick up your aunt's computer. Do you know if she had more than one?" he asked.

"So far, I have only found the laptop out in the office. If you want to meet me out back, I'll get the keys for the office and meet you there."

She slowly closed the front door, signaling that the deputy would not be coming through the house.

Going out the back door, she met Deputy Cleeves, and they walked toward the office building. Denia saw Jorje on his way into the barn with little Billy in tow and waved to him.

"We would also like to get your aunt's cell phone if she had one. We've already gotten the phone records for the land-line phone from the phone company," the deputy stated.

Opening the office door, Denia tried to think if she had seen a cell phone anywhere in the house.

"I'm not sure if she had a cell phone. I haven't found one. I can look around and ask one of her friends if she had a cell phone."

"If you find one, please let us know. We are trying to find out about all of her recent contacts," explained the deputy.

This made sense to Denia since the police were conducting a murder investigation. She noticed that Deputy Cleeves had focused his sight on the painting of Stonehenge on the wall behind the desk.

"It's quite an amazing picture, isn't it?" remarked Denia.

"Yes," he said, still admiring the picture. "I have to say I have never seen a picture of Stonehenge quite like it."

Going to her aunt's empty desk, Denia disconnected the laptop computer and handed it to the Deputy. He wrote the serial number of the computer on the clipboard form and handed Denia a copy.

"Here is a receipt. We will get this back to you as soon as we can," he paused. "I don't suppose you know the password?"

Denia shook her head.

"We'll still be able to get into the files, but it would be easier if we had the password. We'll have to send it out."

Then turning to go out the door, "Thank you for your help, Miss Rawlings. You can call our office if you find a cell phone or need anything. Either the sergeant or I will get back to you."

He waved and took off toward the front of the house and his car, computer in hand.

Absentmindedly, Denia sat down in the chair behind the desk, and gazed out upon the empty yard. Again, she marveled at the organization of the small office space and desk. She opened the desk's top drawer in front of her. Pencils, pens, notepads, scissors, and various other items represented the usual desk drawer fare. Pulling open the topside drawer she found a stapler, rulers, and a computer mouse.

She fought off the idea that she was snooping in someone's things and opened the next drawer. Here she found a small paper calendar. It was the type that a woman would carry in her purse. Entries in the dated little boxes were mostly written in pencil. Denia could understand some of them. There was a star in the box of her birthday, and also for her mother's birthday in May. Flipping through the small pages, stars were found on certain dates throughout the year.

Denia could tell what had been reminders for doctor or dentist appointments, but some of the notations were curious. She noticed that on many weekends the word 'Winery' was written. She also noticed that every date indicating there would be a full moon for that month was highlighted no matter where it fell in the month. She decided to take the little calendar back to the house. She thought this might hold clues to her aunt's activity prior to her death.

Opening the bottom drawer in the desk she found some computer cables, a box containing business cards, and some printer ink cartridges. Denia saw a small book with a scene of Van Gogh's *Cypress Tree* on the cover, which on further examination, turned out to be an address book. The sections were divided by pages with letters on the tabs, in alphabetical order. At once, Denia knew the value of the book. Clues for all the people her aunt knew could probably be found in this book.

Gathering her finds, Denia left the office, walking

toward the door. Small sounds echoed in the large room. She was careful to lock the door, turning in time to see a streak of white heading for her, and watched as it skidded to a stop at her knees. The goat nuzzled Denia's hands.

Jorge laughed from across the yard.

"Carrots," he called. "Miss Linda always gave her carrots."

The goat followed Denia all the way to the back door. Denia laid the calendar and address book on the counter and went to the refrigerator. Finding a bag of baby carrots in the bottom drawer, she headed back out the door where the small animal was waiting. She held out a carrot for the goat, who took it and chewed. Denia gave Billy a second carrot, while patting her on the head. The goat seemed satisfied and ran off toward Jorje. Denia smiled. Who would think she could have a goat as a pet two weeks ago, she thought to herself.

Denia looked at the simple clock on the wall between the pantry and utility room.

"Boy where did the day go?" she commented to herself.

She noticed the late afternoon shadows forming in the corners of the room and found the light switch. Looking around the kitchen, the deputy had planted a seed in Denia's mind. Aunt Melinda may have had a cell phone. She thought if she could find it, the phone would provide a trove of information in the contact list, and possible messages. It would certainly show all the most recent calls prior to her death, as well as the contacts that were routine in her life. Denia thought by using the calendar, address book, and information supplied from a cell phone, she may be able to gather some significant clues, not only as to who might have murdered her aunt, but possibly uncover a motive.

When trying to think where Melinda's cell phone might be, Denia thought of herself and how she would frequently miss calls and messages because *her* cell phone was in her purse, wherever she had left it. A purse - surely her aunt had a purse. Denia had only been in the house for a day, and she did not remember seeing a purse; but then, she had not been looking for one. Melinda's body had been found outside, so it made sense that the purse was in the house somewhere.

Denia pondered the possibilities. The murderer could have gone into the house and taken Melinda's purse. It seemed plausible, but unlikely - unless the killer knew Melinda had a cell phone and that it was probably in her purse. The killer may have known there was information on the phone to connect him, or her, to the murder. The killer would know that the police would soon figure out the death was not an accident.

Scanning the kitchen in her search for a purse, she moved on through to the dining area. She looked at the various piles of paper, unopened mail, and other things taking up room on the surface of the dining table. She checked the seats of all six dining table chairs. Denia looked at the top of the long buffet cabinet sitting under the front dining room window, near the front door.

Gradually moving into the living room space, she shuffled all the sofa pillows, thinking that a small handbag could have gotten wedged down behind them. The desk under the stairwell was stacked with items, but none of them a purse, as well as the large, wooden surface of the old console television. She moved on to the coat closet on the back wall next to the wide, brick fireplace, opening the door.

"Oh, Lord," she commented, as she viewed the interior of yet another packed closet, but no purse came into view.

Denia knew that the elusive bag was not in the single bathroom of the house at the top of the stairs. She also knew she could eliminate the bedroom she was using. That left her aunt's large bedroom as the only place in the house where a purse could have been carelessly tossed by its owner. Denia headed up the stairs toward the bedrooms.

For some reason she was hesitant to enter this very personal space belonging to her aunt.

"Where is your purse, Auntie?" she whispered into the room while standing in the doorway.

Late afternoon light filtered in through the windows, while most of the room lay in silent shadows. The large bed, with covers tossed up, was empty of any other articles. The two beside tables on either side of the bed, held matching lamps, books, phone, and a small crystal clock among other things.

Denia ventured into the room, retrieving the clock, a Waterford, thinking she could use it on her own nightstand, for now. The surface of the long dresser inhabiting the wall opposite the end of the bed held two jewelry boxes, several framed pictures, and other articles, either deliberately or casually placed; but Denia could not find any sign of a purse.

"Hmmm," Denia murmured.

Perplexed by the fruitless search, she left the quiet room, taking the clock to her bedroom next door.

Denia went downstairs to the kitchen and searched for the scrap of paper Batty gave her with a phone number. Finding her own cell phone, she placed the call.

A rather high, squeaky voice answered the ringtone, "Hello?"

"Batty, this is Denia."

"Hi, Denia. Have you heard something about Isis?"

"No, but a deputy was just out here to pick up Aunt Melinda's computer from the office. He wanted to know if she had a cell phone. If she did, do you know where it could be?"

"Yes," Batty answered, "she had a cell phone. It was one of those new smart phones. She didn't use it for half the things you could do on it. It had a sparkly gold cover. She usually had it in her handbag, or in a pocket when she was outside. Half the time she would forget to charge it and it would go dead."

"I've looked around here, and I can't find it. I can't find her purse either. Do you know what her purse looked like and where she usually put it?"

"Usually, she put it on the kitchen counter, or on the dining room table, when she came in the door. I think the one she was using recently was tan and black, with an over-the-shoulder strap. Did you check in the office?"

"Yeah, I looked all around here, and in her bedroom."

"That's odd," Batty said, and was quiet thinking for a

few moments. "Try checking the car. I can't imagine her leaving it in the car, but it's been known to happen. She was a scatterbrain at times when she had something on her mind. Did you check the pantry?"

"No, but those are good ideas," Denia answered. "I'll let you know. Thanks, Batty," she said, ready to end the call.

"Oh, I have to tell you," Batty quickly added, "I spoke with Olivia after I got back from town. She said that she was in the office last Saturday checking on candle orders and had seen Isis. She thinks she may have been the one that accidentally shut Isis in the storeroom. The cats like to take naps on the shelves in there. That's why Melinda had put the food dispenser and water bowl in there. Olivia thinks she may have closed the door with Isis in there."

"That would explain things," said Denia.

"Another thing that's weird," related Batty, "I got a call from the Sheriff's Office, and I must go in tomorrow morning. They said they're gathering information surrounding Mel's death and want to talk to me. Olivia called me because they requested that she come in tomorrow, too. They know we were both working with Melinda and were close friends with her. Why do you think they want to talk to us?"

Denia remembered what Sergeant Nelson had said about not giving out the details of the coroner's report. The people of the town had been left to assume that Melinda's death was accidental, or medical, such as a heart attack.

"They are probably just wrapping up loose ends," Denia replied. "They took quite a bit of information from me and my mother when we first came into town."

"Well, it just sounds suspicious to me, and why would they need the computer?" said Batty.

"It *is* interesting. Maybe I should call Sergeant Nelson," said Denia. "Let me know what happens."

"I will. And let me know if you find the purse. Oh, and call me about Isis."

"Okay, thanks, Batty," said Denia.

Denia wondered if she should tell Batty about the murder investigation. She thought she might wait and see how things went for a while. Batty was obviously very close to her aunt; and she seemed to care about the ranch and the Candlewick business. Denia did not think for a minute that the frizzle-haired lady had anything to do with her aunt's death, but Batty did appear to be involved with many people in the town. She did not want the murderer to be inadvertently tipped off that the police were investigating. For now, she would keep the murder investigation to herself.

Denia went to the pantry to make sure she had not overlooked a handbag sitting on one of the shelves amid the chaos. Looking from shelf to shelf, it did not take long to rule out the pantry. So, she snatched the garage keys from the hook and headed out the back door, and around the back of the house to the garage.

The unattached garage was set back from the road to one side of the house. In front of the garage was a very, large, cement pad upon which her Explorer was parked. Using the garage door opener, the wide, white, double doors opened to expose an expansive interior. There sat the green Range Rover that had been her aunt's car. It was not a new model, but the older, larger model of previous years.

Denia walked to the car and looked in the passenger side door. The tan interior was clean inside, with no handbag or other articles on the seat or floor. Crystal beads hung from the rear-view mirror. Opening the back door and looking into the back of the car, she saw a container holding shopping bags, a flashlight, and rolled up blanket. Denia respected the neatness of the interior which was probably better than her own car. The condition of the vehicle indicated that it had been given good care.

The center of the garage was an open space. The shape of another car, covered by a tarp, was on the far side of the garage. Denia could not resist a peek under the car cover, which revealed the yellow, 1964 Super Sport Impala that she remembered from her childhood. This had been Melinda's husband's car. Denia knew this was a valuable collector's car; but obviously, her aunt had never been able to part with it. For now, it would stay under the tarp. It had been here for years and was not a priority.

She jogged back to the house to get her own car keys, and momentarily was pulling the Explorer into the garage between the two resident vehicles. The space was perfect for another well-loved car.

Going back to the house, she stopped to speak with Jorje who was heading to the barn to put Billy in for the night. He wanted to take Sunday off for a family gathering. Denia agreed to meet him in the morning to learn the daily chores needed to take care of the chickens and the goat until he got back on Monday.

By the time she got back to the kitchen, she was so

hungry that even canned soup sounded good. Mona came into the kitchen looking for another meal. She fed the cat and heated the soup on the stove. Denia pushed a couple of piles aside to clear a spot at the end of the dining room table for her bowl of soup. She found a package of English muffins in the refrigerator and toasted one to have with the soup. Finding a grocery store would need to go on the list for tomorrow.

After eating, she took one of the candles from the coffee table and moved it to the dining room table and lit it. She noticed that Mona was now nestled into the corner of the sofa, sleeping. The house was quiet. Denia sat down at the table and started flipping through the address book she had brought in from the office. Here was an alphabetized list of the people her aunt knew. The name of her murderer could be in this book. There was the rare chance that a stranger had wandered in off the road and killed Melinda, but Denia thought that unlikely. She believed someone who knew her aunt had killed her for some unknown reason. Not being able to find the cell phone nagged at the back of her mind.

Two folded pages fell out of the back of the book, and upon review, turned out to be a typewritten list for sending Christmas cards. Denia was trying to decide how to sort the names in the book and on the card list to identify potential suspects. The police believed the murderer had been a man, so she could start by sorting male names. She could also try to identify service and business acquaintances versus friends. Batty might be able to help her with some of that.

Denia was startled as the phone in the kitchen started

ringing. The ringer must have been turned up as high as possible as the shrill ring cut into the silence in the house. She rushed to reach the phone.

"Hello," she answered.

"Hi, this is Hans," came the male voice.

When there was no response, "Dr. Anderson."

"Oh, yes."

"I thought you would want to know how Isis is doing."

"Yes, how is she?"

"She's perking up a little. She's actually starting to move around a bit. I still have the IV going but cut it down to a slower rate. I think she is going to make it through the night."

"That's great. It's kind of amazing after seeing how she was this morning."

"Sometimes we're lucky," he said. "Also, I wanted to apologize for my comment about your wedding," his voice had softened. "I hope we can be friends, and I know I did not start out well. Can you forgive me?"

Denia believed he was sorry for getting off on the wrong foot, and probably deserved a do-over.

"I guess there was no harm done. I was surprised that someone I have never met would know something about my private life. I just got here and am starting to meet people. I only met Batty this morning."

"I really do know better," he said. "Why don't you let me treat you to a cup of coffee, and a Danish? Our little town is famous for the pastries."

"Maybe I can take a raincheck on that. I've got so much to do around here and I'm still trying to get settled."

"Whenever you're ready," he said. "I'll call you again in the morning after I do the lab work, and let you know how the cat is doing."

"Okay, I'll talk to you then. Good night."

After the call, Denia thought about the young veterinarian. He was about her age, give or take a couple years. He had a little bit of a Patagonia look about him, with his long hair, slim but lithe physique, and beaded band on his wrist. It would be good to start making friends her own age, if she was going to be here for a while. Also, he was a man who was acquainted with her aunt. It would be worth a cup of coffee to be able to scratch him off the list as a possible suspect in her aunt's murder.

Denia settled herself on the end of the sofa not occupied by a cat. Looking around, Denia knew she had so much to do but did not know where to begin. Tomorrow, she had to learn to take care of the animals when Jorje was not here. Tonight, she felt unsettled. What a crazy day it had been! She met two more good-looking men in this town. It must be something in the water, she quipped to herself.

For now, she felt really alone in a strange place. She wanted comfort, but everything around her was not hers, and a reminder of how much she needed to do. Today had been a start. Tomorrow had to have some achievements. She knew she could make this place a good home for herself. Looking around the living room, one thing that was high on the list was to get a television. Living alone in her old apartment she had gotten used to having the TV on, droning away in the background. Somehow it eased the feeling of being alone - and she planned to be alone. It will be a cold day before she allowed herself to get carried away with any illusions of romance.

She stared at her aunt's large TV console taking up prime living room space by the fireplace. It was a throwback to earlier years and didn't work anymore. She could not understand why her aunt hadn't replaced it. It was hard to find a house today without a flat screen TV somewhere. The top of the old console was piled with old mail, catalogs, and more items that needed to be sorted.

Thoughts came to mind as to how to attack the clutter in the house. Possibly, she could use some of her own empty boxes to sort which items to keep, to trash, and which to donate. Paper was valuable. She would carefully sort mail, bills, and other paperwork to get a clearer picture of her aunt's life. She could start with one hour of decluttering each evening. Denia looked over at the dining room with table and buffet piled high. The TV console, desk, and coffee table in the living room could be next. Heaven knows when the good pieces of wood furniture had last been dusted.

Yes, a good plan - but not tonight. It wasn't late, but she was tired. She checked the door locks and turned out all the lights except a small lamp on the TV and headed upstairs for the night.

Denia sat straight up in bed out of a deep sleep. An ongoing pelting sound resonating from above her head had awoken her. The noise grew louder. Coming to her senses, she realized she was hearing an onslaught of rain on the roof over her room. The smell of rain permeated the darkness. Large amounts of water were hitting the steep peaks of the old structure and would run off to the ground around the house. She hoped the roof was in good shape with no leaks.

She felt disconnected. Usually, she would have heard of any forecasted precipitation through television news shows - another reason to get a TV. Rain in California was a big deal, especially over the past few years of dry weather. Any impending rain called for a *'storm watch'* as weather forecasters looked forward to a reason to add some excitement to their usual balmy projections.

Listening to the rain, which was slowing, Denia flopped back down onto her pillows. Thinking about the yard, she guessed at the probable muddy conditions that would greet her in the morning. The weather flaps were still rolled up around the three sides of the chicken coop. The hens should be alright in their nesting boxes. The winter chill had not come, yet. Billy would be okay in her stall in the barn. This was the first rain on the ranch. She could not remember any rainstorms during her summer visits of childhood.

She grabbed the sheet and covers and pulled them up to her chin. What time was it? Glancing to the small bedside table, she could not see the hands on the small crystal clock she had brought from her aunt's room. She looked at the darkened windows where there was no sign of impending morning light. She knew she would probably not be able to go back to sleep. Grabbing a pillow to her chest, she turned to her side seeking a sleep-inducing position.

Nighttime had been difficult for her over the past few weeks. She had problems getting to sleep and staying asleep through the night. Denia struggled to keep her thoughts from straying to Jeff. It was so easy to remember how comfortable it had felt to sleep next to him after an evening of lovemaking. There was the feeling of being held in his arms, being kissed, a feeling of being secure in his love. All of that was gone now.

It had also rained the day after the missed wedding, rare for San Diego in June. Denia had been alone all day and all night in her apartment with the door locked and the phone turned off. The usually unsympathetic sky cried with her, maybe for her.

In May she had been a starry eyed twenty-eight-year-old planning her wedding to Jeff, picking out her gown, and registering at every up-scale store in San Diego. Finally, there would be a home of her own. As a couple, they had spent happy hours searching the neighborhoods north of San Diego for the *right* starter house. She had been looking forward to the children she always planned to have, never sure how many, but she wanted more than one. She had been an only child and knew the pressure of carrying the full load of parental expectations. The Hawaiian honeymoon was bought and paid for. She was to be a June bride.

Her mother was in a state of constant excitement, providing prenuptial details to her many co-workers and friends at the university.

The plan had been for a modest wedding. This had

mushroomed into a hundred and fifty guests due primarily to her parent's large social circle, and the large family on Jeff's side.

Jeff. Now, when she thought of him, much of it was to chastise herself. How could she have been so misled? Maybe she had wanted so much to believe in the dream and the promise. He was thirty, a graduate of Irvine in Engineering, working for a small aerospace firm in North County. She had met him last September, while it was still hot, when she loved to go to Mission Bay for her jogs along the paths at the waterfront. There were plenty of people about and it was a safe area for a woman alone. Jeff was also a jogger, but in better shape than her. He had approached Denia first, saying that he noticed they always got there about the same time, and would she like to run with him. He had been gracious and accommodated her slower pace. Next came the dinner at the chic restaurant in Coronado, with the fabulous view of the San Diego City skyline at twilight and sparkling night lights. There were Sunday trips to Balboa Park for picnics and visits to the museums, and the exploration of the wandering paths of the world-famous San Diego Zoo. She was in love for the first time in years, with an attractive, well-educated, fun-to-be-with guy, who found her attractive with her auburn hair, freckles, and size fourteen jeans. For Valentine's Day he had taken her to the Gaslight District downtown and proposed with a Tiffany solitaire diamond ring. She had cried through her acceptance.

Her parents had been married for over thirty years. Many of Denia's friend's parents were divorced and on their second, or even third, marriages. Denia's mother had wanted to see her daughter settled and was impatient to have pictures of grandchildren on *her* desk at work. Denia knew her mother had almost given up on her, having seen many 'boyfriends' come and go, none lasting very long since one serious romance in college. For years, her mother had dreamed of planning the wedding and being the mother of the bride.

Her father had been a little less impressed. What was the rush for the wedding, he had said? Shouldn't they get to know each other better prior to such a momentous commitment? Mother and daughter had teased him for being a dinosaur living in the sixties; but, despite his reservations, he wrote the checks for all the customary expenses. He never complained about the forty-thousand-dollar price tag which had added up quickly. People had assured them this amount was not uncommon for a wedding and reception of that size.

In the darkness she let her thoughts drift back to the wedding day, where images of the day were burnt into her soul, and the blur of the days that followed. Heather, her best friend at college, and her Maid of Honor had fussed with the full skirt of her flowing, white gown. Her mother came into the dressing room just in time to see the veil added to her upswept hair, and promptly started to tear up. She was given a kiss by the bride and shooed out the door before all were in tears with their make-up destroyed. Her other two bridesmaids, Cindy and Jennifer, flitted about the room in their lime green chiffons, focusing on this and that, taking pictures of the bride for remembrance.

The wedding was scheduled to begin at one o'clock, with the reception from three in the afternoon and into the night at the nearby country club. One o'clock came and went. A knot of anxiety had formed in Denia's stomach. Cindy and Jennifer left the room, as Heather stayed close to her side.

A little after two o'clock, her father came into the room. After seeing the look on his face, Heather quietly left. Her father related the news that Denia already knew.

Jeff had never shown up.

His brother and family had tried frantically to reach him, thinking something may have happened to him; but there had been no answer to phone calls.

No Jeff.

His brother had driven to Jeff's apartment, not knowing what else to do and had found an envelope on the table with Denia's name. Her father handed her the envelope.

The small note contained two words, *'I'm sorry'*, and her world crashed around her.

She never spoke to Jeff again. He never tried to contact her. Everyone has heard of these things happening, but never thought that it *would* happen.

Had there been signs that she missed? Was she too trusting and gullible? Hadn't there been hints of impending disaster?

She went over all of this in her mind time, and time again. The rest of the summer had been spent mostly alone in her apartment. She couldn't really stand spending time with her parents and the sympathetic mood. The people at work and friends initially offered statements of encouragement, but then avoided her.

She understood. What was there to say?

The groom had gotten cold feet. The wedding dress filled with hopes and dreams was sold on eBay, and wedding gifts returned. She could never repay her parents for the money they had spent, and they did not ask for it. Their thoughts were only for her well-being.

Denia noticed the rain had slowed to a soft pattering on the roof. The house below was quiet. The first gray signs of morning appeared at the window. She made a vow to herself to put thoughts of Jeff away in the back of her mind until it was less painful for her. She was convinced the move from San Diego was a good thing for her, and that she could make a good life for herself. She wanted to be helpful to the police in the investigation of her aunt Melinda's murder. That's what was important, now. Her mind went to the present and planning for the day ahead. She was glad she was here. She found a certain freedom from her recent past.

4

THE TURTLES

Denia woke up early and got dressed. Thinking she would be working outside with Jorje this morning, she chose her raggedy jeans and t-shirt. She came downstairs with her older tennis shoes in hand. It was going to be a sunny day after the rain that had come during the night; but she was not sure how muddy the yard would be. She took a quick look out the bay window at the front yard. Raindrops still clung to the leaves on the roses under the window. Puddles remained on the asphalt drive and the small walkway leading to the front door. It was a new day, and her mood had lifted with the sunrise.

She headed for the kitchen in search of a cup of coffee. Mona was waiting for her, sitting patiently in front of the cat food cabinet, lest her new keeper would forget to feed her. The crunch of a vehicle on the driveway caused Denia to look out front toward the road. A small, dark blue, Toyota truck pulled up to the back patio, followed by a knock at the kitchen door.

Opening the door, Denia saw a short, Asian man in a faded baseball cap standing in the doorway.

"Hello, I am Paul Oda. I used to work for Miss Melinda. I am the gardener."

"Oh, hi," said Denia. "I am Melinda's niece. I'm staying here, for now."

"I talked to Jorje, and he told me of Miss Melinda's death," he explained. "I sent a bill for last month with a letter asking if you wanted me to continue doing the yards?"

Denia thought of the stacks of mail sitting on top of the TV console.

"I'm sorry. I just got here a couple days ago, and I have not had a chance to get to the mail, yet. My name is Denia Rawlings."

"Nice to meet you," he said, reaching for a light grasp of Denia's hand.

"I know Jorje is usually out back and takes care of the back lot and orchard. Can you tell me what type of gardening you usually did for my aunt?"

"I provide ordinary gardening services. I mow the front yard and the grass area over in front of the garage every other week. I take care of the planters around the house and trim the bushes as well as the roses. The sprinklers are all on timers, but I do take care of those if there are any problems. I usually come by every Thursday. Melinda used to pay me once a month with a check. I have not been paid for last month."

"I would like to continue to have you as a gardener," Denia decided on the spot. "But I am still in the process of getting my aunt's accounts put into my name. I have to go to the bank. Would I be able to pay you next week? Then I could pay you for all that I owe."

"That would be okay," he agreed. "Would it be alright for me to mow on Monday? It has not been done for two weeks, but right now the grass is too wet from the rain."

"That would be good."

"Thank you, Miss Rawlings. I've been working for your aunt for six years since I moved up here from Los Angeles. I was very sorry to hear of her death."

"Thank you, and you can call me Denia," she said. "I'll see you on Monday."

Denia watched as the middle-aged gardener headed back to his truck. Soon he was turning around and heading out of the driveway with rakes and other tools sticking out of the back of the truck's bed. Denia had a small sense of accomplishment, after making the quick decision about continuing to employ a gardener. She reveled in her new status. She was actually a homeowner with a gardener!

The gardener reminded her she had not looked at any of the mail that was lying in little piles in the living room and on the dining room table. Denia decided that this evening she would collect all the piles and go through them. There were probably other bills than just the one from the gardener. Going through the mail might help her learn more about how the ranch ran, and some of the usual expenses. She could also identify some of the business acquaintances, versus other people, who knew her aunt. *Someone* had killed her aunt and, most likely, it was someone she knew. Possibly someone who came to the house on a regular basis.

Later, after Mona was fed, Denia swilled down a quick cup of coffee and ate some toast with jam. She put on her old shoes and headed out the kitchen door to find Jorje. This should be interesting, she thought to herself, as she knew next to nothing about taking care of chickens or goats. Since she did not see Jorje by the chicken coop, she headed across the lot to the barn, where one of the tall, red doors stood open.

Denia had spoken to the dependable, Hispanic farmhand yesterday afternoon. While Jorje was working for her aunt, he did not usually work on Saturday and Sunday. Since her aunt's death, he had come to the ranch every day to care for the animals, not taking any time off for himself. He lived in the nearby town of Lompoc with his elderly wife. Jorje had grown children who also lived in the area.

Yesterday, he had requested to take Sunday off for a family birthday party. Of course, Denia agreed, despite her anxiety of being alone and responsible for the animals. Jorje assured her that she would be able to carry out the daily feeding and watering.

Walking through the back lot, Denia could not help but notice the old barn was enormous and ancient. The barn and the little bunkhouse on the side looked like it had been built many years before the house. It was a product of the old western days of central California. Denia was not sure what kind of wood was used to build the old structure, but coat over coat of redwood stain applied through the years, gave it a reddish-brown hue. Its rustic form stood majestically, providing a perimeter to the large backyard on one side. Upon entering the high doorway, Denia found Jorje working in the first of the four horse stalls that lined the right side of the barn.

Billy was bleating and prancing about as Jorje used a small pitchfork and shovel to remove the soiled hay from the floor of the stall. After scooping all the discarded hay into a low garden cart, Jorje spread new straw throughout the stall.

Denia thought the goat ate all the time, but that was not the case. The goat was given fresh alfalfa hay placed in a feeding grill on the side of the stall wall. Four cups of a mixed grain and pellets were added to a feeding tray. A red, plastic basin with a brick in the bottom held water and was changed daily. When the stall was ready for the evening, Jorje placed a lead on the goat, guiding her out of the barn toward the pen in the yard. Denia laughed as the young goat fought the lead, making progress slow.

After placing the goat in the pen, Jorje returned to the barn and brought the half full cart and rake out to the pen. The pen did not need much cleaning. Fresh alfalfa was also placed in the feeding grill of the pen, and fresh water filled another red plastic container. Billy's attention was currently occupied, eating the new feed at the grill.

Jorje spoke a combination of English and Spanish with a thick accent, but Denia had no problem understanding his instructions. The goat's stall and pen were cleaned every morning. The goat was put in the pen outside the barn unless someone was in the yard with her. She had her breakfast in the pen, and her second meal in the late afternoon, when she went into her stall for the night.

Jorje had shown Denia how to clean the goat's hoofs with a stiff brush while she was eating and less likely to fight the process. According to Jorje, the hoof cleaning was an important part of daily care. There was also a brush for her coat on a hook outside the barn stall. Jorje explained that the livestock veterinarian, Dr. Peele, came to the ranch once a month to trim the goat's hooves, and check on her general condition. He could be called for health issues, such as digestive problems which were not uncommon in goats. Denia was impressed with Jorje's attention to Billy.

"Why the brick in the water dish?" Denia asked.

"She thinks it's fun to dump over the water pan," said Jorje. "I get tired of filling it up all day."

Denia noticed the goat also had a large, blue, plastic ball and a couple of old tires in the pen for activity. The goat liked to climb on the roof of the little shed in the pen, bleating and looking for Jorje.

With the goat temporarily taken care of, Denia followed Jorje to the chicken coop.

The rest of the morning out back had gone well. Denia felt confident that she was prepared to take care of the animals the next day.

Around noon, Hans called with news that Isis was doing

well, moving around in the cage, and beginning to take water. The cat's lab work showed improvement. Food was going to be offered later. The intravenous line was still providing some fluids, but at a slower rate. Dr. Anderson wanted the cat to remain under treatment for at least another day, to make sure she was eating and drinking before going home. That meant it would be Monday or Tuesday before she was released.

That afternoon, Denia had taken the Explorer out, driving through Solvang in search of a grocery store. She found herself stuck in the Saturday tourist traffic while going through town, both coming and going to the store. Making a mental reminder for herself, Saturday was probably not the best day for grocery shopping. For now, though, the chore was done, and she would have something to eat for dinner other than canned soup.

Denia's aunt had been on her mind all day. Knowing that Jorje would not be coming the next day made her feel a bit vulnerable. Her aunt had been alone here for many years and Denia wondered how she had managed by herself.

She thought of the letter the lawyer had given her when he finished reading Melinda's Will. It was a handwritten letter addressed to her from her aunt. At the time, Denia had put it in the center pocket of her purse. Later, she moved it to the little desk in her bedroom after she arrived at the ranch. She had hesitated in opening it for reasons she could not exactly define. Denia felt that she needed to emotionally prepare herself, knowing this would be the last letter - the last words - from an aunt she had cared for since childhood. Now, she chastised herself for being silly. The letter might contain something that would be helpful to the police and their investigation of Melinda's death. She decided to read the letter.

"There's no time like the present," Denia said, as she climbed the stairs and headed to her bedroom.

She found the slightly crumpled envelope secured in the drawer where she had left it. Holding the letter in her hands, she examined her own name written in her aunt's handwriting. Throughout her life she had seen the same generous script on birthday cards, gift tags, and miscellaneous notes, most of which she had taken for granted at the time. She knew regret was a waste, but it was haunting her when it came to her aunt and her own neglect of their relationship.

Denia decided to open and read the letter at the turtle pond. That would be the right place. Spending time at the pond was part of the bond she shared with her aunt. It was a place Melinda had loved and would always remind Denia of her 'Auntie'.

Heading out back, she crossed the lot toward the gate leading to the orchard. Billy called to her as she went near the pen. The goat had spent a good part of the day in the pen. Denia thought it might be alright to take Billy along with her. She opened the gate to the pen and called for the goat to follow her. Billy was always happy to go through the gate leading to the orchard and followed after Denia with no encouragement.

The August afternoon had been warm and bright, and the landscape gleamed in thankfulness after last night's rain. The sky was blue after the rainclouds had dissipated, replaced by slow-moving, cottony masses. Denia made her way through the rows of broadleaved walnut trees and out to the rural back field, covered in the amber grasses of late summer. Through the years, a natural pathway had been honed, winding in spots, leading through the wide field, toward the large outcrop of rock formations that made a significant divide in the ranch property.

Low hills ran from the frontage road diagonally away from the house and garage. The mounds surrounded a wall of granite blocks gradually forming into a long wall of uneven stones. Out of a crevasse in the rocks poured an ongoing spring of water, flowing from a hidden source. Long ago, Melinda told her of the underground stream that ran beneath the ranch's interesting topography. A natural depression in the ground in front of a large section of rocks, filled with water, forming an oval-shaped freshwater pond. An aged oak tree sprawled its limbs in the protection of the granite wall, dipping its old roots into the moist earth near the pond. A rickety bench, weathered gray and perched under the oak, provided a panoramic view of the pond and field, with the ranch house off in the distance.

Denia followed the pathway across the field. The goat exalted in its freedom, bounding from one place to another, but never straying too far from Denia. A few yards from the edge of the pond was a walkway made up of large, turtle-shaped, paving stones. The turtle stones had been a gift from Melinda's husband on her birthday, many years ago. The turtle stones followed the circumference of the pond and led off to the adjacent rock amphitheater. Denia stepped onto a stone turtle, and then onto the next one, and the next, making her way to the bench under the oak tree.

She settled on the bench, looking at the grouping of the dead walnut trees that had been drug into one end of the pond. Their purpose was to make surfaces for the pond's resident turtles to bask in the sun. Denia saw several turtles of different sizes perched on the old tree limbs, making the most of the late afternoon sunlight. Her aunt brought the turtles here, initially rescuing them from small tanks in pet shops. At first it had just been two turtles, but turtles have long lives, and gradually the pond's turtle population had grown. There was no way of knowing exactly how many turtles made the pond their home, but Denia knew there were a lot of them.

Billy was nibbling at vegetation along the edge of the pond enjoying the exotic menu. Denia scanned the vista, easily falling back into childhood memories. Her mind's eye could see her aunt sitting on the bench with a straw hat while her little girl self ran along the edge of the pond, dragging a stick in the soft mud. This was the place where they used to come in the afternoon to see the pond; to see the turtles. As a girl, she would run in great circles around the field and make games of skipping on the cement turtle stones. She and her aunt would sit on the bench together, watching the sky change through sunset and dusk. Neither of them ever tired of the routine.

Now, Denia held the unopened envelope containing Melinda's letter in her hands, staring at it for a moment before turning it over and tearing open the seal. She unfolded the two-pages, recognizing the familiar script, and began to read.

Dearest Denia,

If you are reading this letter, then you know I am dead and have left you my ranch and the funds to maintain it for some time going forward. As you go through my papers, you will see I have found ways to make money from the ranch, which makes the property self-sufficient, for the most part. This will allow you time to make decisions regarding your life and how the ranch could be a part of it.

It's been a long time since I have seen you, but your mother has sent pictures from time to time. I know you have grown into a clever, beautiful, young woman. Your mother did tell me about the recent end of your engagement. At my age, I have learned that sometimes things happen for the best. The prospect of years spent in a bad marriage could be far worse than the time required to recover from a temporarily broken heart. I know your strong character will see you through.

You have my blessing to sell the ranch if that is what you decide to do. I have currently leased the east ten acres to Samala Vineyards, and they maintain the land and all the grape vines. Keith Clearwater, the owner of Samala, has expressed interest in buying my land in the past. You can contact him if you decide to sell. I am sure he would give you a good price. I would also advise you to work with my attorney, Eugene Sorenson, for any legal advice you require.

I have been very blessed to have made many good friends, over the years, living in this little valley. My small group of ladies, the Doves, which we affectionately call ourselves, will help and guide you in whatever you may need. They are my dear sisters and have my full love and trust. You will not have to reach out to them. They will come to you, for my sake.

The ranch has been my home for many years, so I would love to think of you living here and making it your home. I hold such fond memories of you as a child, visiting here and bringing such a wonderful light to my world. You seemed to be happy here. So, my gift to you is a wish for happiness.

Please know that whatever you choose to do regarding the ranch, you have my love and best wishes for your future. I can picture you sitting out by the turtle pond as we used to do when you were little. Please take care of my turtles.

May the Goddess hold you in her arms and bless you,

Your Auntie Melinda

With tears in her eyes, Denia re-read the letter. She believed her aunt *did* only wish for her happiness and gave to her all those things which were most dear to her. Yet, she also gave her a free rein to sell the ranch, if that was what she decided to do.

Denia knew she was currently in over her head with the ranch, the animals, the Candlewick business, and no experience with any of these things. She was not sure if she would be able to handle everything. Not to mention, the murder investigation - something her aunt could not have predicted.

Melinda had recommended her lawyer, Eugene

Sorenson, who had already been very helpful to Denia and her mother. She had yet to meet Keith Clearwater, who was currently leasing part of the land. Denia remembered the lawyer mentioned that someone made an offer to buy the property prior to her aunt changing the Will. Denia thought this was one more reason for her to start going through the mail and her aunt's papers in order to get a clear picture of how the ranch and Candlewick were managed.

Right now, she had no understanding of the financial arrangements. She knew about Jorje but was not sure how much he was paid and when. She would need to make some decisions about Candlewick shortly, since internet orders for candles were still coming in, and there were people on the business payroll. Just today, she had found out about the gardener and the livestock vet, which also amounted to monthly financial commitments.

She reread the section of the letter that talked about her aunt's friends and immediately thought of Batty. She had not been at the ranch for twenty-four hours when Batty had appeared on the doorstep. She read again about the group of friends called the Doves and remembered the small knot of ladies standing together at the memorial service and the restaurant, afterwards. They had solemn faces, managing tears and tissues. They had supported one another. These must be the close friends the letter referenced. Denia thought she might share her aunt's letter with Batty and talk to her about the Doves.

Denia looked up from the letter and her thoughts to see Jorje waving and calling Billy from across the field. She surmised he probably wanted to put the goat in her stall for the night and go home for the day. As soon as Billy heard him calling, she went running across the field. She watched as Jorje herded the goat back through the orchard and out of her sight.

The sun had gone down behind the western hills, and the sky glowed with the yellowish light of the impending sunset. Denia rose from the bench, following the trail of turtle stones. The path led away from the pond and curved around the front of an outcrop of large stones and boulders. Tall eucalyptus trees stirred overhead with the gentle breeze, their scent flavoring the air. These towering trees had been planted in years past as a windbreak between the acres of farmland on the back side of the rocky hills.

Denia paced steadily forward on the stone pathway that led to a natural rock amphitheater. A great wall of stones formed a circular cul-de-sac which fanned out on both sides in boulders of gradually declining height. This secreted grotto could not be seen by the casual passing observer. Willow trees had been planted to complete the circular space, hiding the rocky alcove. The willows' thick, vertical branches formed an unbroken curtain of greenery. The entrance to the hidden circle was through a camouflaged break in the trees.

The path of turtle stones stopped at the willows. Denia hesitated prior to stepping through the veil of leaves, into the shadowy space. She stood very still, trying to recollect the memory of the place she had once feared, and shied away from as a child. It seemed smaller, as was often the case when returning to places known in childhood. The willows had not been there when she was young, so there had been no feeling of being enclosed, as there was now.

Taking a measure of the space, Denia could see that it could easily hold two or three dozen people.

Pedestals of wood made from thick logs, were positioned vertically around the inside edges of the circle at even intervals. Thick, round candles sat in basins sitting atop the wooden posts. Denia examined the closest candle, which was wax, with multiple wicks around the center. Surely, her aunt had made this. Looking toward the front of the amphitheater, she could see a circle of large stones on the ground that was clearly used as a fire pit, still harboring the remnants of burnt wood.

Denia shivered, though there was no breeze in this hollow. She heard the silence, with no sound of life except for her own breathing.

Suddenly there was a swish of sound, and she turned abruptly to see a dark silhouette standing in her only escape path. Involuntarily, a startled scream filled the silent space, echoing off the rocks, as Denia lunged backward deeper into the circle.

"Miss Denia, it is me," came the familiar accented voice. "Do not come here. Do not come to this place. Come back with me now!" he pleaded.

Denia realized it was Jorje who had come to fetch her. He was clearly afraid of the hidden grotto, but had ventured into the alcove to get her, suppressing his own fear.

"Jorje, you frightened me!" Denia exclaimed with relief, while trying to catch her breath.

"Come back with me. This is not a good place. Come with me and I will walk you back to *la casa*," he implored, as he stretched an arm out in a coaxing manner.

He reminded Denia of a kindly grandfather, here to collect the errant child.

"Yes, I'll come with you. Don't be upset. We'll go back together."

Once outside the circle of trees and rock, the fading daylight allowed Denia to see Jorje more clearly. Here he stood, in obvious distress - the little man who would save her. His thin form was shorter than Denia herself, with his upper back slightly hunched due to aging; but he was an honorable man whose thought was to protect her from whatever it was he feared. Possibly finding his dead mistress had taken a toll on him, fanning his superstitions. Did he dread another death, Denia thought to herself.

"Come, *Señorita*, I will take you back now," he demanded.

Denia walked beside him as they quietly crossed the field. They passed through the back of the orchard, and at last, through the gate to the yard behind the house. Denia noticed that he placed a lock on the large gate, clicking it into place. She followed as he checked on the goat and secured the barn door. They passed the Candlewick building and its dark interior. The chicken coop was quiet, the hens having moved into their boxes, preparing for the darkness. Finally, at the back door, Jorje waited as she went inside.

"*Buenos noches*, Miss Denia," he said, as he waved good night.

A few moments later, Denia heard his little Ford compact go past the house and out to the road as the last rays of daylight faded with him.

Once secure inside the house, Denia felt a little shaken. Jorje's fear of the rock amphitheater was so sincere and exaggerated that it had heightened her own fear. She had to ask herself why the old man had such a fear of the place.

Also, it was obvious to Denia that the grotto was being used, but for what and by whom? Was the mystery of the grotto's use related to her aunt's murder? She just didn't know.

Feeling alone, she checked the back door lock and headed for the living room to close the curtains and make sure the front door was secure.

That evening, Denia's resolve to understand how the ranch ran, and the circumstances of Melinda's life at the time of her death, prompted her to start digging. She gathered all the mail, magazines, and other papers from their resting places throughout the living room, dining room, and kitchen counters. Pushing aside everything on the dining room table to one end, she established a workstation, gathering pencils, writing tablet, a bag for trash, and a box for magazines. She found a stack of unused, manila folders sitting on the desk under the staircase, and thought they may be useful in the sorting process. She sat down and started by dividing out magazines, newspapers, and advertisements, which made a severe dent in the pile before her. Next, she sorted the unopened mail into stacks of possible bills, financial reports, and miscellaneous items.

Two hours later, every envelope had been opened, bills segregated, and some folders labeled. She made a list of unpaid July and August bills. In review of the bank statements, Denia found that her aunt made regular withdrawals of five hundred dollars every Friday, like clockwork. She remembered her aunt's lawyer said that Jorje was always paid in cash, because he was afraid of banks. She knew her mother had given Jorje the envelope of money that Melinda had left with the Will, but Denia also knew he had not been paid for the three weeks since her aunt's death. She knew she would need to pay him soon. There were enough funds in the ranch bank account, but she would need to get access to the account. This needed to move to the top of the 'to do' list for Monday.

For tonight, she felt she had done enough. The day had been emotional, and she was tired.

"Good night, Mona," she said to the cat, still curled on the sofa, and headed up the stairs to bed.

It was Monday morning, and the beginning of Denia's first full week at the ranch. She stood in the kitchen watching Mona eat her breakfast while a bagel for herself toasted in the toaster. The kitchen counters looked a little better, with the piles of paper having been removed; but there was still a lot of unnecessary clutter to be cleared. Sunday at the ranch by herself had gone pretty well, leaving her with a sense of satisfaction.

Yesterday, she completed the chores of watering the herb garden, and planters and pots sitting around the little stone patio by the kitchen. She had cleaned Billy's stall and pen and had let the goat run in the yard while she attacked the chicken coop by herself for the first time.

Denia counted sixteen hens in the coop. Jorje had told her that Melinda always bought two hens at a time, of the same breed, from poultry suppliers. The hens looked different from each other because there were several different breeds in the coop. When she gathered the eggs from the nesting boxes, she had collected eleven eggs in total. Jorje had explained that most of the hens laid an egg every day, but sometimes skipped a day. Denia, who was used to seeing the white eggs from the supermarket, was surprised to see the color of most of the eggs was a light brown, or tan, with the exception of one blue shelled egg that seemed unique. She felt like she had done a good job cleaning the floor of the coop, following Jorje's instructions of using the tools reserved only for the coop. She carefully filled the round food trays and cylindrical water dispensers that hung from cables attached to the crossbeams of the roof. These hung low to the ground for easy access by the birds. The chickens tolerated Denia's presence among them, but flapped and ran about squawking when Billy charged the side of the coop with her head, seeking attention. Denia spread extra feed and grit on the ground, and checked every hen, one by one.

Jorje told her that chickens who were not moving around or standing off to themselves needed to be separated from the rest of the hens, until the health of the hen could be determined. He explained that there was a veterinarian in the nearby town of Orcutt who specialized in chickens and birds. Denia thought to herself…so far, this added up to *three* veterinarians! Animal care was getting complicated.

Denia took the fresh eggs to the office, washed them, and put them into the available egg cartons. Billy stood at the doorway, wanting to come in, but knew she was not allowed into the office building. Mona came out of the house and into the yard, too. She was enjoying a sunbath, her patchwork of fur stretched out on a low cinderblock wall, separating a small area of the yard where Jorje and potential visitors could park cars behind the house.

Denia noticed that the cat ran back to the house, following her after she had put Billy in the pen. Mona had developed a habit of staying near Denia. She was not friendly yet, as she had demonstrated with Batty, but she seemed to like having Denia around.

She spent Sunday afternoon doing laundry and addressing the situation of the stuffed closet in her bedroom. She wanted to get her clothes out of boxes and suitcases and hung up in the closet. In going through the various contents, she assumed this had been an overflow closet used by her aunt to store accessories and older clothing. After piling all the clothing on the bed and establishing piles of shoes and purses on the floor, Denia used her own boxes, filling them with items to be donated.

Denia found her aunt's collection of scarves hanging from hooks along one wall of the closet. They varied from delicate silk to homemade knits, short to long, square and rectangular, light and airy, to heavy and thick. The bright and muted hues of the collection covered an artist's palate, with everything from delicate prints to intertwined Celtic and baroque patterns. Denia decided to keep all but a few of the scarves. She also decided to keep two Coach handbags, one black and one a cocoa brown. These were timeless.

It had taken the best part of the afternoon, but when she was finished her clothes were hung neatly in the closet. Denia appreciated that the space looked larger, now being half empty. She completed the task by carrying the boxes downstairs, out to the car, and loaded into the back of the Explorer for donation the next day.

On Monday morning, Denia's thoughts went to the agenda of things she needed to do that day: go to the bank in Santa Maria where Melinda had her account for the ranch and donate the boxes of clothing and shoes. The kitchen phone rang before she could add any other items to the list.

"Hello," she answered.

"Hi, Denia?" the male voice asked.

Denia thought it was probably the vet calling about Isis but realized the voice was different than she remembered.

"Yes," she answered.

"This is Eugene Sorenson."

"Oh, hi," Denia responded, somewhat surprised.

The image of the handsome attorney sitting behind his

office desk came to mind.

"I was wondering if you could meet me down in Santa Barbara on Wednesday. Santa Barbara is the county seat, and we need to file the papers regarding the change of title on the property," he explained.

"Well, yes, I could meet you if you tell me where and when."

"We need to meet at the courthouse on Anacapa, between State Street and Garden. You can take the freeway to Santa Barbara and exit on State Street. State Street is one of the main drags through town. You'll be going south on State. Watch for Anacapa and turn right. There are signs for the courthouse and parking. Would eleven o'clock be convenient?" he asked.

Denia grabbed a notepad and pencil and was scribbling down the directions he gave.

"Yes, that sounds fine," answered Denia.

"Do you have copies of Melinda's Death Certificate, yet? We will need that."

"Yes, my mother gave me three copies in case I needed them for the banks, or getting the utilities changed into my name."

"That sounds good. Bring one with you. I'll bring the other paperwork. I'll see you on Wednesday. Let me know if anything comes up and you are unable to make it," he instructed.

"Okay, I'll see you then," Denia said, putting down the phone.

Denia was thankful for the call and the offer to help her through the process of getting the title on the ranch changed into her name. She looked at her scribbled directions to the courthouse and made some quick corrections so she would be able to read them later. Meanwhile, her morning bagel had popped up in the toaster, and was now cold.

Again, the kitchen phone rang.

"Hello?" said Denia, wondering who else would be calling.

"Hello, Denia, this is Hans," said another male voice.

"Hello, how is Isis doing?" asked Denia.

This was the call she had been expecting.

"Not as well as I would like," he commented. "She's taking some water, but I still have the IV going since she would not take any food over the weekend. We've tried a couple of different foods, but she just smells it and doesn't eat. I thought she might be able to go home today, but I want to keep her here until she starts eating."

"Why do you think she's not eating?"

"It's hard to tell. She was in kidney failure and may still be nauseated. I'll try giving her something for nausea and see if it helps. In the meantime, what kind of cat food did Melinda use? Maybe she is just finicky and wants the kind of food she usually eats."

"The canned food is called 'Cool Cat', and most of the cans are some kind of chicken," Denia said, reading the can she had opened for Mona that morning.

"Alright, I'll try some of that," he said. "I'll call you again tomorrow."

Denia was thinking about the cat after the call. Isis had been at the vet's office since Friday, which really was not too long knowing she was on death's doorstep when they brought her to the vet's office. Denia was starting to worry, not only about the cat, but how much this was going to cost. For now, she had little choice but to continue the care for the cat. So, she headed up the stairs to get ready for her trip to Santa Maria.

On Wednesday morning, Denia was standing in front of the bathroom mirror with a critical grimace on her face. She had decided on an outfit she used to wear to the office – a pale pink, silk blouse and a straight, maroon skirt. Her bed down the hall was piled with clothing items discarded during the decision process. She had brought few clothes with her to the ranch that were not casual. When she left her San Diego apartment, she packed and stored most of the nice blouses and business clothes she used to wear to work.

She was getting ready to drive to Santa Barbara for her meeting with Eugene Sorenson. Denia had to admit to herself that she was a little nervous to meet with the good-looking attorney; so, maybe she was primping, just a little. Denia knew Melinda had a good opinion of her lawyer. Having met him only once, under rather difficult circumstances, Denia wanted to make a good impression.

She had already applied makeup to her oval shaped face.

Denia used a light base coat to cover her ivory skin and the sprinkling of freckles across the bridge of her nose. She had always wished to have a more olive complexion that would not sunburn so easily; but her mother's heritage had been Irish, hence the genetic pale skin and freckles. She did her best to live with it, sunscreen being a fact of life.

Denia had carefully applied the dark brown mascara to her upper and lower eyelashes. Her dark blue eyes were probably her best facial feature. The blue came from both sides of the family. Her nose was straight, with a rounded tip. Her lips were well-shaped and naturally pink. A rose-colored lipstick completed the effect to her satisfaction.

She had washed and styled her thick, auburn hair, and was now wrestling to get it contained with a clip at the back of her head. She thought the simple style would supply the more sophisticated look she wanted, rather than letting it hang straight. When finished, she stood back and approved the animated portrait looking back at her.

Back to the bedroom she went, to add amethyst earrings and tan pumps. As a final thought, she pulled a silk scarf, with varied shades of pink, from a stack saved from her aunt's collection. She wrapped it lightly around her neck to provide a soft, feminine look.

Situated in the front seat of the car, she put on her sunglasses to block the bright rays coming through the windshield. Denia pulled out of the drive and started the twenty-minute drive from the ranch to where she could pick up the 101 Freeway, going south to Santa Barbara. On the center console of the Explorer, she had her cell phone and the directions the lawyer had given her to find the Santa Barbara Courthouse. The downhill drive toward the

Pacific Coast flowed easily, with light, mid-morning traffic. She took peeks at the sparkling waters of the ocean that came in and out of view on the right. Glancing at the clock on the dashboard, Denia knew she was early, but was glad to have a little extra time just in case she had problems navigating the unfamiliar city streets.

Once in the city, finding the courthouse had been easy using the directions, as well as finding parking. Upon meeting the young barrister on the first floor of the building, Denia was glad she spent the extra time getting ready for the day. The foyer of the building was wide with high ceilings, implying a serious, formal atmosphere. Sorenson looked every bit the professional in a steel gray suit, pale yellow shirt, with a yellow and silver checked tie. His eyes crinkled at the corners as he smiled and gave a brief wave when he saw her.

Eugene Sorenson quickly took command of the tasks *du jour*, leading Denia to the appropriate courthouse office and managing the discussions and paperwork needed to complete the business.

Denia was relieved with how efficiently the process was completed to transfer the ranch property into her name. On the way out of the building, Eugene, as he had insisted that she address him, advised her to make an appointment with him to set up a Will for herself now that she held such a valuable asset as the ranch.

To Denia's surprise, when standing outside of the preeminent building of the county, Eugene suggested they get lunch. It was a short walk to State Street, harboring an eclectic choice of small restaurants serving food for an upwardly mobile clientele. Eugene led the way along the busy street to an unimposing door front, opening one of the double glass doors for Denia to enter.

The interior of the restaurant was lit by dim, overhead lighting, needed due to the lack of natural light filtering in from the street. A waitress led them to a small table along one wall and took their drink order. Contemporary art in black frames was featured on turquois-colored walls. Bright, white tablecloths and napkins lay atop the tables of sleek, dark wood.

Denia sipped from a flute of white wine as they waited for their gourmet salads. She watched the subtle changes in Eugene's chocolate eyes as he spoke of the attributes of the towns lining the California central coast, with Santa Barbara being the diamond in the crown. She was enjoying his smooth, enthusiastic voice. He clearly knew the highlights of the city. He convinced Denia that some the local landmarks, such as the Santa Barbara Mission and the waterfront pier, were worth a visit.

As the waitress brought the salads to the table, there was a break in the conversation.

"I'm sorry," he said. "I'm monopolizing our time. How do you like the wine? It's from a local vineyard not far from Santa Maria."

"It's good," she answered. "It's not heavy. I don't usually drink wine during the day, but this is nice."

The couple spoke back and forth throughout the meal. She talked about the ranch, the goat, and the chickens. He talked about the towns surrounding Solvang, and some good places to look for a flat screen TV. After the meal they had coffee, and the conversation turned to the afternoon.

"I am going to have to get going," he explained. "I have an appointment at my office at three-thirty. I need to get on the road."

"It's already two o'clock, how will you make it all the way back to Santa Maria in time?" she asked.

"Yeah, it's getting late. I'll take the pass. I should make it in time."

"What pass?" she asked.

"It's the San Marcos Pass, also known as the Chumash Highway. It's a very old road that goes through the Santa Ynez Mountains. It connects Santa Barbara to the Santa Ynez Valley, and easily connects with the 101 Freeway. It can cut thirty to forty minutes off my drive."

"Forty minutes!" she repeated, in surprise.

"It's a winding road that really climbs into the hills quickly, but on a day like today, when the weather is clear, it's very scenic and can really save time," he explained. "I wouldn't take the Pass in the rain, or on a foggy day. Lots of people use it every day to commute back and forth for work. There's a famous bridge, called the Cold Spring Canyon Arch Bridge, that you cross when you're coming down into Santa Ynez. The view from the bridge is rather spectacular."

"I haven't heard about the Pass. It sounds like a good shortcut."

"If I'm not in a hurry I still like to go up the coast and look at the ocean, but today I need to take the Pass."

"How do you get to it?" Denia asked, considering the shortcut for herself.

"Actually, it's easy to find from here. You just follow State Street out the same way you came in, and you'll come to a large intersection with lights. There is signage for the San Marcos Pass, Route 154. Follow the signs, turn right, and you'll start going up the hill."

"Maybe I'll try it. Can I follow you?" she asked.

"Well, I'm going to have to leave right now, and race to my car; but you take your time and finish your coffee."

"Oh, alright," she said, a little disappointed.

Then remembering her manners, "Thank you so much for helping me today, and for this wonderful lunch."

"It was my pleasure," he said in a charming voice. "I don't get many chances to have such a good-looking lunch date."

Denia flushed with pleasure.

"Don't forget what I said about getting a Will in place. I'll promise you a discount for the legal work if you will agree to another lunch date."

"That would be nice," Denia responded, trying not to appear too eager to spend more time with him.

"Got to go," he said, rising from his seat. "Have a good drive back."

He turned and left, waving to the waitress on his way out the door.

Denia sipped the rich coffee with cream. She wondered if she could count this lunch to be her first date after Jeff.

Eugene had a better demeanor than Jeff ever had. He was also better dressed. She chuckled to herself. Having been so recently burned, she was not going to allow herself to be swept up by a handsome face. Denia knew she needed to focus on getting her new life in order.

Also, she needed to help get the murder of her aunt resolved, if possible. She took another sip of the coffee. It had been nice, but she needed to get back to her new reality, with the goat and the chickens.

Denia took her time walking back to her car after lunch. Storefronts ranged from small eateries to clothing and specialty shops. Eugene told her there was a wonderful up-scale mall just off State Street, with stores not available in the smaller coastal towns. She knew she would need to come back to become more familiar with Santa Barbara.

It was a balmy afternoon, with a mild ocean breeze – perfect driving weather. Denia decided to try taking the shortcut up through the Santa Ynez Mountains that Eugene had mentioned. The traffic on State Street, going away from the civic center, had not yet reached the evening rush. Denia had no problem finding the turn for the San Marcos Pass. After the turn, the road started out with two lanes of traffic leading up the hill, but quickly became a two-lane highway.

Denia was surprised at how quickly the road changed to a steep, upward grade into hills covered with thick chaparral vegetation, common to the California coast. The lane of traffic going up was on the inside, next to the rock walls carved into the steep hillsides. The reoccurring curves in the road demanded Denia's full attention. Oncoming, downhill traffic rushed by on her left, frequently not seen until she drove around a curve. The speed limit varied from thirty-five to fifty miles per hour, and Denia tried to maintain the proper speed. Other traffic seemed to take the speed limit as a mild suggestion and cars piled up in her rear-view mirror. Twice she pulled over into the occasional turnouts to allow the traffic behind her to pass. Maybe these were commuters who knew every turn in their daily trek. Prior to pulling back into the traffic lane, Denia took in the view of the land laid out below, the coastline, and the horizon of the Pacific dropping off the edge of the world.

The highway crested the top of the hills and started its descent away from the coast. Denia noticed that the vegetation changed on this side of the mountain, showing more greenery. Small ranch houses perched near the road with tree-filled front lots, popped into view from time to time.

Soon, she came to the famous arched bridge. The road led Denia onto the bridge before she realized it. There were no cars behind her, so she slowed her speed to take in the breathtaking view of the valley below. Multiple shades of greens and browns reflected the sunlight. The opposite side of the valley was lined with a flow of rounded hills touching the Scandinavian blue sky. No wonder the Danish settlers of old had found this place appealing, thought Denia.

Once over the bridge, the highway's downward grade was less pronounced, so Denia felt she could safely increase her speed. Convenient passing lanes appeared every few miles, allowing impatient drivers to pass her. There were warning signs posted with pictures of deer. She was enjoying the scenery rushing by the windows.

At some point, Denia became aware of a black pickup truck quickly approaching in her rearview mirror. A sign for an upcoming passing lane appeared on the right. Denia planned to stay to the right of the passing lane as soon as she could, to let the truck pass. She could see the truck was raised on high, thick tires, enabling the driver to look down on her car from his seat in the cab. As the truck moved closer, she increased her speed.

Not a moment too soon, the extra passing lane appeared and Denia stayed to the right; but the black truck stayed behind her, continuing to close the gap with her car. Denia felt a pang of panic and rush of adrenaline go through her. The chrome grill of the truck came so close as to take up most of the view of her back window.

She decided to slowly decelerate her speed, in hopes that the driver of the truck would pass her in frustration. The pickup did drop back, temporarily, only to accelerate again toward the back bumper of the Explorer.

Denia quickly looked to the roadside, planning to pull off to the shoulder, but she couldn't pull over before the grill of the truck once again filled the back window. In seconds, she felt the rear end hit from behind which vibrated through the car, propelling it forward.

In a panic, realizing the attack, Denia jerked the steering wheel to the right, taking the car off the road and onto the shoulder, shredding vegetation as it went. She hit the brakes, trying to control the car to a stop on the uneven terrain, while seeing the black truck speed past her on the left. She could not stop before the car hit a small boulder, halting the car and lifting the driver's side of the vehicle off the ground. The impact caused the driver's side airbag to inflate.

At once, Denia's consciousness faded to black.

$$5$$

THE RAM

Denia's first recollection was of someone calling her name. She tried to move her arm to push the inflated airbag away from her face and chest. She quickly remembered that her car had been hit from behind, and she had been forced off the road. She could see that her car had come to a stop on a tilt. The driver's side door was open.

"Can you move your legs?" came the familiar voice of a man.

Denia realized that she *did* have feeling in her feet and legs. She discovered she could move her ankles. She tried to move her legs from her knees. Her feet and legs appeared to be without injury.

"Yes, I can move," she answered faintly.

"Can you reach down and unfasten your seatbelt?" he asked.

Denia slowly moved her arm, finding the latch on the seatbelt. The seatbelt was holding very tightly against her upper body. Unlocking it, her body jolted toward the center console, due to the car being elevated off the ground on the driver's side.

"Move your legs slowly out the door, and I'll help you down," he said persuasively.

Denia turned her head toward the man speaking and found herself looking into familiar blue eyes.

"Sergeant Nelson?" she asked, surprised to find him there.

"Come on, try to move your legs out the door," he instructed.

With much effort, moving against gravity, Denia managed to get one leg and then the other, out the car door. The sergeant helped rotate her legs, slowly turning her in the seat to face him.

"Put your arm around my neck, and I'll pull you out."

Denia put her arm around his shoulder. He put his arm around her waist and inched her to the edge of the car seat.

"Okay, I'm going to lift you down," he said.

He lifted her out of the car and stood her on the ground in front of him; but Denia's knees would not support her weight and buckled beneath her. The officer was able to catch and steady her, and with much support, guide her to the open door of his police cruiser. Once he had her seated, with her legs out the door and feet on the ground, he fished for the first aid kit behind the front seat. He pulled out a small ampule, crushed it, and waved it under Denia's nose.

"Agh, that's awful," she said, moving her head back, trying to avoid the offensive pellet.

"It's ammonia. How do you feel?"

"I feel kind of shaky," she answered. "Look at my car," she whined.

"It could have been a lot worse," he said, "Do you want me to call an ambulance?"

"No, I think I'm alright, physically - just really upset."

"Alright. Sit there and try to catch your breath. I'm going to call the highway patrol and a tow truck."

"How did you find me?" Denia questioned with appreciation.

"I was down in Santa Barbara most of the day for meetings. Our office in Solvang functions under the Santa Barbara Sheriff. I was on my way back to Solvang, and decided to go over the Pass," he explained. "I saw your car and pulled over."

Sergeant Nelson got on the cruiser's radio and called for the California Highway Patrol and a tow truck, giving the police dispatcher their location on Route 154.

"My purse and cell phone are still in the car," Denia said to him once he came back around to stand near her at the open car door.

"I'll get it."

He went around the back side of the Explorer to enter the tilted car from the passenger side door. He came back with the retrieved purse.

"I got the car registration out of the glove box. We'll need that for the police report on the accident."

Momentarily, a highway patrol vehicle, with lights flashing, came toward them on the road, made a U-turn and parked off the road behind the sergeant's cruiser.

"Hi, Ray," the sergeant greeted the young officer. "How did you get here so fast? I just called it in."

"I was just two minutes down the road at the entrance to the recreation park for Lake Cachuma," he explained. "What happened here?" he asked, looking at the Explorer, assessing how it came to rest on the boulder.

Both men turned to Denia, waiting to hear what she had to say.

"A truck hit me from behind and forced me off the road," Denia said.

"A truck hit you?" Nelson asked. "What kind of truck?"

"It was a black, pickup truck. It was raised up on those big wheels. I saw him tailgating and tried to avoid him. When he had a chance to pass me in the passing lane, he just kept coming up behind me. Then he bumped me, and I went off the road into the bushes," she explained.

"It was a male driver? Was he alone?" The CHP officer asked, while writing on a pad.

"Yes, it was a man. I could see him. He was alone in the truck," Denia reported.

"Can you remember what he looked like?" Nelson asked.

"He had light skin, dark, short hair, and no beard. He looked young."

"Can you remember what model pickup?" The officer asked. "Did you see the license plate on the truck?"

"I remember the grill of the truck had a ram's head in the middle. I saw the license plate - it was a California plate, but I don't remember anything else about it."

The investigating officer and Sergeant Nelson walked over to the Explorer, checking out the back of the car. They spent time discussing what they found, looking closely for signs of a hit from behind. Denia overheard some of the conversation.

"If you're going fifty miles an hour, it wouldn't take much of a hit from behind to force a car off the road," said Nelson.

"You can see where it hit, right here. Not much damage. The front is really screwed up, though," Ray said, walking over and standing by the elevated front fender.

"Yeah, the wheel is bent. There is probably wheel well and axel damage. They'll have to pull it off the rock before they can tow it," Nelson predicted.

"I'm going to call it in. We might get lucky and find this guy still in the area," the officer said as he walked over to his patrol car.

Denia, still sitting in the police car, was becoming more dismayed realizing that her car would probably not be drivable for some time. The next half hour was spent completing the police report. Denia was given the police report number and told to give it to her insurance carrier when she reported the accident later.

"You should take the time to write down everything you remember, including the time, the weather situation, and everything that happened in chronological order. Write down whatever you can remember about the truck and the driver. This may end up as a court case, if he was deliberately trying to run you off the road," advised the patrolman. "Do you think you could identify the driver?"

"I don't know, probably not. I only saw him through the rearview mirror. I know I'll never forget the grill of the truck coming at me," she answered.

The tow truck arrived, taking both policemen off to speak with the driver. Denia felt a sudden rush of relief, thinking that the accident could have ended with a much more serious outcome. She could have been killed. Tears sprang up in her eyes and she started to cry, not understanding the sudden barrage of emotions. Sergeant Nelson returned to his car in time to see Denia fishing through her purse for a tissue.

"Come on, get in the car, and put on your seatbelt," he said gently, and then tried to lighten the mood. "You are going to get a rare ride in the front seat of a police cruiser. Let's get back to town."

He smiled at her as he climbed into the seat beside her and gunned the engine of the car, showing off as he pulled onto the highway.

That evening, Denia was sitting on the sofa with Mona, sipping an after-dinner cup of green tea. She reflected on the day, which had started out so well. The business on the ranch property was completed. She had a wonderful lunch with her attorney. There was the drive over the hills that was a little nerve racking, but incredibly scenic. Then, out of nowhere, the frightening encounter with the rogue truck and the wreckage of her car. Good fortune had been with her since Sergeant Nelson just happened to be traveling on the same road. He was definitely the hero of the day.

She put her cup down on the old coffee table and used a match to light one of the purple candles before her. The faint scent of lavender drifted into the air around her. Denia's thoughts returned to the tall, blonde, police sergeant. He had been very kind and kept the conversation light on the way down to the valley from the accident scene. He made a joke about her riding in the front seat of the police cruiser and swore her to secrecy, saying that he did not need all the ladies in Solvang lining up to get a ride in his car. He had driven her to the ranch and dropped her off at the back door, reminding her to call her auto insurance company to report the accident. He gave her the name of the auto body shop her Explorer was being towed to in Buellton, a small town just down the road from Solvang, near the freeway. Then, he was off.

Denia called her auto insurance company and reported the accident shortly after getting home. She forgot that she had a large deductible which would need to be paid toward fixing the car. Between cats and cars, she was spending money without even trying. She sighed. Denia looked around the living room but did not have the willpower to tackle a clearing and cleaning project. On a whim, Denia picked up her cell phone and placed a call.

"Hello," came the strong male voice.

"Hi, Daddy."

"Hi, Pumpkin. What's going on up there in Danish land?" he asked, jovially.

"I got in a car accident today. The Explorer is at an auto repair shop," she reported.

"How bad was the accident? Are you alright?"

"Yeah, I'm okay. I'm just really upset about the car," she moaned. "I think they'll be able to fix it."

"What happened?" he asked with fatherly concern.

"I was taking a different way back from Santa Barbara and a pickup truck deliberately hit my back bumper and ran me off the road," Denia explained.

"Are you sure you're alright? Did you report it to the police?"

"Yes. I was lucky. The police sergeant who has been working on the investigation of Melinda's death, was on the same highway, coming back from Santa Barbara. He found me off the side of the road, right after it happened. He helped me out of the car and called for the highway patrol."

Denia went on to tell her father the entire story of the day, including a detailed description of the encounter with the truck, the rescue, and the condition of her beloved SUV. They spoke for a half hour. He told her of things going on around home, and some of her mother's latest projects. It was such a comfort to her just to hear his voice, and his unfailing support for her. Denia felt better when the call ended, with her fears put into perspective, and with the reinforcement of parental love.

Feeling emotionally drained, she used her aunt's little, hooded, brass tool to snuff the candle's flame, patted Mona along her curled spine, and headed up the stairs for bed.

The next day, Denia was up and dressed early. Rays of the morning sun came through the windows, and she knew it would be a warm, sunny day. She had gone to bed early, and fallen into a restful, dreamless sleep. She noticed her neck was stiff this morning; but, otherwise, she felt no residual injuries from yesterday's accident.

She had just gotten Mona fed and put a pot of coffee on, when she heard a car come in the driveway, followed shortly by a knock at the kitchen door. She glanced at the clock on the stove. It was only eight-thirty.

"Who is it?" Denia called through the door.

"It's me. Hans," came the male voice.

Denia opened the door to see the young vet with hands full, carrying two boxes. He handed her the smaller box with the label of a Solvang bakery on the front, as he held onto the bigger box, a cardboard cat carrier.

"I brought breakfast. I hope you have coffee," he said, coming through the door.

He walked directly into the dining area and set the cat

carrier down on the cleared-off end of the table.

"I tried calling you a couple times yesterday, but there was no answer."

"I was here in the morning but drove down to Santa Barbara."

"Yeah, we heard about you being run off the road. I figured you were without a car and wouldn't be able to pick up the cat, so I brought her out. How are you doing this morning?" he asked with concern.

It took Denia a few seconds to grasp what he said. Rather than answering him, she wanted to clarify how he would know about what happened yesterday.

"How did you know about that?" she asked directly, with a hand on her hip.

"From my mom. One of her friend's daughters works at the Solvang Sheriff's Office, and another friend's son was the tow truck driver for your car. The phone calls were buzzing last night."

Denia shook her head in disbelief.

"I can't believe this town. I've never seen anything like it."

"Yeah, the FBI have nothing on the way these old crones have this place wired," he agreed. "Don't even get me started on the 'who's-dating-who' grapevine. They're probably already talking about me buying a couple Danish to bring out here this morning."

His mouth quirked in a crooked smile.

"You brought Danish?" she asked, possibly one of her

favorite breakfasts – coffee and a Danish.

"Yeah, I was hungry, so I got us both two." He smiled at her.

Denia looked at the wiry young man, with a tanned, clean-shaven face. His fine, brown, straight hair hung down almost to his shoulders, not yet secured for his vet's office dress mode. He wore a button-down plaid shirt, with khaki slacks, and loafers on feet with no socks. He did not wear a watch but had a beaded leather band around his left wrist.

She could not help but feel an affinity with this guy. He was someone from her own generation. At the moment, the conversation was interrupted by more pressing matters. Stifled cat sounds were being emitted from the cardboard carton on the table.

"We better let her out," the vet said, while opening the two top flaps of the cat box.

Denia expected the captive to try and jump for freedom immediately when the container was opened. Instead, the open lid revealed a calm feline, looking up at them. Denia could not believe this was the same animal that had been on the verge of death less than a week ago. The cat was alert with perked ears, and wide, golden eyes peering out from a feminine feline face. Unlike Mona's rather short-haired coat, the regal Isis, who was perfectly named, wore a longer, thicker coat of midnight black.

Hans picked up the cat and gently placed her on the floor. She stood there for a few seconds, taking in the familiar surroundings, before sauntering off to the kitchen. The two people followed, only to find her at the cat food dishes by the refrigerator, finishing the food Mona had left behind. Denia grabbed the half empty cat food can from the counter and scooped the remains onto the saucer Isis was using.

"I've been trying to get that cat to eat since Monday," Hans said with exasperation. "I took her home with me Tuesday night, so you wouldn't get charged for boarding. She's been turning her nose up at most of what I've been giving her to eat."

"Maybe it's more *where* she eats, rather than *what* she eats," said Denia with a smile. "There's no place like home."

Isis rapidly completed the cat food, took a few laps from the water dish, and headed off to the litter box in the utility room. Relieved that Isis seemed to be doing well with her eight remaining lives, Denia poured two cups of coffee. The Danish looked scrumptious, as she put them onto small plates, and carried them to the table. Hans and Denia sat in contentment, feasting on the confections and sipping coffee.

Mona seemed to sense a change, leaving her spot on the sofa, coming over to the people. Isis was making her way out of the kitchen when the two cats met. Short bursts of cat speak were exchanged, as they walked around each other with their tails up. It was Isis who led the way over to the bay window glowing in the morning sun, jumping up to the sill to claim her spot on her braided rug. Mona followed, circling once before finding the right spot on her rug. Everything was right with the cat world.

"I've got to get a picture of this," Hans said, grasping

his cell phone while walking to the window, and snapping the shot. He returned to the table and sat down, taking another swig of the cooling coffee.

"My mom wanted me to ask you if it would be alright for her to come over in the morning with Batty to check the office computer for any candle orders."

"That's right," said Denia, remembering, "tomorrow is Friday, which is egg day. I'm supposed to go with Batty into town to find out where to take the eggs. Sure, tell your mother I look forward to meeting her."

"She's been talking of nothing else since you got here. You would think you were some long, lost niece of *hers*, instead of Melinda's."

"You're not jealous, are you?" Denia quipped.

"No," he said a more serious tone. "She's just used to spending a lot of time here during the week; and that all ended suddenly, and unexpectedly, with Melinda's death. She lost one of her best friends *and* her job. She's kind of wandering around the house in a funk."

"She probably hasn't lost her job. I just have so much to take care of around here, everything involving big decisions. There is so much for me to learn about. I've barely had a chance to get to the bank and get some of the bills sorted out. And now there's this business with my car. I'm kind of stranded here, for now."

"What about Melinda's Range Rover?" Hans asked.

"Oh, yeah," she said, visualizing the car. "It's just sitting in the garage, but it's not in my name and it's not insured."

"Have Batty drive you to the Department of Motor

Vehicles tomorrow and get all the paperwork started. The registration is probably in the car. You can get it insured with a phone call. It's not good for you to be out here alone without a car," he said with concern.

"Of course, you could always call me. I'll come get you." He gave a charming smile.

"That's nice of you, but the idea about the Rover is a good one. I'll talk to Batty in the morning."

"What are you doing this weekend? It's my weekend off from the clinic and I'm going up to Pismo Beach. Would you like to come with me and see some of the local scenery?" he asked.

"No, but thanks. I'm here with the animals this weekend. Jorje, our farmhand, used to have Saturday and Sunday off when my aunt was here, but since her death he's been working every day except last Sunday. So, I'm taking care of the animals on the weekend to get him back on schedule. He needs to have his days off," Denia explained.

"Well, how about if I come out on Saturday morning to give you a hand? I haven't seen the goat since she was little. My mom says she's really getting big."

"That would be good. Yeah, Billy is a character. I think she thinks she's a dog. She loves to be with people. I'm getting better with the chickens. I think they are getting to know me. I could use some of your veterinary advice."

"Speaking of veterinary advice, for right now, I need to get to the clinic," he said as he got up and headed for the kitchen door.

"Thank you for bringing Isis home," Denia said, following him to the door. "What about the vet bill?"

"You can stop by the clinic and make a payment. If you can't pay the whole bill right now, the office can arrange for payments for you. Gotta go, see you Saturday," he said going out the door.

Denia spent the rest of the morning out back with Jorje taking care of Billy and the chickens. The feed truck came with its monthly delivery, so she got to see the unloading and storing of the various types of feed. She was getting to know where everything belonged. Billy enjoyed all the activity, running from one place to another on the large back lot. Denia did a quick check of the office prior to going into the house for some lunch.

After a bagel with cream cheese and a pear, Denia made her way out to the garage with the car keys for the Range Rover. She wanted to see if the car would start after sitting idle for three weeks. To her relief, the engine started easily, and she let it run for a few minutes to help charge the battery. Looking in the glove box, she found the car registration and the insurance card for Blue Ribbon Auto Insurance. These she took back into the house with her, after locking up the car and the garage.

Once back in the house, she knew she needed to do a search for her aunt's personal papers. Something seemed to be cropping up on a daily basis supporting the need to get the paperwork in order. Somewhere, there had to be copies of the auto and house insurance policies and other important papers. There were only a few rooms in this house, so she should be able to find them. Denia decided to start on the bottom floor, and then go to her aunt's bedroom to search, if needed.

As she scanned the living room, Denia realized she had never checked the little writing desk so neatly stashed under the stairwell. Of course, she said to herself, why hadn't she thought of that? She went over to the desk and ducked her head to enter the small space. A little swivel chair was behind the desk, and Denia eased herself into the seat.

"What a cute little desk," she said out loud, surveying the living room with a new perspective. Mona was curled in her favorite corner of the sofa, and Isis by the window. The wide opening in the brick fireplace was dark and cold, while the face of the old TV stared back at her reflecting the light from the window. At the back of the slanted cubbyhole space, Denia saw a simple, two drawer file cabinet. It was so tucked away under the staircase that she hadn't noticed it before. She turned on the swivel chair, easily reaching the top drawer. Looking inside, she found labeled files containing manila folders. The first was labeled: UTILITIES, and contained folders for Gas, Electric, and Trash. Denia weeded her fingers through the hanging files, finding one labeled: INSURANCE, inside of which were folders named House and Auto. At last, here was all the information she needed for running the ranch.

Denia pulled out the folder for auto insurance and turned back to the little desk. As she moved in the chair, her foot slammed into something on the floor by the desk. She looked down and gasped, grabbing the elusive handbag from the floor.

"Oh, my gosh! Here it is," she shouted to the room.

Immediately, she opened the tan bag, and there, sticking out of the top of an inside pocket was a cell phone with a sparkling gold cover.

"Auntie, your cell phone," she whispered into the air.

Thrilled with her discovery, Denia tried to turn the phone on, to no avail.

"Dead," she realized. "Where would the charger be?"

She looked around the small space. On the desk was a small desk light with a conical lampshade. Denia followed the lamp's cord to a socket on the back wall. She found a black box plugged into the top socket and followed the black wire to the set of narrow shelves lining the wall behind the desk to the phone charging stand on the top shelf. Denia put the phone into the charger and hoped for the best.

Denia knew she would need to call Sergeant Nelson to tell him she found the phone, but not before she copied all the names and numbers from the contact list. She would also check all the recent calls Melinda had made and received within a week or two of her murder. That is, *if* she could get the phone to work.

Denia felt it was imperative for her to solve the murder, not only for her aunt, but for her to go forward living in this place.

In the meantime, Denia gathered all the papers for the DMV she would need the next day to get the car registration changed. She put them in a folder, and put the folder on the kitchen counter, ready for the morning. It eased her mind to know she had a working vehicle at the ranch while the Explorer was being repaired. In case of an emergency, she had a car. Denia didn't want to consider what that emergency might be; but, so far, things had not gone very smoothly since she arrived.

The afternoon was speeding by, denoted by the change in light coming into the house through the windows. Denia felt restless. She thought this was partly due to the fact that she was not getting enough exercise. Upstairs, she dug through the clothes in her dresser for her running pants, a sports bra, and a brightly colored tank top. Quickly donning the outfit, she rummaged around the closet floor for the neglected running shoes.

In less than two minutes, Denia walked up the gravel driveway, looking down the frontage road one way, and then the other. She decided to take the direction going toward town. She crossed the two-lane road to the dirt shoulder on the other side, and started her jog facing any oncoming traffic, but there was no traffic. The road was deserted.

She started running slowly, giving herself a chance to warm up, and then assumed a steady pace. The dirt of the roadside was soft, making the run easier than when running on concrete. The heat of the August day had passed, and a light breeze felt cool against her warming skin. She thought it was good to be running again, while getting her second wind. Denia tried to remember the last time she had run. It had been a while. In fact, the last time she had put on her running shoes had been early in June. She had gone on a run with Jeff at Mission Bay in San Diego. So much had changed since then that it felt like a year ago, instead of three months.

As she ran, she was passing row after row of well-manicured grapevines perched on their supporting stakes like large, feathery, green birds with their wings outstretched. Bunches of dark grapes hung from the greenery. As one field ended, there would be a brief separation of a dirt lane, and another would begin. Strings of tall trees lined the inside of the bordering fence, acting as windbreaks for the pampered vines. After about two miles she came to a wide, dirt driveway leading away from the road around a curved bend. Beside the entrance to the driveway was a large, rectangular, painted sign.

Samala Winery

Denia recognized the name. It was the same winery that her aunt had mentioned in her letter. It was also the same winery that was leasing the back part of her land. It was the owners, recommended by Melinda, that would be willing to buy her ranch if she would want to sell. Curiosity got the best of her, and she started down the curved dirt road.

After about a quarter of a mile, a rectangular building with a central, Greystone façade in the shape of an arch came into view. A large, semicircular, asphalt drive and tree studded parking lot lay directly in front of the one-story, sprawling edifice, with inviting vine laden patios framing each end. Another large wooden sign with the same logo as the roadside sign, identified the winery. A wide walkway led from the parking lot to the two tall doors, painted a grape-colored purple, centered in the middle of the stone arch. Tall, indigo pots overflowing with pink petunias sat on each side of the doors and vines with small leaves clung to the walls at spots, climbing the stone façade. Denia proceeded up the walkway, and pulled one of the purple doors open using an elongated, brass, door handle.

The doorway opened into a wide foyer with a high ceiling that was lit by soft, recessed lighting. Cleverly placed tables and multi-level stands displayed featured bottles of wine. Wine glasses monogramed in gold with the winery label design, cocktail napkins, decorative bottle stoppers, and other items related to wine tasting rested on throws of purple velvet. An entire section of the room was devoted to wine racks of different designs to meet various home decors.

Denia peeked through the doorway on the left to find a room of shelves holding bottle after bottle of wine. The wall at the end of the room was made of diamond shaped cubes stacked from floor to ceiling with various vintages. Sealed cases of wine bearing the Samala label were stacked about the floor for convenient retrieval by customers.

She walked across the lobby and through the welcoming wide doorway on the right. In front of a horizontal, veined mirror stood a bow-shaped serving bar of dark, highly polished wood. Around the interior, windowed walls of the long room were strewn with tall tables and high seated chairs. Views to the landscaped outside made the space appear larger. A welcoming tray of cheese squares, each speared with a plastic toothpick, sat alone on the bar. Looking around, finding no one, Denia took one and popped it into her mouth.

"Hello," she said weakly to the silent room.

Thursday afternoon was obviously not a busy time in the

wine tasting business.

"I thought I heard someone," said a woman entering from the far door leading to the outside patio.

She was about Denia's height with a medium build, wearing a flowered, short-sleeved top over black slacks. Her most noticeable feature was her long, straight, black hair that gently curled at the ends. Parted on one side, the raven mass was held back from her face by a clip bearing gemstones. Her forehead bore a slight crease over black eyebrows and thickly lashed, brown eyes. Creases at the corners of her eyes and by her mouth suggested an age of about forty.

"Hi, I'm Denia Rawlings," Denia introduced herself. "I was out for a run and turned onto the driveway when I saw the sign for the winery."

"Nice to meet you. I'm Karen Peterson. I'm part owner of the winery. I run the store and the wine tasting room. My sister, Kristen, helps here and with the vineyard and bottling processes which are run by our brother Keith," she paused. "I'm forgetting my manners. Would you like to taste some of the wine, or would you like some water?"

"Some water would be good. I didn't bring any with me, and I still have to run back."

"Actually, I'm closing up here. I've been alone here all afternoon. Not a busy day, but I had time to catch up on a few things. I can give you a lift back if you like," she offered.

"That would be nice of you," replied Denia. "I haven't run for a while, and I can tell that my muscles are already stiffening up a bit."

"Keith told me you were staying at Melinda's house. Keith Clearwater is my brother," Karen explained, pouring bottled water into an etched wine glass. "He's on the back of your property almost every day checking the vines. We're close to harvest, so it's a game of watching the grapes and the weather."

"Yes, I know that part of the property was leased to the winery. When I recognized the Samala name, I wanted to see it, so I followed the driveway here."

"I know Lee…I mean Sergeant Nelson…had asked Keith to keep an eye on your place. I'm not sure why. Have you met my brother yet? It's not like him to not be curious about a pretty woman who's new in town," Karen smiled a little half smile.

"No, I haven't seen him yet. I've only been here for a week today and things have been a little crazy trying to get settled."

"So, are you planning on staying?" Karen asked.

"My original thought was to stay," said Denia, sipping the cool water. "Now that I'm here, I realize there is a lot to try to do with the ranch and the animals. Also, we didn't know about the Candlewick business until after my aunt's death. So far, every day has been somewhat of a challenge."

Both women were silent for a moment. Denia knew that she liked this woman. Her curiosity was peeked about the brother. He was a man that would have had easy access to the ranch and her aunt.

"Did your brother have a business relationship with Melinda?" Denia asked, trying to get more information about the man.

"Our family's relationship with Melinda goes way back," Karen said, as if thinking back to the distant past. "When the Greystone property went up for sale many years ago – in fact I was only a kid – my father wanted to buy the land to increase the acreage for the vineyard. The advantage being that it was right down the road near the existing vineyard. At the time, it turned out that our father didn't have the money; so, Melinda and her husband ended up buying the ranch. As neighbors, we always got along. Melinda and my mother were casual friends. That friendship increased to a real closeness in the last two years of my mother's life, before she died of cancer eight years ago.

"Melinda was so supportive and helpful to my mother. She did things for her, especially during the last six months, that my mother didn't want us children to have to do. Your aunt was a very spiritual and caring person," she paused reflectively.

"Anyway, Kristen and I did our best to support our mother through her illness, but Keith was in denial. When our mother died, he just fell apart. Other than working, he just holed up in his little house and talked to no one. He couldn't deal with the grief. Neither our father, Kristen, nor I could get anywhere in trying to help him get through it. Surprisingly, it was Melinda that was able to reach him.

"One afternoon, she saw him sitting out by her pond and invited him down to the house for coffee. From then on, he would stop by and have coffee with her a couple days a week. Gradually, we saw that he was getting back to his old self," she paused again.

"Even though there was a large age difference, Keith and Melinda seemed to have an easy friendship that both of them needed. Keith was so upset when he heard of her death that he could not even deal with the memorial service. He just sent roses."

"I think everyone was shocked at her sudden death," Denia commiserated.

"Kristen and I were sorry that we missed you and your parents at the memorial service for Melinda," Karen said with remorse. "We had a wedding that day and didn't get there until after you left the mortuary."

"Weddings are hard to miss," Denia said with an understanding tone.

"No, it wasn't a wedding in our family. I run an event business: Samala Winery Events. We hold weddings, anniversary parties, engagement dinners and whatever else, here at the winery. We can host up to two hundred guests comfortably. Melinda used to work for me as a manager, with many of the events. Conveniently, she also supplied whatever types of candles we needed. We always paid her and Batty for their help, of course."

"That explains a lot," said Denia. "I found Melinda's calendar, and she had marked 'Winery' in many of the boxes around weekends, and I couldn't figure out what it meant."

"Yes, she spent a lot of time here helping us. She started Candlewick about three years ago, right before I started the event business. The timing was perfect. She had such a knack for doing just the right setting for the event, whatever it was. Fortunately, she helped us build up our supplies for setting the tables and taught Kristen and I how to do a real presentation, not just set a table. We owe her a debt. I hope that you will consider continuing to supply us with candles," she added.

"First, I need to learn how to make them," Denia laughed, skeptically.

"I'm sure Batty and the girls will be able to help you, if you decide to continue the business. Melinda used to do most of the candle making herself, but quite often Batty or Olivia would help her with large orders. When we have a wedding here with over twenty tables needing candles, over twenty-five of the tower candles are needed. If the bride chooses the candelabras for the tables, we may need over a hundred tapers. Melinda would allow the bride or wedding planner to choose the colors. Sometimes she did not have a lot of time to get an order done. She used to call in the gang for help, so they all know something about the process. I'm sure they would all be willing to teach you what you need to know. Once you start doing it, you will learn," Karen reassured.

"Well, I still have not made a decision regarding Candlewick. I haven't had time to really look at the business yet," Denia revealed.

"Don't worry. You have time," Karen said with understanding. "Come outside and I'll show you around. Then I can give you a ride home if you would like."

Karen gave Denia a tour of the grounds around the winery. She explained that the patios were used for small events, and intimate dinner parties. A stand of pine trees lined the landscape behind the building. A large gazebo stood before the evergreens, perfect for small weddings, suggesting a woodland setting. The left side of the winery opened onto a wide, green lawn, perfect for the ten to twenty round tables suited for ten guests. An elevated wooden platform sat on one end of the grassy space. Toward the front, and to one side, stood a ten-foot slab of rough granite with water spilling from the top to a shallow pool around the base. A semicircle of flagstones lay in front of the fountain, wide enough to hold a large wedding party, with space before the flagstones for chairs observing the ceremonies. Denia could visualize potential couples considering the romantic, outdoor venue.

Denia was most impressed with the right side of the winery where a long, arched, vine-laden pergola reminded one of scenes of Tuscany. Long tables were placed in a row, allowing seating for fifty. Denia could imagine candle and flower laden centerpieces, with white china gleaming on colored tablecloths. Romance was in the air, here.

On the short ride home with Karen, Denia learned that Karen was married to a hospital administrator, had a teenage boy and girl and lived in Orcutt. Karen had invited her to come along with Batty any time she wanted to see an event taking place at the winery. Weekend events were already scheduled for the rest of the year. Karen stressed that she could come by any afternoon for a glass of wine, or for a chat. Denia promised to give her a call once she looked into the Candlewick business and decide if she could continue in Melinda's footsteps.

Once home, Denia's focus was for one thing, the cell phone. She called Sergeant Nelson to tell him she had found Melinda's phone but could only leave a message on his voice mail. She knew it was after five o'clock and thought the Sergeant may have already left for the day. For now, her goal was to get as much information off the phone as she could prior to handing it over to the police. So engrossed was she, that she quickly made a sandwich for her dinner to nibble at while working with the phone.

The cell phone had charged during the afternoon, and Denia was able to turn it on and immediately go to Melinda's contact list stored in the phone. She got out the lists she had made previously from her aunt's address book, and the calendar that gave her some idea of Melinda's activities. On a clean tablet she copied the contacts, and associated phone numbers. She noticed that some contacts had a first name and a surname, such as 'Paul Oda', while some contacts showed only the first name, such as 'Batty'. Denia just copied the name and phone number, as it was provided, in alphabetical order.

Once she completed copying the contact list, she went to the phone's text lists. It seemed her aunt had never erased any of the text messages, as some dated back over the past year. Yet, after a brief review, it became obvious that Melinda rarely used the text feature of the phone. The few that were available were Melinda's short responses to texts related to logistics of time and place. There were no insightful conversations, and nothing recent.

A little discouraged, Denia went to the phone call history stored on the phone, which began with the most recent calls. Looking at the date, Denia realized the last few calls Melinda made were on the evening before her death. There were three calls: one was to Batty, one was to Keith, and one was to a person named John.

There were several people with the name of John on the list that Denia had compiled from the address book, but none stood out. The John names listed on the contact list, all seemed to be business acquaintances. Keith was listed on the phone contact list by a single name, and in the address book, under 'Clearwater' with his sister's names. There were several numbers listed, one for each member of the family. Rather than focus on analysis, Denia started copying each call, by date, time, and name. Not knowing what could be important, Denia copied all the calls going back for the time her aunt had the phone, which was almost a year.

When finished, she went over the pages of paper. She needed to learn who the people were, and what their relationship was with Melinda. She felt strongly that these lists held clues for what happened to Melinda. The name of Keith stood out in her mind. The police suspected that her aunt's murderer was male. She knew this man had access to her aunt. He had easy access to the ranch, and a reason for being there. He had spoken to Melinda the evening before her death. Denia allowed the seed to develop which had been planted at the back of her mind.

If anything happened to Melinda, Keith Clearwater would have a chance to buy the ranch and extend the acreage of the Samala Vineyard. Keith Clearwater could have a motive for murder. She wondered if he had been questioned by the police.

Abruptly, Denia looked up from her papers upon

hearing the crunch of a car on the driveway's gravel.

Within less than a minute the doorbell rang, followed by a knock on the front door.

Denia stood up from the dining room table and moved to the kitchen to glance at the clock on the stove. It was eight-fifteen. She tried to think who it could be at this time of night. Disturbed, Isis jumped onto the back of the sofa, facing the door and arching her back. A second knock sounded.

Denia recognized her vulnerability, being alone in the house. Whoever was out there probably knew she was here alone. She decided to ignore the knock and remain quiet, hoping that whoever it was would leave when the door was not answered.

Isis let out a low growl.

6

THE DOG

Denia stood quietly facing the front door when another forceful knock sounded. She held still, barely breathing.

"Miss Rawlings," a man's voice called through the door. "It's Deputy Cleeves. Sergeant Nelson sent me to pick up the phone."

Denia walked the short distance to the front dining room window and moved the drawn curtain aside just enough to allow her to see out the window. She saw the back of the police cruiser in the drive confirming that it probably was the deputy at the door. Switching on the porch light, she opened the door.

"Sorry," she said. "I was upstairs and didn't hear you knocking."

"I thought you might be upstairs," the deputy said in a friendly, understanding tone. "I'm sorry to disturb you in the evening, but I was already out here on patrol when Sergeant Nelson left the message to pick up the cell phone."

"Yes, I left a voice mail for him when I found the phone. Wait a minute and I'll get it," Denia said.

Leaving the deputy standing under the porchlight, Denia gathered the phone and charger and brought it back to the doorway. Deputy Cleeves put the phone in a plastic bag, sealing the top. He quickly filled out a form and handed to her.

"Thank you," he said, handing her the receipt. "This could be a great help to the investigation. Have a good evening."

The deputy was in his car, and leaving the drive as Denia was closing the door and turning off the porch light. She was glad that she had already copied as much information as she could off the phone since her opportunity would have been lost. Denia had not expected anyone to come pick it up so quickly after her call. She did take some comfort in knowing the police were patrolling the area. Looking at the old-fashioned door handle and key lock, Denia knew she needed to do something to improve the security of the house. She thought of the fear that ran through her when the deputy first came to the door, knowing she was alone in the house with no protection. Now, the single locks on the kitchen and front doors did not seem adequate.

In the morning, Denia looked out the front window as she opened the curtains to see another beautiful California day. She had gotten up early, thinking she would have a cup of coffee before taking her shower. Denia planned to go into town with Batty today, so she wanted to look halfway decent to meet the people that paid her for the fresh eggs, and later, Olivia. Scanning the yard, bathed in golden morning rays, she watched as a green pickup truck pulled into the driveway and proceeded along the gravel path to stop beside the kitchen. She knew this was not Jorje, as he was always here early, and drove a small, compact car.

"Now what?" Denia exclaimed to the walls.

This was followed by a strong knock on the back door.

"Doesn't anyone ever use the front door around here?" she asked in exasperation.

The walls did not answer. Denia walked through the kitchen to the door and swung it open. She was not prepared for the tall figure that stood on the threshold filling most of the doorframe.

"Hi, I'm Keith Clearwater. Karen, my sister, told me she spoke to you yesterday. I brought the puppy. He's eight weeks old now and we've got him weaned. Kristen got his shots yesterday; so, he's ready to go."

Denia's mouth dropped open slightly while looking up at the tanned, clean-shaven face, smiling down at her. Large hands held a wiggling, caramel-colored, fur ball with amber eyes, and a pink nose and mouth, struggling for freedom.

"What?" was all that she could get out at the moment,

staring back at the man's hazel eyes showing shots of green in the kitchen's morning light.

A sudden flush came up Denia's neck on the way to her face, as she realized the state of her attire. She was wearing a ragged, oversized t-shirt with the faded image of the Coronado bridge on the front, and stained, charcoal sweatpants. Her thick hair was uncombed, held back by a loose band, with locks escaping to hang around her face. She had no makeup on except the smudged mascara under her eyes from yesterday.

Before she could get another word out, the early visitor brushed past her into the kitchen, setting the wiggling puppy onto the floor. Surveying its surroundings, the puppy took three wobbly steps, stopped, and peed on the floor.

"Whoops," said the stranger, grabbing a paper towel from the roll on the counter, and bent down to mop up the mishap.

"He's still not trained," he said apologetically. "We do have them pretty much paper trained. Do you have newspaper?"

As if familiar with the kitchen, he casually walked to the utility room to dispose of the wet towels in the trash. Then he proceeded to the sink to wash his hands and took a clean dish towel out of the drawer next to the sink for drying off.

Denia had no time to consider answering as the puppy ran to the living room and, of course, directly to the bay window where Mona, aroused from her perch, stood and arched her back at the intruder. Denia rushed to the window trying to intercept disaster, scooped up the puppy and secured it in the crook of one arm. She also grabbed Mona and held her tightly in the other arm. Keeping both animals as far apart as possible, she walked back to the dining room table where the tall man was stretched out on one of the chairs.

"Coffee?" he asked.

"Who *are* you?" she asked, glaring at the grinning face.

By this time Mona had enough and jumped free, only to arch with displeasure at Denia's feet, before running for higher ground. Denia used her now free hand to contain the wiggling, brown mass to her chest.

"Haven't made the coffee yet, huh?"

Denia did not respond.

"Sorry," he said, taking in the perturbed look. "Let's start over. I'm Keith Clearwater. I'm your neighbor," he started to explain. "I own the vineyard across the road. I live down the highway about five minutes. I'm also leasing the back side of the hills on Melinda's property, or I guess, your property. Karen told me you had come to the winery yesterday. I knew you were here since Lee told me last week, but I've been too busy to get over here. The grapes are almost ready, and that rain the other night required a lot of extra work. No one wants moldy grapes."

His explanation did little to appease Denia's ire. She hadn't had coffee yet, either.

"Look," she started, "I just got here. This house is a mess," gesturing to the cluttered state of the dining and living rooms. "I have chickens that I know nothing about except that you feed them, and they lay eggs - lots of eggs.

I have a *goat*, a goat that thinks it's a dog and eats things it shouldn't. I have an elderly, skinny farmhand – who speaks only partial English - holding things together. I also have two cats - one that has already cost me over eight hundred dollars. My car is in the shop. *And now, you want me to take a puppy?"* she finished the tirade.

"Yeah," he said sympathetically, "I heard about the car."

Denia could only stare at him with exasperation. Again, here was a stranger knowing her business. She didn't think she had mentioned the car accident to Karen the previous day.

He sat up in the chair with his elbows on his knees, then continued, *"That* is not an ordinary puppy. He's from champion stock Labrador Retrievers. He's a pick-of-the-litter chocolate lab. Mel picked him out when he was barely crawling around. He's already bought and paid for. Kristen gave her a discount, and sold him for five hundred dollars, because it was for Melinda."

"Five hundred dollars?" Denia asked with surprise at the large amount.

"Hell, the rest sold for seven to eight hundred," he explained. "These dogs are very popular. In fact, Kristen is driving one of that one's sisters up to San Jose today."

As if the matter of her taking the puppy was settled, he stood up and headed toward the kitchen door. "I've got his puppy food and the crate in the truck. I'll bring it in."

When he went out, Denia looked down at the puppy. He had stopped struggling and had fallen asleep against her chest. If there is anything cuter than a sleeping baby, it's a sleeping puppy. Her anger fizzled.

Keith returned shortly holding a bag of puppy food, which he deposited on the counter, and a wire maze that he quickly assembled into a dog crate. Denia looked at the size of the large, black cage sitting in the middle of the kitchen.

The man must have read her mind.

"It looks big now, but he's going to be eighty to ninety pounds when he's fully grown. Let's put it over here," he said, moving it to an empty spot between the doorways to the pantry and the utility room.

"For now, you can put newspaper and an old towel in the bottom and keep him confined when needed. We had him in it yesterday so he could get used to it. He's getting fed four times a day right now at eight, twelve, four, and eight o'clock. You can call my sister Kristen, or me if you have any problems. Kristen is a certified dog trainer. She's had the puppies at her place since they were born. Here is my business card".

He put a business card, bearing the Winery's logo, on the counter. Pulling a pen from his shirt pocket, he started writing on the back of the card.

"Here is Kristen's number, and I put my cell phone number just in case you need to reach me in a hurry."

"Good Lord, why on earth did Melinda want to get a puppy?" Denia asked.

"She said she wanted a watch dog for the ranch. I thought it was a good idea with her being alone here, especially at night. She knew Whiskey, the puppy's mother, from seeing her at the winery; so, when Whiskey was bred, Mel asked if she could buy one of the puppies."

"Did she say why she wanted a watch dog after all this time here?"

"I asked her about it," he said, moving his hand over his chin in thought while leaning on the counter. "She said that she had seen lights out back in the orchard on a few different occasions. Then she found the lock on the garage cut off and thrown on the ground. She said she couldn't find that anything had been taken.

"One morning she found the chicken coop door open and two hens missing. She called me to come over one night in July because she heard noises coming from the area of the turtle pond. It was two o'clock in the morning when I got here. I looked around with a flashlight, but didn't find anyone, or anything. I was thinking it might be coyotes.

"Mel and I just stayed up that night having coffee. I could tell she was upset. I didn't tell Mel but did tell Lee Nelson about it last month at the Rotary Club meeting. He said they would add a night patrol to the road out here."

"You mean, Sergeant Nelson?" Denia asked.

"Yeah, I've known Lee since high school. We've been friends for a long time," he paused. "We were all shocked to hear of Melinda's death. I had just been here the day before," he paused. "Anyway, if you have any problems, give me a call. I can probably get here faster than a patrol car."

"Thanks," Denia said. "I hope I don't need to call anyone."

"I need to get going. It was nice to finally meet you. Mel always spoke fondly of you. Welcome to Solvang," he said, as he left through the back door.

In a second, he was gone. Denia stood there in her sloppy clothes, holding a sleeping puppy, taking in all that the man had said. Melinda had been having strange things happen around the ranch, and then she was found dead.

But why? Denia pondered.

Life with the puppy was going to be disruptive, Denia decided by the time she was dressed. Not wanting to leave him downstairs alone, she took him into the bathroom with her while she took her shower. The puppy cried, making little yapping sounds, and peed on the bathroom floor. Denia took him into the bedroom while she got dressed and did her hair and make-up. The little guy smelled around the room, went under the bed, and peed on the floor in the closet. On her way downstairs, puppy in arms, she took a thin, flannel blanket from the linen closet. Ten minutes later, she had given the new resident half a cup of puppy chow, some water, and took him out back where he *wouldn't* pee. By the time Batty arrived, Denia had arranged the blanket into the back of the dog crate, laid out newspaper in the front, and secured the puppy within his wire safety zone. She glanced at the clock on the microwave noting that it was almost eight-thirty. Sitting on the floor in front of the crate, she felt like she had already had a work-out.

Batty came into the kitchen wearing her Friday casual

clothes, and 'went batty' over the new puppy. Denia refused to let him out of the crate knowing it would take them another half hour before they could leave for town if Batty got her hands on him.

Mona snuck cautiously into the kitchen when she heard Batty's voice. Her eyes on the wire cage holding the whelp, the cat chirped her unhappiness to Batty about the intruder as Batty stroked her head and back.

Later, Denia secured by a seatbelt, tried to control her nervousness with Batty at the wheel as they headed off to town with the cartons of eggs in the back of the purple PT Cruiser.

"Olivia said that Hans brought Isis home yesterday. How is she doing?" Batty asked.

"Hans said that he was having a problem getting her to eat, but she started eating as soon as she got home. She seems to be doing alright. Last night both cats were back to what I guess is their old routine of eating and lying around," Denia answered. "Where are we going to drop off the eggs?"

"The Stork's Nest. It is one of the oldest established restaurants in Solvang," Batty stated, as they bounced along at a high speed on the pitted roadway.

"Ben and Marci Siegel took over the business when Ben's father retired. Mel and Marci had been friends for years, so after she got the chickens and Mel realized that she had more eggs than she or Jorje could ever use, she offered the extra eggs to Marci. Ben insisted that they pay Mel for the fresh eggs, so they send her a check every month, paying by the dozen."

"I *did* find a check in the unopened mail from last month. I didn't know what the check was for, since there was no note with the check," Denia replied.

"Mel said it wasn't much, but pays for most of the chicken feed, and the eggs don't go to waste."

Then changing the subject, as she looked forward at the road, "How's it going with your car?"

"It's in the shop. I called them yesterday, but the man said they would not be able to get to it until next week. I need a car, so I was able to start the Range Rover, which is just sitting in the garage. I found all the paperwork on the car and wondered if you could take me to the Department of Motor Vehicles today after we drop off the eggs," Denia requested.

"Okay," said Batty. "The office in Santa Maria may be the fastest for getting the registration changed. I could drop you off and go to the nearby shopping complex. I need to get a couple of long-sleeved shirts for fall. You can call me when you're finished and I'll pick you up," Batty offered.

"Thanks. I really appreciate it. I hate not having a car, just in case I need one," Denia said. "By the way, do you know anyone named John that Melinda knew?"

"John Waters - he was Melinda's dentist. He's my dentist, too," replied Batty.

Denia was thinking of the information she had taken off the cell phone. She did recognize the name of John Waters from the address book, but she could not believe her aunt had been calling her dentist the evening before her death.

"Were there any other people named John she knew?"

"Hmmm, there's John and Helen Wilson. They own one of the little antique shops on Mission Street in town. We used to go in there from time to time. Mel knew them better than I do. I can't think of anyone else right now," she replied. "Let me think about it."

The car rattled on along the road, with the two occupants focusing on the passing surroundings.

After a few minutes of driving, "Soooo," said Batty, emphasizing what was to come next, "You met Keith Clearwater. What do you think?"

Denia sensed that *this* was what Batty *really* wanted to talk about. She had not yet made up her mind about Keith Clearwater. She was not going to tell Batty that her aunt had called him the evening before her death; or about the questions at the back of her mind concerning his access to the property, and her aunt's trust in the man. He did have a possible motive for getting Melinda out of the way so he could buy the land. Her mind jumped to what Hans had told her about the town's gossip line, and Denia knew that Batty was right in the middle of it. Denia decided to hold her cards close to her chest.

"He showed up this morning before I was even dressed. I was not impressed," reported Denia.

She didn't care if *that* got back to the early visitor.

"The grapes are almost ripe. He spends all day in the fields this time of year."

"Yeah, well, he walked in like he owned the place."

"I mean what did you think of him. Quite a hunk, huh?"

"He's tall."

Then after a few seconds, remembering her first impression of the man, "I could see the family resemblance with his sister."

"Oh, did Kristen come over with him to bring the puppy?" Batty asked, gleaning information.

"Ah, no," she answered. "I decided to take a run yesterday afternoon and ended up at the winery. I met his sister, Karen."

"That's nice. I didn't know that you were a runner."

"I'm severely out of shape, right now. My legs are really sore today. I used to run two to three times a week when I was in San Diego," she said, glad of the change in the conversation.

"Did Karen show you around?" Batty asked.

"Yes, there was no one there for wine tasting, so she took me around the grounds. I didn't realize how much my aunt did with the winery. It also made me think that I need to get up to speed with Candlewick. Karen mentioned that the candle orders could be large for some of the events."

"I've always done the accounting for the business, so I can show you the financial side. Olivia does the day-to-day, so she can show you the ropes, including the actual candle making. She was going to come over this morning and get out as many orders as she could. She'll probably be there when we get back," said Batty with reassurance.

Then going back to her original subject, "Keith does look more like Karen. They both have that thick black hair and the Native American complexion. Wait until you meet Kristen. She's the baby of the three and has honey blonde hair and blue eyes like her mother."

"They're Native American?" Denia asked with curiosity.

"Clearwater, yes, they're Native American. Their father is full Chumash Indian - not many left. He married a Danish girl, so the kids are half Chumash. We do have the Santa Ynez Reservation here, with the Chumash Casino. It brings a lot of revenue to Solvang and the tribe. Prior to the Spanish coming, the Chumash were the original people along the central coast of California, with many settlements up and down the coast. Their populations have dwindled over the years. Keith's father named the winery Samala, after the old native language of the tribe."

"Interesting," Denia noted, as the car screeched to a stop, before turning onto the highway into town.

She now understood the handsome, almost exotic looks of the Clearwater brother and sister.

Denia was lost in thought. She didn't remember her aunt or parents ever mentioning a casino being near town when she used to come here for visits. Maybe it hadn't been built at that time. She felt like she really needed to go out and explore her new neighborhood. There was so much she didn't know.

The meeting with Marci Siegel went well, with Marci making a fuss over Denia. As soon as they drove up to the restaurant parking lot, Denia realized that these were the people who had provided the refreshments after the memorial service for Melinda. She took the opportunity to thank Marci for the unexpected hospitality for her family.

The drive to Santa Maria was scenic, with Denia paying

attention to road signs, trying to get a better feel for the neighboring small residential hamlets. They passed Orcutt and she remembered Karen Clearwater saying she lived there. It took about a half hour to get to Santa Maria.

The visit to the DMV was exactly what Denia expected. It was crowded, with people waiting in lines and in chairs. There were lots of windows with numbers, each governing aspects of the regulations related to driving in the state of California. After checking in, Denia took her seat and waited for her turn at one of the windows. Surprisingly, she was able to call Batty to come get her after only an hour, with the temporary registration for the Range Rover in hand.

On the way home, Batty was determined to take Denia to the pet shop in town for stuff she needed for the puppy. Denia thought she should never have let Batty talk her into it, as she groaned to herself, looking over the seat of the Cruiser at the new travel kennel she had bought which was taking up most of the back, as the car made its way back to the ranch. There were also the 'how to raise your puppy books', the lime green leather collar, the packages of training pads, cleaning spray and stainless-steel feeding bowls.

Batty herself had bought new toys for the puppy, including a package of balls, a stuffed bunny and a good imitation of a mallard duck that squeaked.

"What are you going to name him?" she asked.

"I'm not sure yet," said Denia. "I need to think about it. I want to get to know him. We'll see what his personality is, first."

"Kristen holds puppy training classes at the park, but he's too young right now."

"We'll probably need them. My parents have a poodle, but I haven't ever had a puppy of my own."

Batty pulled up to the stone patio by the kitchen door. Denia rushed in the house to check on the puppy. He stood up from his blanket when he heard Denia. She could see that the newspaper was wet in a couple spots. Opening the wire door, she grabbed the puppy and rushed him out to the edge of the patio, where he immediately squatted and peed.

"What a good boy!" she praised, letting him sniff around as she helped Batty unload the car. "Thanks so much for your help today, Batty. I think I'll be able to take the eggs into town from now on."

"Looks like Olivia is still here," said Batty. "I'll meet you at the office after you get him fed and settled."

Denia spent the next half hour feeding the puppy, taking him outside, and feeding herself. She awkwardly carried the new dog kennel upstairs, thinking that the puppy could sleep in it at night rather than having the puppy downstairs, while she is upstairs. When she returned downstairs, she found the little pooch stretched out asleep on the kitchen floor. She gently moved him into the crate and shut the door. Denia wanted to be able to give her full attention to meeting Olivia at the office.

On the way out back, Denia noticed the small parking area near the office building was full. Batty's car was still over by the kitchen door. Jorje's little car was in its usual spot under the tree. He was always the first one here, so he got the shady parking spot. There was also a silver sedan, which Denia did not recognize, and a well-worn red pickup truck parked next to the sedan.

When Denia entered the office just inside the Candlewick building she found three people in the small, but efficiently arranged space. The person closest to her, obviously Olivia, was standing next to Melinda's desk. To Denia's surprise, Isis was lying on the desktop, paws outstretched. Batty stood at the back of the office in front of the Stonehenge painting, deep in conversation with a large man facing her. Olivia came forward and gave her an unexpected hug, and then started making introductions.

"I'm Olivia as you have probably already guessed. You already know our Bathsheba, and this is Snowy. I had to call him to come out this morning when I couldn't get the printers to work. He does all our technical work with the computers, printers, and anything else electronic in nature," the small, plump lady related.

The man with the thick mass of white hair raised his hand in a wave of acknowledgement toward Denia.

Denia looked at Olivia and could see the genetic resemblance to Hans around the eyes and mouth. Olivia was short, no more than five feet tall. Her fine hair was curled in a short style that flattered her round face. The lack of any deep wrinkles belied the fact that she had a son over thirty years old. She wore light makeup around her blue-green eyes, emphasized by mascara on the lashes. She was well dressed in a long-sleeved, flowery, silk blouse that did a lot to hide her thick middle, flowing over the top of her navy-colored pants.

The man named Snowy was in an animated discussion with Batty, pointing to the upper limits of the painting. "I'm saying that the artist had no concept of the constellations over Great Britain. Their view of the stars is different than ours even though we are both viewing from the Northern Hemisphere."

"The artist wasn't focusing on the little spots depicting the stars here. The painting is depicting Stonehenge. *That* is the subject of the composition," emphasized Batty.

"They always do this," said Olivia to Denia's ear in a hushed voice. "They're always bickering like an old married couple."

Denia regarded the tall man towering over Batty. His broad shoulders and large arms did little to detract from the button-down, plaid shirt stretched tightly over the protruding belly. Under the cap of disheveled hair, blue eyes looked out from the pink face, getting rosier as the conversation continued. The heavy, clean-shaven jowls lent to a man in his sixties.

"I'm just saying that a wee bit of research would have made this painting more believable," he said.

"This painting was not meant to accurately depict reality - it was meant to be mystical," said Batty. "It's meant to appeal to the spirit. It's not a postcard."

"Snowy has a degree in astronomy and is an amateur astronomer. He's pretty touchy about stars," explained Olivia to Denia.

"Are the printers working, now?" asked Denia while stroking Isis along her back.

"Yeah," answered Olivia. "Snowy thinks the problem was caused by the fact that they hadn't been used for a while. I was trying to print labels with no luck. He put in new ink cartridges and sprayed them with something to get them going again."

"Can't you see yourself standing on the plain at sunset looking at the ancient stones?" Batty continued in a voice with longing.

"I'd like to see it, but I'd be looking at all of the visible constellations that came into view as the sky darkened," the man replied.

"Looking for UFOs, no doubt," said Batty with sarcasm.

"There are a lot of well-documented UFO sightings from the British Isles," Snowy defended. "Even the Queen's husband is a believer."

Olivia leaned toward Denia, "He's also a ufologist – stays up all hours of the night on the UFO websites, and the short-wave radio," she said in a low voice.

"Good grief," said Batty, throwing up her hands. "I give up. Come over here and meet Denia."

The large man moved toward the desk, turned to Denia with an outstretched hand.

"Nice to meet you," he said. "You can call me Snowy, like the rest of the girls.

He gave her a charming smile, showing the dimples in his cheeks, reminding Denia of some of the better Santas she had met over the years. Denia reached out and shook the warm, fleshy hand.

"Do I owe you for fixing the printers?" asked Denia. "I've only been here for a short time and I'm going to have to start from scratch learning about this business."

"Nah," he responded. "I only charged Melinda when I needed to replace hardware. Today I just fiddled around and got them going."

"What happened to Mel's computer?" Olivia asked Denia. "Did you take it into the house?"

Denia did not have time to answer. Looking through the large office window she saw Sergeant Nelson and Deputy Cleeves walking toward the office building being led by Jorje. She turned to see them come through the door. The room suddenly became very quiet.

At the site of the uniformed officers Isis sat up alert on the desk. Her ears went back, and she let out a long hiss toward the two men. At once, she jumped off the desk and darted out of the office door like a black flash.

Sergeant Nelson came to stand next to Denia and Olivia. He faced the large man next to Batty.

"John, I'm going to have to ask you to come with us down to our office. We have a few questions to ask you regarding Melinda Greystone's death."

The Sergeant's words hung in the air. Denia looked at the faces of disbelief surrounding her. The man before her was shocked into speechlessness. Batty stood silent, her mouth fell open in surprise.

Olivia reached out and touched the back of Snowy's hand.

"Don't worry, Snowy," she said. "Batty and I were both

questioned. They're just gathering information."

Denia and Olivia moved back allowing the big man to move toward the policemen. His face had gone pale.

"Do I need a lawyer?" he asked the sergeant.

"We are not arresting you," said Nelson. "We just need to ask you some questions. You can request that a lawyer be there if you wish."

Then with his hand on Snowy's arm, "Come on, let's go."

As the three men left the office building, the trio of women stood transfixed, watching through the window as the men walked across the dirt lot toward the front of the house.

"His name is John?" Denia asked in a weak voice.

"His name is John O'Malley, but we've called him Snowy for years," said Olivia.

"Was he a friend of my aunt?" Denia asked.

"Yes, they were close friends. He built the website for Candlewick for her," Olivia informed her.

"Denia, you asked me about the name John earlier today. What's going on?" asked Batty.

"I found Melinda's cell phone yesterday. When I got it working and checked the list of recent calls, it showed that she had called someone named John around nine o'clock the night before they found her dead," Denia explained.

"Well, what's so unusual about that? We always call Snowy when we're having computer problems, or other technical things go wrong," said Olivia.

"And what happened to Mel's computer?" she asked pointing to Melinda's desktop.

"The police have it," answered Denia, "and the cell phone."

Batty had remained quiet, but Denia knew she was starting to understand the truth of the matter. Denia knew it was time. Time to take the risk of telling these two friends of Melinda what she knew about her aunt's death.

"Denia, what are the police investigating?" Batty asked.

Tears sprang to Denia's eyes.

Batty put her arm around Denia's shoulders. "What is it, dear?"

"Melinda was murdered," she sobbed. "They're investigating her murder."

7

THE OWL

"Oh my God," said Olivia, in little more than a whisper. "Mel was murdered?"

"Denia, are you alright?" asked Batty.

Denia looked at her aunt's two best friends, eyes brimming with tears. Somehow, saying the words that Melinda was murdered was a relief, bringing on the surge of emotion.

"Come on, let's go in the house and have a cup of tea." Batty suggested.

She seemed to know that tea and comfort was called for in this situation. Denia nodded her head in agreement, wiping the tears with the back of her hand.

The three women were each struggling with their own thoughts, mulling over the arrival of the police, the taking of Snowy for questioning, and the revelation of Melinda's murder. Olivia locked the door to the office building, and they headed across the back lot toward the kitchen door.

Jorje was doing a last check of the chicken coop. Chickens milled about in their pen as he fastened the coop's door and walked toward his car, ready to leave for the day.

"Is Billy in her stall for the night?" Denia called to him.

"*Si, Señorita*" he replied. "I locked the back gate, and Billy is in the barn."

"*Gracias, Jorje,*" waved Denia.

Then remembering that it was Friday, and he would be off work until Monday, "Have a good weekend."

The puppy was awake and crying as Denia, Batty, and Olivia entered the kitchen. Denia immediately went to the dog crate, rescuing the animal, and taking him out back for a couple minutes.

Batty quickly removed the wet training pad from the cage and spread out a new one at the front. Going to the dining area, she noticed that Denia had cleared most of the dining room table from its previous state of unorganized piles. She moved the remaining mess to one far end, making room for three to comfortably sit and have a talk. She took a light blue candle from the buffet, moved it to the center of the table and lit it with a match. A blue candle to promote calm communication and tranquil spiritual energy, she thought. The candle was not large and provided only a minimal glow in the small, shadow-filled dining area.

Olivia filled the blue enamel teapot and put it on the stove to boil water for the tea. She retrieved the familiar mugs from the cupboard, placing an Earl Grey teabag in each cup. She rummaged around in the cupboard under the counter holding boxed foods, "I can't find any cookies to go with the tea," she lamented.

"We don't need cookies," said Batty, taking her place in the traditional-styled chair on the back side of the rectangular table.

Olivia thought they needed cookies despite Batty's dismissal, but they would have to make do. After a minute, she removed the sodden tea bags from the cups, adding a teaspoon of sugar, and a small splash of milk to each. Making two trips, she walked slowly carrying the overfilled mugs to the table. She sat down opposite Batty, leaving the end of the table free for Denia.

Denia came in with the puppy. The animal had been in the crate most of the day, so Denia thought he needed some time out of the crate while she could keep an eye on him. She glanced into the living room and saw that both cats were lounging there. Mona was among fat pillows in the sofa's corner, and Isis curled on her rug by the window. Denia hastily formed an idea. She pulled the large crate across the kitchen, turning it sideways for maximum length to block the opening between the kitchen wall and counter, making a barrier of black wire. The little pooch would be able to look into the dining area but would still be confined. Putting the dog on the floor he would have the full run of the kitchen, Denia thought, while they sat at the table.

Denia switched on a crystal lamp on the buffet prior to taking the available chair at the end of the table. Silence ensued as they sipped their tea.

"I couldn't find any cookies to go with the tea," Olivia commented, feeling that it was a safe topic of conversation.

"I know," said Denia. "If I *buy* them, I *eat* them, especially in the evening. Besides, it was my first trip to the store, so I was rambling through the aisles trying to find the basic things that I needed – not to mention cat litter."

After another minute of sipping in silence, Batty decided to get to the point.

"Denia, you know we were the two people closest to Melinda. Don't feel like you need to go through all of this alone. Let us help you. Tell us what we need to know."

Denia stared at the tiny flame of the candle on the table and began to speak.

"When my mother and I got here the morning after Melinda was found dead in the yard, my mother had been told to go to the sheriff's office in Solvang. That was when we first met Sergeant Nelson, who told us they were investigating Melinda's death as suspicious. He said her body appeared to have been moved, indicating that her death may not have been from health reasons or an accident. The day before the memorial service he came to the hotel to give us the findings of the coroner's report. The report said the cause of death was asphyxiation due to strangulation," she paused.

Tears quickly appeared in Olivia's eyes, and Batty's mouth formed a thin, grim line.

"The report also said there was a skull fracture at the back of her head, indicating she had been hit with something, which may have happened prior to the strangulation."

After another brief pause, "Sergeant Nelson requested that we keep the cause of death quiet, to give them time to investigate. That is probably why they are questioning the people who were close to my aunt."

"This is terrible," said Olivia, still trying to believe that someone would kill her friend, both hands clutching her mug. "I thought there was something fishy when they wanted to ask me all about the business and the people who came and went from the ranch."

"That's why they wanted to look at Mel's computer," stated Batty.

"Yes," Denia confirmed. "The police wanted to look at the computer for her contacts, e-mails, and anything that could give them clues as to who might have a motive to kill her."

"Well, good luck with *that*," said Olivia with emotion. "Mel was dragged kicking and screaming into the computer age. If it wouldn't have been for Candlewick, and the absolute need for using a computerized system, she would have never touched the thing. She was barely functional. Snowy and I were constantly helping her just to learn how to do basic things with it. Snowy built the website and had to write a step-by-step instruction manual for Mel, just so she could navigate the site. I don't think the police will find anything personal on Mel's computer. We were still teaching her how to use the internet for the news, shopping, and buying the books she so loved."

"What about Mel's phone?' asked Batty.

"Well, remember I asked you about the cell phone? That was because the police asked me if Auntie had one," Denia replied, looking at Batty.

"Once you confirmed that she *did* have one I tried to find it, with no luck. Then yesterday, when I was looking for the papers for the Range Rover, I accidentally found her purse stuffed on the floor by the desk, and the cell phone was in the purse. I was able to get it charged and spent some time taking down names from the contact list and recent calls. Then I called Sergeant Nelson and left a message that I had the phone. The deputy came out and picked it up last night."

"Was Snowy on the lists you made?" asked Olivia

"No," said Denia. "But Auntie did make a call to a 'John' the evening before she was killed. He was listed on the contact list as John, with no last name."

"She did refer to Snowy as John sometimes," said Batty, absentmindedly taking a sip of the cooling tea. "We usually refer to him as Snowy, or the Owl, so when you asked me about the name this morning I just didn't think about Snowy. I knew his real name was John, but it didn't come to mind. That must be why the police want to question him."

"Why do you call him Snowy?" asked Denia.

"Are you kidding? Did you see his hair?" asked Olivia. "Besides, he's had that nickname for years. Not only because of the white hair, but the fact that he's known for staying up all hours of the night on short-wave radio. He's such a night-owl. I always try not to call him before ten or eleven in the morning, because I know he's probably sleeping."

"If he's not on the radio at night, it's the UFO websites," said Batty, sarcastically.

"Really?" asked Denia, trying to ignore the puppy, whining at the wire barrier.

"Oh, yeah, the Owl is a diehard believer," reported Olivia. "He teaches astronomy two evenings a week at the junior college, but I think it's just an excuse to always be looking through a telescope."

"But we love him," said Batty. "He does so much for all of us from computers to TVs and VCRs, or anything else electronic. We're always calling him about something."

"What was his relationship with my aunt?" Denia asked.

"Snowy had great admiration for Melinda. She had built Candlewick from scratch. She became well-known in town over the years, and for the work she did with Karen Peterson with the event business at the winery. Snowy would have probably liked to have a closer relationship with her, but Mel had nixed that early on. He had asked her out to dinner a couple times," Batty confided, as if it were a secret. "In the end, she liked her life the way it was and had no desire to have a serious relationship with a man at this point in her life. She always said that James Greystone was the best husband anyone could have, and she didn't want another one."

"They were good friends, though," put in Olivia. "Mel knew she could trust him."

The three sat quietly, sipping tea, all into their own thoughts.

"Cassie predicted this," said Olivia with a reverent tone, mainly to Batty.

"She didn't predict that Melinda would be *murdered*," Batty came back at her.

"Yes, but she said she had seen Mel's aura darken, and she saw dark clouds hovering around her. That was only a month ago. Now she's dead. Cassie saw this coming," insisted Olivia.

"Who is Cassie?" asked Denia, feeling excluded.

"Cassie is Cassandra Demeta. She is one of our friends. She was very close to Mel – to all of us, really," said Batty.

"She's a psychic. Not one of those '*sign on the front lawn*' psychics. She never takes money for her gift - or curse as she sometimes calls it. She was devastated when she heard of Mel's death. She thought she should have been able to warn her or do something to prevent it. She'll be upset all over again when she finds out Mel was murdered."

At this point, the puppy had enough of being confined in the kitchen. He could see them sitting at the table but could not get to them. His whimpering became full-fledged yelping, forcing Denia to get up from the table, pick him up and bring him back with her to her seat.

"Can either of you think of anyone who did not like Melinda? Anyone that had some kind of grudge or a motive to kill her?" Denia asked the two older women while holding onto the squirming mass of brown.

"I can't believe that anyone had a problem with her. I surely didn't hear of anything brewing, or she would have mentioned it," said Olivia. "We talked about everything."

The candle was sputtering, trying to keep its flame going despite the liquid wax lapping at the wick. Batty used the small brass, hooded tool that was sitting at the end of the table to extinguish the flame.

"We better get going," she said. "Thank you for letting us know what was going on. We'll have to do a little snooping around, to see if we hear anything. If we do, we'll let you know."

"Also, you need to let us know if there is anything we can do to help you. Even if you just want someone to talk to, we can come over," said Olivia. "Oh, that reminds me, I do need to come back on Monday and work on those orders that I didn't send out today. If you have time, I can show you the computer system and how we manage things."

"Monday is good for me," said Denia.

She turned to Batty and asked, "Do you have time next week to show me the financials and the payroll for Candlewick?"

"I'm working Monday and Wednesday next week. How about Tuesday?"

Since plans for the following week were set, Denia walked with the two friends to the back door. Each gave her a hug, and again offered help should she need it. Denia decided to take the puppy out back with her as she checked on Billy in the barn. Then it would be feeding time at the zoo.

The long evening was upon her. Denia had gotten all the animals fed with some distress. The cats were used to coming back and forth into the kitchen for food. Not knowing that his food was not the same, the puppy had already discovered an enthusiastic liking for cat food. Since Denia could no longer leave any cat food down on the floor, she put the puppy in his crate when she fed the cats. They were not happy about it, especially Mona, but they ate their food. Denia felt that the cats and the dog would need to get used to each other, and the sooner the better. The puppy was only going to get bigger.

The phone in the kitchen rang and Denia rushed to get it, wondering who would be calling.

"Hello?"

"Hi, Denia?" a man's voice asked, but did not wait for an answer. "It's Lee Nelson."

"Sergeant Nelson," Denia specified, the good-looking officer's face coming to mind.

"I just wanted to explain what happened today with John O'Malley," he said.

"It *was* a little dramatic," replied Denia. "I had just met him a few minutes before you got here."

"We got his name off the cell phone and matched the number. As far as we know, he was the last person to speak to your aunt before her death, so we did want to talk to him. John shares a small store front in town for his electronic work with Rob King, who does air conditioning and heating. I went over there to bring him in for some questions, when Rob told me he was out at Candlewick. Deputy Cleeves was already in the area, so I asked him to meet me out there."

"Well, did you arrest him?" Denia asked curiously.

"No," he answered. "Not only didn't we arrest him; we've pretty much cleared him of any involvement with the murder."

"Can you tell me why?" she asked, not knowing how much he would be willing to tell her about the questioning.

"John has a really strong alibi for the evening before, and the day of Melinda's death. It seems there is this Perseid Meteor Shower that happens pretty much every year around this time. John and three of his astronomy students, had gone up to the Sierra National Forest where there are some telescopes set up, to view the meteor shower. They were there for two nights. We're going to check out his story, of course, but it looks like he was up in the hills above Fresno and didn't get back here until the next day, after Melinda's death."

"According to Batty and Olivia he was a good friend to my aunt. I'm kind of glad to hear he was not involved," she said.

"He did add a little something to the mystery, though," Nelson relayed. "I asked him why Melinda had called him that evening. He said she wanted to meet with him when he got back to have some lighting and maybe surveillance cameras set up around the house and office building. It seems that Melinda had noticed some strange things happening around the ranch at night. What John told me supported what Keith Clearwater had also told me. Melinda told Keith about some odd occurrences around the ranch, mostly at night. That's when we put the night patrol on the road out there. So far, we haven't seen anything unusual."

"That means you don't have any suspects right now?" Denia asked.

"I have feelers out, and we have a couple lines of information under review. We're sure someone knows something. Don't think we will put the investigation on hold. As time goes by someone may feel they are in the clear and get careless. Don't worry, I won't give up. Melinda was a friend of mine, too."

"I appreciate all of your work on this - so does my mother."

"How's it going with the car?" he asked, changing the subject.

"It's still in the shop, but I got the Range Rover changed into my name today. I have a temporary registration."

"That's good," he commented. "Okay, well, I just wanted to check in with you. Let us know if you hear of anything or come across anything that could be helpful to the investigation. Just give me a call or leave me a voice mail."

"Alright," she agreed. "Good night."

"Good night," he said and disconnected.

Denia liked the sergeant. He was a good man. Batty told her that he was one of the most eligible bachelors in town. He had certainly been considerate of her, but in a professional manner. She was not sure if he was paying attention to her because of the murder investigation, or maybe something more.

"Time will tell," she said to the walls.

Denia came out of the kitchen in time to see Isis climbing the stairs to the second story. The previous evening the ebony feline had disappeared after dinner, and Denia had not seen her until breakfast. She decided to follow the cat, walking up the stairs as quietly as she could, despite the periodic creaking of old wood. Once on the landing the cat made her way in a determined fashion to the far bedroom, where darkness emanated from the open doorway. Denia turned on the hall ceiling light and looked into the room where the cat had disappeared, finding Isis curled up on the comforter covering the empty bed. She walked into the room and stood next to the rumpled comforter.

"So," she said softly to the cat, "you used to sleep with Auntie?"

She patted the curled animal on the head. Isis let out a soft mew of recognition in answer to Denia's question.

"Alright. You can stay here. Good night, Isis."

Denia stood for a few moments remembering evenings sitting next to her aunt in this bed, propped up against pillows, reading *The Secret Garden*.

"Good night, Auntie," she whispered into the dark room, turning to leave.

When Hans got there around eight-thirty on Saturday morning, Denia was almost finished cleaning the goat pen. Jorje usually took the goat out to the pen by seven-thirty during the week. Denia figured she could leave the goat out of the barn a little longer today, and not put her in her stall until after five o'clock.

Speaking of Billy, she was having a great time with her newfound friend. Finally, something with four legs that she could chase. Billy and the dog were a picture of motion. Billy would charge the dog, sometimes butting it with her head, but the puppy was close enough to the ground that he would just roll in a ball. Quickly recovering, the puppy was on his feet again running around the goat. Hans and Denia stood by the pen watching them, laughing at the antics.

"What are you going to name him?" asked Hans. "Have you thought of a name?"

"I've kind of settled on a couple names. His mother's name is Whiskey, so I was thinking of Brandy. I thought that would be something like his mother and went with his coloring."

"No, that one's no good," Hans responded. "Kristen Clearwater is keeping one of his sisters from the litter, and she's already named it Brandy."

"Darn," replied Denia, thinking it would be a good name for a chocolate lab.

"What else have you got?" he asked, running to grab the puppy to save him from another head butt.

"Well, I was thinking that Melinda named the cats after Roman and Egyptian goddesses, and she *did* pick out the puppy, so maybe I should name him after a famous god."

"Do you mean like Mars or Jupiter?" he asked, putting the struggling animal back on the ground.

"I like Angus. He was the Celtic god of love. Auntie was Irish, so I think she would approve."

"It's a good, masculine name," he said in agreement, "and it does follow her tradition."

"Here, Angus," she bent down and called to the brown motion machine, holding out her hands toward him. The puppy turned toward her and came running.

"I guess that settles it," said the vet with a smile, watching Denia snuggle with the pup.

"Are you going to help me with the chickens or not?" Denia demanded.

"Why don't you take care of the chickens, and I'll watch these two."

"Okay, but you're not a lot of help," Denia teased.

"My expertise is more with the four-legged variety. It's not often you can get a licensed veterinarian to dog, and goat sit for you," he said, giving her a charming smile.

It actually was a big help to Denia to let him oversee the playing animals while she took her time with the chickens in the coop. The group of hens were getting used to her, practically ignoring her as she went about the tasks. Jorje had filled the feeders yesterday, and she checked the on-demand watering system to make sure all the little cups were clean and supplying fresh water. She collected twelve eggs from the nesting boxes, adding fresh straw to some.

Jorje had a good system for cleaning the floor of the pen, which Denia followed diligently.

Once finished with putting the eggs away, Denia asked Hans if he wanted to take the animals up to the turtle pond with her. She brought some romaine lettuce from the kitchen and carried a measuring cup full of turtle food pellets. She previously unlocked the back gate when she took the used straw from Billy's stall out to the compost piles.

It was a clear morning with blue, cloudless skies. Hans picked up Angus and carried him through the gate, and Billy followed not wanting to be left behind. Once they got to the edge of the orchard the goat took off running across the field. Hans put the puppy down and he did his best to follow Billy, even though the tall, field grasses were high and frequently swallowed him in some places.

Denia and Hans ambled slowly up the low grade leading to the pond area and the line of rocky hills that divided the ranch property. Denia had to frequently call the puppy moving through the rough.

"These turtle stones are so cool," Hans commented, as he studied the pattern of the stones following the circular edge of the murky pond.

"Yeah, when I was a kid, I counted them once. There are more than fifty of them. Melinda's husband bought them specifically for the pond here," Denia explained, as she laid out lettuce leaves along the edge of the pond. Moving toward the old oak, she spread the turtle pellets all along the far end of the water near the bench.

"Billy!" Denia called to the goat who had wandered far

down the field heading toward the garage and the lavender grove at the far end.

"Billy, get back here," she called again in a loud voice.

The puppy was bobbing his way through the field, coming into sight at intervals. The goat turned around and ran back, passing the puppy on her way.

"My mom was so glad to finally meet you, yesterday. She said you had some excitement out here."

"It wasn't exactly exciting. It was a little frightening to have the police come out here," said Denia, "but they just wanted to ask Snowy some questions."

"Mom was pretty quiet when she got home," he said, "but those Doves are like that."

"What do you mean? How many are in the group?"

"Let's see, now that Melinda is gone there's Mom, Batty, Agatha, Cassie, and Evelyn - five of them."

"How did they get together and start calling themselves the Doves?" Denia's curiosity was peaked.

"I left for college eleven years ago, worked a couple years before veterinary school, so I've been gone most of the time. I'm not sure how it got started. Mom and Melinda knew each other for years from the Solvang Ladies Book Club. Both of them were readers, and president of the club at times. When I left for college, things changed around the house. Dad retired after a while and made one of the bedrooms into a home office. Then Mom took over my bedroom for her books and whatever else. She made it clear that it was *her room* and has a lock on the door. Dad didn't care. When Mom would go off with the Doves and their meetings, he felt less guilty about leaving for his five-day fishing trips. He loves to go fishing. Mom is the only one of the Doves that is married. The rest are all single, older women. Mom was already working with Melinda at Candlewick when I decided to come back here to practice.”

Denia watched as a large turtle made its way to the edge of the pond water to snag a piece of lettuce treat.

“I haven’t met all of them yet,” she commented. “Your mother said Cassie is a psychic.”

“Yeah, they’re all a little weird if you ask me, but harmless. If you pay attention, you’ll notice they are kind of secretive. I mean, they don’t talk about things that they do as a group. Melinda’s death really hit them hard. She was a very strong lady, and they all looked up to her.”

Denia thought of some things Batty had said that *she* thought odd. She had to agree with Hans that there was a little weirdness in what she had seen so far.

Hans suddenly went running to the opposite end of the pond where the puppy had discovered the water and was drinking. He grabbed the dog and carried him over to where Denia was standing.

“It’s getting hot out here. We should probably take them back,” Denia said when she saw the little dog panting.

“You take him, I’ll get Billy,” he said in agreement with Denia.

The rest of the morning was spent in easy back and forth conversation, focusing on Hans’ surfing hobby and recent events at the veterinary clinic. Denia found it easy to talk to Hans, although she avoided the circumstances surrounding her aunt's death.

When he left, Denia reflected on some of the things he said about the Doves and thought she needed to pay closer attention to Batty and Olivia, who may unknowingly hold clues to Melinda's murder.

On Sunday afternoon Denia was cleaning out the large pantry at the back of the kitchen. The floor-to-ceiling shelves were unorganized with cans of food, jars of canned jams, jellies, and tomatoes. Boxes of cereal, and baking products, were placed all askew with rolls of paper towels and empty jars of all sizes. Upper shelves held a collection of multicolored, glass, flower vases, among a mixture of small, kitchen appliances. Her plan was to designate sections of middle shelves for canned goods and other food stuff, upper shelves would be saved for less used items.

She was planning to have a large section of open shelves, thinking of her own kitchen items, now in a storage locker in San Diego. She brought in cardboard boxes and bins from the garage and started unloading the shelves. There were at least fifty glass jars that she considered for candles, so these were going to go out to the office building. She would keep some of the vases, locating them on an upper shelf, and the rest would go into a box for donation. There was a redundancy of appliances – how many slow-cookers and blenders do you need – and most of these ended up in the donation boxes.

So busy was she with her re-organization zeal, that she did not even hear a car come into the driveway. When the knock sounded at the back door, she thought it might be Batty, but when the second knock came, she wasn't sure. Moving the back door's window curtain aside she saw Snowy waiting there. She opened the door without hesitation.

"Hi Denia," he started. "Batty told me you said you needed a television. I know that one of Mel's in the living room died long ago. I had this one at the shop, still in the box," he said holding the large, rectangular box he had which was leaning against his legs.

Denia recognized the familiar, electronic brand on the side of the box.

"I know," he said, "beware of Greeks bearing gifts, or Irishmen bringing a flat screen, in this case."

Denia opened the door wider to allow Snowy to enter the kitchen with the large, awkwardly sized box and its contents. Angus, who had been sleeping under the dining room table, came running to investigate the new visitor. After leaning the TV against the counter, Snowy bent down to fuss over the enthusiastic puppy.

"Would you like some iced tea?" Denia offered.

"I would, with sugar," he said. "It's hot out there. One of the best things Mel did was get central air and heating put into this house."

Denia poured out two glasses of tea from the refrigerator, adding sweetener to hers, and sugar to the one for Snowy.

"I was going to try to buy a TV this week. How much would you want for this one?" she asked handing him the cool glass.

"No charge. This one didn't cost me anything. The guy bought it and had it out in his garage to be installed and found a deal on a bigger one. It was football season last year, and there was a sale. This one never got out of the box. I hung the bigger one for him in his media room, and he gave me this one in trade for the labor."

Walking into the dining area, facing the living room fireplace, "This one is a fifty-five inch and would fit nicely over the mantle there. Unless you want it for your bedroom."

Denia came to stand beside the large man, looking at the fireplace and imagining a TV in the space.

"If we put it there, I could get that monstrosity out of here," she said, indicating the old-fashioned console set.

"Then, I could get a nice lounge chair with an ottoman," she added longingly.

"That would give you more seating than just the sofa," he agreed.

"If I cleared and painted those built-in shelves on either side of the fireplace, I could display nice vases and other things that Auntie has hidden around here. I just found two vases in the pantry that look like they're from the Art Deco era," she said, imagining the far wall.

"Are you sure you would be able to put the TV on the brick?" she queried doubtfully.

"Oh, sure. I have a drill and hanging bars out in the truck. I've gotten good at it. Seems like everyone wants their TV hung over the fireplace these days."

He crossed the small living room looking for electrical outlets.

"You can move that little bookcase from the dining room and move it over here for the cable box and whatever devices you have. I can drill holes in the back for the wires. There are two outlet boxes here…one on this wall and one behind here, on the window wall. You could put a chair and an end table here with a lamp and still have plugs for the electronics."

He looked up facing her, "I can install the TV now if you want, and you can call the cable company tomorrow."

When Denia agreed, Snowy went out to his truck and carried in his equipment, while Denia went back to work on the pantry.

An hour later, Angus, running back and forth keeping track of all the excitement, followed Snowy into the kitchen.

"Come see how it looks," he called to Denia, who was up on the step stool, rearranging a top shelf in the pantry.

She got down and followed him into the front room.

"Wow, what a difference," she exclaimed with approval. "I love it!"

"I got the bookcase ready for you, too," he said.

Denia noticed, with dismay, that he had emptied the contents of the bookcase onto the clean space on the dining room table and moved it to the wall next to the built-in shelves in the corner.

"Would you mind if I took this old set?" he asked, which

he had already moved to the middle of the room. "These were made with good wood, and I have a friend that repurposes old wood into new pieces of furniture."

"Yeah, I would like to get it out of here, but it's too heavy for me to move. I'll help you take it out."

Once the TV console was out of the house, Denia walked back into the living room and noticed the need for a severe cleaning. There was an inch thick of cat hair and dust on the floor where the console had been that spoke to the passage of time. Snowy stood by the bay window petting Mona, who had refused to leave her spot, despite a nosey puppy, the noise from the drill, and the reorganization of furniture.

"I wanted to talk to you about your aunt," Snowy said in a serious tone looking at Denia. "I need you to know that I would have never hurt Melinda in any way."

"Thank you, that's good to know."

"I will miss her terribly," he said. "I already do. She was like an elusive spirit I could never quite catch. Whenever I got closer, she was gone again."

Denia felt the man's desperation, which came through in his voice.

"I was up in the mountains when she called me the last time. We had paid for our time on the telescope for the meteor shower. I was busy with my students and couldn't really talk very long. She wanted me to come by when I got back to put up some lights and maybe some cameras around the house and back lot. I asked her why, and she said that she would tell me when I got here. That was the last time I spoke to her," he said, sighing. "When I got back to town, the news of her death was a topic of conversation. Several people mentioned it to me. I called Olivia, who told me what she knew. We were all assuming the cause of her death was a heart attack.”

“My mother and I pretty much knew from the beginning that it might be something more.”

“Based upon the police questioning on Friday, I knew they were investigating a homicide and point-blank asked Nelson if that was the case. He confirmed it, but told me to keep it quiet, since they were still investigating. I told him I would keep my ear to the ground. I have a few hundred contacts up and down the central coast in the short wave and astronomy networks.”

“Can you think of anything that could help?” Denia asked.

At this point she had pretty much ruled out the big man as a suspect in her aunt’s murder.

“No, I’ve been racking my brain,” he replied. “That’s the thing about this…Mel was so well liked. She was a private person, even though we all knew her. She was very close to Batty and Olivia, and that group, but I always felt there was so much there that no one knew. Like I said…elusive.”

Denia felt an urge to comfort this gentle man who so obviously felt a loss. This was someone who knew her aunt well and was part of her life, and in some ways, was closer to her than Denia herself.

“Well, thank you so much for the TV,” said Denia trying to lighten the mood. “I’ve really missed not having one.”

Snowy fished a bulging wallet out of his back pocket and handed her his business card.

"Here is my phone number. You can call me if you have any problems getting it hooked up; or, if you need anything else."

Denia walked out back with him, since Angus needed a pit stop. Snowy bent to give the puppy a few last pats before getting into his truck. Denia watched as he pulled out of the driveway.

"That was unexpected," she said to herself.

Back she went to the kitchen full of boxes and bins.

Denia went to bed early after the events of the day. She made sure the goat was in his stall and the cats were in the house. The evening had turned cool, as low clouds made their way into the Santa Ynez Valley, putting a ring around the half-moon which hung above the hills.

After a half hour of trying, she realized she couldn't go to sleep. The events of the last few days kept coming to the front of her mind, no matter how hard she tried to dismiss them. She felt tired, both physically and emotionally, but could not seem to relax enough to fall asleep.

She sat up in bed and turned on the hurricane lamp sitting on the bedside table. She always used to read to get herself drowsy, but all *her* books were packed in boxes in a San Diego storage garage. She remembered her aunt had a wall of bookshelves in her bedroom. Bare feet on the floor, she headed out of the room to the nearby doorway and into her aunt's bedroom. She was sure she could find something interesting to read among all of Auntie's books.

Finding the wall switch to the empty room she turned on the inverted dome of a light in the middle of the ceiling. Denia had spent very little time venturing into her aunt's bedroom since she had been there. The bedroom looked lived-in, waiting for its occupant to return at any moment. Bed linens had been left askew in a quick attempt to make the bed. Isis was curled on the bedcover, sleeping. As in the rest of the house, a state of organized clutter prevailed on the nightstands and oversized dresser.

Discarded clothing was piled on the small, upholstered chair by the bed. The old, wood floors, which needed restoration, were covered with various-sized flowered, throw rugs. Pairs of shoes lay here and there on the floor, ready to be put on. Full length, burgundy, drape panels framed each of the four windows, two on the wall framing the head of the bed, and two on the wall opposite the doorway. Mirrored closet doors next to the large dresser reflected the empty room.

Crossing the threshold, the silence in the room was gripping. Denia believed she could smell a hint of her aunt's flowery perfume - rosewater. She could feel her aunt's presence here more than anywhere else in the house – maybe that's why she had been unconsciously avoiding it. A sense of good and warmth came to her.

"I came to borrow a book, Auntie," she spoke out loud into the silence.

The wall which was shared with Denia's room held eight feet of floor-to-ceiling bookshelves. An upper section of shelves was enclosed with several sets of glass doors. The lower shelves were hidden behind wood paneled doors. Behind the glass doors books lined shelves vertically, interrupted at spots with horizontal stacks, titles in view. Empty space was sparse throughout the upper shelves.

Prior to marrying James Greystone, fifteen years her senior, Denia's Aunt Melinda had been a schoolteacher living in Burbank, California. She had never lost her love of reading, and the books in her bedroom were more than books, they were her friends. As a child, Denia would frequently receive books from her aunt, carefully selected to match Denia's reading level at the time. They would read every evening on the summer nights when she used to visit. Some of those stories were still among her favorites.

Denia opened the closest glass door. The middle shelf seemed to hold a collection of fictional novels, divided by authors, not on current day book lists. Book spines reflected authors Denia had not heard of such as Phyllis Whitney, Victoria Holt, and Mary Stewart. There were some familiar titles like *Gone with the Wind, Rebecca*, and *Death on the Nile*. As she reached for a book with a mysterious title, she heard a sharp clatter that sounded like something had fallen on the back patio below. She was startled by the noise breaking the silence of the night.

She stepped to the doorway and turned out the ceiling light and went to the closest window moving the drapery aside slightly to permit a view of the flagstone patio below. The patio appeared to be empty, but a shadow moved along the driveway toward the backyard holding what appeared to be a small LED flashlight. In order to follow the light,

Denia walked around the bed and moved the drape aside on the window overlooking the back. The figure and light moved across the yard heading toward the outbuildings behind the garage. It looked like the figure of a man.

The realization of being very alone on the large ranch ran up her spine. She was a sitting duck; and the figure with the light would have seen the light on from her bedroom.

She wondered if she had she locked the doors?

Where was her phone?

The figure and the little glow from the light disappeared from her view between the office building and the barn.

She ran to her room, looking for the black purse containing her phone. Damn. She remembered she left it on the coffee table in the living room. Her bare feet made noise at she quickly went down the old, squeaky stairs to the dark room below. She grabbed the phone from her purse, and the light from the small rectangle hit her face as it came to life. But who should she call? 9-1-1? She knew no local numbers. She sat down on the floor and cupped her hand over the phone to hide its light and dialed 9-1-1 for the first time in her life.

"9-1-1," stated the operator.

"I need help. I'm home alone and there's a prowler in my yard."

"What is your address?" the voice asked efficiently.

What *is* my address, thought Denia in a panic?

She crawled to the desk and grabbed an envelope from

a stack of mail.

"2663 Castle Road, Santa Ynez," she stated as clearly as possible into the phone.

"What is your name?"

"Denia Rawlings."

"Is the prowler trying to get into the house?"

"No, he was going across the yard in back of the house."

"Are you the owner?"

"Yes," her sense of urgency growing. "Can you please send someone? My aunt was murdered at this house less than three weeks ago," she pleaded. "I'm alone here."

There was a brief silence on the connection, then, "I've notified the sheriff's station in Solvang, and they will send someone out right away. Find a closet to secure yourself until they get there. I will stay on the line."

Denia crawled around the bottom of the stairs into the kitchen, stood up, and hid herself in the utility room at the back of the kitchen. Lowering herself to a small space beside the hot water heater, clutching her phone, she realized she was shaking.

The thought that her aunt had just been killed by someone, for some unknown reason, became a hard reality while she sat in the darkness. She heard Angus crying in his dog carrier upstairs, but she knew he was safe where he was. Fear gripped her.

Why was someone lurking around the house? What did they want?

8

THE DRAGON

"Hello, ma'am?" came the tinny voice through the cell phone speaker.

"Yes," Denia spoke softly into the phone, continuing to crouch on the floor of the utility room.

Mona had made her way into the small room, probably out of curiosity, and sat on the floor in front of her adopted mistress.

"The police are arriving at your location. The officer will knock on the door and identify himself. You can answer the door," reported the 9-1-1 operator.

She had remained on the phone since Denia called a few minutes previously.

"Okay," Denia replied in a shaky voice.

She got up from her uncomfortable position and walked barefooted across the kitchen, through the dining area, and to the front door. Still holding the phone to her ear, Denia heard a succession of short raps sound from the wooden portal.

"Miss Rawlings," came the voice, "this is Deputy Cleeves. Can you open the door?"

"Thanks, he's at the door," Denia said into the phone, and then disconnected the call from the operator.

Denia turned on the porch light and opened the door.

"Miss Rawlings, you reported a prowler?" asked the familiar deputy.

Denia was relieved to see a police officer she had already met, who knew something of the problems that had been occurring at the ranch. His professional manner was comforting at the moment.

"Yes, I was upstairs when I heard something down on the patio by the back door. Then I saw someone moving along the driveway, toward the back, with a little flashlight."

"Do you have any lights out back?" he asked.

"Only the light by the back door," Denia responded.

"Turn it on and I'll turn my patrol car around to shine the headlights back there. Stay here and I'll see if I can find anything. I have flashlights in the car."

"Ah, can you check on my goat? She's in the barn."

"Sure," he said, already turning to get to his car.

Denia crossed the main floor of the house to turn on the back porch light. She looked out the door's window to the flagstone patio and saw one of the ceramic pots broken on the ground, with its plant and potting soil scattered. The deputy turned his car to face the back with headlamps illuminating the chicken coop and the back lot near the house.

She leaned against the kitchen counter, waiting. The house was quiet, but Mona was alert, sitting on the back of the sofa, realizing the happenings of the night were not routine. There was no further crying coming from the puppy upstairs.

The next sounds came from a car pulling into the driveway, followed directly by another vehicle. As Denia moved toward the door, she saw the figures of two men she recognized as Lee Nelson and Keith Clearwater, stopping to speak to the deputy coming from the back lot, flashlight in hand. She watched as they stood in a huddle, the beam of light moving as the deputy talked. Denia saw the two tall men coming toward the door and opened it as they arrived. Lee Nelson paused at the back door.

"You need to get a better lock on this door and the front door," Nelson said with authority, "tomorrow."

"Do you know if my goat is alright?" Denia asked.

"Yes," the sergeant answered. "Cleeves said the goat was fine, but it looks like the lock on the office building was jimmied."

"Oh, no," said Denia, wondering what it meant.

She looked from Lee Nelson to Keith Clearwater. The officer was out of uniform, dressed in casual slacks, and a cotton, short-sleeved shirt. If it was possible, he was more attractive than she remembered with blonde hair falling onto his forehead. Keith Clearwater wore blue jeans and a pristine, long-sleeved, white shirt which accented the tan complexion of his face and neck. There was a strong contrast between the two men.

"How did you know I called 9-1-1 about a prowler?" she asked looking from one to another of the two, not understanding how they would both know, arriving so soon after her call.

"We were having a beer in town after the Rotary Club meeting," said the sergeant. "Cleeves called me on my cell phone, while he was driving out here."

"Do you have an extra flashlight?" Keith asked. "We want to go out back and look around."

Denia went into the now organized pantry, returning with two flashlights, one with a large lamplight, and handed them to the men. Once again, she heard the puppy yapping his sorrowful song upstairs.

"I better go get him," she said to Keith who was smiling as she ran to the stairs.

The men made for the back door.

Vaulting up the stairs to the upper floor landing, "I'm coming Angus."

She quickly unlatched the carrier's small door, and the puppy dashed forward in a burst of speed, elated to be free. Denia stood as Angus ran circles around her feet, catching her own reflection in the mirror over the dresser.

"Oh, God," she lamented to the image.

Her hair was hanging loose, and she wore no makeup. She was wearing a sloppy t-shirt over an old sports bra and plaid, flannel pajama bottoms.

Denia scrambled to change into her jeans from that morning and found a buttercup-colored, knit shirt, easing it over her sports bra. She needed to go out to the office building, so she grabbed socks and sneakers, jamming them onto her feet. Running the brush through her hair and securing it with a scrunchy at the back of her neck was all she could manage with speed.

Coming down the stairs, holding Angus in one arm, she heard female voices coming from the kitchen, and found Olivia and Batty standing by the counter and stove as she rounded the corner.

"What are you two doing here?" she asked with surprise.

"Snowy called us. He's out back with the guys," answered Batty, coming to Denia to pat the puppy on the head.

"How did Snowy know about it?" Denia asked trying to unravel the puzzle.

"Short-wave radio. He has the police frequency going while he's on the UFO websites at night," Olivia replied as she was completing the task of putting on a pot of coffee. "He always knows what's going on in this town."

The networking in this town was beyond belief, Denia marveled to herself.

She stood looking at the two invaders, the sight almost comical, reminding her of old "Lucy" TV episodes. Olivia sported pink, foam curlers strategically placed in her hair.

Her short, pudgy frame was encased in a rose-colored robe tied at the waist over flowered, cotton pajamas. Fuzzy, purple slippers completed the ensemble. Batty's hair was at its frizzy best, sticking out on both sides of her face. A baggy, blue sweatshirt had been thrown over green, pin-striped, pajama bottoms that were too long, overflowing onto canvas, slip-on shoes. Clearly, getting dressed before forging out through the night had not been a priority.

"Are you alright?" Batty asked with concern in her face and voice.

"I am now," Denia replied, "but I *was* scared when I saw someone in the yard."

Denia took Angus out the back door, setting him on the slabs of flagstone, where he sniffed around before doing his business.

"Good boy," Denia praised.

Looking toward the road she saw the pile up of four cars, one behind the other. The night was warm without the hint of a breeze. She looked toward the office where the lights were beaming from inside.

"What are they doing out there?" called Batty, coming out to stand beside Denia.

They stood looking toward the office. Chickens cackled their displeasure with the nighttime disturbance. The half-moon hung above the orchard on its predictable trek.

Olivia came out of the kitchen and joined them.

"What are they doing out there?" she echoed looking down the yard.

"Let's go see," Batty said, charging into the darkness with Angus following.

Denia grabbed Angus and started into the yard after Batty, Olivia followed.

By the time the three women arrived at the office building, they found all four men huddled around the office door examining the lock and the door frame.

"We need a lock with a dead bolt on this door," Nelson was saying.

"How difficult will it be to run some outside lighting out here?" Keith asked Snowy.

"The electrical panel is not that old, and I'm sure there's room to add lighting. We'll need to get an electrician out here to look at it in daylight. I can help add some lights with motion sensors," the big man said, committing himself to needed updates.

"Tell me what's happening," Denia interrupted.

"Here's where the lock was broken. There's not much damage, but this will have to be replaced," replied Nelson. "Be careful not to touch anything but come look in the office."

All the women moved through the door and to the small Candlewick business office.

"Oh, no, my computer's gone!" exclaimed Olivia.

"What are we going to do?" asked Denia, thinking of the business.

She still didn't understand the business and how it was doing financially, but she did understand that it was a website-based business and was dependent upon computer communication. Now, both computers were gone, one with the police and one stolen.

"I still have the website and all of the financials on my computer," offered Batty.

"You may need to get a new desk top computer, but all of the files are backed up every twenty-four hours, so I will be able to get it all back," said Snowy reassuringly.

"The painting," Batty announced with surprise, "they took it!"

All eyes turned to the empty back wall.

"The Stonehenge painting," said Olivia in reverence, trying to take in the loss.

"Was it valuable?" asked Nelson.

"As far as monetary value, I think Mel paid over two thousand dollars for it. The paperwork is probably in the house somewhere. For us and to Mel it was *very* important. It was the inspiration for Candlewick. That's why she had it out here," explained Batty. "I can't imagine why someone would take it."

"Denia, you said you only saw one person around the house before you called 9-1-1?" Nelson asked.

"Yes, he was on the back patio by the kitchen and then he moved off toward the back lot. I lost sight of him before I called."

"With the size of that picture, the computer, and whatever else is missing, I think more than one person was involved in this," the sergeant hypothesized. "I'll get a team out here in the morning to check for any fingerprints. We might get lucky," he paused.

"Denia, I need you and Olivia to go through this place tomorrow and give me a list of anything missing; I'll need it for the police report. Also, see if you can find any paperwork on the painting in the house. There may be some kind of clue there as to why it would be stolen. Keith, tomorrow I want to walk the property including the vineyard area. Keep your crews out of there until we have a chance to look for anything unusual. That would be the closest access to the road, if they didn't come through the front, which is unlikely," said Nelson.

Keith nodded in agreement.

"I should come, too," Denia spoke up, feeling that she needed to be involved.

"Well, we can't do any more tonight. Olivia made some coffee. Let's go back to the house," said Batty.

The next morning started with what was becoming a pattern - Angus crying to get out of his carrier. Denia felt groggy after only a few hours' sleep, as she padded down the stairs to take the dog out. Mona was already in the kitchen waiting for food.

The night before, the large group in the small kitchen and dining room finally dissipated, one and two at a time after the coffee pot ran dry. Batty and Olivia offered to stay the night, but Denia sent them home with assurances that she was alright. When she did get to bed, she had trouble calming herself down in order to go to sleep, with her mind revisiting the night's events.

This morning, as Angus sniffed around, the previously crowded driveway was empty. It was already warm outside, foretelling another hot day. Jorje's car pulled in the drive, forcing her to corral the unpredictable puppy, allowing his car to pass on its way to the usual spot under the tree in the back lot.

By the time the sheriff department's forensic team arrived, Denia had showered, dressed, fed all the animals - giving Angus some crate time - and cleaned the kitchen. As the dishwasher hummed away, filled with coffee mugs and animal dishes, Denia led the two officers to the office building. One was a tall, lanky male wearing thick, oversized glasses, and the other was a talkative female, appearing to be the senior officer who quickly dismissed Denia as they set to their task.

While she was talking to Jorje, filling him in on the prowler and the burglary of the office, a middle-aged man with ginger hair and a dark, blue, work shirt with a patch identifying him with Circuit Electrical Company, came toward her from the small parking area where he had parked his labeled van. He introduced himself as Ron Jorgensen, an electrician who had been called that morning by Snowy and requested to meet him here regarding the installation of outdoor lighting for the property. Denia explained that Snowy was not here yet but gave the man permission to check the electrical boxes for the house and the office building.

When Snowy did show up at the kitchen door a half hour later, he was carrying two bags from an early morning trip to the all-purpose hardware store. He emptied the contents of the bags onto the kitchen counter. There were two new door handle sets with accompanying bolt locks, all in the new brushed bronze finish showing through the clear packaging. These were obviously for the front and back doors of the house. There was also a replacement lock for the office building and an additional bolt lock. The second bag contained several floodlights with motion detectors. Denia was impressed.

"Now if you don't like these, we can take them back and exchange them for some you do like," he explained, displaying the various items.

"No, these handles look so much better than what's on the doors now. I like the finish on these. They will be fine," she said, grabbing the receipt from the counter. "Boy, door handles and locks are expensive. I'll give you a check for all of this."

"We can put these in today. Kevin is coming over with the drill. I didn't have the right kind for the bolt locks."

"Oh, there is a guy out back looking at the electrical boxes," Denia remembered.

"Jorgensen, yeah, I called him this morning. I better go talk to him."

The large man made his way out the back door.

Later that morning, Denia decided there was absolutely no need for her to go into Solvang to meet people, because sooner or later, they would all end up in her kitchen. The latest local was currently removing the old, back door handle, preparing to replace it.

His name was Kevin Henderson, aka the Dragon. The logic for the nickname was obvious, with the blue and green detailed tattoo of a dragon snaking down his right arm. It had a piercing yellow eye, a green snout - slightly open, baring teeth - emitting red flames that flowed to the wrist.

The question of how this person could be Batty's son perplexed Denia. When she first opened the back door this morning she stood eye to eye with the ash blonde, spiky-haired person of a kindred age as herself. The gray-green eyes, probably the only legacy from his mother, peered at her with the same curiosity that she was displaying. His forehead was wide and his nose straight. A clean-shaven face with studded earlobes and a small, silver ring embedded in one eyebrow finished the artistic self-statement of the man. Though not tall of stature, he was wide-shouldered and muscular in a sleeveless shirt, indicating a gym membership. Denia was surprised that during the introductions she barely noticed he was holding an electric drill, and had a coiled, orange electrical cord hanging from his left arm.

Having spent time with Batty, Denia knew she had two children. One was a married daughter living with her marine biologist husband and Batty's two grandchildren in Corpus Christi, Texas. Batty tried to visit them three to four times a year to spend time with the quickly growing children; but most of what Denia heard her speak of was her son, Kevin.

After high school, he left home and enthusiastically

went into the Air Force. He spent several years in Albuquerque, New Mexico at Kirkland Air Force Base. He left the Air Force almost a year ago and moved back in with Batty 'until he could get a job and move into his own place'. Now Batty was impatient to get her two-bedroom condominium back to herself. It was her wish for him to find a girl and *move out*! In listening to Batty ramble about her son, Denia had formed a picture in her mind of what she thought he would look like, so the reality was unexpected to say the least.

"How does that look?" he asked Denia when the new door handle was in place. "I'll put this bolt lock near the top of the door and one at the bottom, which you can set when you're in the house. These kinds of doors are difficult, because someone could just break the window and reach the door handle. You could set these bolts when you went out, but you would have to go out the front door."

Denia agreed, but realized what a hassle this was going to be with the dog going in and out ten times a day. She didn't like the idea of living in fear all the time.

Later, Denia heard the kitchen phone ring beyond the sound of Kevin's drilling.

She motioned to him to turn it off as she answered the phone, "Hello?"

"Hello, Denia?" came the male voice. "This is Eugene."

"Oh, hi," she said, imagining the well-dressed lawyer sitting behind the desk in his office.

"I was thinking of you, and I was wondering if you would like to go out to dinner with me Friday night?"

Denia was blindsided. A date, he was asking for a date. She had not had a real date since the demise of her engagement. She was not sure if she was ready.

"That would be nice," she heard herself saying.

"There is a really good steakhouse just outside of Solvang. They also have an excellent wine selection. Does that sound like something you would like? You're not vegetarian, are you?"

"No, I'm not vegetarian, and that does sound good. How about if I meet you at the restaurant? Then you won't need to drive through Solvang to come get me."

"I don't mind coming to get you, but that would work. It's on the main drag on the way out of Solvang. The place is called *The Grill and the Grape*. Parking is in the back behind the restaurant. How about seven-thirty?"

"Okay, I'll see you then."

"Sounds good. Bring your hungry," his laugh continued as he hung up.

Denia stood looking at the phone. She felt good and vulnerable about her decision to go out with the attorney. She was not sure why she wanted to drive herself to the restaurant. Maybe it could avoid less after-dinner drama. Maybe she felt a need for more control, and to be able to leave if and when she thought things were not going well. Then she chastised herself for the negative thoughts. It was a compliment to have the handsome attorney ask her out for a date.

Sooner or later, she would have to put Jeff behind her. A dinner date wasn't a life-long commitment.

"Hot date, huh?" Kevin the Dragon commented overhearing the conversation.

"It's just dinner," she said downplaying the date, "and I'll come after you with a pitchfork if you tell your mother. I have no need to be part of the gossip mill around here."

"A little late for that," he said, getting ready to start drilling again.

"What do you mean?" Denia asked, piqued at his sarcasm.

"Are you kidding?" he asked. "You've been the hot topic of conversation ever since you got here right after Melinda's death."

"Great," she said with her own sarcasm.

She grabbed Angus, who was sleeping under the dining room table and went out the front door in a huff.

Denia stood in the midday sun as Angus ran around the front yard enjoying the different smells. In a few days he was already learning that outdoors was the place for doing his thing. Denia was proud of his progress, which also required perseverance on her part.

To her surprise she saw a horse and rider coming from the field beside the garage, moving across the cement pad to the grass and fig tree grove next to the front drive by the garage. Keith Clearwater dismounted in the fluid motion of an experienced rider and walked toward her, allowing the russet-colored horse to graze. Denia was impressed seeing the rancher side of him. The man was just intimidating; too much to get her mind around.

"Nelson called me to say he couldn't get away, but he

still wanted us to walk around the property to see if we could find any signs left by the intruders last night," Keith said as he got within hearing distance of Denia.

"I can do it now if you want. Olivia isn't coming over until later. Just let me put him in the house," she said indicating the puppy.

Denia ran in the house, Dragon agreeing to keep an eye on Angus rather than putting him in his crate. She grabbed two bottles of water from the refrigerator, already warm from the few minutes she had been outside. She joined the tall, dark-haired man, handing him one of the water bottles.

"I'm sorry I couldn't get here earlier. We've started harvesting some of the fields, so I had to make sure all the crews were going. I also needed to check in with Kristen and the winery managers to see that we're ready to go once we bring the grapes in," he explained as they walked toward the garage.

"Are the grapes ripe?" Denia asked, knowing nothing about harvesting grapes on a large scale.

"We grow different kinds of grapes, so they get ripe at slightly different times. We'll be doing ten-hour days over the next month or so."

A long rosemary hedge lined the side of the house, only interrupted by the tall brick chimney that loomed to a height over the roof. The garage was built separate from the house on the lot, allowing an open space between the house and the garage leading to the back lot behind the house. Keith suggested fencing with a gate that could be locked to provide better security.

As they walked through the space, Denia could see that

it would only need about fifteen feet of fencing to make the change. The office building had been added to the back wall of the garage, a long rectangular addition that exceeded the length of the three-car garage.

Walking together, the pair inspected the ground around the small parking area and the front of the office building for anything unusual. This area was so well trafficked, Keith did not expect to find anything of value to the search. The black form of Isis was sprawled out on the low cinderblock wall near the parking space. Keith led the way to the alley-like area between the office building and the weathered, wooden barn. The shaded, eight-foot-wide pathway led from the back lot between the building to the open field behind the barn.

Once at the opening to the field, anyone would have choices as to how to leave the property - out across the field, toward the orchard, or by the outer side of the garage to the front road.

"Look here," said Keith to Denia, stooping and pointing to a clump of tall, dry grass toward the center of the pathway.

Denia came to stand beside him. Keith was touching broken stems of trodden plants.

"They probably came out of the office and through here to the area behind the barn. Then they could have gone across the field or back through the orchard."

He stood up and looked across the field.

"It would be good to put a fence across here, too. This opening gives direct access to your back lot and is hidden from view. It provides an easy pathway to the back of the house."

Denia remembered this was also the spot used to hide her aunt's dead body but said nothing to Keith who was already walking back toward the barn. She had to agree that a barrier would add security. They walked along the front of the barn and the attached bunkhouse that Jorje used during the day. One of the tall, barn doors was propped open. The wide, chain-link gate along the back fence stood wide open and they continued to the orchard beyond.

The set of large, rectangular, vegetable boxes lined the other side of the fence, boasting a host of plants and ripening vegetables. Since discovering the garden, Denia had been taking advantage, bringing freshly picked tomatoes, beans, and squash into the house while encouraging Jorje to take home some of the ripe bounty.

Keith headed toward the back of the orchard, where several mounded compost areas had been cordoned off, next to the fence along the property line. Jorje was nearby, attending to the orchard's watering system. Billy stood a few feet away nibbling at the ground grasses and weeds. Jorje stopped what he was doing and walked over to the tall man. As Denia moved closer she could hear them conversing rapidly in Spanish, most of which she couldn't understand.

Yes, the man was intimidating, she thought to herself while studying Keith. She watched Jorje, as he led Keith to the back fence, which consisted of metal stakes in the ground with a thin wire running from post to post at three levels. The fence separated Denia's property from the avocado farm of the neighboring property.

Jorje was pointing to an area where the wiring looked like it had been recently replaced. Denia could see the line of fence was practically useless if someone was determined to enter her land.

The back fence was in better shape, running along the back border of the property, due to a double fence fronted by a long wall of pomegranate bushes, heavy with reddening fruit proclaiming the advent of fall.

Denia knew the property behind hers was a horse ranch. A long, three-railed, five-foot wooden fence had been erected by the horse owners which went the entire length of the back property. A chain-link fence went along Denia's side of the property line.

Keith ended his conversation with Jorje and walked over to join her, where they headed through the orchard to the open field. The orchard was made up of apple and walnut trees and covered several acres.

"Jorje said Mel had found an opening in the wire fencing a couple months ago. Jorje had replaced the wiring, but that part of the fencing along the property was never substantial. Mel told me she saw lights in the orchard one night, and it had frightened her," Keith said as they walked under the shade of the broad walnut leaves.

"That fence looks pretty worthless. I don't understand why they didn't continue the chain-link fence all the way to the back property line," said Denia.

When trees opened onto the wide, dry field, the sun was glaring down and Denia felt the heat. They headed across the field, traversing a slight upward grade of the land toward the line of towering eucalyptus trees. This would be the way to the vineyard area on the property. They passed the dividing rock formations on the right and walked to the top of a small rise under the giant trees. There was a defined path between the trees.

Denia stopped, taking a drink from her water bottle, and admired the view of the vineyard below. Neat rows of grape vines and their support structures filled the space. Moving forward among the rows, the bright green, grape leaves were piled upon each other, with jeweled purple, conical bunches of fruit hanging below.

"Can I taste them?" Denia asked, unable to resist plucking a few grapes.

"Sure, but they're not quite ripe yet. These are Concord grapes. We use them with another grape to make a sweet after dinner wine. These grapes are usually harvested toward the end of the season."

Denia popped two grapes into her mouth. There was a burst of flavor that made her lips pucker, but the taste was not what she remembered from a multitude of peanut butter and jelly sandwiches. It was a distinctive sweet but sour taste. Keith laughed at the face she made.

He showed her around the vines with explanations of the irrigation system and the farming routine. They walked all the way to the gates that opened onto the roadway. The same road that ran along the front of Denia's property curved at the hills embedded with the large, granite slabs and skirted the front of the vineyard land. The wide, double gates were not locked, which made access to the vines easy for Keith and his crews.

Denia bent down and retrieved a three-inch, rectangular

shape from the ground near the gate, that appeared to be a thin magnet.

"I've seen this before. Olivia had it attached to her computer," she said.

"What is it?" Keith asked, trying to make out the strange alphabetic characters.

"I don't know," said Denia, also unfamiliar with the sticklike symbols, "but this does verify that someone took the computer - and probably the picture - out through these gates," she said, putting the magnet into her jean's pocket.

"That would make sense. Anyone could park a car along the road here and come onto the property. I can put a lock on this gate if you would feel better about it."

"I think that would be a good idea for now."

Keith and Denia walked back through the vineyard in silence. Once at the eucalyptus trees, Keith took a sharp turn toward the rocks and the turtle pond beyond. He led along the grove of willow trees and disappeared behind them. Denia followed him through the semi-circle of trees into the opening for the rock amphitheater. Denia stood behind him, as he moved around the natural circle.

He touched the candle on one of the pedestals and stopped, hovering over the centralized stone circle, enclosing remnants of burnt wood. He turned and looked at her. Rays of sunlight streaked into the natural amphitheater from above, enclosing them in golden light.

"What is this, Denia?" he asked. "What is this place?"

"I'm not sure. When I was young and used to come to the turtle pond with my aunt, this was all open. The willow trees were not here then. It was just an outcrop of rocks near the pond."

"This place is being used for something. These pedestals with the candles indicate that it's being used in the evening or at night. This burnt wood is not that old. The fire pit has been used recently."

"Was Melinda using it?" she asked, thinking out loud.

"These could have been her candles, but she never mentioned anything to me about using this grotto."

Then after a pause, "How well did you know your aunt, Denia?"

She took a minute to answer. "You probably knew her better than I did. I used to come here to visit during the summers when I was a girl. Then my mother and Melinda had some kind of falling out. I was never allowed to come up here after I turned eleven, so it was a long time since I had seen my aunt when she died. We got along very well when I was young. I used to look forward to coming here. As an adult, I never came up here, to my regret now. I really didn't know my aunt other than my childhood memories. I was shocked when I learned that she had left the ranch to me in her estate."

"This place could be some kind of a clue to her murder," he said looking around.

"You know that it's a murder investigation?" Denia asked with surprise.

"Yes, Nelson told me. I was one of the first people to be interviewed and give a statement to the police. I had spoken to her about the dog the evening before she was found. Also, I was on the property almost every day. From the questioning I quickly guessed there were more than health reasons to Mel's death, and Lee confirmed it."

"Maybe I should ask Batty and Olivia about this place," she mused. "They have that little ladies club going."

"You should. There's something strange here that is not obvious to us."

"What would that have to do with the prowlers last night?" she asked.

"I'm not sure. See what you can find out from Batty."

Then after a pause, "Maybe your mother knows something that she's not told you about."

"Maybe…," she said thinking about her mother for the first time.

"Well, I need to get my horse and get back to the fields we're harvesting. I'll call Nelson later."

They walked in silence back across the field to the front of the garage. The horse had wandered over toward the hillside and was still grazing the field grass. They said goodbye and split up, with Keith whistling for his horse and Denia walking to the front of the house. She had mixed feelings about the man, but he had brought up some good points. There was something she was missing.

When she got into the house, she found Dragon stretched along one end of the sofa, the puppy asleep at the other end, and Mona on her windowsill rug. The door handles were changed, and the bolt locks installed. Dragon sat up straight when she came in.

"Snowy left the plans for the outdoor lighting on the counter," he reported. "The electrician will call you with an estimate. Snowy and I can help install the lights once the wiring is figured out."

"Okay," Denia replied, thinking that the lighting and the fencing updates could be expensive.

"I needed to talk to you about something," he said seriously, standing up to face her. "My mother actually wanted me to stay here with you."

"What?" Denia exclaimed with astonishment.

"Not here exactly. I can sleep in the bunkhouse or the barn. Just so there is someone here at night, so you're not alone out here. I have my sleeping bag in the car."

Denia looked at him with skepticism.

"I won't bother you. You won't even know I'm here."

Denia thought back to the previous night. It had been disconcerting. There were no nearby neighbors. She really was alone out here. It had taken a few minutes for the deputy to get here last night after she had called for help. Maybe having someone on the property she could depend on would be a benefit. She thought Batty probably did care more about her welfare than her urge to get her son out of the house. Even though the man's looks were rather absurd to her, she sensed a good-natured person underneath and trusted his mother.

"That might work out. Let's go look at the bunkhouse and see if it's doable," Denia replied, tentatively.

They walked out to the barn with Angus in tow, who was quickly joined by Billy, his new best friend. The bunkhouse was ancient and built onto the side of the barn, originally a place for farmhands. Denia opened a squeaky screen door with rusted hinges, used to allow fresh air in on warm days prior to air conditioning. The wooden door stood open to find Jorje sitting in the main room. Denia knew he used this space during the day when he was not working. She introduced Dragon and explained that he was going to be staying here at night. Jorje agreed with the plan. The old man had been worried about Denia's safety since she got here.

The bunkhouse had originally been one big room, and had been somewhat modified at some point in time. Just inside the door was a counter with a kitchen sink in the middle over a small window. There was a cupboard in the corner, and a modern coffee maker. A small refrigerator, with a microwave sitting on top stood next to the counter. A small wooden table hosted two chairs. The living space - that used to house bunkbeds – now had a brown recliner that Jorje used, and a rather well-used sofa. A large square coffee table filled the middle space.

Denia led Dragon through the space to see a very small, but efficient bathroom next to the kitchen. The box of a shower, a toilet, and sink hanging from the wall, were fixtures of an earlier time. They moved to the doorway across from the bathroom where a small bedroom had been walled off, with one window looking out onto the back field. A bed took up the far corner of the room.

"Boy, this place really needs to be painted," said Denia, looking at the peeling walls.

"That would be a good project for me, while I'm staying here. A little work could make this place look a lot better," said Dragon.

"Are you sure you want to try staying here?" Denia asked.

"Sure," he said. "This is not that bad, actually. I would have as much space here as I have at Mom's place."

"Okay," said Denia, "go get your stuff."

Denia left the bunkhouse hoping she had made the right decision about letting Dragon stay at the ranch. She could always ask him to leave if any problems developed. The one thing she feared was the lack of privacy, and all her actions being reported back to Batty. She liked Batty and Olivia, and felt that their concern for her was genuine, but she did not like the idea of everyone knowing her business. She felt smothered by all the attention, well-meaning as it was.

Olivia pulled into the parking space and got out of her car. She walked toward the office door, where Denia met her. The new door locks were open, and Denia explained that all the keys were in the kitchen. Denia excused herself to use the powder room, not having a break for hours. Olivia disappeared into the small business office.

"I can't find anything missing but the picture and the computer," she reported to Denia a few minutes later. "I don't understand why they would want an old computer like that one. Mel was going to buy me a new one but hadn't got around to it."

"Maybe they were just trying to sabotage the business now that Melinda's gone," said Denia. "Was there anyone who had expressed a problem with Candlewick?"

"There *were* some negative online messages about the business due to some of our merchandise. Some people felt that a few of the items we offered were controversial, or what they called non-Christian."

"You mean offensive? Candles?"

"No, no," Olivia said with impatience, "more like paganistic."

"Paganistic?" repeated Denia, questioning.

"Candles are used very heavily in many Pagan rituals."

"Oh," said Denia, starting to see a picture coming together in her mind.

"Don't Pagans celebrate at Stonehenge for the spring solstice?" Denia asked.

"Many different sects celebrate the spring solstice, not just Pagans," said Olivia.

"Do you think the controversy grew into the burglary against the business?"

"I wouldn't think so. I just think it was some kind of nut trying to make a statement."

"How did you know about any controversy?" Denia probed.

"There were e-mails that came in through our customer service mail on the website."

"A lot of them?"

"Not a lot, just occasional e-mails."

"Do you know who was sending them?"

"No, they were signed with weird names like *'Watching*

You' and *'We Believe'*."

"That sounds threatening. Does Sergeant Nelson know about this? He has Mel's computer in evidence right now."

"No. We never thought it was important. Mel just dismissed it, and so did I," Olivia said.

"I think I should tell him about this. It may be important. People can do strange things or act out when they feel they are enforcing their religious beliefs."

"What are all these jars in these boxes?" she asked, changing the subject.

"Believe it or not, all of these came out of the pantry. I was thinking we could use them to make some candles in jars for fall."

"That's a good idea. I can help you get the wax ready. It would get you started."

"Oh, I forgot," Denia said, reaching her hand into her pocket and pulling out the small, rectangular magnet that she had found at the gate of the vineyard that morning. "Wasn't this on your computer monitor?"

"My runes list!" she exclaimed with recognition. "Yes, this is mine."

"I found it on the ground by the gate of the back vineyard. It's pretty clear that was how the burglars left the property with the computer and the picture last night. What is it?" Denia ask, referring to the rectangular strip that Olivia was now holding.

"It's the rune alphabet. There are twenty-four of them. It's ancient Teutonic script. Each symbol has a meaning.

We use them on some of our Candlewick labels just to add mystique," Olivia explained. "Well, I need to get home. My husband is coming home from his fishing trip this afternoon. I'm sure he'll want to have fresh fish for dinner."

Olivia left rather abruptly, leaving Denia to stare after her. The entire conversation with Olivia had been strange and left her with nothing but questions. She walked out into the yard, watching the puppy run rings around the goat. She called the puppy, and both the goat and the puppy ran to her.

"Sorry, Billy, I don't have any carrots today," she said patting the goat on the head.

Jorje came out to get the goat and put her in the pen for a while since she had been out almost all day. Denia picked up the little dog and stood looking at the back of the house.

There were no windows on the first floor that overlooked the back lot. There were two windows on the second story, that looked out from Melinda's bedroom. For the first time Denia noticed an oddity.

When in the bedroom, the windows appeared to be centered on the far wall, but from the outside, they appeared to be closer to one side and not centered on the outside wall. Envisioning the second-floor layout of the house, Denia realized there was something wrong, something she was not seeing.

With purpose she walked directly to the house. After putting Angus in his crate, Denia went up the stairs to the second-floor landing and walked directly to the doorway of the quiet, unused bedroom.

Stepping into the room she examined the walls. The wall with windows overlooking the drive followed the outside wall of the house. Then she moved to the windowed wall looking out onto the back lot. When looking through the window to the outside wall, Denia could see that the end of the room's interior wall did not match the outside wall by several feet. She wondered why she had never noticed this before. Maybe it was the large tree behind the house that shaded the parking area and obscured the view of the back wall of the house. Now, she stood at the foot of the bed staring at the offending wall. She knew this wall did not line up with the exterior bathroom wall on the other side of the staircase.

A long dresser of dark wood was the main piece of furniture centered on the wall next to the wide closet with mirrored, sliding doors. Two, elongated mirrors framed in the same dark wood as the dresser had scrolled accents at the top and were hung evenly spaced on the wall above the dresser with its three banks of wide drawers.

Denia went to the closet and slid open one of the doors. She had come to expect a crammed, unorganized space as was true with all the rest of the closets in this house, but this closet was far more orderly. Dresses, skirts, blouses, and pants hung in an organized fashion from the long bar, with the shelves above filled with neatly stacked shoe boxes of various sizes. She closed the door and opened its counterpart, revealing clothing of a different fashion. Velvets, silks, laces, billowing sleeves, lacings, tiered and ruffled long skirts and dresses. There were several, reversible cloaks with hoods and of varied lengths that hung at the far end. Denia placed her hand on the last garment pushing the clothing away from the closet wall.

There it was. The crack at the back of the closet running vertically from the overhead shelf to the floorboards. Taking a deep breath, Denia pushed against the panel, feeling the easy movement, providing an opening to an unknown darkness. She ducked her head slightly and stepped through the portal.

As Denia stepped into the small room about the size of a bathroom, there was so much to take in that she did not realize she was holding her breath. Afternoon light filtered through tree branches and flowed into the room from a large round skylight in the roof. The entire ceiling around the skylight was a midnight blue and painted with stars. The top of the walls depicted a repeating row of the moons, in the many phases that appeared through the monthly cycles. The walls of the room showed a dark background with hand-painted natural scenes. There were snowcapped, spiked mountain peaks, ocean waves spilling onto a beach, a tornado dipping toward the ground from a mass of gray clouds, a volcano spouting its fiery plumes.

Denia walked to a small desk and chair sitting in one corner. An inkwell sat on the desktop with a plumed, blue pen beside it. Black, leather-bound books with golden suns and stars on their covers sat on the desk. She picked up the closest volume, opening it to the center. Handwritten scrolls of writing filled the pages: *Chant for a Summer's Eve, Charm to Purify Water*, and *Poem for the Hunter's Moon*. She flipped to the front of the book and examined the title page.

Book of Shadows
Vol. 3

Melinda Kelly Greystone
High Priestess of the Doves

An old trunk was centered on the far wall, covered with a golden lace cloth. Towers of candles of different colors, decorated with symbols, were strategically placed on the four corners of the trunk's surface. A heavy, embossed, pewter chalice sat on the surface next to a round, six-inch, turquoise saucer with a five- pointed pentagram etched into the pottery. A wooden wand with an engraved handle, inset with crystals, lay next to the saucer.

Denia's hand came to her mouth as the meaning of the room became clear. The secret discovered…Melinda Greystone was a witch!

She stood for several minutes putting it all together.

'Many different sects celebrate the spring solstice', Olivia had said.

"Oh, my God," Denia whispered out loud, "They are *all* witches."

She left the secret room and went downstairs with determination. Finding her cell phone lying on the kitchen counter, she searched for the picture of her mother and placed the call. Not surprised when the call went to her mother's voice mail, she calmly left the message, "Mom, there are some strange things happening up here. I need you to call me tonight. We need to have a talk about Aunt Melinda."

9

THE DOVES

Denia made herself some chicken and fresh zucchini for dinner. Even though her emotions were jumbled, she had not eaten anything but toast since morning, and was really hungry. She was mentally and physically exhausted with the little sleep she got last night and the events of the day. So much had happened since yesterday.

She sat alone, thinking, reflecting, in the now different atmosphere of her aunt's living room. Everything had changed and it hung in the air. There was the scare from the prowler, the discovery of the burglary, the questioning from Keith Clearwater about the use of the grotto, and the installation of Dragon in the bunkhouse.

By far, the overwhelming event of the day was

Melinda's hidden room and its implications of witchcraft - not to mention learning that the people she had so recently embraced as friends were also witches.

Isis jumped up onto the sofa next to her, offering little mewing sounds of comfort. Denia found herself absentmindedly petting the cat. Feeling the soft fur slipping through her fingertips, Denia spoke to the cat.

"A black cat belonging to a witch – that's just classic."

Denia had never had a cat in her life, but the ranch was the home of Isis and Mona, and they belonged here. She would care for them for her Auntie, and for herself, as an offering of love. Both cats seemed to have adjusted to her being there.

Her cell phone rang, breaking the quiet of the room. Denia saw it was the call from her mother she was expecting.

"Hi, Mom," she answered.

"Denia, what's going on? The message you left was a little frightening. Are you alright?"

"We had a burglary of the office building last night. I had to call the police. Some things were stolen."

"I don't like you being all alone out there at night. Jorje goes home at night, doesn't he?"

"He *does* go home at night, but even if he didn't, he's in his seventies, Mom. I'd be more worried about something happening to *him* than for myself. Anyway, I'm not by myself, now. One of Melinda's friends has a son that's ex-military. He moved into the old bunkhouse today, so I'm not alone here at night. We also changed all the locks on the doors today and added dead bolts," she paused. "That's not why I called you, though. I need to talk to you about Aunt Melinda. Do you know anything about her practicing witchcraft?"

Silence came from the other end of the call.

"Mom, I know about it. I found a secret room Auntie had behind her closet. It contains some of the things she used to practice her magic. You need to tell me what you know about this. Is this why you didn't want me to move up here?"

More silence from her mother's end. Denia thought she could hear her mother crying.

"I need you to talk to me, Mom. This may have something to do with Auntie's murder, and some of the things that are going on around here. You need to tell me what you know about this," Denia said in a demanding tone.

"Yes, I knew Melinda had gotten into witchcraft. I've known for a long time," she admitted. "That *was* the reason your father and I decided not to allow you to go up there and stay with her when you were younger. We didn't want you to find out about it or be involved with it. I always hoped my sister would realize how crazy her paganism was, but she just seemed to become more dedicated as time went by. I knew of her lady friends and guessed they were a secret coven. They had become her family. Her whole life revolved around her spiritual beliefs and her friends."

"How did you first find out about it?" Denia asked.

"To understand, you need to know something of her history. Melinda married a man who was fifteen years older than her when she was twenty-eight. They appeared to have a very happy marriage even though they could not have children. Jim had been injured in his job as a firefighter and was able to retire early with a good pension. They moved to central California and bought the ranch a couple years after going up there. He died suddenly of a heart attack when he was only fifty-two. You were just a toddler at the time," Denia's mother related from her memory.

"Melinda was crushed. I was really worried about her. She was only thirty-seven, so we all thought she was young enough to go back to work and eventually remarry. I encouraged her to sell the ranch and move to San Diego to be near us. She said she would think about it, but she could never let go of the ranch and her memories of Jim.

"She talked about going back to teaching, which she had really loved prior to getting married. She did some substituting at a junior high school for a while, but her heart was just not in it," Denia's mother lamented.

"Her outlook on life changed drastically, and she was a lost soul for a while. After a couple years she decided to go back to school and get her Master's degree in English literature. She was very enthusiastic about it – the first real enthusiasm she had shown since Jim's death – I was happy for her.

"During that time Melinda also started to travel. That was when I first noticed a change in her. She would go on what she called 'retreats' in various states - New Mexico, Washington, New Hampshire - usually out in the woods or mountains somewhere. She talked about her teachers in 'nature appreciation', who came from all different areas of the country. By that time, she had pretty much come to terms with the grief she had the first few years after Jim's passing."

"Mom, what about the witchcraft?" Denia prodded.

"I'm getting to it," her mother said, impatiently. "One summer – you were about five – she went to England for eight weeks to take an anthropology course offered by one of the universities over there. She came back totally enthralled with the place. The course was on the ancient people of the British Isles. She visited all the ancient historical sites. This became her new passion, and she continued her studies when she came home."

"When did you find out about the witchcraft?" Denia interrupted, wanting to get to the point.

"You had been going up to visit Melinda every summer. Daddy and I would take a vacation while you were there. Sometimes you stayed for over a month, not wanting to come home," Helene continued.

"I remember you were eleven that summer, and Daddy and I had gone on an Alaskan cruise. That day, we had driven all the way from Oregon to Solvang to pick you up on the way home. It was already evening when we got there, and Daddy was tired from driving. We checked into the hotel, and I told Dad I would go out to the ranch, stay the night, and bring you back in the morning so we could get an early start for home.

"I'm not sure what time it was when I got to the ranch, but I remember it was already late. The back door was open when I came in. I remember there were candles burning on the dining room table. The house smelled of incense. I went upstairs to use the bathroom and found you already asleep in your bed. I discovered that Melinda was not in her room or in the house. She was boarding horses back then, so I figured she was probably out in the barn for some reason.

"I went downstairs and made myself a sandwich and got something to drink – we hadn't had any dinner. When I finished eating, Melinda still wasn't back, so I found a flashlight and decided to go find her. There were extra cars parked out back, but I really didn't think anything about it at the time. I went out to the barn, but she wasn't there. Walking back to the house I thought I heard voices, like singing, but it wasn't singing. I realized the sound was coming from across the field and noticed lights up by the turtle pond. I started going across the field, soon realizing that it was a group of women with candles. Melinda stood at the front of the group facing me, she stopped the chanting, surprised when she recognized me. All the other women turned around to face me," Helene said, her voice dropping to almost a whisper remembering the traumatic night.

"I stood a few yards from them trying to understand what I was seeing. The full moon was high in the sky that night, with the rocks in the background and the moonlight shimmering on the pond. Even though it was a warm evening, the women were all wearing cloaks with hoods. I remember how beautiful my sister looked in the moonlight and the candlelight. Her hair was flowing, and she wore a jeweled circlet around her forehead. She was taller than the rest of the women, wearing a long, light-colored dress cinched at the waist with a silver belt under her cloak.

When I realized that they were in the middle of some sort of ceremony I turned and ran across the field to the house.”

“Mom, that must have been shocking. I know how I felt when I found the secret room today. You should see it.”

“She came back to the house after a little while,” Helene continued. “Melinda very calmly told me that she was a practicing witch. We had a bitter, angry, argument. Sisters can be brutal when they argue. I sat on the sofa all night until the sun came up and then went upstairs, woke you, and gathered all your things. We left before Melinda was up. You had known something was wrong, but I didn’t tell you anything. We met your father in Solvang and drove home to San Diego.”

“Melinda and I didn’t talk again until Christmas when she called me. I told her I did not agree with her new lifestyle and that you would no longer be permitted to visit her. She said she was very sorry but this was who she was, and she would live her life the way she wanted. Over the years we gradually started talking more frequently and had a fairly good relationship in the end; but it excluded any discussion of the witchcraft. That topic was off limits.”

“So, this is what our separation with my aunt was all about,” stated Denia.

“Yes. Your father and I discussed it and thought it was better for you not to be exposed to it. As you got older and could have understood, I really didn’t want to ruin your fond memories of Melinda. She was my sister and I still cared about her. I would see her now and then, whenever I traveled to northern California for work. I never went out to the ranch again, though…”

"Thanks for telling me, Mom," Denia said with sincerity, knowing that the telling had been difficult for her mother. "I believe this had something to do with Melinda's murder. I'm not sure how it fits in, but at least now I know that some of the undercurrents around here are exposed."

"I don't want to think about witchcraft having anything to do with my sister's murder," Helene said. "It makes me even more fearful of you being up there by yourself."

Then after a rather long pause when neither spoke, "What about your car? Did you ever get it back?" her mother asked changing the subject.

"Not yet. They called and said it would probably be Thursday before it would be ready. I got Aunt Melinda's Range Rover registered into my name. I have that to drive if I need it."

"I want you to call us at least once a week, so we know you're alright. You don't have to stay there, you know. You can always come home."

"Now you're sounding like a mom, Mom," Denia replied, "but I'll try to call more often. Say 'hi' to Dad for me."

"Okay, love you, honey," said her mother. "Good night, Mom."

After the call, Denia thought over the conversation with her mother. It was sad to think her parents allowed Melinda's beliefs to cause such a rift in the small family. Obviously, Melinda was secretive about her practices, and probably wouldn't have exposed a young niece to anything controversial, especially knowing her sister would disapprove. Enough of this, she thought, she needed to go to bed.

On a last trip outside with Angus, Denia could see the dim, yellow light coming through the small, bunkhouse window, affirming that Dragon was there. Once back inside, she took satisfaction in making sure all the new locks were secured prior to making her way upstairs.

The next morning was Tuesday - egg day. Denia was once again up early due to her small, brown, roommate, but felt rested. Once in bed the previous night she had fallen into a deep, dreamless sleep. This morning after some coffee, an egg, and sourdough toast, Denia and Angus were out the back door ready for the day. She saw that Jorje had already arrived and one barn door stood open. She decided to take care of the chicken coop herself and get the stored eggs ready for the trip to town.

On the spur of the moment, Denia thought she would pick some of the late, ripening boysenberries from the heavy vines growing along the fence. Most of the crop's bounty was over, with July being the usual end of the season, but these vines faced east getting the morning sun, so some berries were still ripening. She found a plastic dishpan on a lower shelf in the pantry and spent the next half hour filling it with the purple fruit, native to California.

Almost finished, she heard the phone ringing in the house and ran to answer the call.

"Hello?" she said, using a long reach to get to the receiver on the landline.

"Denia, this is Lee Nelson," he said identifying himself.

"Oh, hi," she answered, "What's up?"

"I was wondering if you could come by the office this morning. There are a couple things I need to talk to you about."

"Actually, I was just getting ready to come into town to drop off some eggs."

"That's good. I'll be in the office all morning. Come by when you are finished with your errands."

"Okay. I'll see you then," she said, hanging up the phone.

She had some apprehension as to what the sergeant wanted to talk to her about. Was it something they found in her aunt's computer or the phone? Her thinking was interrupted when Angus, who followed her into the kitchen, came face-to-face with Mona who immediately took a swipe, with claws-out, at the puppy's ear.

"Stop it, you two!" she yelled at the animals. "Mona, he's here to stay. Get used to it."

Denia loaded the undaunted, enthusiastic lab into his kitchen crate, much to Mona's satisfaction. Soon, the Range Rover was loaded with eggs and the tub of boysenberries, and Denia was off to town.

Denia's first, solo, egg delivery went well. Marci Siegel made a fuss over Denia, and the idea of bringing the fresh berries. Denia learned that Melinda had often brought containers of berries to the restaurant, not wanting them to go to waste. Marci said she would add a little something to the monthly check for the eggs. Denia insisted it was not necessary, but Marci went on about how they could use the fresh berries to dress up breakfast plates and desserts.

Shortly after leaving the restaurant, arriving at the sheriff's station, she took the last remaining parking space at the front of the building. Before getting out of the car she cracked open the windows, knowing the interior of the car would heat up quickly in the hot August sun.

Once inside, a red-haired, female officer in uniform led Denia back to the sergeant's familiar, little office. The desk was unchanged, holding piles of folders. The good-looking policeman was on the phone and motioned to Denia to take a seat on one of the chairs in front of the desk.

"How are you doing?" he asked after hanging up the phone.

"Okay, hoping for a little less drama this week," she answered.

"Yeah, I guess it has been an eventful two weeks since you got here.

"I never realized how dull my life *was* living in San Diego," she commented with some sarcasm.

They shared a laugh.

The man's face became serious and said, "I wanted to see you for a couple reasons."

He brushed the blonde hair across his forehead and continued, "First of all, we are finished with Melinda's computer, and I wanted to give it back to you. We were able to get into the files and could not find anything we thought would be an investigative lead. She seemed to use it strictly for the business. We had to set a new password on it – it's 'Melinda'."

He took the laptop, still in the plastic evidence bag, and handed it back to Denia.

The desktop phone rang as he was sitting back down, and he excused himself to answer it. As he spoke on the phone Denia looked around the office noting that there seemed to be few personal effects. There were no pictures or anything other than work related items. Cluttered though the desk was, it was an organized clutter, everything had its place within easy reach.

The man's uniform was neatly pressed with the top button of his shirt open. He wore no jewelry other than a watch. He gazed out the rectangular, office window with its open, venetian blind as he spoke on the phone, flicking a pencil in his free hand. Denia was not sure but thought that the sergeant was not married. Maybe because he was already married to the job.

When the call ended, he once again turned his attention to Denia.

"About the burglary out at your place, I think whoever did this was professional. Not only does it look like they wore gloves, but it seems that they wiped down all the surfaces. The door, door frame, and desktop had no fingerprints at all, which is not what you would expect. There should have been your fingerprints, Olivia's, and whoever else had recently been in the office building. We would have had to fingerprint all of you to determine if there were some useful prints for the robbery - but there's no point now."

"When you say 'professional' what do you mean?"

Denia asked trying to verify what she suspected.

"Whoever broke into the office building was aware the police would check for fingerprints and took steps to avoid leaving any evidence," he explained. "Did you get new locks installed yet?"

"Yes, yesterday, on the house and the office building."

He nodded his approval.

"I also wanted to talk to you about the incident last week when you were run off the road. We've arrested the person we think was responsible," he said.

"Really?" Denia asked with surprise.

"Yes, he was arrested out on Route 246 last night for illegal street racing. He was driving the same truck as you described, which we impounded. He's still being held at the Santa Maria station. When I heard about the black, Ram truck, I asked the Santa Maria staff to check the right, front grill. They found that not only was the grill damaged, but they were able to get blue, paint samples off the grill. We're having them tested now, but we're pretty sure they'll match your Explorer. I have the guy's booking photos here, and I wanted you to look at them to see if you could identify him as the person who hit your car from behind."

He turned his computer monitor so she could see the pictures.

Denia took her time looking at the photos. Staring back at her was a man younger than herself with a narrow face, long, thin nose, thin-lipped mouth and short, black hair. His eyes were dark and defiant, topped with black, curved brows.

"There is no way I could identify him," said Denia, still looking at the pictures. "He does fit with what I remember, seeing the driver through the rear-view mirror, but I could never be sure enough to identify him in court."

"That's okay," said the sergeant, "I'm going over there this afternoon to try confronting him. We'll see what he has to say when I tell him we took the paint off the grill of the truck. We can prosecute this without your identification, but if it goes to court you would have to testify as to what happened."

"I think I could do that," replied Denia.

"Well, we may not need that if I can get him to admit to it. Sometimes we can convince someone that it's in their best interest to admit to an offense rather than go to trial," he said, standing up behind his desk, indicating he had said all he had to say to her.

Denia stood to leave.

"Oh, by the way," he said remembering another thought, "Keith said you found something from the computer out by the gates to the vineyard on your land yesterday?"

"Yes, it was a little magnet Olivia had on the side of the computer monitor. Keith and I both thought the burglars probably went out that gate. He was going to put a lock on it. I'm also getting an estimate for some outside lighting around the back of the house."

"Sounds good. We'll continue to patrol the road at night out there. Be sure to call me if you notice anything unusual. Sometimes it's just a little something that may seem insignificant which helps the pieces fall into place."

The tall policeman walked her to the front door of the station, giving her reassurances on the way out.

After leaving the police station Denia marveled at how quiet the town was on a Tuesday. There was little traffic on Mission Drive, and Denia saw an almost empty, public parking lot. No hordes of tourists were crossing streets or milling around on the sidewalks. She enjoyed looking at the provincial architecture of the buildings along the street, many with leaded and stained-glass windows.

Denia knew the town was famous for the *bindingsvaerk*, a Danish term meaning 'part timber', which is reflected in the wood strips applied to the outside walls of the buildings as accents. Sharply pointed roofs of different colored tiles or aged copper provide added character as one scanned the tight knit rows of hotels and businesses. Signage for the multitude of small shops and eateries were painted over doorways and hung from shingles in old world script. Denia decided to park the car and check out a small shop displaying women's clothing. She felt she had nothing to wear for her Friday night date with Eugene.

Once in the store, looking through the clothes rack near the door, Denia was trying to decide what she wanted, but noticed most of the clothes were for small sizes. An older saleslady assured her they carried all sizes and led Denia to an area in the store with more appropriate sizes for her. She had some nice, black slacks at home and zeroed in on some blouses that were not overly casual. She wanted something she could wear for the fall season; yet the weather was still warm and would remain so throughout September, as was the norm for California.

She picked a lightweight, flowing blouse with three-quarter, see-through sleeves. The splashes of color were shades of gold, which would go well with Denia's auburn hair.

Back at the ranch, she dealt with some needed phone calls. An appointment was made to get the TV working by getting the cable installed, and to install internet in the house. Speaking with the electrician, Denia found that he would be out on Thursday to complete the wiring for the outside lighting. Lastly, she left a message on Batty's home phone regarding the Candlewick accounts and the need to replace the stolen computer. She spent most of the afternoon out back with the puppy and Billy. She used a rake to do some clean-up around the back lot and brought a few tomatoes and more zucchini into the kitchen.

That evening she was tired but felt the day had been successful. Angus loved having the run of the house under Denia's supervision. Isis was aware the puppy could not yet climb the stairs and would saunter upstairs to escape him as she pleased. Mona refused to give up the spot on the sofa and would bat at the dog with a paw when his curiosity brought him too close.

Denia was sitting at the small desk under the stairs with the drawer of the file cabinet open, searching for the house insurance policy and any documents on the Stonehenge painting, when the phone rang.

"Hello, Denia?" came Batty's voice.

"Hi, Batty, did you get my message?"

"Yes, I heard it when I got home from work, but I just now had a chance to call you back."

"I'm worried we may be getting behind with the candle orders, and I really need to get a better understanding of the business. Now, with Olivia's computer gone, I think we should get it replaced right away, but I don't know where to begin. Do we have money in the accounts to buy a new one? I think I would like to get a laptop with a docking station and monitor. We had those where I used to work and it would be more versatile for Olivia," explained Denia.

"Yes, there is plenty of money in the account to replace the computer. I can call Snowy about it if you want and have him order one. He is up on all the latest systems and will set it up for us when it's delivered," said Batty.

Then for clarification, "So, Denia, are you thinking you want to continue the candle business?"

"I *would* like to try to keep the business going if you and Olivia are willing to help me until I can get my feet on the ground. You would both be on the payroll, of course," Denia replied. "I've never made a candle in my life, but I would like to try. I already have ideas for making some candles with an autumn theme."

"We will definitely help you, but there are some things we need to discuss," said Batty with a very serious tone. "The Doves would like to meet with you. So far, you have only met Olivia and me. You know we were all close to Mel and there are some things you need to know before you go forward. You may decide you would like to take a different course once you meet with us."

Denia wondered if Batty was referring to the witchcraft.

"I agree I do need to meet all of you. How about

Saturday evening?" she offered.

"I think that will be fine but let me check with everyone and get back to you," said Batty.

"Okay," said Denia, not knowing what else to say. "Good night, then."

The phone went dead.

That was the most strained conversation Denia had with Batty since she met her. She hadn't even asked about her son, Dragon, currently installed in Denia's back yard. Did she somehow know Denia had knowledge of the Doves and their true relationship with Melinda? Was she worried that witchcraft had something to do with her aunt's murder after the theft of the Stonehenge painting?

Yes, Denia thought, it was time that she met all the Doves - the rest of the coven.

If Denia thought having Dragon living on the ranch would be intrusive, she could not have been more wrong. It was Thursday evening and she had not seen the missing man since Monday. His car would be gone in the morning, not returning until evening. She knew he was there at night because she would see the lights coming from the bunkhouse when she took Angus out for his last potty-patrol before going to bed at night.

Speak of the devil. After dinner she heard a knock at the back door and opened it to see the man with the spiky hair.

"Where have you been?" she asked ushering him in the

door.

"Oh, my mother is trying to ruin my life," he bemoaned, looking worn-out as he leaned against the kitchen counter.

"Batty? What do you mean?"

"First, she throws me out of the condo, saying she doesn't want you staying here alone at night. Then last Saturday night while she's working at an event up at the Samala Winery, she runs into Kristen Clearwater who tells her she needs a day manager for the wine press, since Keith is starting the harvest.

"Naturally, my mother offers my services. Mom called me Monday night and told me to be at the plant the next morning. I've been out of work since I quit my last job up in San Luis Obispo, which was costing me more than I was making. I worked at the winery the year before last during the harvest, so I know the drill. It's a lot of work over a short period of time, until all the grapes are in and pressed. At least it will give me a chance to get out of the hole and get some money saved."

"So that's where you've been all day," said Denia with understanding. "It does sound like a good opportunity, and the harvest doesn't last forever."

"Yeah, at least the pay is good. Anyway, I was wondering if I could use the washer and dryer in the office building. I've pretty much run out of clean clothes and dread the thought of trying to find a laundromat in town."

"Sure, go ahead."

"I need a key to get in."

"Oh, yeah."

Denia made her way to the pantry, finding the shiny, new, brass key for the office building.

Returning and handing the key to Dragon, she asked, "Can you check on Billy out in the barn for me?"

"No problem," he said. "Do you want me to take him out with me and let him run around while I'm doing the wash?" indicating the puppy who was pawing at Dragon's pant leg, wanting attention.

"Yeah, good idea. Get him tired out before bedtime."

"I'll bring him back in a little while."

Denia closed the door behind the two, smiling to herself. She liked Dragon and felt comfortable with him. She was glad he was there at night. As for the puppy, she wondered how he was ever going to be a good watchdog, when he seemed to love everyone who came near him.

Friday morning, she found herself a little anxious about the approaching date with Eugene Sorenson. She tried to go about the normal tasks of the day. She went into town and delivered more eggs, had sets of keys made, and checked on her Explorer, which was still not ready to be brought home. Next to the auto garage was an American Cancer Society thrift shop, displaying a large, overstuffed green chair in the window.

"What the hell," she said to herself, thinking that the chair would look perfect next to the fireplace where the old console TV had been.

She went into the shop and found the chair was being sold for seventy-five dollars and made an on-the-spot decision to buy it. She also found a round, wooden, table lamp that would fit beside it. After much ado from her, the saleslady, and a male Filipino clerk, the chair and table were loaded into the Range Rover, the back hatch of the car secured with a rope.

Once home, she parked by the front door, and managed to get the lamp table into the house. Fortunately, the cable guy showed up for the one o'clock appointment and helped her drag the large chair into the living room through the front door. While the man worked on getting the TV and internet installed, Denia cleaned the table, moved the crystal lamp from the buffet, and positioned the table and chair in an inviting spot between the fireplace and the window. She stood back, admiring the new addition to the room.

As she looked at her watch, a full-blown flock of butterflies hit her stomach regarding the plans for the evening, and her first real date since the end of her relationship with Jeff. Denia tried to talk herself out of being nervous. After all, it was just a dinner date. She made her plans for the time she needed to leave for the restaurant. She would have to feed the animals and have time to take the puppy out before she left. She also needed time to shower, put on make-up, get dressed, and do something with her hair. Denia decided to wear her black, open-toed, sling-backed shoes, as a thousand thoughts ran through her mind. By the time she got into the Range Rover to leave, she felt some confidence of looking her best, and being ready to face the evening.

As she drove through Solvang, she could see the weekend excitement was already underway with a slow line of traffic heading into town, and people standing outside of restaurants waiting for their tables. Denia had no trouble finding *The Grill and the Grape* and made a left turn into the driveway which led to a large, busy, parking lot behind the building. A back patio extended from the building, holding many occupied tables which formed a semi-circle around a small stage. A guitar player sat on the elevated platform playing formal, Spanish guitar music into a standing mic. Denia looked across the sea of tables, and saw Eugene stand up and wave to her. She made her way to a table near the back of the patio, where the man with luscious, brown eyes pulled the chair out for her.

Denia was relieved she had dressed in slacks, as the handsome man wore a button-down, blue, silk shirt and dark blue, casual slacks. It was the first time she had seen him not wearing a suit. A half-finished glass of wine sat on the table. Another glass of what looked like a rose wine was waiting for her.

After greetings were exchanged, he asked, "Did you have any problems finding the place? I went ahead and ordered you a glass of wine."

"Thank you, no, I'm starting to find my way around," she answered. "I was actually out here today checking on my car in the shop down the road near the freeway."

"Having car troubles?" he asked taking a sip of wine.

"Oh, that's right, you didn't know about what happened."

He looked at her with interest.

"Remember when we had lunch and you told me about the shortcut through the pass to Solvang? Well, I ended up taking the pass that day, and some guy ran me off the road. It was pretty terrifying at the time. So, the car is still in the shop being repaired."

"My God, that's just terrible," said Eugene. "Were you hurt? Did the police get the guy?"

"I was more shaken up than hurt, but it looks like the police may have found the guy."

"Do you need a lawyer?" he asked with a charming smile.

Denia laughed.

"I thought I already had a lawyer," she quipped back, and they both laughed.

The hostess approached the table, ignoring Denia, and made the most of leaning over to tell Eugene that their table inside was ready. Denia followed the hostess and Eugene, wine glass in hand, weaving through the outdoor tables and into the dimly lit interior of the restaurant.

Once seated, they both opened the large menus enclosed in brown leather. Denia was hungry, since she had skipped lunch due to the busy afternoon; but while looking at the dinner choices she was rather shocked to see the cost of the meals.

As if reading her mind, he said, "They have excellent beef here. It's a little pricy but definitely worth it. I think I'm going to have the steak and duck combination. Feel free to order whatever you would like."

"Thank you. They have a wonderful selection," she said,

continuing to peruse the list as she took a sip of the wine.

An overly attentive waiter, dressed in black-on-black, came to take the food order while providing them with a tray of warm rolls and butter. Both ordered steak with Denia ordering the four-ounce filet, served with steamed vegetables. Eugene ordered a bottle of a local, merlot, red wine to accompany the meal.

As they waited for their dinner and munched on the rolls, Denia took in the restaurant's upscale atmosphere as Eugene talked about a recent trip to Seattle. The cozy floor plan provided some intimacy. Their table sat before an unlit, stone fireplace with a thick wooden mantle. Dark, tan tablecloths topped the tables, with forest green napkins that corresponded with the green detail on the white dishes. The walls were covered with a beige, textured wallpaper above the chair rail and a warm, wood paneling encasing the lower half of the walls. Brushed brass chandeliers were hung strategically with dim lighting coming from the half-globes of antique-style, frosted glass. Sconces of the same style dotted the walls at intervals.

Once the food arrived, they had a relaxing meal. Denia felt herself unwinding as the intoxicating wine had its effect. Banter went back and forth, Denia finding she could hold her own with the intelligent man across from her. He, too, feeling the effects of the wine, seemed to be taking pleasure in her company, showering her with his full attention. After the meal, and two glasses of wine, the waiter came to offer dessert. Denia said she couldn't eat dessert but would like coffee before trying to drive home.

"See, you should have let me pick you up, then you wouldn't have to drive," he said to Denia.

"We'll have the bread pudding with two forks, and coffee," he said to the waiter.

After the dessert and coffee was served, Eugene insisted that Denia take a few bites from the large slab of bread pudding, drizzled with caramel, and topped with a swirl of whipped cream.

"There is something else I need to talk to you about concerning your property," he said. "If you would rather I save it, I can make an appointment for you to come to my office next week. No sense letting business spoil the glow from a good wine."

"Well, that's silly. I'm here now. It's been a wonderful dinner, and I don't think you could spoil it," she encouraged. "Besides, you've made me curious, now."

"Alright, here goes," he began. "A guy came to the office on Monday. I'm not sure how he got my name associated with your property, but maybe because I also represented Melinda. He is a vice-president for a development company, and he wanted to put an offer in on your land. According to him, he's also working with the owner of the avocado farm next to you, trying to buy *that* land. The company is called Ricco Land Development and they're interested in putting luxury townhouses on the property for senior citizens. They have gone far enough to draw up designs for the buildings. The pond and the area around it would be formalized into walking trails and a park. There are twenty acres of land, so they could put a lot of buildings on the property. When the man said that they were offering twenty million dollars for the land, I was surprised, but I told him to submit a written offer and I would contact the owner," he paused and took a sip of coffee.

Denia's first reaction was not related to the offer of money but the ranch land.

"They can't put townhouses there; it's not zoned for residential."

"Money talks, and they seem to think they would be able to get a zoning change through the city council."

"Twenty million dollars? I can't believe they would offer that much," Denia said, remembering her relatively small pay checks from her last job. "I probably couldn't make anywhere near that much money in a lifetime."

"Tell me about it," he said, taking time to eat another bite of bread pudding, "but when you think about it, so many people would like to live around here, and there's very little regular housing available. There's the reservation held by the tribe, and most of the other land is in private hands. Then there is the zoning issue you mentioned. Most of the people that work in Solvang live in surrounding towns and drive in for work. This developer is willing to buy the land and then work to get it zoned for the townhouses."

"You know, I just got here. I've just changed my whole life to take over Auntie's ranch," Denia said with some exasperation.

"I'm not telling you to take the deal. I'm just letting you know about it," he said defensively. "I should get the formal offer next week, and I'll send it out to you. I know the front money to buy the land and develop it is being put up by a group of investors. You should probably think about it. I've never had an offer like this come across my desk, but I will support you in whatever you decide."

As much as Denia did not want to let the subject of selling the ranch put a damper on the evening, it did change the relaxed mood that had developed previously. They sipped their coffee as Eugene settled the bill, steering away from the difficult topic.

"Thank you so much for dinner," Denia said, trying to put the topic of the ranch property behind them.

"Maybe we can plan another day," he said. "We could visit the little zoo in Santa Barbara. My family belongs to the Friends of the Zoo organization. It would be a fun day."

"That sounds nice. I would like to see more of the local attractions," she said as he was walking her to the car, guiding her protectively with his hand on the small of her back.

"Are you sure you are alright to drive?" he asked, standing next to the Range Rover.

"Yes, the food and the coffee offset the wine."

"Can I call you next week?"

"Yes, I plan to be around the ranch most of the week."

"Okay. Take care driving home."

"I will," she said opening the car door. "Thank you again for a wonderful dinner. Good night."

"Good night," he echoed, closing the car door for her.

On the drive home, Denia felt like a wet blanket had been thrown over her enjoyment of the evening with the proposal on the ranch property. The cynical side of Denia thought back to Jeff, and how she had been taken in, and swearing never to let it happen again.

She wondered if Eugene had asked her out mainly for the purpose of telling her about the developers wanting to buy the ranch. What did he stand to gain from the deal, if anything, she wondered? Maybe he was just protecting her interests and had nothing to gain. That amount of money was staggering. She could go back to San Diego or anywhere for that matter and do whatever she wanted with her life. Maybe Eugene was right, that she should consider it?

Things had certainly not gone that well since she came to the ranch, and the unsolved murder of Melinda still hung over her head.

Batty called Denia and told her the meeting with the Doves was scheduled for Saturday evening at seven-thirty. They would all be coming to the house, so she spent the afternoon cleaning and dusting, trying to make the place look presentable. With the TV droning away in the background, Denia spent time adding her touch to the now shining surfaces, with articles found throughout the house. She brought some of Melinda's framed pictures downstairs from her bedroom and added some vases and knick-knacks to the white shelves on both sides of the fireplace.

Listening to the news with one ear, she fed herself and the animals and cleaned the kitchen. Then she went upstairs to change into some slacks and a casual knit top. Running a comb through her hair, she chose to let it hang free, while adding a little blush to her lips.

When she first heard a faint knock at the back door, Denia opened it to one of the Doves she had not met.

"Denia, I'm Agatha," she said in a lilting voice, and proceeded to hug Denia. "You haven't changed much since your high school graduation picture."

"Hi, come on in." Denia led her through the kitchen and into the dining area.

"I thought it would be good to use the table," she explained to the stranger.

"My platter," she exclaimed, looking at a large, ceramic, oval plate decorating the center of the table.

An aqua glaze shone brightly, with a brown glaze rimming the outer edges and the circular pattern spiraling in the center.

"I gave that to Mel years ago. I made it for her birthday."

"You made that?" Denia asked with appreciation.

"Yes. Batty should have told you. I'm the artist in the bunch. I have a studio in town. You'll have to come see it."

Denia took Agatha's purse and put it on the sofa, committing to memory the thin lady with long, red, naturally curly hair. She floated up behind Denia and looked around the inviting space of the living room.

"You've done wonders with this place. I've never seen that coffee table or the buffet so clear of stuff; and the table…where are all the piles? We can actually all sit around it. I recognize that table runner is one of Mel's scarves," she said referring to a thin, linen, material, striped with multiple colors of pinks, corals, and turquoise.

"I love it. You have a creative eye."

Another knock was heard from the back door.

"Come in," Denia called.

Olivia and Batty entered the kitchen. The puppy barked, wiggling at the front of the crate, wanting to come out. The two women came into the dining area, each hugging Agatha in turn. They also looked around at the change in the house.

"Is that a new chair? That lamp looks so good there. What a nice little spot to sit; and a TV - did Snowy hook that up for you?" asked Olivia, thoughts tripping over each other.

"Yes, Snowy hooked up the TV and took away that old console set. The chair is used but I thought it would look good there and provide more seating in here," replied Denia.

Batty walked to the fireplace and picked up the framed picture of Melinda, in younger days, standing next to one of the tall, ancient stones of The Ring of Brodgar in Scotland.

"This is nice. Mel would like how you have displayed her things," she said looking at Denia.

Another knock at the back door. Olivia went to open the door, and brought the younger looking, middle-aged woman with perfectly styled hair, into the now crowded dining room.

"Denia, this is Cassandra Demeta, whom we all call, Cassie," said Olivia.

Cassie came directly to Denia and folded her arms around Denia.

"I am so happy to finally meet you," she said.

Denia remembered seeing these ladies at the memorial service for her aunt. Here they were, all together again.

"Where's Evelyn?" Batty asked, directing her question to Cassie.

"She was driving up from Goleta, and was running late," answered Cassie.

"She's my younger stepsister," Cassie said, directing the information to Denia, "and she's usually late getting here."

No sooner had she said this when another car buzzed through the driveway, followed shortly by another knock at the door.

"Come in," Denia called.

Evelyn was obviously younger than the other Doves, with long, blonde, wavy hair held back from her thin, beautiful face with a hairband. She was taller than her sister and thinner in her long, sequined, dress with a V-neck showing creamy cleavage.

"Hello, Denia," she said, taking Denia's hand. "I remember seeing you at the service for Mel."

Then looking around, "Wow, this place looks different…and bigger."

"Now that we are all here, we should sit down," said Batty, taking control of the women. "We're here tonight to meet with Denia. There is much to discuss."

The ladies gradually found a seat around the table leaving the chair at the end empty. As they talked to each other, they had not noticed Denia slip up the stairs. Mona came into the room and was getting lots of attention while the puppy whined in his crate.

Denia came back down the steps from upstairs carrying the belongings of Melinda. The voices at the table ceased, as all eyes followed Melinda's niece. Denia walked to the table and folded her aunt's green, velvet cloak with a silver lining over the back of the empty chair. She laid the black, leather book with golden symbols on the cover, onto the table.

The room was silent, and eyes were filling with tears. Isis, who had followed Denia from her mistress' room, jumped up onto the long table and sat next to the black book, with her head high and tail coiled around her feet. Her amber eyes looked around the table as if to say she would stay by her mistress even in death.

"Melinda's *Book of Shadows*," whispered Cassie.

10

THE KID

The Doves all recognized Melinda's cloak folded over the back of the chair, having seen it in use many times through the years. They all focused on the book, which none of them had ever seen. Melinda's personal *Book of Shadows* – a witch's most private collection of Craft secrets.

The women, each of the witches, had a similar book of their own – written by hand, in secret. Tears spilled over from Evelyn's sea-green eyes and ran down her cheeks. They were quickly brushed away by the backs of her hands. Cassie reached out for her stepsister's hand, grasping it in support.

"We all knew it was only a matter of time before you

found Mel's things and put it all together," said Batty with a soft voice of resignation. "That is why I thought we all needed to meet with you."

"Come sit with us," pleaded Olivia to Denia, her eyes also brimming with tears.

Before Denia could take a seat at the table, a knock came from the kitchen door.

"Come in," Denia called.

It was Dragon. He walked into the kitchen toward the dining room and saw the group of familiar women sitting around the table. All eyes were on him in an unwelcoming stare. The grimace on his mother's face told him everything –this was not a good time to be here, being the least of it. He looked at Denia, with his hand moving to the back of his head, realizing his *faux pas* of non-invitation.

"I just came to take the puppy out," he said weakly.

There was silence. The puppy yipped from his cage. Dragon would take the non-answer as permission, and quickly went to the crate, extricating Angus. The pup wiggled with exuberance at its unexpected escape. Dragon moved across the kitchen adroitly with puppy lapping behind, closing the door soundlessly on his way out.

Denia moved her aunt's velvet cloak to the back of the sofa and sat in the empty chair behind the precious book. Isis stood and walked across the table to rub her head against Batty's folded hands. After a pat on the head from Batty, she jumped down from the table. They all watched as the sleek, black, feline walked to the bottom of the stairway and started to climb, leaving them for her bed.

After taking her seat, Denia broke the silence, "High Priestess of the Doves..." in the tone of a statement more than a question, she posed to the onlookers.

"She was our guiding light," said Cassie in reverence.

"She led us in our practice and our *magick*," said Olivia, emphasizing the last word.

"She held us together as sisters and practitioners," said Agatha.

"We loved her," said Evelyn softly.

"And you are her coven of witches," pronounced Denia, putting the obvious into words.

"Yes," said Batty, the one-word answer confirming all, and supported by the group.

"Who will lead you now?" asked Denia, wondering what would happen to the coven now that their Priestess was gone.

"We will have a ceremony calling for guidance from the Goddess," said Cassie, "and we will select our Priestess from among us in a secret rite."

"Melinda had prepared us for such an event," explained Agatha. "We have all routinely taken turns as leader of our monthly lunar rites and our Sabbat ceremonies. Mel felt we all needed to be able to cast the circle and invoke the Goddess. We were all made responsible for the chants and spells in any ceremony we led."

"Where did you have these ceremonies?" Denia asked, already knowing the answer.

"Up until a few months ago, we always had them up at

the rock amphitheater near the pond. Years ago, Melinda had the willow trees planted to screen the grotto and make it more private," offered Olivia.

"Not only did the willows provide privacy for us," said Evelyn, "they are known for being magical trees. They inspire love, intuition, and wisdom, and are associated with the moon and the water."

"How often are your meetings?" asked Denia.

"We hold lunar rites once a month on the day of the full moon," answered Batty.

Denia remembered how all the dates of the full moons had been highlighted on her aunt's calendar.

"We also celebrate our eight Sabbats during the year. Occasionally we hold a special meeting when an event impacts our coven."

"Such as Melinda's death?" Denia asked.

"Yes," said Agatha solemnly. "We had a ceremony at my studio in town the night of Mel's memorial service. It was to ask for an easy passage to the Summerland for her spirit."

Denia regarded Agatha's golden-brown eyes. Her naturally curly hair shone under the globed lights of the chandelier over the table, giving a halo effect.

"So, are you not meeting at the amphitheater now?" asked Denia.

Then as a second thought, "Is it because I'm here?"

"No, it's not you," answered Cassie. "The place is shrouded in darkness. We haven't used it since our *Litha*

Ceremony – or summer solstice, to you – that was in June."

"Why? What do you mean?" Denia asked with curiosity.

"Mel thought someone was sneaking onto the property to use the amphitheater. She respected my psychic ability and asked me to go there with her one afternoon." Cassie's hands were open in front of her, showing manicured nails with rose polish, and the several unusual gemstone rings she wore.

"When I was there, enclosed among the rocks and the trees, no images came to me, just darkness. It enveloped us. Mel and I decided to try a purification spell the next day, but after a week the darkness remained. The energy there was foreign, and our energy of light could not penetrate. That was when I started to fear for Mel. It was like she had gray clouds following her. My psychic ability does not work on demand. I warned her, but I never had a clear vision of the threat. I was too late to save her," she said with remorse.

Denia remembered Jorje warning her away from the grotto. Had he felt a dark force? Denia knew he was Catholic, always wearing a crucifix on a chain around his neck. She also remembered Keith Clearwater saying the place had been used recently. She wondered how she would be able to catch the strangers using the place if it were true.

Could this be the reason for Auntie's murder? She thought.

"When was all of this?" asked Denia, realizing she was dealing with belief systems she did not understand.

"The beginning of July," replied Cassie. "There has been a dark mist surrounding this place. We have all been worried about you being alone here."

"After the robbery I had to send Dragon out here, so I could sleep at night," said Batty.

"Do any of you know anything that will help the police solve Melinda's murder?" she asked, scanning the troubled faces around the table. "Or who might want to break into Candlewick and steal the Stonehenge painting?"

"Not many people knew that painting was there," said Agatha, "so, possibly the picture was taken as an afterthought, thinking they could make a quick buck. I've had my studio in town for over twenty years. Most of the established California artists that focus on the tourist trade know each other either directly or by reputation, each of us with our own specialty. I have been gently probing online with other artists for any news about the painting. There is an underground market for the occult, and the painting may fit into that following. I'm working on getting some contacts, so if it comes onto the market, we will hear about it."

"We've all been quietly working on gathering clues. There *must be* a local connection of some kind. The question is who and what," said Olivia.

"We are all searching for the answers and will tell you if we find out anything that sounds even slightly important," said Batty, "but there is something else we all need to speak to you about."

Denia remained quiet, allowing Batty to go on with what she wanted to say. She knew she had an agenda for this meeting, and she knew Batty had one also.

"The Doves, our coven, was founded by Melinda Greystone almost twenty-one years ago. Olivia is the only one of us who was with Mel in the beginning, so she is our group's historian. I have belonged for seventeen years. I was there as a novice the night your mother came out to the pond and found us in the middle of our lunar rites. We have always been a rather small coven, never more than seven members at one time. A few witches have come and gone over the years. Two, including Agatha's soulmate Reanne, have passed on to the Summerland."

"We have a code we live by to obtain our desired goals. It is sometimes called the witch's pyramid, that has the four base actions needed for accomplishment: To know, To Will, To Dare, and To Keep Silent. We are silent about our practices, whether it is personal, or our communal practice. The stigma associated with witchcraft has plagued practitioners all through our history and is alive and well today. The fact that we practice with the energy of light, and our ethics demand our practices will not promote harm to anyone, doesn't matter. Some people might persecute us or shun us if they knew of our coven."

"We have all built up a network of relationships here. I've been at my accountant job for fifteen years and have access to the finances of at least half of the businesses in town. Agatha has her studio and shows her work at galleries up and down the coast, not to mention her Saturday art classes. In town, Cassie owns her little shop that she set up on the bottom floor of an older house, while living on the top floor. Olivia not only helps with Candlewick, but volunteers at the library two days a week.

Evelyn teaches at a dance studio in Goleta, and is a renowned harpist, with her side business of playing at weddings and other events. We are all pretty dependent in keeping our coven and our practice of the Craft a secret. We are all here to offer support and love to you as Mel's friends; but, also, to request your silence about our coven."

When Batty finished her speech regarding the Doves, Denia looked around the table at the faces of the women. They all looked like the ordinary person you would run into at the market. Except each face held the hint of a common emotion: fear. They all feared what Denia's knowledge, if made public, could do to upset their day-to-day lives.

She looked at Batty, who had done nothing but help her and ease her path since she arrived. Olivia, in her motherly way, had embraced her as a friend. The coven's devotion to Melinda could not be questioned. These people reached out to her as her aunt's letter had said they would – *'They are my dear sisters and have my full love and trust…they will come to you, for my sake'* – were Melinda's words.

Denia got up from the table, went directly to the far kitchen cupboard containing the fine dishes and removed six crystal, cordial glasses. She returned to the table, placing one glass before each witch, and one next to the leather-bound book. She went back to the kitchen and retrieved a bottle of wine from the wine rack in the pantry. After a little struggle in opening the bottle she returned to the table, filling each glass with the dark, red liquid. She took her seat and lifted her glass to the ladies.

"For the love of Melinda Greystone, and the kindness and acceptance you have given me, I vow to hold the secret of the Doves close to my heart." Denia sipped the rather dry wine, and watched as relief, smiles, and tears came from the faces around her.

Sunday was another sunny day that started out at a slow pace. Denia worked out back taking care of the daily animal chores since Jorje was off for the day. Billy was out of the pen, so Denia had to keep stopping what she was doing to get Angus or Billy out of whatever they got into. Dragon's car was parked out back, so he was probably catching up on his sleep on his one day off from the winery. Snowy showed up before noon and spent an hour in the office. Once done, he announced that Olivia's new laptop was installed and online, ready for business on Monday. Denia was finally going to get together with her to learn the Candlewick website. If there was time, they planned a walk-through for making some candles the next day.

A little after noon, Dragon emerged from his cocoon and helped Snowy install the double-headed, light fixtures on the back corners of the house, garage, and office building. A large flood light was being added over the two, tall, barn doors, requiring work from both men - Dragon up on a long ladder and Snowy holding it while he worked. A small porchlight was being added to the doorway of the little bunkhouse attached to the barn. The electrician had talked Denia into three pole lights that would add to the coverage of the wide lot. These were evenly spaced between the chicken coop and the goat pen along the fence. The good thing was, all the lights, except for the small light at the bunkhouse, were controlled by two new switches installed in the pantry. Denia felt the lighting would add to the security on the property and was worth the investment. The bank account for the ranch had stored extra funds. She decided to wait a month before she tackled the needed extra fencing.

At one o'clock, Denia stopped the men from their tasks to call them in for lunch. She made sandwiches, cut up a fresh cantaloupe, and made a new pitcher of iced tea. The men sat around the table, talking about the Mars Opposition which would be occurring the next few nights. Snowy would be working with a group of his astronomy students trying to get the best photographs they could of the red planet, while hoping the infamous, fog bank that frequently blanketed the central coast would stay out to sea.

Both Dragon and Denia had never heard of the Mars Opposition, so Snowy explained in too much detail. He told how this occurred about every two years when the sun, Earth, and Mars all lined up in their orbits, and the two planets were both on the same side as the sun. It was a time when Mars was close to the Earth and could easily be seen by the naked eye in the sky if you knew where to look.

"What was going on last night with my mom and her crew?" Dragon asked Denia, wanting to change the subject.

"Not much, really," said Denia, wanting to downplay the gathering of the previous evening. "I wanted to meet the rest of my aunt's close friends, and your mother arranged it. It was just a little wine and cheese party."

"Well, it looked a little intense when I came in," he said taking another bite of the sandwich.

"They had just gotten here, and we had just finished the introductions. You surprised us, that's all," she lied.

"Thanks for taking Angus out, by the way. That dog thinks if people are here, he's supposed to be out of his crate."

There was a lull in the discussion as the eating continued. Denia thought she would take advantage of Snowy's broad base of contacts on computer and radio networks.

"Snowy, do you know of any underground or occult organizations around here? Have you come across anything like that?"

"Are you kidding?" said Snowy. "Half of the UFO crowd are nuts, which makes it hard for those of us that are trying to pursue the science. Occult? Let me think about it," he paused.

"I saw a *real* nut the other day," jumped in Dragon. "I was at my tat shop, thinking of getting more ink. I saw this picture of a baby dragon coming out of its egg, and I thought that would be really sick for my left calf. Anyway, there was this guy in there getting ink on his back. It was a big tat, taking up most of the surface of his back, and Craig said the guy had been coming back a few times to get it finished. I had never seen anything like it. It was some kind of symbol. It had spirals and what looked like a blade going through it - very weird. Something like you would see on those Viking TV shows. The odd thing about this guy was that he was not young. He was older with gray in his goatee and hair. He must have been in his forties or fifties. Kind of old for the tat shop's usual clients."

"Hmmm," was all Denia could get out, while her mind was whirling away. Denia knew ancient Norse and Celtic symbols were often confused.

"I can ask Craig at the tat shop about him, if you want," Dragon offered.

"That could be something," said Denia. "Do you think you could get a name, and where the man lives around here?"

"Sure, I go in there pretty frequently. Craig and I go out for a beer now and then. We're pretty tight. He's ex-Air Force, like me. That's how I started going to his parlor."

"In the meantime, can you both put out some feelers about anything related to the occult, or let me know about any scuttlebutt you may hear regarding the Stonehenge painting? Agatha seems to think someone may try to sell it."

The two men finished their lunch and went back out to complete installing the lighting fixtures. Denia decided she would spend the evening on the internet herself, looking for chatrooms, and just generally trying to educate herself about the occult.

She also wanted to look around the house for books. Melinda was old-school and relied on print. There *had* to be books around here relating to 'the Craft', both the history and the practice.

Denia knew if she was going to keep the Candlewick business she needed to get in there and roll up her sleeves. She had a master's degree in business administration from college and knew a lot of theoretical basics. Unfortunately, some of the largest businesses of the time were internet-based businesses that had thrown most of the MBA rule book out the window.

She spent most of Monday morning working with Olivia on the Candlewick internet website. By the time they were finished, Denia was able to check on incoming orders for candles, look up inventory, and find and use the customer service area of the website. The afternoon was spent packaging and getting out the current backlog of orders.

Olivia worked at the library on Tuesday, and Denia took the boxed candles to be shipped out. The day before, she told Olivia of her idea to use the fifty-some empty jars she had taken out of the pantry for seasonal, fall candles. Olivia thought this would be a great way to get Denia started on the candle-making process. It would be easier than starting off using the molds. So, she told Denia to run all the jars through the dishwasher and make sure that the glass was clean and free of any traces of labels.

Denia stopped at a craft store and bought decorative ribbon of the various fall motifs. She also bought a glue gun with glue sticks, and foil stickers of autumn leaves. When she got back to the office, she spread newspaper on the worktables in the office building and sprayed the jar lids with gold paint.

Wednesday, she had her first experience with melting, coloring and pouring the paraffin wax. Olivia guided her through the steps, and the use of the wick bars, needed to make sure that the candle's wick ended up in the center, where it needed to be. Thursday was another library day for Olivia, but Friday was productive in learning how to order supplies, mainly wax, coloring – both liquid, and solid, and various scented oils that were running low.

Denia was shocked to find out that Candlewick had sold over five-hundred black candles last September and October, noticing there were few black candles on their shelves. She realized this was going to be a very busy six weeks. The sooner she got up to speed with the candle-making, the better. Karen Peterson ordered twenty-five, gold-colored tower candles for a wedding reception which was coming up in two weeks at the Samala Winery. So today, Olivia was going to teach Denia how to use the molds. They would only melt enough wax to do six tower candles at once, which turned out to be a lot of wax. Coloring, that would be a shade lighter when the wax cooled, had to be measured exactly, so all the candles would match in the end. Like anything else, Denia knew she would need practice to become independent, but for the first week she was feeling good about her progress.

Evenings around the ranch had fallen into a pattern. Denia would make some dinner for herself and feed the animals. Angus would run around the house as she cleaned up the kitchen while listening to the news on the TV. She was opening the mail every day, working on getting utilities into her name one by one, and getting a handle on the monthly expenses associated with the property. Dragon would usually come by every evening after he got home from the winery, with a fast-food bag in hand, and would take Angus out to the bunkhouse for a while and for a run in the back lot.

As he promised, Eugene Sorenson forwarded the offer on selling the property from the Ricco Land Development Company. It turned out they were offering a million dollars up front for the property, with the balance to be paid within a year of the first townhouses going up for sale. This did not sound like the great deal that had originally been presented by the handsome lawyer.

Denia thought if she did decide to sell the property, she would rather offer it to the Clearwater family first. At least she would know how the land would be used, and as her aunt advised, they would give her a fair price. She wasn't sure she wanted her Auntie's beloved ranch to end up as townhouses. Eugene had not called her for the day in Santa Barbara they discussed. So much for the Solvang dating scene, Denia thought, dismissing thoughts of a real relationship.

She was finally able to pick up her Explorer. Batty drove her to the auto shop. She had to admit it looked as good as new, and she felt comfortable driving the now repaired car.

Lee Nelson called her to say she would not need to go to court over the accident, since the man responsible had agreed to plead guilty to the lesser charge of reckless driving. Between that and the charges for street racing the culprit would probably lose his license. Denia was alright with that since his insurance had paid for all the repairs to her car. Evidently, she heard, the offensive truck had been repossessed for lack of payment.

As far as the Doves were concerned, Denia spent time

searching for any books her aunt had collected focusing on witchcraft and any books related to the ancient history of pagans. She found more than she expected. The house had books tucked in all nooks and crannies. There were books for the care of chickens, cookbooks, books for making jelly and jam, and canning tomatoes. These 'how to' books were all delegated to a section on the pantry shelf with her own 'how to train a puppy' books.

At last, Denia found several textbooks on the history of the British Isles related to anthropology of the ancient peoples and their religions, including Druidry and Paganism. These she had carted into her bedroom from the lower bookshelves in her aunt's bedroom. More books were found in Melinda's secret room. These were directly related to witchcraft, astrology, annual almanacs, and more. She hauled them all into her bedroom.

Her idea was to read for an hour or two every evening to broaden her knowledge, and possibly find clues that could lead to solving Auntie's murder. At the very least, she could better understand the background and be able to better communicate with the members of the Doves.

It was Monday morning during a California September when the wish for the fall season was in the air, but the heat of summer persisted. Denia was cleaning the sink and loading the dishwasher, with Angus scampering around her feet and licking water from the open appliance door. The gardener was in the front yard pursuing his usual task, his lawnmower accenting the sounds of morning. The cats had been fed and had already taken their spots on the living room windowsill for a quiet sunbath. Denia proceeded with the chores of straightening the puppy's crate for later, and changing the cat litter when a knock came from the back door.

Walking through the kitchen from the utility room and peeking through the sheer curtains in the door's window Denia saw Paul Oda the gardener, standing outside, his Asian eyes wide with concern. Denia did not delay in opening the door, not knowing what to expect from the quiet man.

She saw he was holding a wooden, kitchen mallet, dangling from two fingers. It was the kind used to prepare meat. One side of its head was a flat surface, and the other side was covered in small, diamond-shaped projections. The mallet was coated in dirt, but Denia's eyes were drawn to what was hanging from the tool's handle. There were fine, long, strands of what looked like hair, coated with an occasional clump of dirt.

Denia knew immediately what this was and, as the bile rose in her throat, she swallowed hard to suppress it. She went to the drawer in the kitchen which held plastic freezer bags, bringing one back to the gardener and carefully enclosing the mallet in the bag before sealing it.

"Where did you find it?" she asked the solemn man.

"Beneath the rosemary hedge on the other side of the house," he said, understanding that his find could mean something.

"I need to call the police about this. Can you stay here to talk to them?"

"Yes, I still need to mow and clean over by the garage. Do you think this is important?" he asked.

Paul Oda knew there was a rumor circulating through the town that Melinda Greystone's death had not been due to her health or an accident.

"I'm not sure," answered Denia in a noncommittal tone, "but it may be. Thank you for bringing it to me."

"Okay, I'll just go back and finish my work. I'll check with you before I leave," he said turning away from the doorway.

Denia closed the door and went right to the phone. The clock on the stove said eight-fifteen. She was not sure if Sergeant Nelson would be at work yet. She found his business card that she had stuck in the catch-all drawer by the phone and punched in the numbers.

"Solvang Sheriff's Station," answered a female voice.

"Is Sergeant Nelson there? This is Denia Rawlings," she said identifying herself.

"Just a minute," came the efficient retort.

"Denia, this is Lee Nelson. What's going on?"

"I think you need to come out here," Denia replied. "The gardener found a wooden mallet in the bushes, and it looks like it has hair hanging from it. I put it in a plastic bag without touching it."

It took a few seconds for the officer to understand what Denia was implying.

Once awareness struck, "I'll come out. Is the gardener still there?"

"Yes, I asked him to stay."

"Alright, give me a few minutes to get there," he said, and disconnected.

In a short while, Denia was opening the door to admit the uniformed sergeant. She showed him the plastic bag containing the mallet lying on the tiled counter. He agreed that the strands hanging from the mallet could be hair. They were looking at the potential weapon used to kill Melinda.

"Your aunt was cremated, wasn't she?" Nelson asked. "It would be good if I had some of her hair for analysis."

"Just a minute," replied Denia, already running for the staircase.

Presently she returned, holding a hairbrush, taken from the long dresser upstairs. On examination it was clear the bottom of the brush held a collection of silver hairs belonging to Denia's aunt. She took another plastic bag from the kitchen drawer and sealed the brush in the bag.

"That's good," he said retrieving both bags. "Now, is the gardener still here?"

"Yeah, he said he would be working over by the garage."

"Let's go see him."

The gardener had seen the police cruiser drive onto the lot, and stopped what he was doing to walk over to the kitchen. He was just entering the flagstone patio as Denia, and the sergeant came out of the house.

After carefully securing the two bags in the front seat of

the police car, the sergeant turned to the gardener, introducing himself.

"Can you show us exactly where you found the mallet?" the sergeant requested.

Paul Oda led them around the front of the house, past the rose garden, and around the corner to the rosemary hedge. They walked along the hedge, stopping near the far corner, where he pointed to a spot under the rosemary bushes.

"How often does this hedge get watered?" the sergeant asked the gardener.

"Rosemary is draught resistant and does not take a lot of water once it gets established. Right now, the sprinklers for this side of the house are set for once-a-week watering," Paul responded.

"So, the mallet probably got water on it four or five times since Melinda's death," guessed the officer. "I'm going to take some pictures of this area. Do you have a ruler I can use for a marker?" he asked Denia.

"Yes, in the house. I'll get it."

After the police sergeant and the gardener left, the importance of the mallet struck Denia. If fingerprints could be found on the mallet, the murder of Aunt Melinda could be solved. Once again, it was a waiting game - waiting for what the police would discover, if anything. Denia looked forward to calling her mother and telling her the investigation was over; but in her bones she felt a darkness still hung around the place, as Cassie had said.

At the end of the week, Denia pulled the Explorer around back and loaded the boxes of candles for delivery to the winery. When she got there, Karen helped her load them into the large storage room used to hold tables, chairs, and other paraphernalia for events at the winery. Shelves held stacks of linens, white china, dinnerware and glassware. Denia looked around at the large spools of ribbon hanging on a rack, with all the popular bridal colors represented. Several shelves held candle holders for tower candles, and various oversized, glass goblets also used for candles, and several silver candelabras. Another shelf held various types of dried flower rings, and sprays, fitting various seasons of the year. Denia was impressed at the large collection.

"I have Batty coming to help me with the wedding Saturday evening," said Karen, securing some raven hair behind her ear. "Would you be interested in helping with the event? I have people to help me set up for the event, and people to clean up after, but the catering staff is slim, and I need a few other people to help."

"Well, my dating calendar isn't exactly full," remarked Denia with a smirk, "so I *do* happen to have Saturday open."

Karen chuckled.

"I worked my way through college waiting tables, and I do have some experience with serving and handling banquet settings."

"That's more than I could ask for," said Karen. "The wedding is at four o'clock at the Mission in town. Then they are taking pictures. Drinks and appetizers are scheduled from five-thirty to seven, so you would need to be here by five o'clock. We'll start serving dinner at seven. You and Batty would be able to leave after the cake and coffee are served."

"I'll see you then," said Denia, already turning to leave.

"Oh, I forgot to tell you," called Karen after her, "the wedding is formal, and the bride is requesting that the staff wear long dresses."

"Okay," said Denia waving.

Great, she thought to herself. She didn't *have* a long dress at the ranch. She didn't want to spend all the money she would make on the job buying a new dress. She thought of Auntie's closet, housing many long, flowing, dresses. Melinda had been a little taller and thinner than Denia; but, just maybe, she could find something that would work.

On Saturday night, Batty offered to pick Denia up and drive to the winery. This would free up one more parking spot at the front of the building, leaving room for the cars of a hundred or so expected guests. Once again, Denia belted herself into the front seat of the Cruiser and steeled herself for the short drive down the road to the winery. Batty wore a lace, crocheted, coral dress in A-line style, which she hiked up over her knees for driving. Denia had been lucky enough to find an amethyst-colored peasant dress, with a scoop neckline, capped sleeves, and smocked waist, which allowed her to wear a dress from her slimmer aunt's wardrobe. The dress was long, made of a gauzy material with a pattern of eyelets. Denia found a delicate, glass-beaded belt she hooked at the side allowing the long, beaded strings to hang down the skirt to the knee. Thin, strappy, tan sandals with a small heel finished the outfit. A little proud of herself for putting the ensemble together, she thought she was ready for the evening as she surveyed the outcome in the mirror.

When she came to the side lawn of the winery where the round tables were set for the wedding guests, Denia was enchanted by the scene. Her golden candles were set on pedestal bases in the center of tables surrounded by large, multicolored autumn leaves and baby pumpkins at the base. Tablecloths and napkins were of gold linen with glassware sparkling next to silver flatware. Burnt orange ribbons, also decorated with leaves, hung down the backs of the individual white chairs.

Denia was surprised to see Evelyn already in place at the front corner of the winery's tasting room, sitting behind a large harp. Batty and Denia greeted her. Although she was at least fifteen years older than Denia, Evelyn looked like a Grecian goddess in a gossamer, sleeveless, jade-green dress that flowed over her knees to her ankles. A golden braid was woven through her luscious curls, and her beautiful eyes made up to accent their sea-green color. Batty explained that Evelyn frequently spent her weekends playing harp at all sorts of gatherings.

Denia had no problem fitting into the busy serving schedule. The winery's lobby and tasting room was used for the open bar and the circulation of the appetizers, as guests milled about and sat at the high bar tables. When it was time to be seated for dinner, she helped guests find their places at the tables set up on the lawn. At dusk, the candles were lit, and well-positioned floodlights provided romantic, evening lighting.

Every winery post and tree were wrapped in white fairy lights, and Moroccan lanterns with candles hung from low branches. As darkness fell, the magic of the night only increased. For just a moment, Denia remembered with sadness the wedding reception her and her mother had planned just a few months ago, that had never happened.

As the cooling evening passed, Keith Clearwater and Lee Nelson stood by each other holding bottles of beer next to one of the trees circling the reception area. Open tuxedo jackets were still on both men, but the ties had been undone.

"God, she looks great," said Keith, watching Denia as she leaned over a table, refilling glasses from a wine bottle.

Tendrils of hair had escaped the bronze clip at the back of her head, and hung along her cheeks, with her face and neck glowing in the candlelight.

"Yeah, that hair," said Lee with admiration, "and that dress hugs in all the right places."

"Have you asked her out yet?"

"No, I can't ask her out," he answered with some exasperation. "We're still trying to solve her aunt's murder. I have to stay professional. Besides, her mother calls about once a week. The timing is just not right. I wish I could wrap it up. The gardener found something I think was used to hit Melinda in the back of the head – a wooden mallet thrown under a bush. It still had hair on it. It's at the lab."

After a brief pause, "We *did* get the guy that ran her off the road, a real smart-assed jerk," he said.

Then, what he really wanted to know, "Have *you* asked her out?"

"How can I ask her out?" said the tall, dark-haired man. "I'm in the middle of the harvest. I'm up at five, and falling in bed at ten every night, dead tired. I shouldn't even be here tonight."

"Tomorrow's Sunday," said Lee, implying a day off.

"Just because the crews are off on Sunday doesn't mean I'm off," the vintner bemoaned. "It's my only day to catch up on the payroll, and all the other crap I can't get done during the week."

"Batty said Denia rode here with her. Maybe she'll need a ride home," said Lee.

"Someone should take her home. I think that place is not safe at night, even with Dragon staying there," said Keith.

"Yeah, one of us should offer to take her home."

"My house is closer than yours."

"What does that have to do with it?" said Lee. "That's a pitiful excuse."

"I'm taller and better looking than you."

"Also, *older*. I thought you were tired, with lots of work to do tomorrow. Pitiful."

"Want to flip for it?" Keith asked, pulling a quarter from his pocket.

He flipped the coin and covered it with his hand. "Call

it."

"Heads," Lee said.

Then "Damn!" as the tails side of the coin was revealed.

The cake and coffee had been served for those who wanted it. Many of the guests were on the dance floor, as the music had gone from something for all generations to the hotter dance music of the day. Others were well into the glow of the rich dinner and wine and lounged in their chairs at the half-empty tables.

Batty was ready to leave and was looking around for Denia, only to be waylaid by Keith Clearwater.

"Hey, Batty, you don't mind if I give Denia a ride home and take a look around the place, do you?"

Batty was pleasantly surprised by the offer. Not that she didn't want to take Denia home, but by the show of interest by the good-looking bachelor. This would be a good little tidbit for the grapevine tomorrow, she thought.

"No, that would be great because I'm bushed. I just want to get these stupid shoes off and go to bed."

Batty's hair had escaped its restraints on both sides of her face framing her face as she yawned.

"Okay, you go ahead. I'll find her."

Denia was surprised to learn Batty had left without her, but Keith made the excuse that Batty's feet were hurting so badly, she needed to leave. It was just a little exaggeration, he thought.

Since the ranch was just down the road, it had taken them longer to walk to Keith's truck then it took to drive to the dark, little house.

Once there, Denia invited him in, mainly to show off the newly installed lighting they had discussed on the way over. Angus was not in his crate, but Denia saw a note from Dragon, written on a pad propped up on the kitchen counter which said he had the puppy in the bunkhouse.

Denia flipped the light switches and led Keith out back to see the improvements. Dragon's car was parked in the usual spot, yet the lights were out in the bunkhouse. Denia wondered if she should wake him to get the dog.

"This is much better," said Keith, admiring Snowy and Dragon's handiwork. "Are you keeping the lights on at night when you go to bed?"

"Yes," she said. "If anyone is sneaking around, I want to be able to see them. Hopefully, the lights will make them think twice. The chickens don't like it. I had to put a tarp over the side of the chicken coop."

Denia headed across the yard to the barn.

"I need to check on Billy."

Denia opened the barn door. Light from the new floodlight shone into the barn giving Denia a clear view into the first stall, Billy's usual spot. She stepped into the barn for a closer look, and then panicked.

"She's gone," she yelled out to Keith.

He ran into the barn, checking all the stalls.

"Did you leave her in her pen?" he asked.

"No, I put her in her stall and fed her before I got dressed to go to the winery. Oh, God, did someone take her?" she said, verging on hysterics.

She ran out of the barn and pounded on the wooden bunkhouse door. When not answered immediately, she pounded again.

"Dragon, Dragon!" she called, continuing to beat the door.

A light flipped on inside, and the door was yanked open.

"What's wrong?" asked Dragon as soon as he saw the expression on Denia's face.

"Billy's gone! She's not in the barn!"

"I checked on her. She was there when I came in for bed."

At the same time, Keith ran through the alleyway between the barn and the office building and looked back and forth across the vacant field. He thought he saw a light flicker up by the eucalyptus trees.

"Dragon, get a flashlight and come up to the pond!" Keith yelled, already on his way.

Dragon slammed his feet into untied tennis shoes, and grabbed the flashlight he had on the counter by the door. He ran out the door, closing the puppy in, with Denia following behind.

Denia could not keep up with the two men, with the heels of her shoes sinking into the dirt of the uneven ground, making it difficult to run. She had to stop several times as debris slipped into the open sandals. She could see the beam of Dragon's light flashing sporadically up ahead as he ran to catch Keith.

When she got to the secluded grotto, she could see the glow of a fire that was burning in the fire pit before she burst through the stringy branches of the willow trees.

As she ran into the circle, she saw the two men bending over a white form on the ground.

"Billy!" she screamed, running to the goat.

"Give me your t-shirt," Keith demanded of Dragon.

Dragon took off the shirt, handing it to Keith. In a strong yank, he ripped the shirt, and twisted one side into a strip of cloth and tied it around the goat's neck where dark red blood was escaping along a cut line.

"I'm going to carry her to the house, so put your hands over the neck and apply pressure."

All three started across the field to the house. It was a slow, awkward procession. Tears were running down Denia's face, not believing this could be happening.

When they got to the house, Keith laid the barely conscious goat on the only nearby flat surface – the dining room table. He motioned to Dragon to grab a discarded dishtowel to press against the still bleeding wound.

"Call Hans. Get him out here!" he said to Denia, as he applied pressure to the goat's neck.

"Dragon, get my cell phone out of my pocket and call Kristen."

Denia didn't have the number for Hans on her phone, so she called Olivia, waking her.

"Call Hans. We need him out here right now. Tell him to bring his medical bag and IV fluids."

Olivia promised to get him out to the ranch and hung up.

Keith, in the meantime, had reached his sister on the phone as Dragon held pressure on the goat's neck.

"Kristen, I'm over at Mel's ranch, and there's been an accident. Can you bring your medical kit for the horses, and get over here right away?"

After a brief pause, he called a new number.

"Lee, I'm out at the Greystone Ranch. You need to get out here and get a patrol car out here. There's been another problem."

Denia sat at the head of the table, patting Billy's head and talking to the goat, as tears flowed unchecked.

11

THE SNAKE

The pleasant evening had turned into a nightmare. After calls for help, the driveway held a parking lot full of cars belonging to responders to Denia's ranch.

Outside of the house, standing by the police cruiser, Lee Nelson was face-to-face with Deputy Cleeves, showing his extreme displeasure.

"If someone's coming onto this property they're not *walking out here*! They have to be parking vehicles somewhere," emphasized Nelson.

He had changed out of the tux and was now wearing

jeans and a polo shirt.

"When was the last time you patrolled that road before ten o'clock?" he demanded of the deputy.

"I've been running the road every three hours, so the last time was a little after nine," the deputy responded. "There was no activity, and I didn't see any parked cars – I would have noticed them."

"Alright, we need to switch it up. Do every two hours starting at eight in the evening. Look along both sides of the road for any side paths where cars could pull off and hide behind brush. Check the horse ranch next door and see if there are any places to park that would go unnoticed and check around the avocado farm."

"A fire was still burning up there. We should go have a look," said Keith Clearwater, standing a few feet away from the police car and the irritated sergeant.

The men took off across the field toward a faint glow emanating from behind the cluster of willow trees, each holding a flashlight. The night was quiet and still. The full moon was high in the sky adding a silvery light to the landscape.

Inside the house, Denia was in a haggard emotional state, sitting on the sofa with her knees drawn up to her chin. She still wore the smocked dress she had worn all evening. Olivia quietly sitting nearby, tried to offer comfort by just being there. Batty stood at the end of the table, also still wearing the dress she had on at the winery, watching the activity of trying to care for the goat. Olivia picked Batty up on the way to the ranch, after she alerted Hans and made sure he was on his way.

The beautifully polished table had been transformed into an operating table. Dragon stood to the side holding up a bag of IV fluids flowing into the goat through narrow, plastic tubing and a needle Hans had placed in Billy's foreleg shortly after arriving on the scene. Kristen Clearwater stood beside Dragon on the back side of the table applying pressure to the goat's neck wound while Hans made ready to examine the cut and stop the bleeding. He had already given Billy a sedative to keep the goat still during the procedure.

"Okay, here's what we're going to do," said Hans when he was ready. "First, I'm going to remove all the rags, then I'm going to flush the wound with a disinfectant and try to find the site of the bleeding. Then I'm going to try to clamp off any bleeder and suture the vessel. We'll flush the wound again, put in a couple drains, and close the cut. Are you with me?"

"I'm ready," said the determined, short-haired blonde, totally absorbed in working with the young veterinarian.

"Do you still keep a bottle of whiskey for a nightcap?" Batty whispered into her son's ear.

"Yeah, it's in the cupboard over the sink in the bunkhouse," he quietly answered his mother.

Batty slipped out the back door, going directly to the bunkhouse. She opened the door, and the forgotten puppy charged her before she could turn on the light.

"What are you doing out here?" she said to the excited

dog, as she took the bottle of liquor down from the shelf.

She grabbed the puppy as she went out and closed the door. Batty saw the three men were returning from their trip to the grotto and entered the lit up, back lot from the alleyway between the barn and the office building.

"Did you find anything?" she called to them.

"We didn't find any intruders, but it was obvious several people were there by the condition of the dirt inside the grotto. The place is filled with footprints. The fire they lit is still burning itself out right now. Whoever was there carried in wood for the fire and tied the goat to a slab of rock someone had moved over by the fire. I would guess at least five people were there - or maybe more," reported Lee Nelson.

"With all of these things happening, it's like someone is trying to scare Denia away from here," suggested Batty.

"It really does look like that," agreed Keith. "First Mel is harassed and killed, now Denia is being terrorized. I think she's in danger. I'm going to get a couple guys to patrol this place at night."

He brushed his formal shirt, which was no longer white, showing blotches of dirt and blood. His black pants were discolored with dirt from kneeling on the ground.

After Sergeant Nelson dismissed Deputy Cleeves back to his patrol car, the remaining three went back into the house. Batty put the puppy into his kitchen crate, not wanting him to be underfoot, and checked on what was happening at the table. The goat remained on her side on the table. Kristen had one hand holding the goat at the jaw, and the other holding a cloth by the wound site. Hans explained that a blood vessel had been nicked which was the site of the blood flow. He was now finishing sewing up the fairly clean cut across the neck, the gloves he wore stained with blood.

"What are you going to do now?" asked Batty.

"We don't usually take livestock into the clinic, but we're going to make an exception and take her in. I'll stay with her tonight," replied Hans. "We're going to carry her to the back seat of Kristen's truck, and I'll stay in the back with her while Kristen drives."

Once assured that Billy was in good hands, Batty turned to check on Denia who had not moved from her spot on the sofa. She was no longer crying but was non-communicative, staring across the room. Olivia sat nearby sipping from a cup. Quickly evaluating the girl, Batty returned to the kitchen, poured a small amount of whiskey into the bottom of a glass and returned to the living room.

Denia had retreated into herself. The room was full of people she barely knew and none of them could console her. For the first time since coming to her aunt's home she had a strong urge to go home. She wanted her mother. She wanted her father to wrap her in one of his bear hugs.

Whatever made her think she could take this on, especially after they were told Melinda's death was a murder? She now believed someone was threatening her for some unknown reason. Someone was trying to scare her away, and she *was* scared.

Batty stood in front of Denia, handing her the glass. "Here Denia, you've had a shock. Sip on this."

Denia took a gulp of the amber liquid and immediately

broke into a spasm of coughing and sputtering.

"What *is* this stuff?" she asked when she was able to catch her breath.

"Hey, that's my Black Label whiskey," Dragon called from his spot at the table. "It'll grow hair on your chest."

Denia had to smile through her misery.

"Keith, can you help us get Billy into the truck?" asked Hans. "We've got the bleeding stopped and the neck wound closed. Now I need to get her into the clinic and do some lab work. I think we caught the bleeding in time."

"Whoever was up there with Billy thought they were in the clear. When Denia turned on the lights out back, they saw it and fled," said Keith. "We were lucky to get there when we did."

No one in the room wanted to think of what the alternative would have been.

Once Billy was on the way out to the truck, Denia finished the remainder of the whiskey. The warmth of the liquid spread through her. She was depressed and felt drained - drained of tears, drained of emotion, drained of hope for the future. She stood up and walked to the foot of the stairs.

"I'm going to bed," she mumbled, not caring what the rest of them did as she started up the stairs.

The next morning when she awoke, the house was quiet except for the distant noises from the puppy who was still in his crate downstairs. Denia lay on her back looking at the ceiling. It was Sunday. She needed to take care of Angus, feed the cats, and spend time in the chicken coop. She thought over the previous evening and her thoughts of going home.

For today, at least, she was stuck here. If she decided to leave, it would take some preparation. Again, the sounds of the little dog carried up the stairwell, so she got up.

The afternoon was busy. Denia had spoken to Hans who was on his way home to get some sleep after the long night. He reported that Billy was awake and up on her feet, taking up one of the boarding pens used for large dogs. She was drinking water and ate some oatmeal Hans had brought in from a restaurant down the street. They discussed bringing her home the next day, but Denia was afraid to bring the goat home. Hans said he would ask Kristen Clearwater if she could board the animal for the time being.

After hanging up, Denia remembered she had not thanked Kristen for her help the night before. In fact, she had hardly taken notice of her. She had been just another person in the crowded house last night, and Denia was barely thinking straight at the time.

Dragon knocked on the back door and came into the kitchen, after Denia had called to him to come in. Angus was at his feet, while Dragon poured himself a glass of iced tea. He went over to Denia who was at the table with her laptop open in front of her.

"How are you doing?" he asked, unsure of her state of mind after the previous night.

"I feel better, but still upset. Billy is doing alright - she's eating. Hans thinks she can go home tomorrow, but I'm not sure it's a good idea to bring her here."

"Are you going to bring her home?"

"Hans is going to see if she can be boarded at Kristen Clearwater's place. Whoever tried to harm her will not know she survived."

"That's probably a good idea. Kristen will do whatever Hans would ask. She's totally into the vet," he agreed, relaying the grapevine gossip.

"Hey, I wanted to tell you I had a beer with Craig last night before I came home. I asked him about that guy with the strange tattoo."

"Did he know anything?" Denia asked with interest.

"Yeah. He said the guy's name is Dylan Blackwell, and he lives in Sacramento, California. The man told Craig he was going to be down here on business about once a month. He stays at one of the hotels in Solvang when he comes here."

"Did Craig say what kind of business?"

"No, but he's come back to get work done on the tattoo three months in a row. Craig is still adding color."

"Can you get a copy of the tattoo?" she asked.

"I can try. Why? Do you think it has something to do with the break-ins around here?"

"Well," she said, thinking, "if the tattoo is a symbol, let's say Norse or Celtic, we could try to find out its meaning, or its association. Usually when someone gets a tattoo it has some sort of personal meaning to them. It could be a clue.”

“Okay, I’ll try to get it or draw it from what I remember. I only saw it for a second, but I was impressed by the size of it.”

“Agatha knows a lot about this sort of thing. She may be able to recognize the symbol. In the meantime, I’ll call Snowy and see if he’s heard anything of this Dylan Blackwell. Maybe he can find something on one of his networks.”

On Monday morning, Jorje showed up at his usual time but went to Dragon when he found Billy missing from her stall. Dragon explained as best he could what had happened on the previous Saturday night. Jorge said little to Dragon but gathered his few things from around the bunkhouse and left in his car without talking to Denia.

When Denia took the puppy out in the morning, she was surprised to not see Jorje’s car. She wondered if he was sick; or even worse, had he heard about Billy, she thought? She knew he was very attached to the little, white goat.

Denia went ahead and took care of the chicken coop, just in case he did not show up at all.

Lee Nelson called Denia just as she was on her way out to the office building for more candle making with Olivia, who had just arrived.

“I wanted to see how you were doing and get back to you on what we found on the mallet,” he said.

"I'm concerned," she replied. "I think someone is spying on me and taking advantage of when I'm not here. I'm not sure what I should do. I can't tell my mother, or she'll be up here in a heartbeat demanding I come back to San Diego."

The police sergeant didn't have an answer that would make whatever was happening go away.

"We have increased the patrol on the road out there to every two hours after eight o'clock in the evening," he offered. "Also, we did get a report back on the mallet. The hairs did indeed belong to Melinda. The handle had fingerprints from your gardener and one other good print. The only problem is that, so far, we haven't been able to match it. We'll keep trying."

"That's better than the last time. At least you got one print," she said. "I do have a question, that you may or may not be able to help me with."

"What?"

"Can you do a check on a name? This guy is coming to Solvang once a month, possibly on business. His name is Dylan Blackwell, and he lives in Sacramento. It's just a hunch, but if you could check on it, I would appreciate it."

"Do you think he has something to do with the murder or trespassers?"

"It's a long shot," she said, "but my aunt was killed in July, the robbery was in August, and this latest thing was in September. It may be nothing, I know, but if it's not too much trouble I would appreciate it if you could do a check on him."

"I can run a check, but don't get your hopes up. Lots of people travel on business and in cycles due to their work. We have a better shot trying to identify the fingerprint from the mallet. The mallet was found on the property and can be linked to your aunt by the hair."

"I know," she sighed. "I'm just grasping at straws."

"Well, keep grasping. We're going to put this all together," he said with encouragement.

Later that day, the candle making went well with Olivia's guidance. Denia learned when she *did* make a mistake, usually the wax could be reused in batches of candles of the same color. Olivia tutored her in her first try at making taper candles. This process was totally different than using the molds, and a lot messier. It required dipping, cooling, and re-dipping into the hot wax. The candles were made two at a time on the same wick that could be cut when completed. Four dozen uncut tappers hung on the drying rack by the time they had finished. Making these candles took more time.

Olivia left around three o'clock, so Denia decided to close the office for the day. She got the chickens ready for night by putting the tarp over one end of the coop and went into the house for the evening. Dinners had been pretty uninteresting lately, so a well-made meal sounded good. She could always save the leftovers for later.

Deep in food preparation mode, she was surprised to hear a knock at the back door. Denia knew it was too early for Dragon to be home from the winery. When she looked out the window, she saw a man who appeared to be Hispanic, standing on the patio holding a straw cowboy hat in his hands.

"Hi, Denia, I'm Caesar Hernandez, Jorje's son," the man said through the door's glass window.

Denia swung the door open, "Come in. Is he alright?" Denia asked immediately.

Denia led the man into the living room, and they sat down on the sofa.

"Yes, he's at home. He's very upset. I guess he heard about the goat from the friend of yours that is staying in the bunkhouse."

"It was an awful night here, on Saturday," Denia replied. "The good news is that Billy is going to be alright. Please tell him. We're not going to bring her home right away, though."

"I'm here on a rather difficult task," he began. "I'm here to tell you that my father will not be coming back to work here."

Denia could not hide her surprise. She had developed a good, working relationship with the dependable farmhand. He always treated her with such respect and even affection. He had a kind heart and took good care of the animals. He would caution her for her safety and had encouraged her to get the outdoor lighting installed after the robbery. Jorje did as much around the ranch as he was physically able to do; and even though she paid him every Friday, she always felt his dedication to the place was about more than the money. So Denia knew this must have been a difficult decision for the man.

The son continued, "He was going to quit the job after your aunt died. He took her death very hard. They had worked together for so many years, and they had a close personal relationship. Your aunt was always concerned that my dad and the family were doing well. She paid for medical bills for our family many times over the years. When he found out that *you*, her niece, was going to stay at the ranch, he felt he owed a debt to Melinda to help you even though he was uneasy."

"What do you mean, 'uneasy'?" Denia asked, with concern.

"My father is an old Mexican. He's very superstitious. He believed that a curse had come over this place, even before Melinda died. Lately, he feared for you and feared for himself. The robbery last month frightened him even more. The attack on the goat was just the last straw. He came home crying this morning, and my mother called me."

"Oh, I'm sorry." Denia didn't know what else to say.

"My sister has a house in Ensenada, Mexico - it's right on the ocean. She has been trying to get my mother and father to come there for years. She even built them their own little cottage on the back of her land with a wide front porch. Dad can have his chickens and a garden in the yard. He can enjoy his grandchildren on the beach. When your aunt left him that money in her Will my mother pleaded with him to go, but he felt there was unfinished business here and decided not to leave.

"Me and the rest of our family are encouraging him to go to my sister's house. He's old and has worked long enough. My sister will see that my father and mother are well taken care of for the rest of their lives. They deserve a peaceful life," he concluded.

"That does sound wonderful. I would want that for him, too," said Denia with understanding.

"I have a nephew, named Joe. He's nineteen and going to junior college. He needs a job and could come out here before school and after classes. My father is already drawing up a list of all the things he would have to do around here. Dad thinks he would be a good person to take his place for now, until you could hire someone else. Here is his phone number," Caesar said, handing Denia a slip of paper.

"Thank you. Please tell your father 'thank you' for all the help he has given me. I will miss seeing him, but I will think of him walking on the beach in Mexico," she said.

Hernandez stood to take his leave. "Oh, I forgot. My mother and father sent this for you," he said, pulling a silver chain out of his pocket and handing it to Denia.

Denia looked at the small, oval medal hanging from the chain. It was a religious medal with the image of the Lady of Guadalupe showing through the turquoise, enamel paint.

"Oh, thank them for me. This is beautiful."

There was nothing left to say. Denia walked the man to the door and closed it behind him. Denia felt another blow to her support system, slim as it was.

The next day, after thinking over the offer of Jorje's grandson coming to help her on the ranch, Denia called the young man and made arrangements to meet him that afternoon. If she was going to stay at the ranch - or until she decided whether or not to leave - she would need some help around the place. The apples and the pomegranates were ready to harvest, the irrigation system for the orchard was a little beyond her, and she knew she could not keep Billy with Kristen for very long. Dragon's current work schedule did not allow for him to be of help, and Denia felt he was already doing what he could to support her by being there at night and helping with the puppy.

In the meantime, she finished the morning's chores and took the fresh eggs into town, following the usual schedule for a Tuesday. Although Olivia was not at Candlewick today, Denia decided to check the website for any new orders and found two. After writing them down, she went to the shelves to find the requested candles and put them and the order slips at the packaging station. Then, using one of her aunt's recipe cards, she followed it carefully to make six, four-inch, lavender scented candles using molds. The lavender candles were one of their best sellers, not dependent on the time of year. She also spent time adding autumn ribbons to the previously completed jar candles. Once the labels were applied, and they were divided into lots of various size, they would be ready for sale.

She already made arrangements for selling them. Cassie wanted some for sale in her shop. Agatha wanted them for strategic placement in her small studio among paintings, sculptures, pottery, and jewelry displays. Karen Peterson wanted some for tables in the wine tasting room at Samala.

The largest batch was going to the same restaurant that took the fresh eggs. Marci wanted each table to have one of the seasonal candles. Small as it may be, Denia felt a sense of accomplishment as she tied the last decorative ribbon.

Denia went through the motions of continuing, as if her future was in Solvang with all the new people she had met since coming here. Surely, she did have people that offered support. The episode with Billy made her face the fact that she was not dealing with ordinary trespassers. Someone, maybe among those appearing to be helpful, was a threat to her. Inside herself she was thinking about what she would do *if* she would feel the need to abandon the ranch; and the thought of carrying on the ranch and the Candlewick business.

Plan B was formulating in the back of her mind. Self-preservation needed to be a priority, and she was taking the warning signs seriously.

Keith Clearwater was up to his neck in the grape harvest. He could sigh with relief now that the bulk of the fields had been handpicked, grapes pressed, and the processing was in full swing. As he sat on his horse, riding from row to row among the fields being worked, thoughts of Denia and the scenes of the previous Saturday night haunted him. He remembered her from the winery working at the wedding. It was the first time he had seen her well-dressed.

He previously noticed she was pretty with a voice that

made you want to listen but watching her flit from table to table that evening, he realized he had underestimated her beauty and charm. He enjoyed the short ride to her ranch, wishing it could have lasted longer.

Later that night, he had seen the terror on Denia's face after finding Billy in the secluded alcove. There was the look of someone lost and afraid after the goat had been laid on the table in the house, as she helped to hold the animal still while waiting for Hans to arrive. Finally, he remembered the look on her face as she sat on the sofa, only half aware of what was happening around her, totally despondent.

Now he was prompted to take the precarious situation in hand. Just a couple months ago he had failed to take action after sitting in Melinda's cluttered living room sipping coffee in the middle of the night. He had listened to her fears, but held off, not realizing the seriousness of the string of observances the old woman espoused. Then she was dead. Her death had shocked him to the core. He could not relieve himself of the guilt. He thought he should have *done* something.

Now he was determined that history would not repeat itself, ending in Denia's death, if it meant *he* had to sleep in the field keeping watch over the ranch.

Denia was in the kitchen making a salad with the leftover chicken. It was another hot day and going to be a warm evening and she wanted something cool and crisp for dinner. The cats were happy having already eaten.

Angus was sniffing around her feet hoping Denia would accidentally drop another piece of chicken. Mona sat on the table, making little chirping noises, trying to taunt the little dog. She knew he could not reach her. The patchwork cat accepted that the little, ragamuffin was not going away, but she was going to let him know that she was the one in charge here.

Denia heard a gentle knock coming from the back door, and she turned to see Keith Clearwater's form filling the door's window. A sudden burst of nervousness hit her.

"Now what?" she said to the walls.

She was at the end of her rope as far as taking in any more bad news. She wondered what he could want as she opened the door.

"What's wrong?" she asked immediately, ushering him into the kitchen.

"I was checking the grape field and came over for a drink of water," he lied, laying his tan cowboy hat on the counter.

"I have some cold iced tea, if that works."

"Sounds good."

"I was just getting ready to eat; do you want some salad?" she asked.

"Sure, if you have enough. I skipped lunch."

"I have enough. I always make huge salads," she replied as she tossed on the sesame salad dressing.

Denia took two plain, white plates from the cupboard to hold the salad. Keith washed his hands in the kitchen sink and sat down at the table, now restored to its clean, polished state. Angus came over and put his two front paws on Keith's knees.

"He's really growing. He's like his sister Brandy - all legs."

"He's really a good boy. He hasn't had an accident in the house for some time. I had him out in the office building with me today. He loves to run around in there," she said, placing the heaping plates on the table."

"This looks great," he said, as he wasted no time in picking up the fork.

"My specialty, Chinese chicken salad," she replied.

"Did you hear that Jorje quit?" she relayed, changing the subject.

"You're kidding?" Keith responded in surprise.

"No. He came to work on Monday, Dragon told him about Billy and that was the end for him. His son came over that afternoon and said he would not be coming back. He and his wife are moving to their daughter's house in Mexico."

"Do you need me to try to find someone to help out?"

"No, I've already hired Jorje's grandson. He comes every morning, and after his classes in the afternoon, three days a week. I'm thinking I can make that work," she said, thinking as she took a bite.

She continued to explain. "The good thing is that he speaks perfect English, understands ranch work, and is already teaching me the irrigation system for the orchard."

The two focused on the food and ignored the whining puppy. They both stole glances at each other between bites. Denia felt her usual intimidation being so close to the man. His straight, black hair was mussed, probably due to wearing the cowboy hat all day. In the lessened light of the late afternoon his eyes appeared green, in contrast to the blue, cotton shirt that was open at the collar. Every place his skin was exposed was bronzed confirming the long hours out in the sun.

They talked as they ate, and the subject turned to Kristen, who was currently keeping Billy, the recovering goat.

"Yeah, the whole thing is laughable," he said. "Kristen has had a crush on Hans for years. She's constantly dragging dogs into the clinic for one reason or another. Hans asked her if she could keep the goat until she was healed. He knew Kristen built a dog run with kennels on the ranch and takes in dogs for the local pound, waiting for adoption. Of course, Kristen says yes to keeping Billy, thinking this is more of an opportunity to see Hans. So, Hans brings the goat over, and Kristen puts her in one of the large dog kennels. Yesterday afternoon, when she got home from the plant, she felt sorry for the goat being cooped up all day and took her into the horse coral for some exercise. When she turned her back the goat was gone."

"What? Did she find her?"

"It gets better," he said with animation. "Kristen calls Hans at the clinic and says he needs to come over right away and help her find Billy. In the meantime, Gil our ranch hand, and Kristen are out beating the bushes for the goat. By the time Hans gets there, the sun has gone down, and the light is fading. Kristen starts yelling at Hans for not coming sooner, and Hans is yelling at Kristen for not realizing the goat could get out of the corral. After more searching, it's gotten dark, and they figured there was no way they were going to find her in the darkness. On the way back when they went by the horse stalls, there was Billy, curled up, sleeping on a pile of hay in the corner of one stall."

"Oh, that's like her stall here," said Denia, feeling empathy for the poor, lost animal.

"Gil said they were both relieved to find the goat, but Hans left in a huff. Gil was telling me about it this morning, blow by blow. My dear sister seems to have lost *this* round."

"Is that bad?" asked Denia, not knowing Keith's opinion on the match.

"Oh, he's doomed," Keith said smiling and leaning back in his chair. "Kristen is relentless and always has been. She was the baby and always got what she wanted. Karen and I are resigned that we'll eventually have the handsome Hans in the family."

"Is that bad?"

"Hell no, maybe we'll save some money on vet bills," he laughed and Denia smiled, enjoying his sharing the story.

Denia cleared the empty plates from the table, rinsing them for the dishwasher. Keith followed her into the kitchen, bringing the empty glass.

"I was wondering if you wanted to come for a ride with me?" he asked. "I'd like to show you where my place is located down the road."

Denia was surprised. She couldn't think of any reason to refuse. "Okay, let me put the puppy in his crate and leave a note for Dragon."

As they were going out the back door, Keith reminded her, "Don't forget to turn on the outside lights. It will probably be dark by the time we get back."

Denia went into the pantry and hit the light switches and took her keys before following Keith out the door.

"Where's your truck?" she asked, seeing the vacant driveway.

"I didn't bring it," he said, leading her around to the front of the house.

Rounding the corner, Denia saw two horses grazing near the garage.

"Do you ride?"

"I haven't ridden a horse since college," she said, looking at the animals with a measure of hesitation, following the tall man to the horses.

"This is Alice," he said, patting the neck of a dark brown horse with a black mane. "She's a real sweetheart. Come over here, and I'll help you up."

After three tries and a boost from Keith, Denia sat in the saddle, trying to remember how she used to work the reins. Keith was up on his russet horse, named Wheaty, in one bound. He slowly walked his horse across the vacant field.

The gentle slope of the expanse was shining in the late light of the day. Slowly they rode toward the turtle pond. Denia tried to relax in the saddle as she guided Alice after Keith and Wheaty.

By the time they reached the edge of the pond, the task of horseback riding was coming back to Denia. Keith pulled up and Denia was surprised to see a man standing by the old bench. A thermos and what looked like a lunchbox sat on the bench. Out of the way, behind the old oak tree was a small, one-man tent already pitched. Denia walked the horse over to stand next to Wheaty.

"Denia, this is Carlos. He's one of my field managers. He's going to be staying on the property all night to keep an eye on the grapevines and the house. We're almost ready to harvest, and I don't want any problems."

Denia knew the vintner's concern was not for the grapevines, but for her. Normally she might try to argue, saying it was not necessary to have someone keeping watch all night. She couldn't argue the need though, considering the last few weeks.

"Hello, Carlos," she said. "Thank you for helping. I really appreciate it."

Then thinking of the man alone out here all night, "I'm usually up until at least nine o'clock, so if you need coffee come knock on the back door and I'll make you some."

Keith spent a couple minutes speaking to the man, telling him to call if he sees or hears anything unusual. Then he turned the horse's head and started toward the silent, hanging, willow trees. He stopped the horse in front of the hidden grotto.

"We know someone is using this enclosure for something, and something that is not good," he said to Denia, who had stopped Alice beside him. "I think you need to get these trees cut down and expose the rock walls."

"When I was a kid, those trees weren't there, but my aunt planted them," Denia said in a noncommittal statement.

"Take these trees out of here, remove those pedestals inside, and get rid of the circle used for fires," he reiterated. "Clean out this place."

Denia's thoughts went to Batty and the Doves. She could not explain to Keith that this alcove was made private to shield the small band of witches for their monthly practices. However, what Keith was proposing made sense under the circumstances. She thought the Doves might agree to clear out the grotto but felt that she would need to talk to them first.

"Give me the word, and I'll get a crew out here," Keith pressed.

"That might be a good idea. Let me sleep on it," she said. "This place had a very special meaning to Auntie. When my mother comes up, we're going to scatter Melinda's ashes here, as she requested."

"Just as long as we aren't scattering anyone else's ashes," said Keith, disappointed with her lack of enthusiasm for what he felt was needed.

A chill ran down Denia's spine.

Keith kicked his horse's sides and started off to the path

through the towering eucalyptus trees, and on to the concord vineyard. Denia followed, getting the feel of the gentle horse beneath her.

Minutes later, they exited Denia's land through the large gates near the road. Keith got off his horse to replace the large chain and lock for the night.

Keith led the way along the side of the road, bordered in a wide shoulder of soft dirt, perfect for the horses. No cars were in sight. Denia had always turned into her driveway and never followed the road beyond the ranch. She knew it curved around her property with its large outcrop of rocks, the road changing direction to the north after the curve. Now, she could see it led on to the front of the horse ranch next to her property.

"Boy, this is a large horse farm," she called to Keith.

"Yes, the Kellogg's have owned this ranch for as long as I can remember," he said, slowing his pace to ride beside her. "They raise quarter horses and show them. Their son, Ron, is pretty much running the ranch now. Harry and Kim are always off somewhere."

They rode on at a slow pace for another fifteen minutes. Small farmhouses lined the road from time to time. Keith explained that this was part of the Samala land, and the acreage behind the farmhouses was planted in vines. Denia noticed a young boy, chasing his older sister in one of the front yards, playing in the evening's fading light. Keith explained that he rented the houses to his field managers and their families.

Soon, Keith led the horses into a dirt, tree-lined driveway that partially hid a small, blue house with white shutters and trim. To the side of the front yard was a large, maple tree. Its immense, white trunk narrowed as it rose above the house and was lost in the mass of smaller branches and leaves. Keith progressed past the front of the house, on to the garage and horse stalls, where he reined Wheaty and dismounted.

"This is it," he gestured toward the back of the house. "You did pretty well for not being on a horse for a while," he said as he helped Denia down.

She was relieved to put her feet on the ground.

"So, this is your house?" she asked. "It really *is* just down the road from me."

"Yes, this is the original house my mother and father lived in when they started the vineyard," he said. "I have to take care of the horses and feed them before I can come in but go on in and look around. The back door is open. I'll be in once I get them settled."

Denia walked across the dirt lot passing a line of rose bushes. A thick honeysuckle vine circled the back porch and climbed onto the gray, shingled roof. She opened the wooden, back door which led into a large rectangular kitchen holding a round, wooden table and chairs at one end. The yellow tile on the backsplash and counter dated the room. White, wooden cabinets went to the ceiling on both of the long walls. Only the stainless-steel appliances spoke to the modern times. The walls were a dark beige, and the floor was made up of squares of light green linoleum, also from an earlier time. A wide doorway led to another rectangular room where the linoleum ended and worn, wooden floors flowed. The opposite wall held the front door and three large windows, all to one side of the door. A stone fireplace took up the center of the far wall with a rough, wooden plank serving as a mantel.

The room was sparsely furnished. A fat sofa lined the wall opposite the windows, with the obligatory side chair. An oversized, brown, leather recliner was placed near the fireplace. A table lamp placed next to the recliner was piled with books and papers. Denia went to the fireplace, looking at a small array of pictures on the mantel. One framed portrait showed a mother, father, and three smiling children. The father, and the two older children with black hair, and the pretty blonde, blue-eyed mother, holding the youngest child, with bright hair like her mother. Another picture in a gilded, oval frame was a wedding picture of the mother and father. Last was a modern picture of Karen, with her husband and two children, which must have been taken several years ago, judging from the age of the children. Denia knew Karen's kids were now teenagers.

Denia wandered past the front door to the back of the house. The first bedroom she came to held a king-size bed that took up most of the small room. A chair sat in one corner, covered with discarded clothing. The bed was partially made, with the comforter thrown over pillows. A TV covered a good part of the wall opposite the bed. The closet door was open, exposing a stuffed interior. The next room was a bathroom. Most of the room was as dated as the kitchen, again hosting the small squares of outdated, green tile around the sink and the wall behind the tub. A large, modern looking shower with a clear, glass door and enclosure took up all the back wall.

As she continued down the short hall, Denia came to a

second bedroom, not holding a bed but a desk, bookcases and shelving. A file cabinet stood in one corner with a printer on top.

Denia heard Keith come up behind her in the narrow hallway.

"All three of us kids were in this room, until Dad could get the big house finished. When Mom got pregnant with Kristen, she insisted on a bigger house. It took Dad two years to get the ranch built over by the winery. Kristen uses that house now. Dad stays there when he comes down from Washington."

"This place is small," Denia said, knowing this man could afford to build a small mansion if he wanted one.

"It is small, but it's just me here. This place has lots of good memories. Also, I'm close to a lot of our fields and vines."

Denia realized this was not a materialistic man. His lifestyle was obviously simple. The land and the grapevines were his life. Denia wondered why the good-looking, wealthy man had never married. He had to be in his mid-thirties. Maybe he had not met the right person. Denia would have to ask Olivia what she knew. The infamous Solvang grapevine had to know something about Keith Clearwater.

Later, Keith drove her home in the truck, which he parked by the back door for Denia.

"Now that you know how close I am to your place, don't hesitate to call me if you have anything strange going on around here. I can be here in a few minutes," he offered, "and think about what I said about cleaning out those willow trees."

"I will" she replied. "Thank you for the horseback ride. I think I better go in and take a warm bath. I can already feel my leg muscles tightening up."

"I'll stop by when I'm around. Call me if you need anything."

"Good night," she said, closing the door to the truck.

Keith waited until she was in the house before using the circular drive to pull out onto the road, using the far driveway to exit.

What a strange, unexpected evening, Denia thought to herself while lounging in a tub of warm water. She could tell her legs would be sore the next day from the unplanned horseback ride. She found that she liked Keith Clearwater, but she didn't *want* to like him. He was too big, too right about things, too everything. Maybe the man was a womanizer, going from one to another, never ready to settle down. She knew she didn't need that right now, she couldn't handle any more problems.

Yes, she thought, Keith Clearwater could be a big problem if she thought seriously about him. Look at Eugene. He hadn't called her since their dinner date. The thought of a love life would need to be postponed.

Then there were the Doves. She had promised to keep their secrets. It was not just for them, but also for Auntie.

Keith's suggestion of removing the trees from the grotto

was a good one.

Denia was overwhelmed at how her life had gotten so complicated in such a short span of time. She sighed and scrunched down into the water.

All was quiet on the western front, and Denia's life settled into a routine over the next couple days. She would get up in the morning and feed the menagerie that kept growing. The rest of the day she was in the Candlewick office checking orders and adding to the growing stock of candles.

Billy was back home in her stall at night and in the pen every morning; however, she brought a friend home with her.

Kristen had Billy in one of the dog pens while she was at the plant during the day, and the goat had formed an attachment to an old greyhound in the next pen. The brindle-colored dog, named Roxy, was waiting for adoption after being turned in to the pound by an elderly man who, tearfully, could no longer care for her. The dog was being boarded by Kristen, with finding a 'forever home' unlikely due to her advanced age. Kristen took the two animals out with Brandy, her puppy, and Whiskey for exercise every evening. The goat and the old dog would lay next to each other with only the pen's chain link fence between them.

When Denia went to pick up the goat and saw the two together, she agreed to take the dog; so, when Billy came home, Roxy came home too. The large dog was as big as

Billy and would herd her along as they walked side by side. She slept in the barn with Billy at night, protecting her new charge. She had found her calling and a new home. *That* dog understood how to be a watchdog and barked for unexpected noises. During the day, Angus made sure that both Billy and Roxy got enough activity, annoying their peaceful lives with his unbounding energy.

Joe, Jorje's grandson, was working out and worth the money she paid him. The young man didn't miss his fast-food job in Lompoc. He had single-handedly harvested all the ripe pomegranates from the bushes lining the back fence in the orchard. Using only sunlight and water, the mature bushes produced large fruit, containing the red seeds bursting with juice and the mouth-watering tart flavor for which they are known. Keith hooked her up with a buyer, who took all the overflowing baskets of the red, autumn fruit. This brought an unexpected windfall of money to the ranch budget.

This weekend Dragon had a rare Saturday and Sunday off and decided to paint the bunkhouse!

The previous weekend, he had tackled the bathroom, putting in a new toilet, sink with faucets, and fixtures for the shower. He almost asphyxiated himself cleaning the shower tile using ammonia and bleach cleaners leading to toxic fumes, but the old tile sparkled. He installed a new cabinet around the sink, allowing for some storage, and added a new mirror and light fixture over the sink. He painted the walls and added white wooden paneling to the lower walls, and a new shower curtain depicting ocean waves.

Denia was amazed at the transformation and said that

she would repay him for all the expense. He refused to take any money since he had been staying there rent free. Besides, he wanted to clean up the place and make it more livable.

He started by moving all the furniture out into the yard Saturday morning and heading off to the big-box hardware store to buy paint and more painting supplies. Denia told him she thought he should wash down the walls before painting, but he said he would get a good primer, thinking that the aged walls would soak up the paint and would need at least two coats. Joe had agreed to come by and give him a hand as it would give him a little extra spending money.

Sunday morning, the two men were once again at the task that was taking longer than they thought it would. The first coat of paint was dry. Dragon had slept on his mother's couch the night before to avoid moving the bed back in and stay away from the paint fumes.

Denia was in the living room watching the Sunday morning show – one of her favorites – when Joe burst through the back door yelling for Denia to call 9-1-1. Denia jumped up from the sofa, trying to make sense of what the stammering young man was yelling about, clearly catching the word 'rattlesnake'.

Picking up the phone, she dialed 9-1-1 with the knowledge sinking in that Dragon had been bitten by a rattlesnake when he opened the cupboard under the sink in the little kitchenette of the bunkhouse.

Once Denia was assured by the operator that paramedics were on the way, Denia sent Joe out to stand by the entrance to the driveway, to flag the ambulance into the graveled pathway to the back lot when it arrived. Her adrenalin was flowing and her hands shaking as she wet a clean dish towel and headed for the bunkhouse.

She found Dragon lying on the floor just inside the door. He had wrapped a paint rag around the affected ankle. A dead, decapitated rattlesnake was on the floor over by the refrigerator. The shovel used to kill the snake was propped against the sink.

Denia dropped to the floor kneeling beside the sweating, pale face of Dragon. She lifted the paint rag and saw the two small holes that penetrated the white flesh just above the ankle. Denia replaced the paint rag with the clean, wet dish towel, covering the site of the snakebite.

"Keep still," she ordered. "The ambulance is on its way."

Dragon did as he was told, beginning to feel the effects of the snake venom.

Denia tried to appear calm. Dragon looked awful. His breathing was labored, and the sweating had increased, beading on his forehead.

Denia could hear the siren from the ambulance increasing with vehemence as it approached.

Finally, she heard the crunch of the tires on the gravel outside the barn and footsteps on the ground. She moved away as the two paramedics came into the small space with their equipment, needing to do their initial assessment. They took no time at all deciding to load Dragon onto the gurney and get him into the waiting rescue vehicle.

Denia watched them as they pulled out of the yard with

lights flashing and siren blaring. They were headed for Santa Maria and the closest trauma center, where anti-venom serum awaited their victim. The relatively short-lived peace at the ranch was broken. Denia rushed to the house to call Batty and head for the hospital herself.

12

THE STAGS

Hurry up and wait – that is the modern day emergency room experience. Waiting rooms with plastic, uncomfortable chairs spaced too closely together for the congregated crowd. Persons sniffling and coughing sitting beside the crying babies and unattended, bored children. The entire family that showed up with Grandma, all crammed into this designated space – waiting. All in this realm are overseen by a long, reception desk and staff wearing different shades of uniforms looking like pajamas called 'scrubs'. Large identification tags, somewhere on the front of each staff member, providing the only hint of their place in the ER hierarchy.

Wide, double doors separate the waiting area from the rooms in the back, where the *real* professionals work, and restrict entrance without invitation.

Looking around the busy room on a Sunday morning, Denia sat next to Batty, trying to be supportive. The events of the morning had already been thoroughly discussed. At this point boredom had set in. She wished she had the forethought to bring a book as she rushed out of the house. She had already exhausted the news apps on her cell phone.

She glanced sideways at Batty who did not look her best. Her worried face showed every line, aging her in the process. The unruly hair was at its worst, only partially held in place by the clip at the back of her head. She sat up straight in the hard-backed chair, hands clasped together on her knees, shredding a lone tissue. Her eyes darted frequently to the double doors leading to the back of the unit where Dragon was being treated. The rest of the time she watched the staff milling about the reception desk, waiting for word on her son's condition.

Denia sympathized knowing that *her* mother would be reacting in the same manner under the circumstances. It had to be the 'mother gene' that kicked in somewhere during pregnancy, Denia thought. They had already been there for two hours with no communication on Dragon's condition.

Denia thought back to her panic as the ambulance had pulled out of the driveway. She had made a bee line to the house to call Batty. When she explained what happened and that Dragon was on his way to the hospital, Batty was totally flustered trying to decide what to do. This time

Denia took charge of the situation.

"I'm coming over to pick you up and we're going to the hospital. I'll be there in ten minutes."

Without hesitation, she tore out of the house to the Explorer, and barreled out of the driveway toward Solvang. It was Sunday, so once in town, pedestrian traffic and vehicle traffic conspired against her meeting the ten-minute promised arrival. Batty lived on a side street where houses were placed closely together and looked like any middle-class California neighborhood, absent the architectural charm of the Solvang business district. Batty was standing on the porch of her condominium, with the usual tan purse hanging from one forearm. Once Batty was in the car, Denia made her way despite obstacles, as quickly as possible toward the 101 Freeway, in the northern direction.

The largest and most specialized hospital in Santa Barbara County was in Santa Barbara which could be a forty-to-fifty-minute drive with a victim needing rattlesnake anti-venom immediately. The paramedics told Denia they would be taking Dragon to the hospital in Santa Maria. The Lompoc hospital was closer, but the ER there was managing patients from a three-car accident, so paramedics were deferred to Santa Maria. Santa Maria was a straight shot up the road, and the modern, Spanish-style facility could be seen from the freeway.

Denia was startled out of her thoughts when Batty reached her breaking point.

"I'm going to check with those people, and they better let me in there!" she said with determination and stomped off to the reception desk to deal with emergency room bureaucracy.

Denia watched as the reception staff dealt with the full force of an angry mother. The nurse Batty spoke with listened, and then disappeared into the forbidden, back space. When she returned, she directed Batty to the green, double doors. She met Batty at the door and escorted her into the bowels of the emergency department.

Denia waited for another half hour, occasionally glancing at the TV set showing the Sunday golf tournament. Finally, Batty emerged, looking relieved, and came over to where Denia sat. Denia stood up to meet her.

"He's okay," she reported. "He's in bed and not allowed to get up. His foot is really swollen but the doctor said it will look worse before it looks better. He has an IV and they've given him the anti-venom and pain medicine. He has feeling in the foot and the leg. The doctor said that was a good thing. They're going to admit him to a room upstairs."

"Thank goodness," said Denia with relief. "What do you want to do?"

"I'm going to stay here until he's settled in a room. Olivia is coming over to see him, so she can take me home later."

"Okay. Tell him that I'll come to see him tomorrow, a*nd* that this was a pretty shabby way to get out of painting the bunkhouse," she said smiling.

"Uh oh," said Batty looking toward the ER lobby.

Denia turned around to see Keith Clearwater and Lee

Nelson walking toward them. Keith held Angus to his chest in an escape-proof grasp.

"What are you *doing* here with him?" she asked Keith as soon as he got close enough.

"He was running around the yard when you left. I didn't know what to do with him."

"We came to find you," said Lee, out of uniform on his day off. "I think that snake was deliberately planted. This could be an attempted murder charge if we could prove it."

"How is he doing?" Keith interrupted, asking Batty about Dragon.

"He's had the anti-venom and they're getting ready to admit him. He's drowsy due to the pain medication, but he's doing okay for someone that's had a rattlesnake bite," answered Batty.

"What do you mean?" Denia asked Lee, questioning what he had said.

"Someone *put* that snake into the cupboard in the bunkhouse. It didn't get in there by itself. Someone came through the back fence of the orchard. We found the wires cut," Lee explained.

"I'm confused," said Denia. "How did you two even hear about this?"

Denia knew she had not had time to call anyone except Batty.

"You remember that I have Carlos watching the place at night?" reminded Keith. "He called me a little after six o'clock this morning. He saw two guys come over the fence into the vineyard. I got in my truck and drove over there."

"And got me up to come out there," Lee added.

"We were over at the back gate, still looking around the vineyard when we heard the ambulance," explained Keith. "By the time we ran over to the house, the ambulance was gone, and you were pulling out of the driveway."

"We found Joe, who told us what happened. I put the snake in a bag and took it out of there after I took some pictures of the place. Joe said Dragon hadn't slept in the bunkhouse last night because of the painting. The bunkhouse door had been left open all night to air out the paint fumes."

"We think the guys coming into the vineyard were just a diversion, while someone was putting the snake in the bunkhouse," said Keith. "Whoever it was, seems to know that Dragon is staying there."

"Excuse me," interrupted a nurse in pink scrubs, who broke into the small circle of people.

"You can't have that dog in here. You're going to have to take him outside," she said looking at Keith.

"Oh, yeah, okay," Keith stammered.

"Now," said the woman with final authority, not leaving.

"Alright. I'm going," said Keith turning to leave.

"I'll be outside," he said looking at Denia.

"Batty, I better go take care of things," Denia said.

"Go ahead. I'll call you later and let you know how

things are going."

Denia gave the little woman a hug and went to find the dog and the man holding him.

When Denia got home to the ranch she found Joe in full-swing, painting. He had already finished the small bedroom and was on to the common room, roller in hand. Denia put Angus in the pen with Billy and Roxy and picked up an extra roller. By four o'clock the second coat was on the walls, and they were cleaning up. Denia could not stop thanking Joe and promised him full pay for the day.

After dinner she was unwinding on the living room sofa with the TV on. Angus had run out of energy and was taking a power nap curled at her feet. Mona had taken up her spot in the far corner of the sofa, snuggled between pillows. Isis, when not on her rug on the windowsill, had adopted the new, green chair by the fireplace as a throne fit for a goddess.

Denia had gotten into the habit of checking the Candlewick website on her laptop. Olivia was right about the orders for black candles, as they had already started to come in, and here were three more. Maybe black candles were not very available in stores, she thought to herself. She made a plan to work on more candles with Olivia the next day.

Surprised, she heard a crunching on the driveway gravel. Who could be visiting on a Sunday evening? Denia got up to go to the back door, Angus following.

Before she could knock on the door, Cassie saw Denia opening the door.

"Hi," said Denia. "What's going on?"

Denia noticed that Cassie was carrying a large satchel hanging from one shoulder.

"I came to keep you company tonight," Cassie came through the door and headed for the living room.

"Batty called you and told you what happened?"

"Yes. She's still at the hospital with Olivia, but she said they were coming home soon."

"How's Dragon doing?"

"She says his foot and leg are hurting, but he's been sleeping on and off."

"What's in there?" Denia asked as Cassie put the satchel on the sofa, causing Mona to complain and jump off.

"I thought I would stay here tonight," she answered, casually.

"Why?'

"I felt that I needed to. I can't shake this feeling I have. I'm worried about you."

Cassandra Demeter was known within the Doves for her psychic abilities. Denia didn't want to question them. Cassie lived her life based upon her feelings and intuition, not logic.

"Believe it or not I had a premonition about a snake, but I took it to mean an evil *person*, not literally a snake."

"Lee Nelson seems to think that it *is* an evil person. He

thinks the snake was deliberately put in the bunkhouse."

"Denia, that is just frightening. Dragon could have been killed. I didn't want you to be alone here, so I thought I would stay the night."

"I actually don't have an empty bed," said Denia apologetically. "I've been working on the house, sorting things out and all, but I haven't gotten to Auntie's room yet. I haven't even changed the bed in there since I've been here. I *do* plan to move into that room eventually and make my room into a guest room for my parents or friends when they visit."

"No problem, dear. It won't be the first time I've slept on this couch. I've stayed with Mel many a night."

"Would you like some tea?" Denia asked, resigned to the overnight visitor.

Later, the two sat watching the Sunday evening news show while they sipped at their tea from familiar, porcelain mugs.

Denia noticed that Cassie was definitely the most stylish of all her fellow sisters in the Doves. Her hair, golden with highlights, was cut in a short hairdo that framed her round face. Her bangs were a little long to provide height above her forehead where they were combed to one side. Denia had never seen her without make-up. Her nails were always manicured and polished, her long fingers showing off unique, gemstone rings. Her clothes, though casual, were not the usual fare but high-end and perfectly suited to her curvy figure. Even though Cassie could not be called pretty, she took the time to make sure she looked her best. Denia respected that.

The previous week, Denia visited Cassie's store in town to drop off some of the seasonal candles she had made with the jars from the pantry. The 'what not' shop took up the first floor of an older two-story house just off the main street in Solvang and attracted a lot of foot traffic. Cassie lived modestly on the second floor which she had remodeled to have a small kitchen and sitting room that added to the bedroom and bathroom which were already there.

Denia marveled as she walked around the store on the lower floor. The small rooms of an older time held tables, bureaus and tall china cabinets with shelves. Every niche was laden with meticulously placed merchandise calling 'buy me' to the customers. Denia's candles fit perfectly in the main front room, currently filled with items speaking to the autumn season and fall colors.

Cassie broke the silence that had settled over the room.

"Denia, have you thought seriously about leaving here? The danger I feel from this place has continued even though Mel is gone."

"Yes, I am thinking about it," Denia replied truthfully. "I felt like leaving after Billy was attacked. I *want* to stay here but there just seems to be one crisis after another. Now Dragon is in the hospital. I feel some responsibility for that. Then I think, what would I do with all these animals? I wouldn't be able to take them with me. Well, maybe I could take Angus. I think Keith Clearwater may be willing to buy the ranch if I make up my mind to leave. I keep hoping Lee Nelson will find whoever is behind my aunt's murder and all of these other things. I *do* feel that someone is trying to drive me away from here. Whatever they want, they thought they would get once Auntie was gone. Then I showed up and moved in. I don't think that whoever it is could have predicted that."

"This is no ordinary criminal. Melinda was murdered during the day. Dragon was bitten in the morning. This person is willing to do whatever is needed to drive you out," warned Cassie.

"Keith has a man staying overnight up by the pond to keep an eye on things. He also wants me to let him get a crew up there and take out the willow trees to better expose the rock amphitheater near the pond."

"That sounds like a good idea. Are you going to do it?"

"What about the Doves? Where will you have your meetings?"

"Denia, you are a dear, but you cannot worry about that," Cassie said, putting her empty mug on the coffee table. "Our spirituality and witchcraft are *not* attached to a place. It's something that we carry inside of us. We will all support your decisions. We're more concerned for your welfare than for a few trees. Besides, you being here hasn't stopped us from having our meetings or celebrating our lunar esbats."

"But Auntie planted those trees," Denia said mournfully. "I hate the thought of cutting them all down."

"Your safety is more important than a bunch of trees. Maybe you should sleep on it. Consider the ongoing events since you've been here, each more dangerous than the last. I *feel* the darkness over that grotto," she said with a shiver.

"Cassie, how does this psychic thing work for you? Is it

visions? I don't understand it."

"I wish *I* could understand it," she exclaimed. "It's a clairvoyance that just comes to me. Sometimes it happens right when I'm ready to fall asleep or early in the morning. It's always accompanied by a strong emotion. Then I have to try to make sense of it. Sometimes – like now – I would like to force it, if I could get an answer or be led in the direction to solve the dilemma; but trying to make it happen never works. I can't use my abilities on demand. It's more of a free-floating thing that will come when it's ready. My fears for Mel were too nonspecific and came too late to save her. It's very frustrating, even painful at times."

"How long have you had this?"

"Oh, I've always had it, for as long as I can remember. When I was a child, my mother thought it was dreams, or an overactive imagination, until some of my predictions came true. I remember telling her that Daddy was going to leave us. I was about five years old at the time. He left my mother a few months later. Several times things like that happened. Gradually, my mother came to realize I had some sort of psychic ability, although she never spoke of it to others or encouraged it. I think she feared my gift, if you would call it that."

"When Evelyn and I first met each other, I was a teenager, and she was a child. We were immediately drawn to each other, not only because we shared the same father but because we both sensed a psychic bond, even when we were young. Both of us have abilities but access them differently. She is adept at scrying, using a crystal ball – yes, there is such a thing – and tea leaves. She also uses tarot cards. I think we would both agree my predictions are less frequent than hers, but more specific and accurate.

"For now, I sense the same dark energy has hovered over this place since before Melinda's death. The Doves have focused on trying to bring an energy of light and dispel the darkness during our meetings, trying to combine our spiritual strength. We feel helpless as these events keep happening here. Maybe you should think about coming to stay with Batty or me for a while?" Cassie offered.

"That's so generous of you," said Denia with all seriousness. "I treasure the support the Doves have given me. I'm at the point of being more *angry* than scared about what's been happening. I believe I need to pursue this, both for Auntie's sake and my own. I need to get off the defensive and take action. I want to find out who killed Auntie. I feel an urging to do it. I think I *will* talk to Keith about changing the grotto. Trees can grow back. It would send a strong message to whoever is haunting this place."

Denia enjoyed her evening with Cassie. The psychic had no complaints about the bed Denia made for her on the sofa and juggling for the use of one bathroom had not been a problem. After coffee and a bowl of Cream of Wheat, Cassie had left in the morning looking like she had spent the night at a comfortable resort. Denia had developed a healthy respect for the good witch.

Today was another day. Cassie helped her think through her confusion over what to do about leaving or staying at the ranch ending with resolve – she would fight back.

"Hi Keith," she said when the strong, male voice

answered her phone call.

"Denia," he said in surprise at her call, "what's wrong?" immediately jumping to the probability of another problem.

"I wanted to talk to you about clearing the grotto as you suggested."

"Yes, I think we need to do that - the sooner, the better."

Denia felt a sudden spike of anger at his possessive use of the term 'we'. She felt strongly that this was *her* decision to make, not his, and there was no 'we' about it.

"Can you get someone out here this afternoon?" she asked, trying not to show her impromptu feelings.

"Yeah, I can knock off around three o'clock and get there with some chain saws and a trailer to haul the stuff away. I'll bring Carlos and a couple extra hands."

"I want to be there," Denia insisted.

"You don't need to come. We can take care of it," he said dismissively.

"Yes, I *do* need to be there. You are not in charge of this, *I am*. If that's not good for you, I'll call someone else."

"Too much coffee this morning?" he asked in a sarcastic tone.

"What?" she asked, temporarily bewildered, then understood his sarcasm.

"I appreciate your help, Keith, but this is still my property and my decision."

"Right," he answered, giving up on dealing with her

bitchy mood. "I'll see you around three."

He abruptly disconnected the call.

Denia stared at the phone in her hand, irked by his sharp disconnect.

"That didn't go well," she said to Angus at her feet.

The man had a way of taking charge of things that ticked her off. Then Denia considered that he was used to running everything in his world, so what did she expect? She wondered if she would be able to stand her ground against him. Well, if she couldn't deal with Keith who proposed to help her, how would she be able to defeat those conspiring against her, whoever they were?

That afternoon, she made sure she was sitting under the old oak tree by the pond when Keith arrived with Carlos and two other men. They carried two chainsaws and towed a trailer behind a tractor through the string of eucalyptus trees around to the rocks by the enclosed grotto. Keith rode in on Wheaty and led him over to the pond near Denia before dismounting from his horse.

"I want to look at the place with you before you get started," Denia said, quickly taking charge. "I don't want to cut down *all of* the trees. My aunt planted these trees, so I would like to save some of them."

Keith was quiet. He followed her as they walked along the path of the turtle stones to the hidden rock amphitheater. When they reached the spot where the willows thinned, Denia pushed the long branches aside and entered the enclosure.

Standing at the back of the circle Denia tried to look at the space through her Aunt Melinda's eyes. She imagined the Doves standing around the fire pit, casting their circle, calling on their Goddess and practicing their magic. The place so reflected Melinda, the high priestess, that Denia felt a strong hesitation for making changes. It was the same hesitation she felt when she thought of changing her aunt's bedroom - as if in making a change, she would lose more of the woman's spirit or essence. She wanted to hang on to this piece of Melinda – a sacred place for the Doves - her coven.

"Let's just cut the front of the trees to about here," she indicated.

Denia walked over to where the trees started to form the side of the circle furthest from the pond. Her thinking was that instead of a circle, a U-shaped space would remain once some of the trees were removed, with the front open to view from the field.

"Are you sure that's all you want to take out?" Keith asked. "It's not even half of the trees."

"Well, it would open the space and provide a sightline into the circle from the field and orchard. It would be much easier to see any activity at night, especially if there is a fire. It would also allow us to save some of Aunt Melinda's willows. They *are* really beautiful."

"What about the stone, fire circle and the pedestals?"

"Leave them," she said with firm finality, and walked away from the tall man and out of the circle.

Keith shook his head at her decision, watching her back as she walked away. He couldn't figure her out, but he was sure he was seeing a stubborn streak. What good was taking out few trees going to do? He grumbled to himself. Denia was obviously determined to save most of what made up the enclosure. He frowned thinking this would not solve the problem with whoever was sneaking onto the land to use this grotto.

The days were starting to get shorter. Late that afternoon Denia made sure that Billy and Roxy were fed and, in the barn, ready for the night by five o'clock. She put Angus on a leash, leading him out the back door and started across the field from behind the garage. Normally, she would just let the puppy follow her out to the pond, which she did frequently in the afternoon, but she knew he needed to start his training to walk on a lead. He was not happy about it, alternating between pulling and running in front of her as she walked. It took about three times as long to cross the field from the house to the pond due to frequent stops to untangle the leash from his little legs. Denia wanted to see the changes at the grotto now that Keith and his crew had left. She waved to Carlos at his small campsite behind the old oak while following the path of turtle stones on to the work site.

She carried a full box of table salt which she opened as she walked through the new, wide opening made by Keith and his men. Tree stumps had been cut even with the ground, surrounded by light colored sawdust shreds. The grotto was no longer secluded. The entrance opening was wide enough to be seen from the orchard, barnyard and office building across the field, providing a clear view of the rock walls. She let go of the puppy's leash and he ran into the circle toward the high, granite wall at its front.

Denia walked to the first pedestal holding a candle on her left and sprinkled salt into the shallow basin around the candle. She proceeded to the next pedestal sitting in front of remaining willows and added some salt. She continued around the semi-circle until she reached the rock face.

Angus found the fire pit and removed a partially burnt stick dragging it around the space, his new leash trailing in the dirt. Denia noticed the men had removed the long, flat, stone slab to which Billy had been restrained. She was glad. She had not mentioned it to Keith, but she never wanted to see that again with its stain of the goat's blood.

Across the space, the natural rock wall protruded on the right side with boulders of declining height before another screen of willow trees began. These trees blocked any view of the oak tree on the other side and the pond, but breaks in the boulders allowed points of view. At a few places from the outside one could peek into the semi-circle where willow branches did not completely obscure the view between the rocks.

Denia continued along the interior of the circle, placing salt in each pedestal basin on the remaining side. Last, she walked to the center of the space. Denia knew nothing about witchcraft or their practice of magic, but she knew that Batty had put salt around her house for protection on the first day she met her. She filled her hand with a mound of the white grains, closed her hand, and began to twirl around with her arm outstretched allowing the salt crystals to escape through her fingers as she spun.

Not knowing any of the deities held close by her aunt, Denia said her own silent prayer to any goddess of light who might hear her plea for protection. She continued the rotations until the salt box was almost empty. Angus, thinking this was a new game, ran about barking in puppy yelps.

Finally, picking up the dog leash, she moved to the newly formed opening of the circle. Using the last of the salt she drew a line across the entrance. As she walked back toward the house, with daylight fading, Denia felt a sense of accomplishment. She had drawn her own line in the dirt, *her* dirt.

The next morning Denia had just completed her 'egg run' into town and was mentally preparing for an afternoon in the Candlewick office. Driving home, she thought about all the sudden orders that came in for candles over the last week, many requesting overnight delivery. She asked Olivia why the spike in orders.

"Oh, it's Mabon, dear. This happens every year at this time."

"Mabon?" asked Denia trying out the strange word. "I've never heard of that."

"You've heard of the fall equinox, haven't you? Mabon, which is one of the Sabbaths that witches celebrate, takes place on the fall equinox, in our Wheel of the Year. It's one of the three Sabbaths during the autumn season, celebrating the harvest. The Equinox is usually toward the end of September, around the twenty-first of the month – next week. So, that's probably why the rush on candles. Next comes Samhain, or Halloween, to you. At the end of October, we start with the holiday candles."

"I can run these to town to get shipped this afternoon," said Denia, indicating the stack of packages ready to go.

Denia had been trying to get at least two batches of candles done every day. She had missed on Sunday due to Dragon's snakebite, but had been keeping up, otherwise.

Now she parked the Explorer in the driveway without putting it into the garage knowing she would be going back to town later.

She was walking toward the back patio of the house when a green pickup truck pulled into the driveway. The truck came to a stop near the back door just as Denia got there. Keith jumped out of the truck and bounded to meet her on the flagstone patio.

"Hello, there. What are you doing here in the middle of the morning?" Denia asked, knowing he was usually in the fields during the day.

"I was driving by and thought you might have some leftover coffee. Also, I wanted to find out if you approved of the work we did removing the trees."

"I think I can scrounge up some coffee. In fact, I could use some myself before I hit the Candlewick building. Come on in."

Keith breathed a sigh of relief as he followed her into the kitchen. Denia seemed to be in a good mood, and friendly, which was a change from their last couple encounters. Denia let Angus out of his crate and Keith offered to take him out back for a potty break while Denia started a pot of coffee.

When he came back in, he found Denia making a couple of peanut butter and jelly sandwiches. She cut them in half and put them on little plates. Cutting up a pear, she evenly distributed the pieces beside the sandwiches. Keith followed the puppy into the living room and took up residence on the green chair. Denia carried the plates into the room, putting Keith's on the little lamp table, and went back to the kitchen to retrieve the coffee mugs. Denia sat down on the sofa and took her plate onto her lap.

"This chair is comfy," said Keith, taking a large bite out of the sandwich. "You don't always have to feed me you know, but this is good."

"It's the least I can do after the quick job you did up by the pond."

"Is it what you had in mind?"

"It's *exactly* what I had in mind. It looks more open, and I still have most of my aunt's willow trees. Thank you for helping me with that."

"It did turn out better than I thought it would."

Denia noticed Keith was wearing an aqua, polo shirt and tan, casual pants instead of his usual jeans. He didn't have his cowboy hat, either.

"How come you're not working in the middle of the day?"

"We're done," he said between bites.

"Done with what?"

"The harvest. The grapes are all in as of yesterday. Every year it's such a relief when we're finished. Of course, Kristen and her crew are still busy as hell getting them all pressed and the wine in barrels. I'll go over and look in on it this afternoon."

"What will you do now?"

"Oh, there's still loads to do, don't get me wrong; but I always give my field managers and permanent crews a couple weeks off after the harvest is in. We've been working six days a week and long hours, so it gives everyone a chance to spend time with their families. I want to take some time to relax myself. I plan to play some golf next week."

Denia jumped up from the sofa as the phone in the kitchen rang, and she went to grab it from the counter.

"Hello?"

"Hi, Denia?" a familiar male voice asked. "This is Eugene."

"Oh, hi," Denia said in surprise.

She had written the attorney off for expecting any further dates.

"How are you doing?" he asked, but not giving her time to answer before continuing. "I'm sorry I haven't called sooner, but it's been busy around here the last couple weeks."

"I understand. I've been busy myself getting this candle business up to speed again."

Denia wondered why this guy was calling.

"I needed to touch base with you about the offer on the land. The development company called me first thing this morning wanting to know if I had heard anything from you."

"I've decided not to sell the land. Please tell them that I appreciate the generous offer, but this is a rural area, and I can't see my aunt's land being turned into a lot with townhouses. Somehow, I don't think she would want that."

There was a moment of silence at the other end of the line.

"Are you sure? This is probably a once-in-a-lifetime offer," the attorney questioned.

"Yes, I'm sure. We're in the middle of horse and grape country here. We don't need the development."

"Okay, I'm just thinking of your best interests. I'll let them know," he said. "In the meantime, how about dinner next week? I know of a great, little, Italian place in Pismo Beach."

"Actually, I'm really pretty busy here getting this business going again, and I already have a golf date lined up for next week. Can I take a raincheck?"

"Sure, I'll check back in a couple weeks," he said, feeling Denia's coolness through the connection. "Talk to you soon."

"Okay, goodbye."

Denia walked back into the living room where Keith remained in the chair by the fireplace, with a coffee mug in his hand and Angus curled at his feet.

"I couldn't help but overhearing. *Were* you thinking of selling the place?" Keith asked, his mind racing with how he felt about that.

"No, not really. I had an offer from a development company. They wanted to build townhouses."

"Townhouses?" he asked. "That would really change the neighborhood, *if* they could get it through the zoning committee."

"Yeah, can you imagine what my aunt would have said about that?"

"So, you have a golf date next week?" he asked with a knowing smile, changing the subject.

"No, I was just letting him down easy. We've had one date that was nice, but there were no sparks, if you know what I mean. And he hasn't called me for a while."

"Do you think *we* would have sparks?" he asked, smiling, putting her on the spot.

"Only if you think you can tell me what to do, then there'll be sparks," she said lightly, but with a grain of truth.

"Me?" he said innocently. "I wouldn't do that."

Denia felt relieved that afternoon, after the little lunch and coffee with the good-natured man and his hazel eyes. She thought through the comfortable conversation over peanut butter and jelly. It was nothing like the restrained dinner with the handsome attorney. Mutual respect was established between Keith and Denia, and some ground rules were defined.

A calm evening set in. The cats were fed and settled. The puppy dozed, having sweet dreams of romping in the yard and those good doggy treats. The TV mumbled in the background as Denia searched on her laptop computer when she heard a knock at the back door. Thinking it might be Cassie again, Denia was surprised to see Agatha waiting on the doorstep.

She opened the door and immediately noticed the overnight bag that the redhead with long, naturally curly hair, carried in one hand. Her almond-brown eyes were smiling, with crinkles at the edges.

"So, did you draw the short straw to stay overnight on my couch?" Denia asked as she ushered her in.

"No, I volunteered," she answered. "Actually, when you visited the art studio you mentioned something that perked my interest. I want to see the secret room of Melinda's that you spoke of."

Denia had not seen Agatha since she stopped by her Solvang art studio on her quest to deliver the remaining seasonal candles she had made. The name of the studio – Art with Agatha – was in letters on an awning over the blue enamel, front door and written in gold letters arching across the front window. The studio was just off a main street in the town across from a small, public park. It was set in between an antique store on the corner and a jewelry store featuring American Indian workmanship.

At the time, Agatha had stopped her work on a watercolor canvas to give Denia a tour. The front of the shop held a glass counter that displayed jewelry. Large gemstones were set in silver metal on gleaming chains. Moonstones, amber, amethyst and other precious stone pendants vied for space on velvet display trays. Towers with dangling earrings stood on top of the counter. Shelves behind the counter held vases of various colors and size, made from blown glass, or glazed pottery. Tables in the shop showed multiple pieces, each featuring an artist, sometimes kiln-fired pieces, sometimes sculptures. A set of shelves along one wall highlighted objects carved from wood, with smooth edges and high polish that emphasized the curving woodgrains. The front room of the studio primarily held smaller works of art, which opened into a large, back room that was divided into spaces used to show framed paintings of all sizes.

Brochures were available to provide information about the various local artists. Denia noticed a staircase in the back corner which disappeared as it led to an upper story. It was closed off with a velvet rope holding a sign marked 'private'. Denia wondered if that was where the coven of witches was meeting since her aunt's death.

Tonight, Denia understood the conspiracy among the witches. They were trying to protect her from harm or being alone. The animals seemed to be getting used to the frequent guests. After refusing tea or coffee, Agatha and Denia discussed Dragon's progress. It happened that he was discharged from the hospital and was once again staying with his mother. His foot was bandaged and propped up on pillows on Batty's flowered sofa. Batty had instructions to bring him back to the hospital daily for wound care and dressing changes, since he was unable to drive himself.

"Do you really want to see Auntie's little room?" Denia asked.

"Yes, I would like to see it."

"Okay. It's a small space beside her bedroom."

"That's funny. I always imagined she would have a little space out in the workshop in the garage. Her husband built the garage, and he had added the little workshop because he wanted to make furniture. He actually built the shelves on each side of the fireplace there, and the book cabinets up in the master bedroom for Melinda. I think he did the shelves in the pantry, too."

Agatha followed Denia up the staircase of the two-story house holding the flashlight Denia had given her. The dim overhead hallway light cast long, thin shadows on the wall. Agatha peeked into the bathroom and Denia's room as she walked along the upstairs landing.

"You really should be seeing this during the day when the light is better," Denia said as she walked into the bedroom, moving to the closest bedside table to turn on the dragonfly, Tiffany-style, bedside lamp.

Isis stirred from her spot on the bed but did not leave. Agatha stood looking at the bookcase taking up most of the wall and its crammed shelves.

"She loved her books. These must have been her favorites."

Agatha turned and looked around the bedroom.

"Denia, this room looks like you expect her to be coming back."

"I know," Denia said somberly. "I *do* need to get in here and clean it out. I admit, I've been procrastinating. I haven't been ready to deal with all of these very, personal things of Auntie's."

"Maybe you should invite all of us over for an afternoon and we can help you," suggested Agatha referring to the Doves.

"That's a thought. For now, I'd just like to know that whoever killed her was behind bars. *That* is more important to me than getting this room cleared out."

Denia walked to the closet, sliding back the door concealing the clothes Melinda used for coven meetings. She pushed the hangers toward the middle of the rung. Denia fixed the beam of her flashlight on the non-apparent doorway and pushed against it with her free hand. The panel opened. Denia moved into the small, dark room followed by the curious Agatha. Some light flowed into the little space from the bedroom, but the space was also lit in a ghostly manner by light flowing down from the large, round skylight. The moon had risen early, and though it was not yet overhead, some of its light filtered in. Evening stars could be seen with their pinpricks of light from the distant sky.

Agatha gasped as her gaze was drawn upward. She panned the beam of her flashlight to see the painted stars on the ceiling and the band of moons in their phases lining the top of the walls. She noticed the small desk with its stool, and the dressed alter at the far end. Most of her time was spent examining the paintings on the walls, depicting objects of the earth and its atmosphere. She was amazed at the active volcano, the spinning tornado, and the peaceful scenes of a quiet beach and snowcapped mountains.

Denia remained silent, giving Agatha all the time she needed to take in the magical, but personal room. She heard Agatha sniff and could tell she was moved to tears. Denia moved out into the bedroom, giving Agatha some time to herself. She sat on the bed and stoked the soft fur of the black cat.

When they left Melinda's bedroom and went downstairs, Agatha was quiet, still trying to take in all she had seen.

"You know we all have a space in our homes, a special area where we can do daily devotions and practice our magick," Agatha said referring to herself, and the other Doves. "Olivia has a whole bedroom set aside that she calls 'her study'. Mel never ceased to amaze me - her spirit, her strength, and her magick. That room is so special. You could get rid of it and enlarge the bedroom, but I would hate to see it lost."

"As long as I'm here, it won't be lost. I can't imagine painting over those intricate paintings Auntie did by hand to make a larger closet. No, Auntie's secret room stays as it is."

"There was something I wanted to talk to you about," Agatha said after they were settled on the sofa. "It may not be important, but maybe it is. You remember I have been trying to identify any art buyers who were focusing on the occult since the Stonehenge painting was stolen?"

"Yeah, have you found something?" Denia asked expectantly. "I would love to get that painting back."

"No, nothing about the painting, but I did have an interesting encounter at the studio last Saturday. Two men came in and were browsing through when they came to stand by a set of carved wooden plaques I imported by an artist in Ireland. They're mine and not for sale. I have them displayed behind my desk at the back of the studio. One of the men was young and good looking, and the other older with graying hair, and a little beard. They started asking questions about the plaques and how much I was charging for them. I explained they were not for sale but gave them the name of the Irish artist and his contact information."

"Are the plaques something of the occult?"

"No, but it does have something to do with our spiritual beliefs. The magick we practice involves the use of energy – our personal energy – and the energy of the earth and universe. The essence of the energy that comes from the earth is divided into four elements: earth, air, fire, and water. When you look at the pictures Mel painted in her room, they are depicting various forms of those elements. There are the mountains, the land, or the earth. The breeze, the gale, the wind, are all components of the air. The flame of the candle, the fire in the hearth or circle is the energy of the fire. The droplet, the stream, the oceans, all represent the energy of water. That is what the set of wall plaques in my studio are about. Each carving is a scene of nature featuring one of the elements, and together they represent the source of our energy, the energy we draw from to practice our magick.

"Most people would look at those plaques and think

they were nice, picturesque, wood carvings. But the two men that came in on Saturday *knew* what they were and understood what they represented. I almost asked them if they were associated with a coven, but that is just not done," Agatha finished. "I just thought it was unusual."

"Did you find out who they were?" Denia asked.

"No, they didn't buy anything, so there was no chance of looking at a credit card. They looked like tourists. They came into my studio after going through the antique shop next door."

"Do you know of any other covens in the area?"

"There are always lone practitioners who aren't associated with a coven. Some networking goes on, especially now that so many people use social media. I haven't heard of any male covens in the area, but that doesn't mean they don't exist. There are many covens that have male and female members."

Denia mentally stored the information Agatha reported, not sure if it meant anything related to the things going on around the ranch. In the back of her mind, she felt the person or persons who plagued the place were male. Her aunt's killer was probably not a woman due to the force of the blow to her head which caused the skull fracture. She had *seen* the prowler who looked like a man. She couldn't fathom a woman taking Billy to the grotto to kill her or putting a rattlesnake into the bunkhouse. Not only did it seem to be a man, but possibly a *group* of men. Maybe these men Agatha saw were somehow involved.

The rest of the evening was uneventful, ending with the tasks of getting ready for the night. Agatha settled in nicely, making herself comfortable. Denia retreated to her bedroom early giving Agatha the privacy of the living room. Lying in bed she tried to decide what she should do. Her resolve to stay on the ranch vacillated in the darkness.

The next day, Denia was in the nearby town of Orcutt, at a second hardware store looking for 'No Trespassing' signs. Lee Nelson had called that morning telling her she needed to post signs so the police could arrest anyone found on the property without permission. At last, she found the signage section of the store harboring 'Beware of Dog', 'For Rent', and 'Yard Sale' metal placards. At the bottom of the shelves, she found a sign – 'Private Property – 'No Trespassing' – with red block letters on a white background. There were five similar signs, and she bought them all.

Once home, after finding a hammer and nails in the garage workshop, she put the first sign up at eye-level on the orchard side of the back gate. She had a harder time nailing the sign into the stucco of the office building by the door. She posted two more signs at both driveway entrances at the front of the property.

Last, she jumped into the Explorer taking the remaining sign and tools. She drove out the driveway and onto the road leading toward the vineyard. She studied the roadside for unfamiliar vehicles as the road curved to the north encircling her land. She parked the car directly in front of the locked, double gates leading to the now empty vineyard. Again, she nailed the sign to the fencepost next to the gates. She stood back looking at the sign, thinking she should have put up the signs sooner.

That afternoon Denia was holed up in the small office in the front of the Candlewick building, looking out across the yard at the chicken coop. She had already made a set of cranberry-colored tapers, and a set of cinnamon tower candles. Denia looked at Mona, who was stretched out on the low wall outside. Angus slept on the floor after a flurry of activity in the yard with Billy and Roxy.

Using the large desk, Denia had removed Melinda's computer from the police evidence bag where it had been for the last couple weeks, and plugged it in and turned it on, allowing it time to boot up. She was now familiar with the Candlewick website. She knew where to find the new orders and how to process them. Olivia was still coming in at least two days a week, and the employee continued to train her boss. Denia was still far from self-sufficient both with the website and the candle-making process.

The Candlewick website never clearly said the candles were made for those practicing witchcraft; but some of the labels and advertising of the merchandise gave hints of possible use for magical practices. Only those knowledgeable would discern hints of the spirituality. There were two places on the website where customers could give feedback on the candles or the service. One was by using the *Customer Service* tab. The other was the *Contact Us* tab. Olivia had once mentioned that they had gotten some negative comments.

Now, Denia wanted to find them.

She started with the *Contact Us* log and scrolled back to

January. She read every entry, many expressing satisfaction with the products, some discussed problems with the shipping process where the candles arrived damaged. Denia mauled on through the log until she got to April, where one entry stood out.

"You may be able to fool others, but this business is evil, pandering to the occult, Beware, God is watching you."

Taking out a pad of legal paper, Denia logged the date and time of the entry. She continued her review and found another entry two weeks later.

"This is a website for witches and their practice. God will punish you."

Then in June, the rhetoric appeared even more lethal.

"The evil that you practice will come down on your head. Beware of the hand of God!"

The hairs at the back of Denia's neck prickled. That was a threat. She continued to go through the log, noting the date and time of any entry that struck her as negative, threatening, or referring to witchcraft.

When she was finished, she unplugged the computer and placed it back into the police evidence bag. She was angry. Why had no one reported these threats to the police? When the police were looking at the computer, had they missed these communication tabs on the Candlewick website?

After putting Angus into the house, she took her purse and keys and locked the door. She went to the Explorer and put Melinda's laptop and her legal pad on the front seat, as she started the car. She drove out of the driveway and headed toward Solvang, for the second time in one day.

The parking lot at the Solvang Sherriff Station was almost empty when Denia pulled into a space. The uniformed officer at the front desk called back to Lee Nelson at her request, and shortly later he came out to meet her.

"If someone was sending threatening messages to Melinda's business, would you be able to trace who was sending them?" she asked the sergeant.

"Yes, we should be able to do that through the IP address. What do you got?"

"Here's the employee log-in for the Candlewick website. On the website is a tab that allows customers to contact us. Under that tab I've found some threatening notices. Here is a list of them, with the dates and times of when they were sent. They stopped in July around the time when my aunt was killed."

Lee Nelson took the legal pad, scanning Denia's research.

"Here's the computer back. Only internal Candlewick employees can get into the log with their log-on, and this computer allows access. The customer can enter their statement, but what other people have entered can't be seen, only their own entry. The log shows *all* of the comments from the customers, and they are all dated."

"Okay. This is a good lead. I wish we would have found it sooner. Let me make some phone calls. I might have to drive this down to Santa Barbara today and get our data experts on it right away. This is a murder investigation, so I have some clout. I want to talk to them and take your list and we'll see what we can find. Hopefully, these messages were sent from a personal computer and not from a public computer in some library."

Later, Denia was working on getting a supply order ready for the next day. She needed to order more paraffin, and decided to order some bees wax for customers preferring candles made from the natural substance. She also needed some wick spools, which she added to the order when she heard a knock at the back door.

Denia sighed and got up, expecting to find another one of the Doves standing on the patio. When she went to answer the door, she was surprised to find the big man known as the Owl...Snowy.

"I hope you don't think *you're* going to spend the night on my sofa," she said to the tall, wide figure with his shock of white hair.

"No, I brought my sleeping bag. I can sleep in the bunkhouse."

"I'm beginning to think you are all taking turns babysitting. Who called you?" Denia asked, wanting to know.

"Batty," he said, with his gruff voice. "Believe me, she would rather be here herself. Kevin is driving her nuts. He's bored. He's fairly immobile and expecting her to make at least three meals a day."

Denia laughed. She had already heard the tirade from Batty about Dragon when she called that morning.

"Yeah, she's pleading with me to take him back."

"He's got me involved, too. He wants me to hook up the TV in the bunkhouse while I'm here so he can use it when he comes back."

Then remembering, "Oh, and he wants you to bring the puppy over. He's afraid Angus will forget him."

"Oh, please," Denia replied. "Batty says he's hobbling around the house and is on the phone to everyone he knows trying to get sympathy."

As they came into the dining area Snowy noticed that Denia had her computer open.

"Oh, good. There was something I found online last night that I think may interest you."

He sat down at the table in the chair next to where Denia had been sitting and pulled his nifty Dell Tablet out of the backpack that had been hanging on his shoulder.

"What's in the backpack?" Denia asked, noticing the severe bulging from the pack.

"Other than some clothes for tomorrow, I brought some papers I need to grade for my new astronomy class. It's an accelerated course in the evening. We cover a lot of ground, or should I say sky, in a six-week term. I need to have these ready to hand back by next Tuesday night."

While talking, Snowy was deftly working on his tablet keyboard.

"You're not going to try to talk me into any alien abduction theories, are you?" she chided.

"Remember that guy named Dylan Blackwell, you

wanted me to try to find? I searched several of the sites and chat rooms I routinely use and found nothing. Then last night I was in an educational website and found the guy's name which led me to this. Here, take a look."

Denia looked at the page displayed on the tablet. "Sacramento State University?"

"Yeah, the guy is on the faculty there. That was the *last* place I thought to look. I had been looking on some underground sites on the dark web."

Denia looked at the page displayed on the tablet. There was a black and white photo of a fifty-something man. It was a pleasant looking face with short graying hair, a narrow nose, and serious eyes looking into the camera for the picture. His mouth was closed with thin lips. He was clean shaven, other than a small goatee that ended below the line of the chin. There was a brief bio beside the picture:

Professor Dylan Blackwell was born in Cardiff, Wales, Great Britain. He took his undergraduate studies at Oxford, and received his B.D. at St. Andrews University, Fife, Scotland in Eurasian History. He began his academic career at the University of Edinburgh in Scotland, and later taught at Queen's University in Ontario, Canada. Coming to the United States in 2010, he taught Neolithic and Mesolithic Eurasian Studies at the University of Washington in Seattle, Washington. Currently at Sacramento State, he teaches both Early Eurasian History and History of the British Isles.

"Hmmm. I wonder if this could be the guy Dragon saw at the tattoo parlor. Agatha also described a man who visited her studio on Saturday. I asked Lee Nelson to check on the name for me and he said the guy had a driver's license, but there was not so much as a parking ticket."

"Well, if it is him, at least you know something about him," said Snowy. "There may be some connection here with his field of study. If we are looking at the occult, Paganism actually started in ancient Eurasia. Just a thought," the college professor side of the man showing itself.

"The real question is, does this have anything to do with the problems we've had around here of someone coming onto the ranch property, or my aunt's death?"

"Not sure kiddo, but let's keep the lights on out back. I'm going to get my sleeping bag and tool kit out of the car and go on out to the bunkhouse. Call me if you need something," he said, slipping his tablet back into his backpack.

It was a sunny, fall day in September. Denia felt the subtle change in the air that morning when she was out with the chickens. Joe was taking a college class, so he would not be there until afternoon. She already cleaned Billy's stall and put her, Roxy, and Angus in the fenced pen. Thinking, Denia pushed her hair back from her face. She was ready for a cool day. It had been a prickly heat summer.

She went into the house when she heard the phone ringing as she watered the plants on the patio and the small herb garden beside it. Angus followed her through the door.

When she answered, she found it was Batty with her usual morning call. She listened as Batty talked about Dragon who was doing pretty well three days after discharge from the hospital. Batty said he was hoping to return to the bunkhouse the following week. Denia asked what day, thinking she could get a few things for the little refrigerator in the bunkhouse. She had already found a new comforter set for the bed and a cover for the seen-its-better-days sofa. Denia knew Angus would be glad to see him come back.

During the conversation, Denia noticed an air of excitement coming from Batty that had nothing to do with Dragon.

"What's going on?" Denia asked, suspecting something.

"It's our Mabon celebration tonight. We're all baking something."

Denia knew Batty was referring to the Doves.

"What are you making?" Denia asked, knowing Batty did not have a reputation of being a great cook.

"I'm making half-moon sugar cookies with blue sprinkles."

"Um, sounds good – save me a couple."

"I will if I can keep them away from Kevin."

"Where is your meeting?" she asked, curiously.

"We're actually celebrating with another coven that Evelyn keeps in touch with down in Goleta. It will be in a wooded glen on a piece of land that overlooks the ocean.

We couldn't refuse the invitation. It will be a sunset ceremony."

"Well, enjoy," said Denia. "I'm just going to have a quiet evening now that none of you will be showing up to sleep on my couch."

They both chuckled.

Then, in a serious tone, "We will be thinking of Mel and you. Blessings upon you, Denia, and may the winds be fair."

"Thank you, Batty. Say hello to the sisters for me."

Denia was dreaming and in her dream, she could hear someone calling her – 'Denia, Denia.' It was an almost forgotten, female voice that she knew at once. 'Auntie,' she called back to answer in her dream.

When she came out of her dream, the darkness of the night surrounded her. She heard a soft whine from Angus, so she knew he was awake in his crate. She listened in the darkness. The house was silent. Then she heard it, a dog barking in the distance. She sat up in the bed, and the realization sunk in that it was Roxy barking in the barn.

Denia bolted out of bed, trying to think what to do as she grabbed her yoga pants, putting them on under her long, cotton nightshirt. She needed shoes to go out back and her black well-worn flats were the closest, lying by the nightstand.

Angus whined again, as the distant barking from the

barn continued.

"You stay here!" she called to him running out the bedroom door and down the stairs.

She went to the pantry and took the closest flashlight from the shelf. Going to the back door, she threw open the locks and ran toward the barn. The newly placed floodlights did their job giving her a clear view of the lot which she scanned for any movement.

Again, she heard Roxy's bark coming from the barn. She suddenly berated herself for not bringing her cell phone. She should have called Keith Clearwater, but it was too late as she was already at the barn.

When she pulled the heavy door open, she found Roxy at the stall gate, alert, with Billy awake and standing next to her. Shining the flashlight around the barn, she saw nothing out of place. Though awake, both of the animals appeared to be alright. Knowing she was alone and defenseless if someone was lurking around, she put the flashlight down and took the small pitchfork she used to clean Billy's stall. She let Roxy out of the stall and called for her to follow as Denia left the barn and struggled to open the gate to the dark orchard beyond.

She made her way along a nearby row between the trees toward the edge of the orchard that bordered the field. Now open to view, a shock went through her when she saw orange light coming from the amphitheater by the pond. Once again strangers had come onto her land uninvited. Anger filled her being as she started across the field, Roxy at her side.

A round, white moon was high in the sky surrounded by

gray clouds. As sounds came from those in the grotto, Roxy barked announcing their approach. Denia's anger over the intrusion overshadowed any common sense. She wanted to see who they were. She wanted to confront them. As the sounds from the semi-circle grew louder, Roxy loped ahead of her with the grace of a greyhound. Denia stopped at the threshold of the grotto taking in the sight.

Robes. There were men in robes. They stood facing the fire pit in black and green robes. At the front of the semi-circle, standing near the fire were two men in white robes. These two men wore headpieces – the antlers of stags. They faced the group of at least twelve men. As the man in white stopped speaking and focused on a point behind them, they turned to face Denia. Their chanting stopped.

"Welcome, Denia. Did you want to see who was here?" asked the man in the white robe, with the small beard.

A hush filled the air around the robed figures.

Denia must have looked comical to the group. She stood on the border of the circle holding a small pitchfork. Her hair was falling around her face and onto her shoulders and nightshirt. She must have looked small with the firelight reflecting on her as she stood with the black night in the background.

Denia's eyes widened, and mouth opened as she recognized the man who had spoken as Snowy's professor. Her breath caught in her throat as she recognized the man next to him in white – Eugene Sorenson. Now this was starting to make sense to her.

"Get off of my property! You are trespassing here!" She

said in a clear, unwavering declaration.

"We have done our best to buy this land in a fair way, first from your aunt and then from you," said the older man in white, "but it was to no avail."

"Why?" Denia asked. Her voice sounded small but resonated within the circle. "Why here?"

"We are the New Druids, Denia. We are growing our community in California. This is just the beginning for our sect. The central coast is at the center of the state, and we come here from the north and the south. There are hotels in Solvang. It's a tourist town. We can come and go unnoticed, as tourists do.

"But it is the *energy* of this place that draws us here. We will make it our sacred meeting place with this magnificent rock wall, the air currents finding their way here from the seacoast, and the water sounds coming from the spring flowing from the rocks. Your aunt was correct in finding the magic of this place. We can *feel* it. We can *use* it. Oh, yes, we knew of your aunt and her little coven. Their amateur wand waving cannot be compared to our ancient scripture and magic. We are strong and their clumsy ways could not deter us. When we learned the land would be left to you upon her death, it sealed your aunt's fate."

"Now it comes to you, Denia," Eugene said. "You also refused to sell. However, your Last Will and Testament *donates* this land to the Brotherhood of the Stone Circle."

"I have no Will," Denia said, unsettled to her core.

"Oh, but you do. It is already signed by you, and witnessed by a Santa Barbara Courthouse clerk," the attorney assured her.

Denia remembered the day at the courthouse when she signed several papers put in front of her by this man, one after another. Her anger deflated as the seeds of fear took root.

"I will give you another chance to sell the land to us," said the older Druid. "What say you?"

Denia took a deep breath and straightened her spine. "You will not have my aunt's land. You will not have her circle. You will not take over her magic," she said forcefully.

A murmur went through the crowd of robed men.

"Are you sure, Denia? You could be rich and find another place," asked the handsome man in white in an almost pleading voice.

When she didn't answer, he continued, "No one will be able to connect any of us should you have an accident on your land at night – while out for a walk with your dog."

The threat was spoken.

Suddenly frightened, Denia looked to her left, as the closest robed figure removed the cowl of his black robe to reveal his identity. Deputy Cleeves looked directly at her with a stare that filled her with dread. A tremor of fear ran through her body. These men had murdered her aunt for a bit of land, and she could be next.

Denia threw the pitchfork toward Cleeves and ran from the grotto, following the path of the turtle stones toward the pond. Her mind racing, she thought if she could run past the pond across the field to the house, she might be able to get to a phone or get the keys to the Explorer for an escape.

She heard footsteps on the ground coming from behind her but could not spare the time to look at her pursuer. She focused on covering as much ground as possible using the pale moonlight to find her way. She knew she was beyond the oak tree, near the far end of the pond when she felt a hand grab for her shoulder. She shrugged to dislodge the hand and temporarily increased her speed.

Disastrously, she could not match his gait. At last, he was close enough to grab her, and he threw her sideways onto the ground. She knew it was the deputy, and he was overpowering. He picked her up and tossed her into the shallow water at the far end of the pond. She turned and got to her knees in an immense effort, crawling to get away. Animal instinct told her that her life was in danger.

The man was adept and was immediately on her, grabbing her under the arms and forcing her face down into the shallow, black pond water. He straddled her body with his hands on her shoulders, holding her down. With great effort she raised her head from the water, coughing, gasping for a breath before his hand hit the back of her head forcing her face into the pond silt under the muddy water.

She held her breath and said a last prayer. She was not ready to give up but knew she had lost. She needed to breath. Within a few long, dark seconds, the moon stood witness as the night claimed her.

13

THE DRAGONFLIES

Keith Clearwater was in his truck driving home from the winery. He had been helping Kristen with pressing the last of the grapes. They had worked well into the night, not wanting to stop until it was finished.

He was proud of his little sister, who had been at every grape pressing since she was a child, curious and underfoot. For her, the process of changing the grapes into wine was what it was all about. Both Keith and Karen had to bow to her diligence and expertise in all the nuances of putting up the fruity liquid that would age into the wine. She was her father's daughter.

The familiar roadway was dark and deserted. Keith

slowed his speed as he passed the Greystone ranch, noticing that Denia had the lights on in the back lot. Everything seemed quiet. He planned to park by the back gates and walk onto the property. He had his sleeping bag in the back. Carlos was on leave with the rest of his crew after the harvest. So, unbeknownst to Denia, Keith had been sleeping up by the pond to keep an eye on the place at night. He would go home in the morning and catch a couple more hours of sleep in his bed before starting his day. So far, it was working. Keith felt he was taking the necessary action to watch over his friend's niece.

A sense of foreboding set in as he rounded the curve in the road that approached the back gates to Denia's land. First, he passed one car parked along the soft shoulder, then two more. That was unusual. He pulled onto the wide, well-used ground next to the large, double gates and parked. He threw his sleeping bag over the gates and opened the lock which was still in place. He reclosed the gates and started up the vineyard row between the picked-over vines, on his trek up the slow incline to the eucalyptus trees standing guard at the top of the hill.

Suddenly, he saw two black figures darting though the line of sentry trees on the crest of the hill, followed by three others. At first, he thought they were wearing dresses, but realized they seemed to wear cloaks that were flying out around their legs as they ran. They darted into the rows of vines, fleeing toward the road. Keith thought for a second to take after them, but feared what they may have been running *from*.

He started running himself, knowing instinctively where the center of the action would be. Thinking he needed help, he pulled out his phone and used the keypad to call Lee Nelson's number. He held the phone to his ear as he went. Getting a voice mail response, he yelled Denia's name into the phone. He placed the call for a second time, trying to give emphasis, should Lee see the second call.

He reached the eucalyptus trees and ran toward the rock amphitheater. When he arrived at the recently cleared opening, he paused. He found the circle deserted, a roaring fire still burning within the fire circle. He looked toward the house and barn, and finally toward the orchard. Two figures in white were quickly disappearing into the trees. He started across the field after them when the barking of a dog caused him to look back toward the pond.

In the moonlight next to the pond, he saw a moving figure seeming to be crouched to the ground. He could not make out what he was seeing until the light shone in a manner that let him see the figure was doing something with a dark shape below him, seeing a splash of water echoing in the quiet night. The dog barked again.

Instantly, Keith stopped and changed direction, taking long strides toward the pond. The figures became clear as he approached the pond, and his heart came into his throat. He saw the material of the nightshirt pillowing on the surface of the water. He knew it was Denia in the water, and what was happening here.

The determined would-be murderer was so focused on his task he had not heard the approaching man until a second before the full force of a flying body hit him, knocking him away from his prey and sending him, momentarily stunned, to the ground. The weight of the large man lifted as fast as it came. He moved to the water to retrieve the now limp body of the woman, dragging it to the water's edge. Looking at the man who had arrived from nowhere, the deputy knew his only hope was to flee, believing the dead could not be witness.

In his attempt to save Denia, Keith Clearwater may not have yet identified him as the killer. The dog continued to bark and pace him as he took off across the moonlit field toward the front road.

In the first hint of awareness there was darkness. A repeating, ticking sound was emanating from somewhere near her head. There was a smell. She struggled to identify the smell. Was it a disinfectant? Becoming more aware, she knew she needed to breath but started to panic as she fought for her breath. She couldn't breathe. Was she still in the pond? There was something there, in her throat.

She opened her eyes in the darkness, and the alarms from machines filled the air. Her throat. She tried to reach for her throat, only to find her hands restrained to her sides. The panic intensified as the alarms continued to blare at their individual pace. She saw the L.E.D. light panels of the machines on both sides of the raised head of the bed. She saw two figures enter the room. A dim light was switched on overhead.

"Go call R.T. to get up here, she may need to be suctioned. I'll sedate her, first," instructed a calm female voice.

Some of the alarms ceased. Denia saw hands bring the needle to the Y in the plastic IV tubing and inject the contents of the syringe. Denia felt a soft wave come over her almost immediately, and she sank back into her cocoon of unconsciousness.

Dreams came and went. Sometimes she was a girl, walking on Ocean Beach. Other times she was running along the waterfront at Mission Bay. Although she could not see him in her dream, she knew Jeff was there running beside her. She knew the puppy needed to go out. She was hot, wanting to throw off the covers. She wanted to turn over. She was running on the turtle stones. She fought to get up. She needed to go but was not sure where. Behind it all was the need to breathe. In and out she went, like the waves on the shore.

When she next became aware, she heard soft voices, as if off in the distance. The ticking of the machine continued somewhere near her head. She tried to move her hands, only to find they were still restrained at the wrist. She heard a familiar voice known all of her life. She opened her eyes. It was daytime and light filled the room, the brightness almost hurting her eyes.

"Denia, you're okay, honey," she heard the familiar voice say.

She felt the grasp of her hand, and her mother's face hovered over her. Tears sprang to her eyes. She never needed to see her mother as much as at this moment.

"It's alright, Denia. Don't try to speak. You have a tube in your throat. It's helping you breathe."

Denia's mother used a tissue to wipe away the tears running down her face.

A tall, bald man came into the room accompanied by her father.

"Hi, pumpkin. I'm glad to see you've decided to come back to us," her father said, standing beside the bed and stroking her hair, moving it aside from her face.

"The doctor said they're going to try to take that breathing tube out today. Do you understand?"

Denia nodded. She was no longer alone. Her parents were here. She was safe. The nightmare at the pond was over. Emotions overwhelmed her. She reveled in being the child again…their child. She could relax now, as she drifted back to sleep.

Two days later, Denia took another bite of the cherry gelatin that had been part of her breakfast tray. She grimaced as she swallowed. They had removed the respirator tube from her throat two days ago, leaving her with an oxygen tube and breathing treatments. Once the respirator was gone, she had been moved to another room, outside of the Intensive Care Unit.

Once alert, the doctor explained to her that she had bilateral aspiration pneumonia. During the struggle she had inhaled pond water into both of her lungs, which had wreaked havoc and caused infection. She was told that she had a concussion, which explained the headache and the dizziness when she stood up. There were no broken bones, but the front of her ribs had multiple bruises.

She also had the worst sore throat of her lifetime, accompanied by laryngitis. Swallowing anything, even water, was painful. Talking above a whisper was squeaky. By far the worst of this recovery was the coughing. Every cough was painful. The respiratory therapists told her that she needed to cough, but she dreaded the coughing spells when they came, causing tears of pain to run down her face. She was on her sixth day in the hospital and just wanted to go home. She still had an IV and was getting antibiotics and breathing treatments on a regular schedule.

Later in the morning, her mother came in. She pulled up the usual chair next to the bed. She went into all that had gone on since the previous afternoon. Her father left for home that morning. Her mother had taken him to the small Santa Barbara airport, so he could leave the car.

"Where are you staying, Mom?" Denia asked.

"With Batty, for tonight."

"What?" Denia asked with surprise.

"She offered and I accepted. I have my own bedroom and bathroom. It was very nice of her."

"Where's Dragon?"

"If you mean Kevin, as his mother calls him, he moved back to the ranch two days ago. Between him, Joe, and Hans, they're taking care of your little zoo."

"Have you been out there?"

"Yes, Batty and I went out there late yesterday afternoon

while Dad was on a conference call. I met Olivia, and she showed me all of the candles. She said that you have been a quick learner, and the business is doing as well as it did last year. I think you've done wonders with the house. It's the neatest I've ever seen it. Melinda was a bit of a pack rat. And I love the puppy, he's something else. But a goat? Denia, she's cute but what was that about?"

"Melinda bought the goat. She was going to make soap from goat's milk."

"And the puppy?"

"She wanted a watch dog. She had already picked him out from the litter."

"You've made a lot of good friends here in a short time. Look at all of these flowers!"

"Yes, Mom. A lot of those friends are witches."

"I know," her mother said, reflecting on her previous views on witchcraft. "I shouldn't have let Melinda's beliefs separate me from my only sister."

"I still haven't spread her ashes at the pond as she wished," Denia said with regret.

"Let's wait until you're fully recovered. Daddy and I will come up and we will have our own little ceremony to do that."

"The Doves have to be invited."

"The Doves… is that what they call themselves?"

"Yes, but I've promised them secrecy about that."

"You will keep your promise. We are in debt to them

for all they have done to help you. We can invite them without any mention of witches, but as friends of Melinda's."

"Thanks, Mom."

"Alright. Daddy and I can try to get some time off work. Speaking of work, the doctors are going to discharge you tomorrow, so I need to drive home in the morning. We just started the term at school, and I need to get back. I spoke with Batty. She and Olivia are going to take you home. I think they are planning a little welcome home party for you."

"Well, I hope Olivia drives, I can't handle that PT Cruiser and Batty's driving. I just want to take a shower and get this horrible hair washed. Seeing a bunch of people is the last thing I need."

"Let me talk to the nurses. Maybe you can take a shower this afternoon."

That evening Denia raised the head of the hospital bed so she was in a sitting position. She felt so much better and was looking forward to going home in the morning. She had her last dose of IV antibiotics, and the nurse had removed the IV. Her mother had gone shopping and returned with shampoo and a frilly, cotton nightgown with matching terrycloth slippers. She also brought Denia clothes from the house needed for the ride home the next day. Her mother persuaded the nurse to call the doctor to get an order for a shower for Denia.

Finally, Denia felt clean, with the horrible leftover smell of the pond water gone from her hair. She brushed out her damp hair as it air-dried. Her mother flitted about the room getting things ready for her discharge, throwing out some of the now wilted and dead flower arrangements. Her mother carefully saved all of the cards and get well wishes that would need to be acknowledged by thank you cards.

A little knock came from the door of the room and both women looked to see the tall, blonde, police sergeant still wearing his uniform. Denia waved him into the room, and he came to stand by the side of the bed.

"You look *much* better since the last time I saw you," he said to Denia; and then, "Hello, Mrs. Rawlings."

"I understand we owe you a debt of gratitude for getting Denia to the hospital in time using your police car," Helene said, smiling at the police officer.

"I was just the taxi driver. The fact that she's sitting here today is thanks to Keith Clearwater. He pulled her from the jaws of death, believe me."

"I don't remember *anything* after I was attacked," said Denia. "The last I remember, I was running to get back to the house when I was attacked next to the pond and held under the water. It was terrible," Denia related in a low, shaky voice.

"What I didn't know, and you probably didn't know, was that Keith had been sleeping in a sleeping bag up by the pond at night, in order to keep an eye on the place. He was late getting there that night because he had stayed working at the winery," related the sergeant.

"He said he came onto the property and realized there were intruders who were in the process of running away. He told me that he started to go after them, when he heard your dog bark and saw activity up by the pond. He saw the man holding you down in the water and jumped him. Then he went to pull you out of the water and tried to get you breathing again. He said he pounded on you and got some of the water out from your lungs, and that you coughed and started to breathe. Then he called 9-1-1 and carried you across the field to the house, thinking that's where the ambulance would come.

When I got there, he was by the back door trying to get you breathing again. We knew we needed to get you to the hospital and couldn't wait for the ambulance. We put you in the back seat of the police car. Keith kept working trying to keep you breathing while I drove with the lights and sirens going. I called ahead to the hospital, so they were ready for you when we got there."

"Oh, my God," said Helene, hearing the details of her daughter's near death for the first time.

"How did you know to come to the ranch?" asked Denia.

"I had two calls come in close together on my phone that I wasn't going to answer since I was in bed. When I checked the phone and saw it was two calls from Keith, I listened to the voice mail and all he said was your name. I put on some pants and sandals and ran for my car. Fortunately, I had brought the patrol car home that night," he said, pausing.

"Right away, Keith gave us the name of the assailant and I put out a warrant for him within minutes of getting you to the hospital."

"Deputy Cleeves…," said Denia, in a flat tone.

"Deputy Cleeves," Lee Nelson confirmed.

"One of your officers?" Helene said with surprise.

"Yeah, he normally worked the night shift and was responsible for watching out for problems on the ranch after we knew Melinda had been murdered. He was in the middle of all the things that were going on at night at the ranch, including the burglary. The plan was to scare Denia into selling the place."

"They almost did. I was actually considering it," said Denia.

"Were you able to catch him?"

"Oh yeah. He's been arrested for attempted murder. He's going down," he said with a matter-of-fact tone.

"The highway patrol picked him up the same night in Carpinteria. He didn't get very far. He's been cooperating with the investigation, hoping for leniency. That's not going to happen. There's nothing worse than a dirty cop. I'm afraid you'll have to testify for the court case," he said looking at Denia.

"I will. Gladly," Denia replied.

"I wanted to come here tonight because I knew you would both be here," the officer said looking from one woman to the other.

"I have information on Melinda's case, and I wanted

to tell you that we've made an arrest."

"What?" said Helene in surprise.

"Like I said, the deputy is cooperating with the investigation. He seems to have gotten caught up in a cult, or religion, or whatever it is, and was heavily influenced by these people. He gave us the name of Eugene Sorenson as one of the leaders of this group."

"Melinda's attorney?" asked Helene.

"Yep. We found out that he had been working with another man to buy the property from Melinda. We have chains of e-mails as evidence. He was also the attorney that drew up Melinda's revised Will and knew the property would go to Denia upon Melinda's death. When Melinda refused the offer to sell, he killed her."

"*Who* killed her?" interrupted Helene.

"Sorenson. You remember we had a fingerprint on the mallet? When we brought this guy in for questioning on conspiracy of attempted murder in *your* case, we got his fingerprints and found a match for the suspected murder weapon in Melinda's case. We think we have a pretty, solid case against the guy for murder-one."

"I can't believe it!" exclaimed Helene.

"I can," said Denia. "He really played me, pretending to want to date me while he was just trying to get me to sell the ranch."

"We got a search warrant for his house and office and found more evidence against him. He was heavily involved in this religious movement, and it was all over his home computer. By the way, we matched the IP address to those threatening notices sent to Candlewick. We also recovered the Stonehenge painting, covered with a tarp in his garage.

Unbelievably, he had the old Candlewick computer sitting on top of a workbench in the garage. You would think he would have gotten rid of it. Anyway, we added a burglary charge, but that's the least of his problems. Cleeves is willing to testify that Sorenson threatened to have you killed that night."

Denia's mother gasped, bringing a hand to her mouth.

"In his office at the law firm, we found a Will for you where the land would go to some Brotherhood. We also found paperwork on an equity loan for a hundred thousand dollars against your property that was approved two days prior to Melinda's murder with Addison National Bank. We think it was a forgery."

"I've been making payments on that loan," said Denia indignantly. "I couldn't find what Auntie did with the money. It didn't go into any of her accounts."

"Sorenson closed on buying a house with fifty thousand dollars down two weeks after your aunt's death. He's been spending money like water, furnishing the place and buying a new car. I'm pretty sure we're going to put this guy away for a while."

"It's astounding," said Helene. "Who would kill people just to get their land?"

"What about the other guy?" asked Denia. "That Dylan Blackwell was running the show at the grotto that night when they tried to kill me."

"That one is a little more difficult," Lee started to explain. "He's already hired a high-power attorney that we need to work through. It would be your word against his about him being there the other night. He has three people attesting he was in San Francisco that night, and Cleeves refuses to say he was there. Sorenson won't give him up, either.

"As far as buying the land from you, he says he gave legitimate offers and has the money in the bank to show he could have paid you for it. The guy is loaded – old family money. He has vast land holdings in Wales. He says he had no idea that Sorenson was up to anything illegal. We'll take it to the District Attorney, but as of right now we don't have enough evidence to charge him with anything."

"So, he just gets away?" Denia asked, not believing the professor would get off with nothing charged.

"I can't lie to you. Unless Sorenson or Cleeves are willing to testify against him, we have nothing to go on. He's very clever. Even the e-mails from him to Sorenson are benign and appear above board. Most of what they discussed was about references to books and religion."

"Wow," said Denia, shaking her head.

They all heard a knock at the door and turned to see a man with a puppy coming into the room.

"You can't bring him in here," said Denia, as Keith Clearwater put the puppy down on the bed with her.

"I can until they kick us out," he said in mock defiance. "How are you feeling?"

Denia was temporarily trying to control the little

chocolate lab who was up in her face, licking and wiggling with delight. Helene Rawlings stood up and walked around the bed to stand next to the man with a tanned complexion and jet-black hair.

"I'm Helene Rawlings, Denia's mother," she said holding out her hand.

"Keith Clearwater," he said, gently taking her hand.

"I understand that you are the hero responsible for saving my daughter's life."

"We were just very lucky with the timing, both for me and for Lee getting there in time."

"Well, her father and I would sincerely like to thank you. She's a strong, young woman and we are very proud of her, but I think she's a little too independent at times," she said, leaning over to hug Denia and getting a puppy kiss.

"And stubborn," he said with a smile.

"Hey, I'm sitting right here," Denia said, smirking.

"Are you going to be here for a while?" Keith asked Helene.

"No, I have to get back to work. I'm leaving in the morning. Batty and Olivia will be taking Denia home and keeping an eye on her for the next few days."

"I think we're *all* going to keep an eye on her," said Keith. "She has a way of attracting turmoil."

A nurse walked into the room and took a moment to take in the crowd, as well as the puppy on the bed.

"Visiting hours are over," she said. "Please say your

goodnights."

She walked out of the room, deciding not to make an issue over the dog.

"Yeah, we better go," said Lee. "We'll be in touch with you to come into the station and give us a statement as soon as you feel up to it."

He started walking toward the doorway.

"I have to get this little guy home before Dragon comes after me," Keith said, lifting the puppy from Denia's arms.

"See you soon," he said looking at Denia, as he made his way to catch up with Nelson.

After they left the room, "Two good looking men. Are they married?" Denia's mother asked lightly.

"Mommm," Denia groaned.

Her mother picked up her purse and prepared to leave.

"I'll stop by early in the morning. I have a long drive home tomorrow. Good night, honey."

She leaned in and kissed Denia on the forehead and squeezed her hand.

"Sweet dreams."

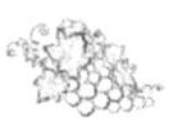

At mid-morning, Olivia and Batty showed up at the hospital to take Denia home. Denia was already dressed and packed all of her personal belongings, which were few. For the remaining flowers in vases that were retaining their freshness, she donated them to the nurse's station and the nurse's lounges as a little thank you.

Batty was excited to see Denia. She had obviously taken extra care in dressing this morning, wearing a dress and a string of pearls. Her hair was tightly reined in with combs and a clip at the back of her head. She had even bothered to put on some light eye makeup and lipstick.

Olivia also looked nice in her department store pant set, made in such a manner as to be kind to the more mature woman's figure. She was a vision in shades of peach. Olivia went to tell the nurses that Denia was ready to leave, taking charge of the discharge procedure.

After signing multiple pages and acknowledging discharge orders, Denia was put into a wheelchair and taken to the front lobby. Outside, they waited in the loading zone while Olivia went to get her car. Batty loaded the back seat and got in, while the nurse supported Denia getting into the front, passenger seat.

Other than some small talk, the ride to Solvang and through the little town was quiet. Now that she was out of the hospital and on her way home, a renewed thankfulness for being alive struck Denia. The colors of the tree leaves impressed her with their simple beauty. The flowers along the main street were brighter. Even the air held the scents of the town.

A lump rose in Denia's throat as they came upon the little house with its tan exterior, happy front windows and charcoal roof. Olivia pulled into the driveway and parked by the back patio. Denia was determined to walk to the back door by herself, though there was a touch of dizziness when she stood up to get out of the car.

As she opened the kitchen door, she could smell the freshly brewed coffee and saw trays and platters of different kinds of food lining the kitchen counters.

As she walked through the kitchen, moving into the dining area, Denia saw that all of the Doves were here to see she had a welcome home. Cassie and Evelyn sat on the sofa, while Agatha standing behind them, came to hug her. Snowy's large frame stood by the fireplace and Dragon sat in the green chair, his injured foot encased in a medical boot. Welcomes came from all corners, including from two cats and a puppy.

Lunch was served as everyone filled their plates from the smorgasbord of food in the kitchen. Olivia had made chicken soup and brought Denia a bowl at the table, with a soft, buttered roll. Denia was hungry and the warm soup felt good on the back of her throat. Gentle conversation buzzed around the room, as Angus went from one person to the next trying to get a little snack.

Everyone was quiet when Denia told them about the night up at the pond and the band of men in cloaks. They could have heard a pin drop as she relayed the information Lee Nelson had told her and her mother the night before. The murder of Melinda Greystone had been solved. Snowy was surprised that the man who appeared to be the mastermind, or at the very least the instigator of the crimes, had gotten away with no charges.

"I have my own group of followers on several websites and in chatrooms, not only on some of the shall we say unusual 'unorthodox' websites, but the more established educational communities. I can get the word out about this guy. Maybe I can be helpful in exposing him and give warning to potential followers."

"Let's talk about something else," said Olivia. "We need to celebrate the fact that Denia is here with us."

Evelyn and Cassie disappeared into the kitchen, only to bring out dessert. The top of the cake was decorated depicting the rock alcove, old oak tree, and pond with a *'Welcome Home'* message inscribed in the icing.

Denia cut the cake, dishing out large portions onto the colorful paper plates that Cassie provided.

After everyone had eaten, it was clear that Denia was tired. This had been the longest she had been out of bed since going into the hospital.

"I really want to thank you all for this little party, but I really think I need to lie down. I'm feeling pretty wiped out."

Snowy came and gave her a hug, saying he needed to get home because he needed to get ready for his class that night. Dragon, who thanked Denia for all of the little improvements she had made to the bunkhouse, said he was going to put his foot up for a while before starting on any afternoon chores around the back lot, and left out the back door.

The Doves gathered around the table.

"We'll help you upstairs," said Batty.

"I can probably make it alright," said Denia, hoisting herself up from the chair.

"We'll go up with you," insisted Cassie.

Denia got to the bottom of the stairs and stopped.

On the wall at the base of the stairs, Denia noticed a new addition. A long, thin, wood-framed mirror with a curved decorative top hung in a convenient spot for the last-minute checking of hair and makeup. It looked familiar to Denia, but she could not place where she had seen it before. She continued up the stairs with Batty beside her. Another mirror, a duplicate of the first, hung on the wall at the top of the landing, new to the space.

"Aren't these the mirrors from Auntie's dresser?" Denia asked as the recognition dawned.

"Yes, I think they are," sounded Olivia from behind her.

Denia walked past the bathroom and on to the doorway of her room and stopped. The floor of the room was littered with cardboard boxes.

"What…?" Denia started to say.

"I hope you won't mind that we've made a few changes while you were gone," informed Batty. "We've packed most of Mel's things and moved you into the larger bedroom."

Denia walked to the entrance to her aunt's room and stood astonished as she peered in. This was not the same place.

"Go on in," Agatha encouraged.

Denia did not know where to look first. Probably the most obvious change was that the bed had been moved to the opposite wall. The room looked clean and new, having been painted a pale shade of green. The old, maroon curtains were gone, replaced by long, pale gray panels that framed each of the three windows in the room. Next to the large, floor to ceiling bookcase sat a comfortable, upholstered chair and matching ottoman. A tall, floor lamp finished the look for the perfect reading nook. Her aunt's large dresser had been moved to the other side of the room, taking up much of the wall opposite the bed. Its old, dark wood had been refinished, and was now an Ashwood tone, also used for the two bedside tables.

The top of the dresser was covered by a crocheted scarf that Denia recognized as previously on the buffet downstairs, prior to Denia removing it in her cleaning and polishing frenzy. Above the dresser was a large, rectangular, modern mirror, with a beveled border. Her things had been brought from the other room and took up residence on the dresser, along with a framed picture of her as a girl sitting next to her aunt on the old bench up by the pond.

Looking around, she saw the headboard of the bed had been removed. Horizontal, wooden panels, stained a dark grey, were attached to the wall, with the head of the bed pushed up against them. A textured, silver comforter with matching pillow shams highlighted the bed.

Not all of Melinda Greystone's things had been removed. The Tiffany, dragonfly lamps sat in their usual spots on the two bedside tables. The lamps and the multicolored, Persian rugs provided the accents of color for the room with its otherwise cool colors.

"This is amazing. It no longer looks like a room left

over from the old days. It looks so comfortable and modern, other than the lamps. I'm so glad you saved them," said Denia as she ran her hand along the comforter.

"Do you *really* like it?" asked Batty, with the excitement of a someone far younger than herself.

"We had some fun and only a few squabbles designing it," said Agatha. "Cassie and I refinished the furniture. Snowy put up the stained wood panels for the headboard. Evelyn found the chair and the ottoman. Dragon painted, and Batty and Olivia packed Mel's things and did the rest of the decorating."

"I love it. I would have never thought to do all of this, like moving the bed, painting the furniture. The headboard is so modern, and rustic looking," said Denia.

"Come on, it's time to get you into bed. You're still not fully recovered from all of the excitement in your life," said Olivia, while she motioned to shoo everyone but her and Batty out of the room.

Batty turned down the bed while Olivia helped her change into a comfortable shift.

"I've picked out a couple books and put them on the bedside table if you feel like reading later. I'll go downstairs and bring you up something to drink. You need to keep up your fluids," Olivia admonished.

"You can trust Olivia on the books after twenty years of working in the library and running a monthly book club," said Batty.

Suddenly, Angus bounded into the room heading for Denia, sitting on the side of the bed.

"Oh, yeah," said Olivia, "he's learned how to come up the stairs. He couldn't stand it when all of the action was happening up here, and he was left out."

"Looks like it's the beginning of the end of keeping him in one place," sighed Denia, shaking her head at how fast the puppy was growing.

"We put his crate in the corner, over there," said Batty.

"Okay, little guy, you're coming downstairs so Denia can get some rest," said Olivia, picking up the dog with some effort.

"I can't believe how tired I am just from coming home from the hospital," Denia said, finally getting a chance to lie down.

"You're recovering from pneumonia and a concussion and need to rest for the next few days. This was probably a little too much excitement for your homecoming, but I couldn't hold them back. They all wanted to be here."

"Batty, what's happening with the Doves? Are you the new high priestess for the coven?"

Batty laughed.

"We do have a new leader, although she does not want to be called the 'high priestess'. She feels that she would need to grow into that title."

"It's not you?" Denia asked with surprise and curiosity.

"No, it's someone much more qualified than me. Of

all of us, she is the most knowledgeable and skillful in her craft."

"Who?"

"Olivia, of course. She was with the coven from the beginning. She was Mel's greatest support. The two of them built Candlewick. I just do the bookkeeping."

"Olivia," Denia said, trying to picture the short, plump witch leading the Doves in their circle.

"Well, the grotto is still here for all of you. Auntie would be happy knowing you are still using the place she had made for you. Besides, it will be good to have *friendly* lights and voices coming from across the field."

"That's kind of you, dear. Now you need to get some rest. We'll clean up downstairs and take Angus out to Dragon."

Batty left the room, and all was quiet. Denia looked around, again marveling at the transformation of the space with a peaceful enjoyment. In came Isis. She jumped up onto the bottom of the bed and meowed a greeting to Denia. She did a turn and nestled into the new comforter, her midnight black standing out on the silver background. Denia closed her eyes, thankful to be home.

Epilogue

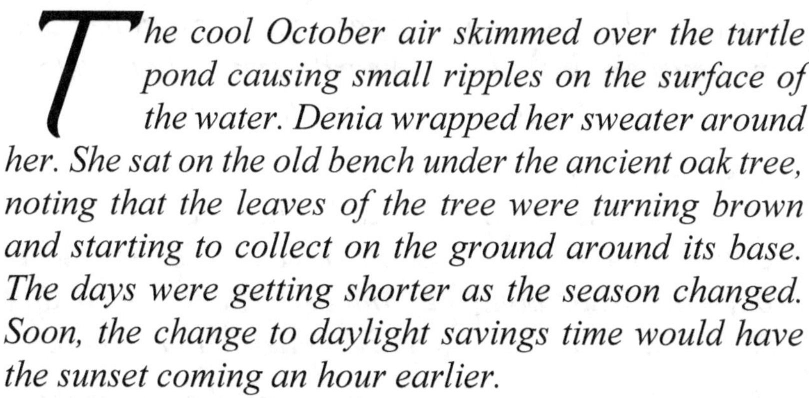

The cool October air skimmed over the turtle pond causing small ripples on the surface of the water. Denia wrapped her sweater around her. She sat on the old bench under the ancient oak tree, noting that the leaves of the tree were turning brown and starting to collect on the ground around its base. The days were getting shorter as the season changed. Soon, the change to daylight savings time would have the sunset coming an hour earlier.

The little town of Solvang had embraced autumn with an air of excitement, looking forward to the quickly approaching holidays and the gusts of visitors that would come. Candlewick was thriving and Denia had discovered beeswax for making candles. Long pieces of wax, rolled into tapers, set in copper base, with a thin *ribbon and a sprig of rosemary was the new best seller, appealing to those demanding the natural elements. She spent several hours a day in the office building, with the cats and Angus wandering in and out.*

She watched as Roxy, Billy, and Angus ran around the field taking full advantage of the openness and the early evening change in scenery. What an odd little trio they made, Denia thought. Billy couldn't resist eating the long, dry grasses and weeds. Roxy loved the expanse, allowing the greyhound to run as she tried to recapture her younger days. Angus was growing quickly, awkward with the long legs. Denia remembered that he started his puppy classes with Kristen on Saturday. He would be a large dog, and a loving companion - another gift from her aunt.

She was going for a run in the afternoon every day to recapture her strength after the hospitalization. Sometimes she would run toward town, only to detour to the Samala Winery for a chat with Karen.

Like Melinda, she planned to work at the winery events with Batty, as her schedule allowed. Other days, she would run the other way on the road's soft shoulder, around the bend, along the front of the horse ranch, and on to Keith's little house, enjoying her neighborhood.

Halloween was only days away and the Doves were preparing for their Samhain celebration. They would once again be using the rock amphitheater next to the pond for their ceremony. Batty was going on about the veil being the thinnest on that day, and they would send their love to Melinda. Olivia invited Denia to attend but she gently declined. She felt better hosting an after-

circle coffee and dessert, rather than being the interloper. She cared for all the women she now considered her friends, but she was not ready to embrace their beliefs.

Denia heard his horse before she saw him come around the bend. He must have let himself in through the vineyard gates. Wheaty came to stand by the tree, already anticipating where Keith would lead. The tall man came to sit beside her. Quiet conversation ensued. There was no talk of traumatic events.

There was no fear of unwanted trespassers. There were just the simple updates of the day and the plans for tomorrow.

The sun dropped below the hills. Glorious golds changing to shades of pink, painted the western sky. A breeze came from the north and the crescent of a moon rose in the east. Melinda's turtle stones stood vigil around the rim of the pond, their flat backs reflecting the fading light.

EILEEN RAYE

ABOUT THE AUTHOR

*E**ileen Raye** started on the road to being an author several decades ago, then life happened. Now a retired nurse, the blank page was calling. Ms. Raye is a supporter of the printed page, bookstores - new and used - and encourages reading for all age groups.*

She currently lives in Boulder City, Nevada - near Las Vegas - with her husband. Her hobbies include reading, writing and attending a book club. Retired from a fulfilling career in nursing, Ms. Raye also enjoys gardening, jigsaw puzzles and a robust "Harry Potter" collection. Family, grandchildren and pets bring a sweetness to her life.

ACKNOWLEDGMENT

I would like to thank my editor and friend, Lady Leanne E. Staback, Ph.D., in helping me make this book a reality. She is also an author, and her books can be found under Leanne Staback and Leanne E. Staback, Ph.D.

RESOURCES

"Museum Replica-26." *Medieval and Renaissance Store*, www.medievalandrenaissancestore.com/p-296-medieval-monks-robe-hood-set-larp-sca.aspx. Accessed 19 May 2024.

O'Brien, Sam. "Why 18th-Century Scots Performed Mock Human Sacrifices over Cake." *Atlas Obscura*, Atlas Obscura, 4 May 2023, www.atlasobscura.com/articles/how-to-make-beltane-bannock-oatcake.

Puchan. "Big Moon Stock Photo. Image of Grey, Water, Reed, Black - 30703208." *Dreamstime*, 12 May 2013, www.dreamstime.com/royalty-free-stock-photos-big-moon-over-wild-lake-image30703208.

Vostrikov, Maxim. "Elegant and Woman in the Red Evening Fluttering Dress Is Capture in Move, Running Away from the Ceremony Stock Image - Image of Attractive, Away: 120417349." *Dreamstime*, 3 Nov. 2015, www.dreamstime.com/elegant-sexy-woman-red-evening-fluttering-dress-capture-move-running-away-ceremony-elegant-sexy-image120417349.

www.ingramcontent.com/pod-product-compliance
Lightning Source LLC
Chambersburg PA
CBHW072002190726
48293CB00001B/128